"Why do you wa

He shrugged. "I'
it into words. Wh
Constantinople, I v
bored, and lacking challenge in my life. Perhaps
you'll think me mad, but I've always wanted to
live as one with nature, with no limits but the
sky. And," he admitted, "when I saw you again,
I knew my decision was the right one."

How had he read her heart so easily? April
drew in her breath, startled by Damien's revelation. He was turning his back on his other
world for her, as well as for himself. Did he
also feel the same powerful urge to link his
body with hers?

April didn't know the answer to the question,
but she could not quell the rapid beat of her heart
or a soft moan when he suddenly leaned close and
pressed his mouth down upon hers . . .

PATRICIA McALLISTER

GYPSY JEWEL

ZEBRA BOOKS
KENSINGTON PUBLISHING CORP.

ZEBRA BOOKS are published by

Kensington Publishing Corp.
475 Park Avenue South
New York, NY 10016

Copyright © 1993 by Patricia McAllister

Zebra, the Z logo, Heartfire Romance, and the Heartfire Romance logo are trademarks of Kensington Publishing Corp.

First Printing: September, 1993

Printed in the United States of America

To those who inspired . . . Candace and Bertrice;
to those who believed . . . Kim, Doris, and Aunt B;
and last but not least, to my husband Kevin
and son Kyle . . .
for keeping me in hot coffee and sticky kisses
the entire time.

Or were I in the wildest waste,
   So black and bare, so black and bare
The desert were a paradise
   If thou were there, if thou were there

Or were I monarch of the globe,
   With thee to reign, with thee to reign
The brightest jewel in my crown
   Would be my queen, would be my queen.

                 —*Robert Burns*

Prologue

The Caucasus Mountains
April 1837

The gypsy's bare feet were blue and icy as she carefully threaded through the forest. Like most Romany, Tzigane disdained shoes, preferring to feel the bare mother earth on her soles. And the *phuri dai* was too absorbed in her pursuit right now to care that she risked frostbite on this bitter day.

Though it was early spring, the narrow passes that led from the fertile Russian steppes up into the high mountain meadows were still dusted with snow. As the gypsy band drove through the upper pass of majestic El Bruz, the snow-capped peak that overlooked the Romany summer camp on the shores of the Black Sea, a thin, keening cry reached Tzigane even from where she perched in the seat of her gaily-colored wagon. The fortune-teller's alert eyes and ears at once sought the source. None of the others seemed to have heard the peculiar wail that sounded like a small animal in distress. Since she was the last wagon in the caravan, efforts to stop the others proved futile.

Tzigane drew her little mules to a stop, and went in search of the injured animal. She had no idea what she would do with the creature when she found it; perhaps it would be enough to put it out of its misery. So she brought along an ornate, ivory-handled stiletto, now tucked securely in the symbolic sash at her waist.

As always, Tzigane wore the *pomona* skirt of bright red to signify her state of mourning. She had worn it faithfully on each anniversary of her beloved husband's death, not caring that some of the others muttered she was mad.

As her Bal had once been *Rom Baro*, king of the gypsies, Tzigane was now *phuri dai*, wise-woman of the Lowara band. And because she had been the matriarch for over twenty years now, nobody questioned her fancies, not those in the band, and certainly none of the *gaje*, or outsiders, who came covertly at times to partake of her gift of foresight.

The whimpering was closer now, and Tzigane continued cautiously toward the source. Her amber-colored eyes bright against the dark matte of her skin, her chapped hands shaking as she drew the knife, she peered ahead into the mysterious shadows cast by the towering trees.

The unblemished virgin snow was awash with scattered footprints that indicated the hasty departure of someone just moments before. Tzigane strained for a glimpse of a fleeing figure in the dusk, but she saw nobody. Then the *phuri dai* caught her breath sharply in disbelief.

There, left beneath a gnarled, ancient pine, a naked newborn baby howled in the snow. Jolted out of her shock by the realization that the child was freezing, the gypsy woman hurried over and snatched it up against her breast.

The child's cries were muffled as it instinctively, greedily rooted for food. It felt its cold, hostile world give way to comforting warmth, and its screams gradually subsided to gasping sobs. Tzigane smoothed the fine, pale down on the infant's head and crooned softly to the squirming bit of flesh.

Who would abandon such a perfect child to die? The baby wailed again, blinking back great tears, and Tzigane saw that its eyes were a beautiful sea-green color. Exposure would have claimed its life within minutes more had she not appeared.

Noting the sex of the child as she hastily pulled off her heavy winter shawl, Tzigane wrapped it snugly around the babe. The infant girl had been left totally naked, but a small, green velvet pouch dangled from a silken cord around her neck. With an uneasy gaze at the darkening woods around her, Tzigane decided she could wait to pursue the mystery after she returned to the safety of the gypsy camp.

Whoever had left the child had surrendered

all rights to her in any case—for, at the will of the gods, Tzigane had just become a mother. And only the silent trees knew the truth, of how and why the baby had come to be there . . . except for the EVIL ONE who had abandoned the child to die.

$\mathcal{O}ne$

Constantinople
Summer 1850

"Halt! Thief!"

The hoarse, angry cry echoed in her ears, but the young girl dared not stop now. With a wild jangle of jewelry, she dashed down the alley, her kerchief flying off to sail away in the brisk wind. A wealth of blonde hair unfurled behind her, momentarily confusing the shop owner who was shouting for help.

"Stop that gypsy! She stole my fruit!"

Glancing down to see an apple clutched in her sweaty hand, April nearly tripped in a tangle of colorful cotton skirts. She had just passed a fruit stall when the apples the hawker had been stacking too high came down in a bouncing heap all over the street.

Without thinking, April had reached down to help him pick up his spilled goods. But the moment her hand closed around the nearest apple, he had started shrieking at her in rapid-fire Turkish. Who would believe her now? To anyone who looked, she appeared to be a gypsy girl with "stolen" goods in hand!

Gasping for breath, April burst from the alley, wildly looking in every direction for any sign of the gypsy caravan.

She had only wandered a few streets away from the others to gawk at the colorful crowds in Constantinople. Who would have guessed that a thirteen-year-old girl could get herself into such trouble in a matter of less than five minutes?

Behind her, April could hear the fruit seller still babbling urgently, no doubt directing the city soldiers her way. And if they caught her, she knew her goose was cooked, as the *gaje* would say. Soldiers had a notoriously dim view of gypsies in the best of circumstances, and given any excuse to persecute them, they eagerly seized the chance.

Shudders coursed through April at the thought, and with a Romany oath she dashed off in the direction in which she hoped to find Tzigane. She had left her mother telling fortunes across from a mosque near the Golden Horn. Ironically, that was where the *phuri dai* usually found her business was the briskest, near churches or holy sites. But it seemed now that all of Constantinople was a maze of minarets and golden domes, and the girl could hardly choose which way to flee.

Poised in mid-flight, April threw the unfortunate apple back over one shoulder, hoping that might appease anyone who took up the chase after her. She jumped guiltily when someone stepped out from the shadows of an overhanging shop awning and spoke softly in her ear.

"I think you dropped something, *madamoiselle.*" The man's voice was deep and smooth, his Turkish as flawless as her own. Whirling around in a flurry of skirts, April's green eyes widened in surprise.

She looked up into a strikingly handsome male face framed by waves of night-dark hair. Eyes the color of the Caspian Sea twinkled at her from beneath dark brows arched in apparent amusement. Obviously a gentleman, the young man's expensively tailored suit fit his tall, broad frame like a second skin. He had walked out from the silk shop and caught the flying apple just as she had hurled the evidence away.

Immediately, April knew enough to be wary. Why should a stranger bother to address a gypsy girl so politely? Was he possibly a *shanglo,* a policeman? April doubted it, quickly sizing up his fine clothes and lack of weapons, but for a long moment her heart was in her throat.

The man extended the bruised apple in one well-manicured hand to her. He was a young man, though April was in too much of a panic to note much more than that. She could hardly tear her own thoughts away from the alley she had left a moment ago, where the stallkeeper's curses still echoed off the stone walls.

Shaking her head to refuse the apple, April started to back away. But something in the stranger's approach froze her for a moment, and like a bird fascinated by a snake, she waited to see what he would do.

"Are you afraid of me?" Damien Cross asked the obvious, wondering why the gypsy child was poised like a tawny tiger prepared to spring. By her defensive stance and glittering green eyes, she clearly expected him to injure her in some way. But nothing could be further from the Earl of Devonshire's mind.

Damien knew the girl was a gypsy, both by her clothing, a bright blue layered skirt and loose white cotton blouse, and the fact that she was brown-skinned and barefoot. She wore a dozen bangles around each slender wrist—real gold, if Damien was any judge—and large hoop earrings that just touched her shoulders. But instead of being dark, her hair was the color of summer wheat, pale gilt and gold swirling in a lustrous sheen all the way to her small waist. She was an unusually beautiful child.

Before April could reply, the apple seller burst from the alleyway and came storming toward them. Damien adroitly palmed the apple into his silk-lined pocket and gained a look of surprised admiration from the girl for his sleight-of-hand.

"Gypsy filth!" The Turk, short and fat and

huffing with indignation, hawked and spat to one side as he rushed toward April with one finger wagging. "You give me back my fruit, or I'll have you sent to prison, eh? You understand?"

April raised her chin and held her ground. The earl could only watch in admiration, for the girl had definite poise and an inner strength that was obvious even to the Turk. For a moment even Damien was forced to wonder if she was really a gypsy. There was something almost aristocratic about the way she stared the other man down.

"What do you mean? What fruit?" Her innocent reply, delivered in perfect Turkish, caused even the fruit seller to hesitate and fumble for further ammunition. He sputtered for a second, impotently waving his chubby arms, and then Damien coolly intervened.

"If you're suggesting this girl has stolen goods, sir, I must admit I'm surprised. As you can see, she is clearly empty-handed, and only stopped here because I asked her to give me directions to the Hagia Sophia . . ."

Was April mistaken, or did the handsome stranger slip her a sidelong wink? It seemed incredible that a *gajo* would ever stoop to interfere in street matters, especially when a gypsy's life was at stake!

Yet she couldn't help but feel grateful when the merchant finally shook his head, more puzzled than angry, threw up his hands in a dramatic display of surrender, and stalked back to his display.

April's pounding heart gradually subsided and she glanced up at the stranger again, suddenly shy. She had no idea why, for she was not afraid of him, and he *had* helped her out of a very sticky situation. But a sudden urge to find the Romany band and escape to the sanctuary of the mountains pulled at her. With a brief nod of thanks, she turned to go.

"Wait." It was a gentle command, but a command nonetheless. April paused, feeling those light blue eyes holding her in place. And then the man was beside her, taking her hand and wrapping her fingers around the apple which had mysteriously reappeared.

She reddened with insult. "I didn't steal it—"

"I know. I happened to look out from the shop window into the alley, and I saw what really happened. But this apple is all I have to give you, little girl, and you deserve something for your courage just now."

While he spoke, Damien studied the sweep of golden-tipped lashes on the child's rosy cheeks, studying the fine details of her features. Someday, when she was older, she would be a beauty to be reckoned with. And woe to the man, or men, who tried to break her spirit, he thought. There was fire in this little one's green eyes.

Suspicious that he seemed to want no more from her, which was clearly out of character for a *gajo,* April asked boldly, "You saved my life. Why?"

Why, indeed? The earl wasn't sure he could answer her, and his shrug made April wonder if he had heard her at all. His blue eyes distant, Damien finally murmured, "Sometimes a man sees all the injustice he can take in one day." As the young girl's brow furrowed in deep thought, Damien broke from his dark mindset to give her a kindly pat on the shoulder.

"Maybe I'll be in a position someday where you can return the favor, all right?"

With a show of generosity, April offered eagerly, "If you ever want your fortune told, I'll do it for free. I'm almost as good as my mother now!"

A smile tugged at the corners of the earl's mouth. "I'm sure you are. Will you predict good luck or bad for me, do you think?"

"Good, of course!" She looked offended by the question.

Lord Cross laughed, displaying even white teeth against skin bronzed darker than her own. "I can use all the help I can get, little girl! And if I ever have the good fortune to run into you again, I'll take you up on that . . . right now, though, I'm due to catch a ship home. Promise me you'll stay out of trouble? You're far too young yet to go courting disaster."

Her heart-shaped mouth pursed at the unfamiliar word. "'Courting'? What's that?"

"No doubt you'll find out soon enough,"

Lord Cross replied a little dryly. The earl gave her one last wink, then strode off down the street. April stood watching him for a moment, twirling the apple in her hands. Then, before she went in search of Tzigane again, she put the fruit to her pink lips and took a huge bite.

Tzigane was getting old, and the harsh Russian winters had not agreed with her. What had once been rich, sable-brown hair was now liberally streaked with gray, and hours of meditation upon her tarot cards had ringed her sad eyes with dark circles and bags.

With gruff honesty, Tzigane admitted to herself that looking in a mirror now only revealed the hag she was labelled by the *gaje*. But her crone-like appearance actually made for better business. The *gaje* women shivered with delicious fright when she cackled over their cards, and even their men could not disguise interest when old Tzigane spewed out their respective fates in a dramatic, croaking voice.

The gypsies themselves agreed that Tzigane, though a widow, more than paid for herself and the keep of her daughter, April. Especially in the winter months, when boredom and confinement drove the *boyar* aristocrats in search of amusement, Tzigane could often be found huddled in her colorful little wagon with a circle of wide-eyed young ladies from the nearest town.

After almost thirty years of plying her trade,

Tzigane's skirts were heavy now from the gold coins sewn safely in the hems. But money paled beside Tzigane's secret purpose: to secure for her daughter April a better life. Many a time the *phuri dai* had watched the fine ladies upon gentlemen's arms as the tribe passed through various cities, and she gnawed thoughtfully upon her plan.

Close study of her foster daughter always reassured the old woman of her eventual success. April was a beauty, and had been turning men's heads ever since she had tagged along at Tzigane's skirts. Of the girl's true heritage, the seer still knew nothing. Even her cards were silent on April's past. But it was enough for Tzigane that April was pretty, clever, and quick to learn, and therefore able to fulfill her foster mother's dreams for her.

Tzigane plotted most carefully. Nowdays, a gentlewoman knew how to ride, hunt, and even shoot alongside men, and she also spoke several languages. From childhood April had been well-versed not only in her native Romany, but in Russian and Turkish as well. The real obstacle had been getting the girl exposed to the more refined languages, such as English and French. Fortunately, the Lowara band was comprised of many from varied backgrounds, and Tzigane paid several of the other women to instruct April in their spare time.

There was a fiery, dark-eyed girl who had immigrated from a Manouches gypsy band on the outskirts of Paris, and another who had been an English lady's maid until she had been dismissed for stealing. Both agreed to teach April what they could of their languages, and reported to a satisfied Tzigane that they had been surprised at how easily the young girl learned new things.

It had not surprised Tzigane. April had always been like a sponge, soaking everything up, incessantly curious, sometimes to the point of annoying the elders in the camp. But though she had exasperated them as a child, she worried them more as a young woman, riding her black stallion astride and causing the young men of the band to fight amongst themselves for the chance to race or chase her in the woods.

When April had turned seventeen this past spring, it was agreed among the elders and the *Rom Baro,* Jingo, that it would soon be time to put an end to Tzigane's crazy whims. Bad enough that she let her daughter run wild like a boy, but she had made no marriage plans for the girl. And while most young women April's age were already wed and with child, it infuriated the women and concerned the men that the *phuri dai's* daughter should be given preferential treatment. There was no doubt Tzigane had sufficient dowry for the girl, so when would she settle April's future?

But April's future was exactly what the seer had in mind one late summer day as she spread out the arcana and peered at her tarot cards, trying to read the hazy signs that signified her daughter's destiny. Once a day she had April shuffle the well-worn, colorful cards, and though the young woman was impatient with the task, she still agreed to it out of love and respect for her foster mother.

Tzigane always spent hours pouring over the meaning of the cards, pondering and weighing her next move, and today was no exception. But something was wrong . . . never before had the cards been so clear, so defined, in telling her that April was in grave danger.

Dabbing at her sweaty brow with the tail of the kerchief that bound back her peppery hair, Tzigane stared at the picture of the mighty ivory and onyx tower surrounded by a boiling, blood-red sea. Red was the color of death to all Romany, and to see it surface made the old woman shiver with fear.

The Tower meant calamity coming soon. Crossed over the Queen of Diamonds, April's card, it was as obvious as a warning shout in the seer's ear. Rising abruptly with the ominous card still in hand, Tzigane hobbled as quickly as she could on her arthritic legs to the far end of her wagon.

Leaning out the back, She croaked anxiously at the children scampering nearby, "April! Where is April?"

The boys stopped scuffling in the dirt to regard the *phuri dai* with wary respect. She

21

seemed ancient to them, and they knew the respect she commanded in the tribe. Still, she frightened them, for her bony fingers shook at them and her raspy cry was like that of an angry crow.

"Where is April? You must find her for me!"

The oldest of the boys, and the bravest, risked Tzigane's wrath by shouting back, "She went to the woods!"

"Alone?" The old woman looked close to toppling out the back of her wagon, as she leaned dangerously and trembled like a leaf in the wind.

"No . . . a bunch of the girls went berry hunting together."

Tzigane visibly sagged with relief, then muttered to herself, "Perhaps she is safe . . . oh, *Del,* watch over my *chavali,* my little girl . . ."

But even as she prayed, the *phuri dai* could feel the sharp edge of the tarot card cutting into her clenched fist, and when she looked down, there was blood on her hand.

"He'll be the death of you yet!"

As a familiar horse streaked by him on the forest path, Nicabar shook his fist after the girl who flew by like the wind. The black's hooves tossed up chunks of soft, dark earth that spurted in every direction, and one of the clods hit the young man squarely on the cheek. With a furious gesture, he wiped off the mud and started to run after her.

Ahead of him, the stallion and the carefree Romany maid shot from the trees into the glorious sunlight of an open meadow. Riding bareback, the young woman wore slim-cut black trousers like Nicabar's, but there was no mistaking her for a man. Nature had conspired in the last few years to make April unmistakably feminine, and just to watch her ride astride was enough to make Nicky's loins throb.

He caught up with April when she drew Prince Adar down to a canter and circled ahead in a clearing. Pausing on the forest's fringe, Nicky took the opportunity to covertly observe the girl. Eyes shining with exhilaration from her wild ride, April leaned down to stroke the arched neck of the horse as she finally brought the animal to a stop in the knee-high, lush grass.

Sliding down from Adar's sweaty back, April pulled off the simple harness to let the horse graze. She leaned over to scratch the stallion behind his ears, while the black emphatically rubbed his head up and down against her. "Is that the spot? Yes? I know what you like, itchy boy!" Laughing, April let her horse eat in peace then, content to watch him rip the rich grass easily from the moist earth.

Hands on her slim hips, April turned to survey the view, drinking deeply of the clean, crisp mountain air. Surely there was no place as close to paradise as the Lowara's summer range, where sea and sky met in a clash of awe-inspiring, perfect blue. Plucking a stem of grass for herself, April chewed absently on the tender white root as she gazed westward.

Out there, just beyond the craggy slopes of the high mountains, the Black Sea crashed unrelentingly upon white sand shores. She sniffed, imagining she could smell the salty sea tang. When the heat became unbearable at lower altitudes, the band always retreated to the cool shadows of the forests. There the Lowara would remain until the decision was made to head south again. Though April enjoyed the sea, she felt more at home here in the blessed peace of the mountains, and the tension drained from her now as she surveyed her beloved homeland.

Someday, she thought, she might ignore King Jingo's orders for her to stay close to camp, and ride over the next rise just to see what was there. April had a burning desire to learn about the world. She was glad she was a gypsy, for she had seen the constriction the *gaje* girls endured. Never to ride free, never to speak one's mind . . . how close to suffocation that must be! Her life now was almost paradise by comparison.

Yes, it was paradise, but frustrating too . . . she was still a young woman, after all, and the others endlessly reminded her of that. Everyone in the band wanted to know when she would marry and settle down. She was aware of the boys' heated stares, and the scandalized looks of the other girls when she refused to wed. But there were no young men in the band who interested her.

April heard a low chuckle and whirled in consternation to find that her secret meadow had been discovered. Nicabar, the tribe's horse trader as well as a renowned thief, stalked through the lush grass toward her. The young man's onyx eyes burned into April, and she returned the stare with thinly-veiled contempt. Nicky was *gitano,* a Latin gypsy from Spain. With his mother, Belita, he had joined the band two years ago, offering to train and sell the Romany horses.

But it was not out of love that Nicky worked with animals. It was purely for profit, and April did not mistake the gleam of cruelty in his eye whenever he broke fresh horses to his hand.

For that reason among others, the animosity between the two young people had been almost instantaneous. April hated the way his dark eyes always followed her, hungry and sly. Nicky was annoyed by the control April had over her stallion, Prince Adar. Why the wild stallion had not killed her yet was a mystery to most of the camp, but Nicky suspected it was only witchcraft that kept the horse so biddable.

After all, hadn't April been raised by that old hag who told the fortunes? Perhaps the girl practiced dark magic, too. April's uncanny green eyes challenged him now, and Nicky felt the blood surge hotly in his veins.

"You nearly ran over me back there!" His arrogant voice rang out as he approached. "That horse should be gelded, girl. And you must learn proper respect for men!"

April almost laughed, for Nicky was barely older than she. Though she supposed some might consider him handsome in a Latin way, April was repulsed by his leering mannerisms and greasy, black hair. She was not taken in by his charms like the other girls were, but they were goose-brains anyway, and desperate to marry. April had no wish to wed, not when it meant her will would be completely subject to another's.

Nicky was eying Prince Adar now with his usual greed, unaware that the girl had not dignified his complaints with a reply. "I'll still give you three hundred *lires* for him. I just took in a little bay mare that's nice and gentle. It's a good trade and will save your pretty neck in the end."

A short burst of laughter came from April's lips. "I'm in more danger from you than Adar," she said, never suspecting how close to the truth that was.

Raised alongside the Romany boys in the band, April was nearly fearless, and for years she had tussled with them like a wildcat in the woods. She had learned to knife-fight when she was eight, and the Greek gypsy who had trained her had once been a slave. Dinos had taught April to be ruthless where self-defense was concerned, and she had learned well. She eyed Nicky now with the same contempt she had reserved for the bullies she had faced in the past.

Nicky said in a low voice, "What you need is another sort of stallion, April. You should be married and having your own children."

"And I suppose you have someone in mind for their father?"

Nicky grinned, his small black eyes glittering. That she was not afraid of him was all the more exciting. He expected women to cringe and tremble in awe of him, and the fact that April seemed unable or unwilling to do that was nothing more than a challenge.

He took a slow step toward her, raising his hands. "I'll take the fight out of you like I do my mares," he whispered coarsely, and when her green eyes widened slightly, he laughed. "The first trick is to gentle you to my touch."

Adrenalin shot through April as she read the intent in his eyes. "Stay away from me," she ordered him, but she could not summon further words before his hand shot out and caught her abruptly by the wrist, yanking her into his arms.

For the height and weight he lacked, Nicky's strength was like iron. As April struggled in his arms, he wrenched her hands behind her back and forced his thin, hard mouth down on hers.

27

"Bitch!" He spat out the word along with a bright bead of blood as April sank her teeth into his lip. With the momentary release of his hold, the young woman fled.

April ran toward her horse, who stopped grazing and regarded his mistress with a look of alarm. Scenting fear on her, the stallion shied away just enough to prevent April from scrambling up on his back. Without the harness, she had no way to hold Adar still.

Soon it was too late. Nicky ran up behind her, shoving April to the grass and reaching out to soundly slap the horse on the flanks. The black bolted instantly, lashing out his back hooves in a fit of upset before he tore off toward the woods.

Dazed, April had no time to recover her feet before Nicky dropped on her. In one smooth move he pinned her with a knee on either side, and brutally twisted her wrists above her head. The young woman had the feeling he had either done this before, or had planned it down to the last detail—perhaps both.

"Go ahead," Nicky panted down at her, "fight! I like a woman that fights!"

"Pig!" she spat up at him, setting her teeth with the effort of trying to throw him off. She had the satisfaction of seeing he kept well away from her mouth this time, pausing to lick his already bloodied lip.

Nicky's nostrils flared as he drank in the sight of the golden beauty splayed beneath him.

She was like a young filly, his for the taking and training. He knew now why the mothers in camp murmured restlessly about April, and what a temptation she was for their sons. They would never admit they were jealous themselves, jealous of her fairness and her slim, proud figure that so easily set men afire.

April's green eyes shot sparks of hatred up at him, and her long legs flailed wildly in the attempt for freedom. Nicky glanced over his shoulder at the sight of her hips snugly encased in the tight trousers, and he felt the sharp swell of his desire.

"Relax, *chula*," he chuckled lewdly as he settled himself firmly into the saddle of her hips, "you'll only hurt yourself. I'll ride you, cat-eyes, and curb your spirit! Soon you'll beg me for more."

His leering face deserved only one thing. April spat up at him and had the satisfaction of seeing Nicky flinch.

"You still think you're too good for me, eh? I'll show you, witch!"

While Nicky muttered his vile plans for her, April held down the nausea and the fear enough to construct one of her own. Suddenly she remembered the small dagger she had tucked under her belt that morning, a gift from Tzigane several years ago. She had never had the need to use it until now. With Nicky pinning her hands so effectively, it was unlikely she could reach it anyway. Unless . . .

Swallowing her revulsion, April whispered softly, "Please."

Nicky paused and savored the word with obvious glee. "What did you say? I didn't hear you!"

April licked her dry lips, straining against the burning hold he had on her wrists. "Please, Nicky. Please don't hurt me. I'll do anything you want . . . just don't hurt me."

When she suddenly ceased struggling, Nicky stared at April suspiciously. But there was a glimmer of tears in her eyes, real enough to stroke his ego. He had no way of knowing they were tears of rage, not fear.

"Anything?" he rasped, roughly shaking her for confirmation, until she nodded wildly, anxiously. "You know what I want, April. Will you give it to me?"

Again she nodded, and her silky voice stirred hope in the depths of his burning loins. "I . . . I've wanted you to teach me things, about men and women," she stammered convincingly, and blushed a little, which was not difficult.

Actually she could imagine nothing less appealing than letting the *gitano* touch her in any way, but she knew her very life depended on her ability to act. When April quickly rimmed her lips with a moist tongue, Nicky groaned aloud. Then gradually, she felt the tiniest loosening of his hold upon her wrists.

"I knew it," Nicky panted, "you've just needed a real man to teach you some tricks, eh? You've been driving me mad all for nothing, witch! But I can train you well, and I will."

The young man released her hands then, but before April could reach down to grab her dagger, he had seized the front of her silky white blouse and ripped it halfway down. Rage engulfed April when he buried his dark head between her breasts and began to slobber wet kisses all over her skin.

Her own hands fumbled desperately about her waist for the handle of the knife, but her palms were sweaty and slick. When she finally found it, it took several tries to tug it free from her tight waistband.

Thinking April groped for something else between his legs, Nicky grunted encouragement. He never had an inkling as to what was really happening until he felt the sharp point of a dagger digging into the tender flesh at his neck, and his head rose with a jolt.

"No more sudden moves," April hissed as she kept the razor-thin stiletto pressed to his jugular. The horse trader was furious, but he wasn't foolish enough to jerk away. One thrust, even an awkward one, would mean a ghastly wound, or even death.

"Now, get off of me . . . slowly!" April followed his every move with the waving blade, and there was bloodlust in her eyes. When they were both on their feet, April collected herself again. It had taken all of her self-control not to gut Nicky like the dog he was, and her grip trembled on the little knife, but did not loosen.

Nicky's eyes burned like live coals in an otherwise expressionless face. "Give me the knife, April," he said in a soft, cajoling voice. "You know you don't need it. I won't hurt you."

He took a single step toward her again, and she tensed with fury. "I will kill you if you touch me again, Nicky!"

"Women." He gave a deprecating little laugh. "Come on, April, I was only playing. You knew that, didn't you?"

The sound of distant voices in the nearby woods caused April's head to turn in hopeful expectation. Seeing his only chance, Nicky feinted to the right and lunged at the girl again. But he had forgotten how resourceful she was, and April pivoted smoothly and avoided his grasp.

Knowing she was in dire danger as long as they were alone, and seeing the madness in his eyes, April finally chose to run. She was only a few steps ahead of Nicky as they crashed wildly into the woods, and she gasped for breath to scream just as he seized a handful of her hair from behind. Pain exploded in her scalp, but instead of trying to tear free again, April spun around and lashed out with the dagger, carving a thin ribbon of blood along his left cheek.

"April!" Nicky cried her name and it echoed

32

throughout the woods. It sounded strangely forlorn coming from the young man, but April was too angry to notice. She watched in bitter satisfaction as Nicky crumpled to his knees, bright red blood trickling through his hands and spotting his shirt.

"Why, April? Why did you try to kill me?"

Nonplussed, April stared at him as Nicky continued his surprising plea with arms outstretched in supplication.

"I told you it was over long ago! I will marry Marya instead!"

April heard a sharp intake of breath nearby. Shocked, she glanced over to see that Nicky's performance had been for the benefit of an audience. She recognized three girls from the camp standing there watching the drama with berry baskets in hand.

The dagger fell from her numb fingers as she opened her mouth to speak. But already she could see Marya's eyes hardening on her, and the other Lowaran girl drew herself up with a hiss.

"So, you jealous witch! You've been trying to steal my man, eh?" The unmarried daughter of the copper-worker Bruno spat out the words as she ran to Nicky, kneeling by him and gasping in horror at the blood covering his hands. "You tried to kill him!" she accused, whipping the kerchief off her dark hair and dabbing at the wound on Nicky's cheek with angry, curt motions. She glared at her supposed rival for Nicky's affections.

"No, that's not true! He attacked me in the meadow!" April heard her own voice coming as if from a great distance away, and realized she had spoken in a dazed whisper.

She was no match for Nicky, who gazed up at Marya with soulful, dark gypsy eyes and murmured, "April lured me to the woods and then threw herself at me. I told her we were to be married, but she wouldn't listen. And when I tried to leave, she came after me with that knife . . ."

"Liar!" April lashed out, unable to listen any longer. She indicated her torn blouse clutching it to cover her breasts, and shook with indignation. "How do you think this got ripped to shreds?"

Nicky closed his eyes in apparent anguish. "You were foolish enough to offer yourself to me, knowing I would never betray Marya!"

April made an exasperated noise, but when she saw the faces of the other two girls, she paled a little. Both Beti and Dodee were staring at her uncertainly, and she could see the conclusion they were coming to.

"It's not true! He tried to rape me!" Her desperate cry, however, was lost in the sudden flurry of activity as Nicky rose to stand and Marya rushed to assist him.

He moaned dramatically and clutched his

bleeding face. "Please . . . lead me back to camp. I can't see . . . my eye . . ."

Knowing she had not come anywhere near his eye, April burned in helpless frustration. But the moment she moved in the direction the others were headed, Marya screamed at her to stay put.

"You evil thing, stay away from us!"

As the three girls turned to help him limp from the scene, Nicky glanced over his shoulder and gave April a smug, victorious smile.

Knowing it would be pointless to run or hide when the men from the camp came in search of her, April waited there until they arrived. After all, she was not the guilty party. Everyone knew that Nicky was cunning and cruel, even to his prized horses.

She intended to face her accuser with dignity. Even if it took everything she had, April would see that the truth was dragged into the light of day, and of course her people would believe her.

Wouldn't they?

Two

"We are not going over this again."

Damien Cross spoke with exasperation over the dramatic sobs which trailed him down the curving mahogany staircase to the front door. Pausing on the landing behind her son as he gathered up his overcoat, Marcelle de Villette, a countess of Normandy in her own right and also the widow of an English earl, wiped at her streaming dark eyes and cast another plea after him.

"Damien! You cannot rush off like a madman to your certain death like this! How can you leave me here alone while you go running off to heathen lands again?"

Gathering his patience, the Earl of Devonshire turned to face the tear-streaked, beautiful face of his French mother. Long used to Marcelle's tragic scenes, he said rather dryly, "The moment I am gone, *Maman,* you will doubtlessly decide to retire to Versailles once more to take

36

the spring air, and be comforted by your many admirers."

Not consoled in the slightest, Marcelle sniffled and dabbed at her delicate features with a lace-edged handkerchief. It was easy to see where her headstrong son had gotten his brooding good looks. His thick, blue-black hair and stubborn air were perfectly reflected in her own. But above Damien's firm, square-cut jaw, his father's ice-blue eyes stared her down from beneath the dark pair of brows, and Marcelle was unhappily reminded of Edward Cross's famous stern looks.

"Bah," she sniffed at last, in perfect imitation of her English dowager friends, "I can see you have no sympathy for your poor *Maman,* none at all! Well, perhaps I *will* go to France then, and try to distract myself from the thought of your certain demise."

"Don't forget your mourning gowns, then," Damien reminded her briskly as he shrugged an overcoat onto his muscular frame. Like Edward, he was a tall man, but it was his coloring that instantly drew the eye. The unusual contrast of light eyes and dark hair had made the young Earl of Devonshire quite the "light o' love" of many young ladies at court.

But court could not be farther from Damien's mind now. Faced with a war looming on the Russian front, while Czar Nicholas prepared to invade Turkey, he felt doubly obligated by virtue of his mixed heritage to enter the fray for both France and Britain. Thus he had volunteered to step from drawing room to battlefield, even though it was a prospect that obviously did not sit well with Marcelle. She had wailed and weeped for days after he had received his orders.

"You are gentry!" she cried desperately now in a final gamble. "The last of the male Cross descendants. Surely it must be considered by the queen!"

"It was," Damien reminded his mother with annoyance. "But Her Majesty felt I might serve as a useful liaison between our two nations, and she also recalled my previous campaign in Algeria under Louis-Philippe."

"More barbarity!" Marcelle shuddered and covered her eyes. "I thought you lost then, too."

"Maman," Damien changed his tactics swiftly, "you know I must go. Why not accept it? It is not the first time I have left, nor likely to be the last. Once you would have cheerfully waved me off, or even thrown a *fête*. What is so different now?"

Reluctantly, Marcelle realized he was right. But Damien was thirty-one now, and Edward was no longer there to console her. She was beginning to feel her own age, no matter how youthful she still appeared. Her dark eyes brimmed with tears as she reached out to her son with open arms.

"You are my only child," she whispered, and

she saw his blue eyes soften slightly. For all his curt ways, Damien was not as hardened as he appeared.

With an inner sigh, the earl lingered one last moment to kiss his mother goodbye. He believed Marcelle truly grieved to see him go, but he also knew the moment he was gone, she would once again be caught up in the intrigues of the French court, and be honestly surprised when he turned upon her doorstep at Chateau de Villette.

Marcelle tended to be flighty and forgetful, though he loved her dearly. His only regret was that if he were to die overseas, it would likely be months or even a year before she heard of it, and she would need every moment of that time to secure herself a husband and assure another heir for her French estates.

After the emotional parting with his mother, Lord Cross strode briskly outside and down the long row of small steps from the stately manor house. Pausing before he got into the waiting coach, he let his gaze sweep over the grand estate overlooking the sea.

Here on the Devon coast, the jagged cliffs appeared to be all that kept Mistgrove Manor from being swept away by the angry gray waves. The channel was torrid and treacherous, and often covered with dense fog, but the humid air that had given Mistgrove its name never seemed more exhilarating than when Damien rode his hunter at a fast gallop through the ancient oaks bordering his lands. He always felt a rush of pride to gaze upon the legacy that Edward Cross had left him, and a deep contentment too, whether walking through the apple orchards or just watching the fat Devon cattle greedily grazing for miles in every direction.

His mother was welcome to France and to their fine chateau there. He found it pleasant to visit on occasion, but Mistgrove . . . Mistgrove was home. Damien burned it into his memory once more before he left, in case this time proved to be the last he set foot on this rich, dark earth.

It felt good to be out again beneath the open sky and stars. Damien breathed deeply of the tangy salt air during the long days and nights aboard a ship christened *Adelaide*.

Bound for the Mediterranean via the Strait of Gibraltar, Lord Cross had secured permission from the queen to stop in Cherbourg and tend to business matters, for he also had his estate near Rouen to see to. By way of telegraph, he sent brisk instructions to the staff at Chateau de Villette. Even in his absence, Damien was a meticulous man.

Reassured that the estate would be kept running smoothly by his steward, Guy Fontblaine, he then resumed the arduous journey by railway toward the heart of the Crimean front.

During the following weeks, Damien met with men traveling under similar orders, gentry and commoners alike, many of whom were old friends and were delighted to be able to serve with the well-liked nobleman on the latest campaign.

Stories of Damien's former success in Algeria were quickly recalled and spread to eager ears. There were many who remembered him as a favorite of King Louis-Philippe's before the Republic, and Damien's high honors earned as an officer in the French Foreign Legion were much envied. A tale of how Lord Cross had singlehandedly convinced the Arab king Abdel Kader to give up his long battle after years of bloodshed was now told with great embellishment.

As Damien smiled and laughed among the lesser men, it was hard to imagine he had ever seen bloody battle or strife. Such a handsome face seemed better suited to an indolent court life, or upon a portrait hanging in a hall. But the dubious few who glanced upon Damien's hands, expecting soft white skin, saw instead callouses and faint scars that lent truth to all the fantastic tales.

By early autumn, soldiers and officers alike found themselves on another ship threading the Grecian isles and at last arriving at the Bulgarian port of Varna. The city which would be the main base of operations for the combined allies was a popular vacation spot, though it served a grimmer purpose now.

Now only the Black Sea, an ancient and strategic body of water, remained between them and the enemy. One hundred fifty allied naval ships, warships, and transports lurked just offshore Varna and awaited further commands from the admirals.

As they dropped anchor, Damien Cross went to the rail of the *Constant Star,* moving hawk-sharp eyes along the rugged coastline, mentally mapping familiar routes of old. Though only thirty-one, he had the experience of a well-seasoned traveler, and it was not hard to see how his sun-bronzed skin and black hair had blended in well with the natives during his years in Algeria.

When he was summoned for consultation with Admiral Brady in his quarters, Damien was not terribly surprised. He expected he would be briefed about the men he was to command in the coming battle. He had shed his fine waistcoats and trousers long ago, and appeared in the admiral's cabin wearing only canvas trews and a plain white shirt like the rest of the men. He saw that his simple attire took the commander off guard.

"M'lord," Admiral Brady acknowledged gruffly, sizing Damien up and obviously startled to discover a strong looking, virile fellow instead of the mincing nobleman he had expected.

Here was no court dandy! Clearly uncomfortable with formalities, Admiral Brady overlooked further polite conversation and invited the earl to a whiskey.

With equal directness that pleased the Irishman, Damien took his measure of drink and sat down, obviously prepared for a serious discussion as he rolled up his shirt sleeves and glanced over the map Brady had laid out on the desk.

"I've heard you've had experience here before," Brady began without preamble. "I need some advice on going in."

"Surely you have your orders already from Her Majesty's naval advisers," Damien said with some surprise.

"Aye." Brady's Irish accent was still strong even after years of living on English soil, and the shorter man scratched at his close-cropped, coppery beard as he stalked the confines of the cabin. "But it's not that simple, Cross-ah, m'lord."

Like many of the Gaelic, Brady had an aversion for titles, and he coughed irritably and rushed on. "As you know, we're land-locked here, and it makes navigating much more dangerous than the open sea. Most of us in Her Majesty's command are more comfortable without such land constraints, but the Russkies know this body of water like that of their wives'." He slapped the small blue circle marking the Black Sea on his map, and waited for Damien's remarks.

"Unfortunately, I can tell you little more than your own men. There are many who have been here more often than I. I'm certainly no sailor to be advising you on strategy where your ship is concerned. My earlier campaigns were all done on land."

"I'm not asking you to navigate the ship," Admiral Brady clarified, "but I've heard you've a ken of the folk here, and some grasp of their ways."

"I did spend three years in Sevastopol, before the present war. I understand the language and, to some extent, the mindset of the people." Damien did not feel it necessary to add that he had also been to the Russian court in those days. He had managed an amiable discourse with Czar Nicholas, whom he still admired even as he prepared to take up arms against that same ruler now.

"I will admit to being somewhat familiar with Turkey and her sultan too. You see, according to Czar Nicholas, it was Abdul Medjid's obstinance that led to this conflict, and the eventual intervention of both France and England. Several years ago, I served as an ambassador to the Ottomans. I was stationed in Constantinople, so I have a passable grasp of Turkish."

"Then surely you see why that makes you invaluable now. This war may well hinge on men like yourself who understand the heathen mentality."

Damien gave the admiral such a look with his keen blue eyes that Brady soon realized the error of his words.

"Heathens, Admiral? I assume you refer to a lack of Christian beliefs rather than the fighting capabilities of the Turkish army. For the Ottoman Empire may indeed be a sick old man as Czar Nicholas claims, but I can assure you it still kicking hard."

Admiral Brady took the rebuke with good grace. "I ask only for your advice on taking in my own ship, m'lord. The others may blunder where they will, but I always turn to an experienced man."

"Fairly said." Damien set down his whiskey and motioned Brady over the map. "I will show you what I feel would be a prudent course, but it's not without some risks. I've been called reckless by some, but as you see, I've outlived them to defend my actions." He grinned at the memory, and for a moment looked a decade younger, with a slight dimpling in his left cheek.

"That's good enough for me." Brady returned a wry smile as he prepared to listen to the young earl. "For I've been dubbed a crazy man myself, m'lord, and I don't dare disappoint my critics now."

After spending several hours closeted in the admiral's cabin pouring over maps, Damien was relieved to escape to the open deck again to get his bearings.

Since nightfall, the shipboard activity had gradually lulled, broken only by the rhythmic slapping of the waves against the great vessel and the occasional off-tune whistling of a sailor swabbing the deck. Looking out across the water, Damien could see the winking lights of the Bulgarian coastline where Varna lay.

Somewhere in the dark, the remainder of the combined forces of Her Majesty Queen Victoria and Napoleon III also lay in wait for the orders that dawn would bring. Earlier that day, Damien had spotted the smaller Sardinian fleet and six heavily gunned Turkish warships riding low in the water to the east. Under the recent treaty, the allies had agreed to wait for Sultan Abdul's word before attacking the Russian front in unison.

It turned out to be weeks before anyone saw further action. Damien measured the span of days with a variety of diversions, such as playing cards with the other men and bettering his sea-faring skills. He was unused to sitting still, and frustrated by the lack of exercise. But at least this was a pleasant contrast to the busy intrigues of the European courts, and not having to fend off any fluttering females made it a decidedly relaxing change.

Finally, after a series of cloudy, rainy days and freakish storms that hailed the onset of winter, the *Constant Star* received her orders.

She and several other ships were ordered to pace the land armies now headed toward Sevastopol. The bad weather had delayed the invasion and forced the foot soldiers and cavalry to land in less hospitable terrain nearly thirty miles from their goal.

Following Damien's advice, Admiral Brady took a quicker, more dangerous route and easily outdistanced the other ships still getting underway. Theirs was the first battleship to escort the landward troops, and they arrived in the waters outside Sevastopol just as the combined armies under Lord Raglan and Marshal Saint-Arnaud struck at the gates.

With the planning of one of their brilliant engineers, Colonel Todleben, the Russians had set up their base in an ancient fortress, capable of withstanding the greatest of attacks. As Admiral Brady shouted commands to bring the warship about, Damien gazed out with frank admiration at the stronghold that awaited them.

Czar Nicholas was nothing if not industrious. He had combined the naturally defensible position of Sevastopol with the walls of an ancient Greek city near the sea, and so constructed a virtually impregnable barrier from which to strike out at the Turks.

Obviously the czar had expected the sea to be his friend here, but in his ambition he had failed to take into account the traditional fighting skills of the Turks upon water. Off starboard, Damien watched while a heavily laden

Russian ship struggled to come about in time to deflect a two-fold attack from a pair of lighter, fleeter Turkish vessels.

As Damien had expected, the larger ship could not right herself in time to evade the stream of shot that erupted into her bowels. While he watched with his hands clenched on the rail, the Russian brig listed and sank, men screaming and diving from her decks. Those that surfaced were quickly cut down by Turkish marksmen firing a hail of bullets into the churning seawater.

Such was the insanity of war, a fact Damien had long grown used to but still bitterly resented. He himself had no permanent ties to either France or England, but many men had wives and families for which this campaign would bring nothing but grief and hardship.

"Lord Cross!" One of the sailors was shouting for Damien's attention, hands cupped to his mouth from the crow's nest. "Brady is looking for you!"

Nodding his understanding, Damien hastened through the bustle above deck to Admiral Brady's side, where the Irishman was squinting through a spyglass at the massive sea walls surrounding Sevastopol.

"Where should we point our cannon? It all looks a lost cause to me!"

Damien scanned the seemingly impenetrable walls, now swarming with men firing haphazardly out at the *Constant Star,* though she was still out of range.

"Come round to the left a bit; as I recall there's some old damage from previous wars that has yet to be repaired."

Admiral Brady did as advised and soon they could make out faint chinks in the stone where a hasty patch had been made.

"Bless ye, m'lord," Brady cried, "we'll take her yet!" The admiral hollered orders at his men again, and black smoke belched from the ship's belly. Damien soberly watched several distant soldiers on the walls of Sevastopol hurtle to their deaths.

In his excitement, Brady's voice took on a stronger, more pronounced accent. "We'll hit again in the same spot and rub them right sore! See if that bloody czar doesn't wet his trews to be staring down our cannon now!"

Damien made no comment, but privately he thought that if Czar Nicholas even bothered to be on the front with his men, which was very unlikely, he would surely not gamble his life peering out over the walls at one ship among many.

"They'll curse us now!" Brady shouted, his ruddy face taking on a sheen of pure devilish glee as the guns roared again. But during the fighting they had drifted closer in, and were near enough to the city now that some of the Russians were finally able to hurl back fire of their own.

Just to Damien's left a soldier took a ball in his chest and fell screaming to the deck. As the earl ducked and crawled to the man, he heard more shot whistling overhead, and the curses and cries of other men randomly struck.

"Renault, can you hear me?" Damien shouted over the fracas as he looked down into the agonized face of a fellow French officer who had served with him in Algeria.

"Must you shout even at a dying man? Sweet *Jesu,* I had enough of that in Constantine!" Even as he weakly joked, blood began to bubble from Jacques Renault's lips, and Damien ground his own teeth in mute despair.

"I'll find the ship's surgeon. You must hold on, man!"

But in the next few minutes as Damien's eyes desperately sought the bloodied decks for any sign of the physician Lindley, he also knew with gut-wrenching certainty that it was too late for his friend. In his growing delirium, Jacques lapsed into French and began to mutter longingly of Paris and her pleasures. Damien could only murmur in commiseration with the dying man until at last Renault was silent and still.

Damien bowed his head to the deck and mourned for a friend who had joined him eagerly in this latest campaign. Like all the others aboard ship, he was to stare Lord Death in the face many more times that day, but it never got any easier, and he only grew more hardened as the Black Sea quickly turned to red.

What began as a straightforward intervention to check Russia's ambitions in the Mediterranean soon deteriorated into a vicious, bloody battle that saw thousands of unnecessary deaths on each side.

Getting supplies overland was all but impossible, and when Damien and the other men were at last able to go ashore, they found fellow ground forces already covered with chilblains and frostbite, their boots literally worn off their feet, but no replacements to be found. Unused to the brutality of a Crimean winter, many of the European soldiers were losing limbs and their lives in the harsh climate.

The weeks that followed were hardly more than a living hell. A blizzard struck in early October, and men died like flies from the cold and the cholera. Half-frozen corpses were left lying scattered where they fell, the ground being too hard to dig graves. Damien took a wound in his upper right shoulder at the conflict along the Alma River, where over eight thousand men had died.

For two weeks he carried his useless arm in a filthy sling, using his left hand for any necessary work. Then, when a fellow officer insisted the wound be looked at in the medical tent, Damien was one of the first to receive the gentle ministrations of one of the recently arrived and desperately needed nurses. It was from her that he learned of the true horror of this war; more than twice the men were dying from disease than from battle wounds.

After only a month of fighting, the harbor was blocked by sunken ships and it was obvious that no more supplies were forthcoming by sea. Admiral Lyons was in charge of the port blockade, and though he periodically sent small boats in with foodstuffs and medicine, the provisions never lasted more than a few days.

Between skirmishes, the British had managed to set up a permanent base at Balaklava, and the French at Kamiesch. Damien stayed with the British contingent to rally his men. It would have been easy to avoid the battlefield as many of the other commanding officers had done, sending out the enlisted ranks to fight and die like animals. Damien's conscience would not let him do so, and his popularity with the soldiers grew by leaps and bounds.

But behind his optimistic facade, Damien burned with helpless frustration. He was forced to watch as disheartened British soldiers broke and ran, scattering the lines, and he heard boys too young to grow beards scream with agony when their frozen limbs were amputated in the medical tent. In his own numb, mindless world, the earl took one day at a time, serving on the front lines and then falling back to recoup, sometimes assisting the too few physicians in hasty operations by holding a man down or pouring rot-gut into an open mouth to ease the agony.

Though it initially appeared that the Russians would have an easy win, used to the weather as they were, the slow passage of days finally saw the tide beginning to turn. More soldiers and fresh supplies occasionally arrived from Europe, boosting morale and resolve in the wearied troops.

Damien received word from his mother at last, after having been seven months away from home, and a wry grin twisted his mouth as he read the familiar spidery scrawl on rose-scented parchment dated four months ago.

Mon fils, I hope this letter finds you well and alive after so long away. Of course I realize that the mail service is dreadful during wartime, but I have heard nothing from you or of you . . . and if you are injured or not. However, as you suggested, I have taken respite in France and returned to the chateau to pass the dreary winter months. Mistgrove is closed up and I dismissed the servants with ample wages until your return. Dear Henriette is as frantic as I for word about you. I told her I had heard nothing, but she still calls on me every week. Please, if you find a moment to spare for your poor Maman, write to me here at Villette. In the meantime, I will drown my sorrows with the distraction

of a fête at Fontainebleau, for which I will
wear half-mourning in a lovely dark purple
velvet until I hear from you again . . .

The rest of the letter went on to detail several other gowns Marcelle had purchased for the dramatic effect she so loved, and Damien shook his head with a smile as he folded the letter and tucked it away in his shirt pocket.

His mother was still young enough to be courted, having had Damien when she was only sixteen, and Marcelle had often been accused by the other court ladies of having some secret potion that kept her so beautiful. Damien suspected that his mother's secret was having a host of lovers half her age. It was not hard to imagine how even his staid, proper English sire had succumbed to Marcelle's sparkling charm. The harder question had always been why Damien did not have a dozen brothers and sisters, considering how much time his parents had spent in their bedchamber. Now that he was older and wiser to the ways of women, Damien supposed that Marcelle had merely availed herself of one of the tricks that were popular for preventing pregnancy.

But since Edward Cross's untimely death due to a heart condition, his widow had spent less and less time at the Devon estate. Longing for France as she always had, Marcelle was a hothouse flower that quickly wilted in the cold English winters and rainy springs. Damien expected his mother would eventually declare a firm preference for Chateau de Villette and leave the management of the Mistgrove estate entirely up to him.

In his youth, Damien had spent equal time in both countries and found advantages and drawbacks to each. In the queen's court he was a noted favorite and had only to ask for what he desired. The same had once been true when France was a republic, but in the new empire Damien was less sure of where he stood. Still, his mother's name was not without its influence there. In their day, the de Villettes had been a powerful and wealthy family, and their holdings in the north of France were still considerable.

Naturally, the pressure had been upon Damien since he was barely out of nappies to secure a fine match and produce more heirs for the earldom in England. He had been betrothed twice, unbeknownst to him until Edward's death, to two different girls of approved families. His father had apparently not considered Damien's wishes of much import, and so the younger man had been rather surprised, and outraged, to learn of such machinations when Edward suddenly died.

The third earl of Devonshire had always been a decisive man, with all but his wife Marcelle, who had somehow always managed to wheedle and charm Edward into doing her bidding. Such was how Damien had come to have a French first name, though by tradition eldest boys were usually named for their sires. By guile or wile Marcelle had wrangled that feat, as well as many others during her marriage.

By now Damien had also learned that it was his mother who had saved him from disastrous marriages to either of the two debutantes Edward had selected—young ladies who both later turned out to be vicious shrews who drove their respective husbands to early graves.

Women, Damien had decided a decade ago, were better kept for pleasures of the moment, not years of conjugal misery. He had mistresses in both European courts, one of which was the delectable Henriette his mother had referred to in her letter, but he was always careful to choose ladies who were wise enough not to press him for commitments. Someday, he supposed, he would succumb to society's standards and take a wife pretty enough to pass court inspection and mindless enough to produce the necessary sons year after year.

Sometimes, though, he envied the men who spoke wistfully of their country wives, women without ambition who placed no shrill demands upon a man's time or money, and who were a species apart from the helpless butterflies that flitted around the European courts, scheming only to snare rich husbands.

Damien was astute enough to realize that the beauties he dallied with at court would never spend time with him if he lacked or lost the fortune that he had now. With an idle smile, he

56

found himself recalling the pretty gypsy waif he had rescued from likely disaster several years ago in Constantinople. How long had it been— three, four years? And he imagined that if that little one had fulfilled her promise in this time, she was no doubt a bright, beautiful young woman. And also, no doubt, long wed as well.

Perhaps there was no woman in the world who could suit Lord Cross. It would, he thought ruefully, take a remarkable girl indeed to fulfill his desire for beauty and intelligence. He found stupid, pretty women exasperating, and bookish females usually had faces and figures to match. Somewhere, someday, he hoped to find a lady who could outshine them all. And, if she also had an adventurous spirit to equal his own, he would count himself then among the luckiest of men.

By mid-October, the Russian commander Prince Alexsandr Menshikov had pulled back to regroup, but still clung stubbornly to Bakhchisarai. Meanwhile, French Marshal Saint-Arnaud finally succumbed to the cholera that had plagued him since the onset of the war. His funeral was hasty and grim, as there was no time to waste on formalities during war.

At the dismal field quarters at Balaklava, Damien grew increasingly bitter. He could hardly blame his men for not wanting to follow in the footsteps of fallen comrades. It was all he could do himself to pick up a gun and slog through the stinking red snow, never knowing what waited ahead.

Eventually it occurred to him that a quicker solution might be found if only they could read the czar's mind, but of course that was impossible. The combined efforts of France and England to insinuate spies in the Russian court had only met with disastrous results.

If only they had a better, less obvious way to tap the secret rivers of information. Damien had mentioned this once to his comrade in arms, Lord Raglan, who had led the British army in the initial attack on Sevastopol. Often the two men met to pass the time and discuss different strategies.

To Damien's surprise, Lord Raglan reminded him of his idea when next they happened to share a rare moment of peace in the officers' quarters on the field.

"I've been thinking of your remark since last we met, about how we might ford the shield around Nicholas and get an insight into his next move," James began as he carefully poured steaming tea into a set of mismatched, chipped cups for Damien and himself.

Though he had lost his right arm at the age of twenty-seven at Waterloo, Fitzroy James Henry Raglan, the Earl of Somerset, had used the ensuing years to master even the most intricate tasks with ease. Given his peerage late in life, Lord Raglan was the epitome of British nobility.

Raglan thought a moment before proceeding with his discourse. Not a man given to quick passions, he had proven his careful style often on the battlefield. And he had watched Damien Cross closely over the past month, both in amazement and admiration at the way the younger earl maintained optimism in the ranks even at the worst of odds.

"As you know," Raglan said at last, "Nicholas has set his sights on reclaiming Constantinople, and he's apparently determined enough to keep up this bloody war for years, if need be."

Damien nodded as he sipped his tea. "I can't see how the czar can afford to lose as many men as he has. Only a madman would keep going under these circumstances."

Lord Raglan chuckled and leaned back in his collapsible canvas chair. "I suppose the same could be said for us! But who can say what a madman will do next? Even the queen's most brilliant advisers have been unable to predict his next move. At Pembroke Lodge they all huddle and murmur like a pack of old women, but only a man on the front can reasonably predict the enemy's next move."

"Which still does not give us one whit of insight into Nicholas's master plan," Damien pointed out.

"Precisely. That is why it occurred to me, after our last visit, that your idea about a different sort of infiltration makes perfect sense. The Russians clearly expected spies in St. Petersburg, and took severe steps to silence our internal networks. I don't need to tell you how many have been caught and killed, but suffice it to say that we are badly crippled at this point as far as news from the north goes."

"Which suggests to me not only a different strategy, but a different course entirely," Damien said.

"Yes. It's amazing how much more successful a plan can be with only a slight twist of logic to make it completely invisible to others. For example, I've been thinking how much more effective we could be if we planted someone in a less obvious place."

"Other than St. Petersburg, you mean?"

Lord Raglan nodded. "It is far too obvious for my taste. I think we would see results faster and easier if we made an indirect route toward Moscow, skirting the larger towns and provinces, listening instead for the rumors among the common folk. As you know, even the most outrageous rumors usually have a grain of truth hidden somewhere in their core."

"Are you suggesting native spies?" Damien frowned as he considered that idea. He'd spent enough years in the East to know how loyal certain factions were. Especially among Russians, who were descended from closely-knit tribal groups, there was a fierce patriotism that could not be easily bought or sold when it came to their country.

The older man read Damien's expression and shook his head. "No, I know that would likely only complicate things, or even come back to haunt us in the end. But you know the people here better than I. What do you think would be the best way to undertake such a feat?"

Damien thought a moment while he finished his tea. Setting the cup aside as carefully as if it were fine porcelain, he rose from the crate he had been using as a chair and paced the length of the tent as he spoke.

"One of our best men, someone who speaks Russian well, could be outfitted as a peasant or tradesman and sent on a circuitous route toward Moscow. His reports would be sent back either by bribes or carrier pigeons, though I think the birds would be the safer route."

Lord Raglan nodded his approval. "Go on."

"He would have to be convincing enough to get into the confidence of the locals. It would take time—several months, at least, to cover a stretch from here to Moscow and back across enemy lines."

"Suppose he took a longer route, say through the Caucasus, by way of Rostov," Raglan suggested.

"It would mean a month longer, but it might be worthwhile to avoid detection," Damien mused. "The enemy is expecting us to strike directly at the capital. We'll have to lull them into thinking we've given up. It could work."

Lord Raglan allowed himself the luxury of a smile, something he hadn't done in months. Like Damien's father, the Earl of Somerset was generally a sober, conservative man who rarely displayed emotion. This war was the closest he had ever come to real despair, but he was careful not to let his men see that. It had been agonizing to watch British ships sitting in full view of Sevastopol with ready supplies while his soldiers died for want of a pair of shoes. This bloody, stupid war had tried his patience dearly. Lord Raglan looked older than Damien had ever seen him as he passed his hand over his graying brow.

"You've run with some gypsies before, haven't you? You mentioned it once before in a previous conversation," he said, gaining Damien's surprised glance and a hint of a grin.

"Yes. It was a long time ago, when I was a far more impulsive youth. I ran away from my father to spite him on a trip to Paris, and joined a band camped on the outskirts of the city. I was sowing my wild oats, I guess, and even stayed with them for several weeks."

Raglan chuckled at the thought. "I can imagine your mother's reaction."

"Marcelle was distressed," Damien admitted, a twinkle in his blue eyes to recall his beautiful *Maman* wringing her hands and scolding him

62

shrilly. He had returned long-haired and filthy and wearing a grin a mile wide. It was less pleasant to remember the whipping Edward had given him for worrying his parents so much, but Damien saw now that he'd probably deserved it.

"Then you know their ways," Raglan continued thoughtfully. "It occurred to me that gypsies are free to move anywhere, from country to country, without passports and the like. They apparently consider themselves a separate nation."

"Exactly. Subject to the rules of no land, nor bound by invisible borders. Though they have been persecuted for years, some countries still give them free passage to go where they will."

"It would seem a perfect cover for our agent," Lord Raglan said. "And I consider you the prime candidate for such a venture."

Damien raised a hand in immediate protest. "Wait a minute, James. I didn't claim to be a gypsy myself. You have to be born into a band to have true kinship with their kind. The closest an outsider, or *gajo,* could ever come to gaining their trust would be what's called a *romani rei,* though they rarely grant that privilege to anyone nowdays."

"Seems to me you could earn that rank quickly enough, if you worked at it," Raglan mused. "What does it take to prove yourself to them, anyway?"

"Every band differs. Some only require that

you accept their ways, like the Manouches did outside Paris, but the Romany in general are often an exacting lot and have some rather unpleasant initiations. I've heard of men being asked to steal or even kill for their tribe. Sometimes marriage is the only direct way in, though that's hardly the least painful route, in my own estimation."

Lord Raglan grinned mischievously. "But I should think that would be the easiest way in for you, Damien. I've seen precious few ladies at court who could resist your charm."

Damien sighed and shook his head. "You might be surprised. There's no telling with gypsy girls. Now granted, James, it's a good idea, but I don't relish the thought of being deep in the heart of the Russian front like that without access to weapons or a means of communication. It could take months to get even the tiniest scrap of valuable news."

"But as you pointed out before, we have nothing now, and it would certainly be worthwhile if we could bring this war to a close. If only we knew the czar's intentions . . ."

Damien paused his pacing to think for a moment. But when he made up his mind, he did so quickly and without reserve. "All right," he announced suddenly, "I'll give it a shot. But I'll need support from you, patience from the queen, and a considerable dose of courage for my own part."

Raglan smiled. "My boy, I don't think you're

lacking for that in the slightest. As for support and patience, I personally guarantee that if you make this attempt for England, you'll be buried in medals back home. Which, as you can see, is a bloody sight better than being buried *here*."

Three

It had grown unexpectedly warm during the night, and April thrashed restlessly under the blankets on her pallet in the wagon. Knowing the men of the band had all gathered in the king's tent to mull over her fate had not made sleeping any easier, and the dreams she did have were full of strange, frightening shadows and sounds.

April tried not to disturb Tzigane, but when she sat up at last with silvery tears streaming down her face, her muffled sobs caused her foster mother to whisper across the wagon.

"Hush, *chavali,*" Tzigane soothed, using the same gypsy word for daughter that she had so often crooned in baby April's ear. "All will be right in the end, you will see."

April knew then that Tzigane had not slept either, but also lay awake and listened to the fateful murmur of the men outside. She wished she could believe the seer, but the prickle on the nape of her neck told April that something bad was going to happen.

The young woman clenched the patchwork quilt in her hands. By the thin stream of moonlight coming through the open cooking vent in their wagon, her lovely fair features were touched with silver cobwebs of shadows and her hair gleamed palest gold. Tzigane could see the glistening teardrops on her daughter's cheeks.

"I could run away," April choked out, but there was no heart in her words. To leave the Lowara would be to lose her heritage and her life, and even banishment would be better than such a coward's choice.

"Tonight you can do nothing but get some rest." Even the superstitious Tzigane could be practical at times. "Morning may bring a solution to us, who knows? You will only call to the dark spirits if you let such thoughts take over."

April could hardly believe the fortune-teller could stay so calm. Tentatively she asked, "Have you seen something else in the cards?" She hated to admit it now, but she hoped Tzigane had seen something good, and that it was going to come true.

Her mother was silent for a moment. When she spoke again, her voice was rasped with age, and April was painfully reminded that this woman who had saved her life as an infant was no longer young and strong.

"Daughter, I have always told myself that when the time was right, I would show you something that would change your life. Seeing only darkness surrounding you now, I think that there is no better time than this. If nothing else, you may be comforted to know that I have planned for your future, and have not forgotten the joy you have brought me."

April was bewildered. She knew Tzigane kept a small cache of gold coins securely knotted in a kerchief under her bed, for she had shown the girl where to find the money if ever her guardian should meet with an accident and April was left alone. But aside from that and her pack of tarot cards, April knew of no great treasure which Tzigane had that could avert the calamity they were facing now.

"I don't understand," she said as the old woman sat up and began to fumble for a tallow candle to light. "What could you possibly share with me now that would make any difference?"

"On this day, perhaps nothing." Tzigane sighed to admit it, blowing on the candle as she struck a spark to light. "Ah. That's better. Now I can see your pretty face when I give you your rightful *sumadji.*"

"Inheritance?" Now April was openly curious against her will, and temporarily forgot her troubles to swing her legs over the side of her bed and lean toward the *phuri dai.*

"Yes. I have kept it hidden these many years

68

because you were too young to understand, and I was afraid if the others should find out."

April tingled with the suspense of it. Her voice dropped to a whisper to match Tzigane's as she asked, "Is it so terrible then?"

By the candlelight Tzigane's eyes glowed like golden coals. "Terrible only in that man is greedy, and what he see, he wants. The same is true for woman, but to a lesser degree. However, none must know of what I show you now . . . your birthright and your heritage."

Tzigane reached around her own neck to lift a small velvet pouch dangling from a plain cord. She had worn the amulet for years, telling everyone it contained a magic pebble for good luck, and none had questioned the fanciful old seer. April remembered seeing the worn green pouch many times, though Tzigane usually kept it hidden under her blouse. Now she pulled it off and handed the smooth little sack to April. The girl felt it curiously for a moment, looking at her foster mother in confusion.

"Isn't this your magic rock? It feels like it."

Tzigane smiled, eyes glinting with her inner knowledge. "No, *chavali*," she whispered triumphantly, "it is *your* magic rock. Open it!"

As April's trembling fingers fumbled with the tight drawstring, Tzigane went on to explain, "When I found you, a tiny babe in the woods, you were naked and completely exposed to the cruel snows. But around your neck there was this pouch, this little mystery . . ."

April gasped as she shook the velvet bag open and something round and hard tumbled into her palm. There, reflecting prisms against her face, lay a huge and perfectly faceted diamond, the secrets of her origin stored in its sparkling clear depths.

"Even King Jingo does not know of it. When he saw that I was missing, and took me back to camp," Tzigane continued, "I was careful to hide it once I had seen what it was, and have kept it secure at my breast all these years."

April rolled the beautiful gem in her fingers. "What does it mean? Who would put such a valuable thing around a baby's neck that they abandoned to die? I don't understand!"

Her voice was ragged with grief and upset. Putting an arm around the girl, Tzigane said, "I have only guesses to make, and have made many over the years. Perhaps your mother had to hide you from evil ones, and intended to hurry back when she could. Maybe the jewel was stolen, maybe you were too . . . who knows? Your past is silent even in my cards. But the jewel is worth a great deal, and its sale would last you to the end of your days."

Instead of comforting April as intended, the tale only seemed to embitter the girl. "So I was cast off like an unwanted kitten to die, with a thing of great worth wrapped around my neck. Why did my mother not just strangle me and be done with it?" She tossed the glittering gem

70

back in the pouch and pushed it at Tzigane. "I don't want it! And no *gajo* would buy such a gem from a gypsy, they who call all of us cutpurses and thieves! I would be hung if I tried to sell it in a city!"

Tzigane let the girl rage for a moment, then tentatively began, "Well, whether you want it or not, it is yours. Your birthright—"

"And my curse!" April cried. "Keep it yourself; you have earned it caring for me all these years."

The seer's face reflected hurt. "April, I would not have taken you in had I not truly wanted a child of my own. My greatest heartache when I was young and married was that I could not give my beloved Bal a child. He, too, often spoke longingly of the children we would have someday—brave strong sons and beautiful daughters to dote on in our old age."

Tears dripped and slid silently down the old woman's creased face as she swallowed hard and went on. "And when I found you, I was overcome with joy. . . . Bal was gone but I felt he had left me a legacy in the wood, a love gift to remind me of what little time we did share in this world. That is why I gave you the name of the blessed month in which I found you, so I would always remember the beauty of spring and the flowers blooming, even in the snow."

April cried too as she embraced her foster mother then. She cared nothing for the jewel, precious though it might be, for it paled to insignificance beside this true gem of a woman who had given an orphaned babe her heart and home. They clung to each other and wept softly in unison, in loving joy and deep despair, until a cock's crow signaled the day of reckoning had arrived.

Four

When he arrived in Sukhumi, Damien appeared no different than any of a dozen other passengers disembarking from the Turkish cargo ship. Without much effort he had been able to adopt the look of a down-on-his-luck tramp. His hair had long since grown out to his shoulders and was held back with a bit of string. By deliberately letting the sun fry his skin to a rich, golden brown, he had perfected his cover.

For several days he and Lord Raglan had planned how best to enter Russia. The idea of a gypsy musician seemed the most believable, and his own men had tried to run him out of camp when he first appeared in filthy, torn clothing and bare feet.

Damien's hands were calloused enough to pass close inspection, but his soles were still tender after walking the hot deck at sea. Only time could toughen the skin there, and he set his teeth as he marched ashore across sharp rocks and bits of broken glass lying in the

73

sand. The extent of his worldly possessions, a worn canvas bag and a small wicker cage of cooing pigeons, were slung over his left shoulder.

Aware of the close scrutiny of several idle Turkish soldiers, Damien did his best to scowl and curse under his breath like a genuine vagrant. He hoped his rank smell and appearance would be enough to discourage any questions, and soon enough the soldiers' eyes had moved on to more likely prey behind him.

Leaving the port area, Damien looked immediately to escape the Turkish city and further his plans. Lord Raglan had given him enough money to purchase a small used wagon and a tired nag, and after a few hours of perusing the docks, he finally secured these and other supplies and made his way into the hills.

Damien spent the first night camped under the stars. It was refreshing not having to share the company of snoring shipmates. The cool, crisp air and painful silence of the thickly wooded land all around him gave him a sudden, sharp pang of homesickness for England. Then he remembered his mission, and quelled any further longings by rolling over and firmly shutting his eyes.

By overland route his way would be both difficult and dangerous, separated as the Caucasus was from mainland Russia. However, he and Raglan could dredge up no better plan for the moment, and to tell the truth, Damien enjoyed the ruggedness of this high-altitude mountain terrain.

Unfortunately, the nag he had bought was stupid as well as old, and had to be cajoled into entering the high mountain passes dragging the wobbly wagon behind. Damien spent the better part of the second day cursing the horse and the burning soles of his feet in alternate refrains. When he stopped to eat, the dry jerky and even drier bread did little to improve his temper. In the thinner atmosphere, the sun burned unmercifully on Damien's already sun-baked body, and by the time he came across a cold, inviting stream the following afternoon, he stank so badly he didn't give a second thought to stripping completely and plunging right in.

Damien surfaced with a strangled gasp of exhilaration, and the frigid water did wonders for his mental attitude. It was a world apart from the luxuries at Mistgrove, but there was something elementally satisfying about a dunk in an icy mountain stream.

After he completed several leisurely laps across the water, Damien paused, feeling a ticklish sensation race down his spine. He was being watched. Alert in battle and still alive to show for it, he drilled a narrow stare through the thick underbrush across the stream.

There was subtle movement in the thicket, and he began to swim slowly in that direction. Although he didn't sense any real danger, and it was probably only a curious forest creature, he wasn't taking any chances.

As he brushed against the farthest bank, the rustle of someone moving to flee was obvious. Damien saw a flash of color, and knowing then that his observer was human, he leapt stark naked from the water and hurled himself in a flying tackle after the fleeing figure.

Thud! They impacted hard and rolled together on the carpet of grass and leaves, and Damien found a wildcat in his arms. With a hiss and a screech, the beautiful young woman struggled in vain to free herself, her blonde hair whipping wildly from side to side.

"*Ciel!* What's this?"

Too surprised to be embarrassed, Lord Cross spoke in French. He stared down in wonder at the vision of loveliness trapped beneath him, the dilated green eyes which, cat-like, watched his every move.

"It seems I've caught myself a pretty spy!"

"Spy?" Curious against her will, April repeated the unfamiliar word in her otherwise perfect French. Then, like a tiger in a trap, she tried to thrash free again, but the earl's strongly corded arms pinned hers firmly to her side.

April's green eyes widened. Wrestling with her first instinct to fight a stranger, her hesitation proved her doom. She wanted to be as furious at this man as she was Nicky, but there was no comparison. Against her will, April felt her anger quickly draining away. She was drowning in his blue, blue eyes . . .

"Mon Dieu!" Damien exclaimed, daring to hope, daring to dream. "It's you, isn't it? The little gypsy girl."

April stared up into the burning eyes of the man who held her. Yes, she had seen him before. But where? When she suddenly remembered, her soft lips parted in shock.

"Non!" she whispered.

"Oui," Damien countered. "You do remember me!" Not knowing why, Lord Cross was pleased. There was danger in recognition, but he would have been absurdly disappointed if she'd failed to respond. He felt her slim body move beneath his, his nudity barely concealed by the flowing lines of her full yellow skirts, and his eyes darkened as he drank in the changes time had wrought.

Lovelier, if anything, now that she was a woman grown. She reminded him of a golden lioness with her tousled mane of sun-bleached hair spilling across the ground in a blaze of light. He moved one hand to pick a leaf from her tangled tresses, and held his breath awaiting an attack. Surprisingly, it never came.

April's thoughts whirled wildly. She could no more fight him than she could herself at the moment, and the sensation of water droplets trickling from his bare chest through her thin white blouse made her shiver with strange sensations. Why did it seem so oddly right that he should appear in her life again? Yet she had never dreamed that a simple walk through the forest this morning would completely change her life.

Here she was, about to stand trial for attempted murder, and yet all she could think of was running her hands through a stranger's thick, black hair, and gazing breathlessly up into his sea-blue eyes . . .

With a wry smile, the earl said, "It seems we haven't been formally introduced yet. My name is Damien." For some reason, he didn't want to lie to her.

April accepted his word, asking only, "Is that a French name?"

He nodded, which seemed to satisfy her, and waited for her to respond in kind. Instead, her next comment made him laugh.

"You're naked!"

"We seem to have gotten ourselves into a compromising position this time," he agreed, glancing momentarily away to focus on the sight of his clothes neatly stacked a measure downstream. "Have you any suggestions?"

"Certainement! You can get off of me!"

Damien gave a low chuckle. "As I recall, I've earned a favor, little girl, from saving you all those years past. How quickly women forget their champions!"

"I promised to tell your fortune, not roll with you in the grass!" April retorted quickly.

"More's the pity. By the way, where did you learn French? You speak it like a native."

"I know several languages," she said, distracted by a lock of wavy black hair which dangled from his forehead. "Gypsies travel a great deal, and I wanted to learn all I could. It's useful for telling fortunes, you see—"

"And charming men?" Damien wondered why the thought sent a sharp pang of jealousy through him. "But surely you cannot be old enough for that. How old are you now, about fifteen?"

"Almost eighteen!" April sputtered, coming up on both elbows when he freed her. Thankfully her skirts covered him all the way up to the waist, but she could not avoid a glimpse of his broad, bronzed chest, heavily furred with dark hair.

Averting her gaze, she asked, "Why are you pretending to be *romani?*" She took careful measure of his wagon and the old horse standing patiently in the traces.

"I have decided to become Rom," Damien replied, keeping his voice even. "I would like to join your band."

She was silent a moment, as if testing the sincerity of his words. *"Gaje* before you have claimed they wish to follow gypsy ways. Usually they quickly change their minds."

Her tone was full of warning, but Damien did not notice. Instead he fought off the longing to run his hands down her smooth bare arms one last time, and asked huskily, "Why were you watching me swim just now?"

His question startled April, but she quickly replied, "I often walk in the woods alone like this."

"To meet a lover?"

"Of course not!" *Not until now, anyway.* The unbidden thought sprang to her mind, and April willed it fiercely away. She dared not admit, even to herself, that for several minutes she had watched Damien swimming, admiring his muscular arms cutting the water in smooth, clean strokes.

"At your age, most girls are married," Damien mused in a low voice as he looked down on her. He resisted the urge to toy with a lock of golden-blonde hair, or to capture her sweetly curved lips beneath his own. Dear God, he was as smitten with this wild-eyed wench as none other before, and he didn't rightly know what to do about it. English lords simply didn't keep company with gypsy girls. Not that he wouldn't mind right now, but he had a mission to complete, and he'd best keep his mind strictly on that.

"I choose not to marry," April announced proudly, daring him to dispute it with a flash of her green eyes.

"Why not? I should think it would be rather advisable for a young girl of your ah—er—rather obvious charms to have a protector."

"Men!" she sniffed her opinion of them, for

a fleeting moment reminding Damien of his own mother. He stifled the urge to laugh. Her brow was puckered in obvious upset. "They only want one thing from women."

"Ah." He nodded grimly as if in understanding. April was forced to wonder if Damien might well be contemplating such a thing himself!

"I'll get my clothes," he said at last, after a long silence during which they simply looked at one another.

April rose and turned the other way while Damien got up and donned his clothes. The earl dressed swiftly with his back to her, anxious to find out more about the young woman who intrigued him so. Like a schoolboy with his first crush, he wanted to know her name, her dreams, and everything else about her.

His heart pounding with anticipation, Damien turned to face her again. The rustle of trees in the breeze was all that greeted him. Silent as a cat, she had disappeared.

And except for the imprint where their bodies had lain together in the soft grass, it was as if she had never existed.

Later that afternoon Damien arrived at a clearing surrounded by towering oaks, the site where the gypsies he sought had laid out their summer camp. Clustered wagons kept the smaller domestic animals in place, and here and there horses were scattered all among the trees. He guessed there were about thirty or forty in the band. The large size of the group suited him well, since he would be able to blend in more easily.

As he drove his wagon into camp, children and dogs came running, making a wild uproar of excitement. The earl was surrounded the moment he stepped down from his wagon, and a surge of curious gypsy hands reached out to him.

Damien sought for any sign of the lovely blonde from the forest, but these folk were all dark. He was startled when one particularly hard-looking older wench with dyed red hair licked her full lips at him in invitation. None of the men seemed to mind this, so perhaps the woman needed a husband, but Damien quickly sidestepped her wet kiss a moment later.

From amid the ruckus a large Slav finally pushed his way thorough, going directly up to Damien and speaking in *romani.*

"Who are you?"

Not intimidated by the husky growl, Damien introduced himself to the *Rom Baro,* the leader of the Lowara. Built like a tree trunk, with muscle to spare, the middle-aged Jingo would have intimidated a lesser man. But Damien looked past the brute strength to note that the king's dark eyes held intelligence and kindly curiosity. Their brief exchange proved the earl correct. Jingo was a friendly man, but he was also cautious. Damien respected the request to have his wagon searched, and he presented his careful tale.

At last the king seemed satisfied, or, Damien thought, perhaps just a little weary of all the noise. Jingo ordered the others to disband, and then invited Damien to his tent for some talk.

"You have come very far, if you have come from France," the king began as he gestured to a comfortable mound of pillows where visitors could recline.

"Have you been to my country?" Damien asked politely as he sat down and leaned back, crossing his ankles in imitation of Jingo. He knew enough to reflect the king's habits with his own, lest he arouse suspicion. He also did not refuse the drink that was offered him.

"I have heard of it," Jingo replied. "There are some who were once Manouches in our band now. You will meet them later. Perhaps you share the same friends."

Damien decided to be direct with this man, whom he wished to deceive as little as possible. "It's not likely," he admitted, "for I am not Rom by birth, but only choice."

Damien proceeded to tell Jingo a somewhat exaggerated story, though still holding a kernel of truth, about how he had run away from his family and joined the Romany. Since then, he added, he had traveled widely, visiting with different bands, but staying with none for long.

"I have chosen the wind for my brother,"

Damien said, quoting a phrase he remembered one of the gypsies saying in the camp he had visited when he was fifteen.

Jingo smiled in appreciation of the meaning. How well he knew a young man's urge to escape and wander the world, and how sometimes, once it was in the blood, a man was called to seek such a life forever. With keen eyes he assessed this *gajo* stranger, this *romani rei,* who seemed sincere enough and truly interested in the Lowara people.

"Which way did you come?" he asked, and listened intently to Damien's story. Then he said, "I have heard of this war in the north. I had thought to delay our next move until things were settled."

"You are wise. The fighting has spread to many of the mountain passes, and travel is no longer safe," Damien agreed. Then he gave a whittled version of what he actually knew of the latest troop movements. The two men talked for a time of the foolishness of *gaje,* fighting over land that should belong to everyone, and warmed to each other in the process. Contrary to expectations, Jingo's imposing size was complemented by a merry, gentle nature. And the king found his unexpected visitor informative and amusing after long weeks on the road.

Considering carefully what Damien had said about the war, the gypsy king confessed, "Even with the war, we must move on soon. For several weeks we have been searching for another band of Rom."

Even Damien knew that was unusual for gypsies. "You are having a reunion or a wedding?"

Jingo sighed and shook his wiry dark head. "No, nothing so pleasant. There has been great conflict in our tribe recently. The Lowara are torn between two of their own." He saw Damien looked curious but unwilling to pry, and it gave him greater respect for the man. "Something bad happened. One of our young men was attacked in the woods."

"Was he hurt?"

Jingo shook his head again. "More pride than flesh was hurt that day. You see, the one who attacked him was a young woman. She claimed he was forcing himself upon her."

Looking puzzled, Damien ventured, "I don't understand. You said they were both of your tribe?"

"Yes. There were three other witnesses who claim the girl invited him, but others believe the boy to lie. It is not a simple thing to find someone who does not know either one of them. The tribe is divided by their stories."

"So you are looking for another band from which to draw an impartial judge," Damien filled in. "It seems the wisest course."

"But we have wandered for over two weeks, and the war has driven most Rom off," Jingo explained. "So my people grow frustrated with the delay in justice. Half think the girl should be banished, but there are young men who beg to have her hand in marriage just to save her from a terrible fate."

"She must be quite a woman," Damien remarked lightly, imagining for some reason the brassy, full-blown wench who had been making eyes at him earlier.

Jingo said soberly, "She is like no other here. I admit I do not know what will happen to her. The mood of the camp changes each day. Lately the rumors have been leaning toward the boy's tale."

"Why do you tell this to me?" Damien asked.

Jingo shrugged. "You see my plight. A decision must be made swiftly before someone is hurt. We need an outsider," and his dark eyes bored into Damien's directly, "to settle their differences as soon as possible."

Naturally hesitant to get involved, Damien tried to demur, but Jingo proved most insistent.

"I ask only this one thing of you. Nobody knows you here. My people have not seen a *romani rei* before, but your kind are met with respect among Rom, and I myself will be responsible for your decision. Please, will you not help me to settle this matter and ease the hearts of my people?"

Though his conscience warned against it, Damien considered it long enough to be swayed. He finally accepted Jingo's request, saying, "Does this mean I can stay with the Lowara?"

Privately he was thinking that nothing would be easier; first making an impartial ruling on the incident in the woods, then cozying into the camp as one of the gypsies himself. It would open a back door into Czar Nicholas's homeland. And, if he could find the lovely young nymph who had haunted him at the stream, then so much the better.

"You are welcome to stay as long as you wish to," Jingo said, and once reassured of the newcomer's assistance, he was even more friendly. Damien let out a deep breath of relief as he realized he had secured the necessary cover for entering the Russian front.

"There's the *gajo*," April told Tzigane. She was careful, though, not to let her obvious interest show as she gestured out the back of the fortune teller's wagon toward the figures of Jingo and Damien walking through the gypsy camp.

"He's not a *gajo*, he's a *romani rei*," Tzigane corrected her daughter. Letting the flap fall closed again, the seer returned to her sewing and bit the length of string dangling from her needle and tied it off.

Holding up the beautiful skirt she had just finished, of bright emerald green muslin with a satin-like sheen, Tzigane nodded with satisfaction. By the light of the lamp she worked by, the skirt danced with tiny reflections of gold along the elaborately embroidered, layered flounces.

Across from her April returned to stabbing ineffectually at her own material, pushing the needle hastily through the cotton of the white ruffled blouse on which she was working. She tried to wrench her thoughts from Damien, but couldn't. To deny her own curiosity, April said firmly, "He's not one of us."

"Not of our blood, but of our beliefs," Tzigane answered. "There are a few who understand our ways who are not born Rom. This man is one of those. I could tell at once."

"You are not suspicious of him?" April asked curiously. Tzigane rarely trusted anyone at first sight, and her foster daughter was frankly amazed.

"I have seen him in the cards," the seer replied vaguely, but said nothing more. Instead Tzigane smiled in secret pleasure as she finished hemming the green skirt with its swirling gold embroidery. She had coaxed April to work on the blouse under the pretense of making it for another woman in the band.

Restless tonight, April proved an impatient pupil. She knew why, though she did not wish to admit it to Tzigane or even herself. She was thinking of Damien, of the way his blue eyes had caressed her, as his hands had obviously longed to. And she had felt the strangest, bittersweet sensations pulling their souls together, even as she had fought to keep their bodies apart.

Tzigane could tell something was troubling the girl. She assumed it was because of the trial to come, where April's fate as well as Nicky's would be decided. If Jingo did not find someone to resolve the conflict soon, there would be grave trouble. Her motherly heart bled for the beautiful child-woman who was bent over the blouse now, tears of frustration in her eyes.

"The *rei* will distract the others for awhile," Tzigane said, "and I saw he carried a violin. Now that everyone's attentions are occupied, you will perhaps be able to do more."

"Can I ride Prince Adar?" April asked, her voice raw with longing and an inner pain reflecting deep in her eyes as she looked over at her mother.

Tzigane hesitated. She knew how vehemently the others had insisted that April be forbidden access to the stallion. "We will ask Jingo," she said, not daring to give the girl any shred of hope for fear of disappointment.

Then, to break the gloomy silence, Tzigane decided to surprise April. Rather than save the skirt for a special occasion, she reasoned it would mean more right now.

"April," she began innocently, "I think you are the closest to Choomia's size. Would you try on the skirt now and let me make the final fit?"

The girl set aside her own project gladly and slipped out of her own skirt. After Tzigane helped her put on the new one, April stood still and let the old woman adjust the folds and gathers.

"It seems just right," Tzigane said, pleased with her work, which was a perfect color for April's eyes and hair. "Put on the blouse too so we can see the whole outfit."

April exchanged blouses and let her mother fuss again with the ruffled neckline. The blouse was made to be worn off the shoulders, and April did not protest as Tzigane tugged each side down a few inches, revealing the girl's smooth, golden skin.

Tzigane pursed her lips in consideration. "It needs something more. Will you get me my box?"

Puzzled, April did as her mother asked. She brought Tzigane the carved wooden jewelry case that had been passed down in her own Romany family for several generations.

Pawing carefully through the stash of jewelry, Tzigane selected a matched set of gold coin earrings, a necklace and a thick gold arm band. She persuaded April to put them on and stepped back for a look. She smiled and nodded at the picture she saw.

April was a golden beauty, her blonde hair curling about her hips and her stance still proud and resolved. For all her misery the girl would not buckle, and she more than deserved the gifts Tzigane gave her now.

"These things are yours now," the fortune-teller stated as she closed her box and put it away. "Bal gave them to me, and I want you to have them. Wear them with pride and remember you are always a Lowara woman . . . no matter what any of the others say."

Stunned, April fingered the rich fabric and looked at Tzigane. She was too moved to speak, and when the old woman urged her outside, she could not protest strongly enough to make any difference.

"Go," Tzigane said abruptly. "For once you will go out and enjoy yourself by the fires. The others are too busy with the stranger to take much note of you. You may find a moment of peace in which to gather your thoughts."

Giving the generous woman a grateful hug, April blinked back the threat of tears. Then, taking a deep breath, she slipped from the tent and melted into the shadows of the night.

As Damien had feared, it was not long before the gypsies called upon him to demonstrate his musical prowess. As a people they loved music, and almost all were gifted with dancing or instrumental skills. They would be suspicious if he could not match them song for song, and so he gave in at last and went to fetch his violin. Fortunately, in his youth Damien had taken fourteen years of music lessons at his mother's strict insistence. After all, Marcelle had said, only the *bourgeoise* had money without talent!

Damien shrugged aside the last of his worries and rejoined the others. He knew he had a good ear for music, and he thought he would be able to bluff his way through most of the unfamiliar songs.

The entire camp gathered around the largest fire built in the circle of wagons, and dark eyes shone with excitement. Even the older folk, initially distrustful of the stranger, had finally been swayed by Damien's fascinating tales of countries far afield. They all circled round to provide a clapping, cheering audience for his music, and the moment he launched into the first song, they were keeping time with tambourines as well.

April heard the music from a distance, poised on the edge of the woods away from the busy camp. Her keen ears immediately registered the glorious solo as something out of the ordinary, and as if drawn by an invisible cord, she found herself walking back toward the orange glow of the bonfires.

There she hovered in the shadows and tried to peer through the milling bodies for a glimpse of Damien. The music struck a chord somewhere deep in her breast, though it was a song she had never heard before. It reminded her of cool, smooth-flowing water, the melting tones almost hypnotizing her as the bow was drawn with unequalled skill.

Stepping cautiously between two tethered horses, April leaned out for a better look. Her green eyes widened at the sight of Damien standing in the midst of the circle, gently coaxing magic from the violin. As he slowly revolved, mesmerizing the crowd, the firelight danced off his features and reflected back an image that instantly reached out to her.

Her heart pounding for a reason she did not yet accept, April closely studied every inch of the *gajo's* face. His black hair was now tied back with a blue kerchief that one of the women had coyly tossed at him earlier. He was different from the Romany men. Though also dark, he towered above the others, his height drawing attention to his lean, muscular body.

Dressed in canvas-colored trousers tied loosely about his waist, Damien's white peasant shirt was unbuttoned just far enough to reveal the thatch of black, silky chest hair. He easily caught the eye of all the young women, including April. But she was angry at herself for being intrigued by a *gajo,* an outsider.

Damien continued to play his violin like a lover, his long fingers caressing the neck of the instrument as they slid smoothly on the strings. His notes rang clear and lovely over those of the others who had joined in, and April ached in silent appreciation of his gift, enfolding him with her gaze. The music made her more and

93

more restless as he moved from rippling tones to increasingly bolder crescendos, pausing on trembling high notes that sent shivers down her spine.

Then she realized with a start that he was staring directly at her. He had come around to face her side of the circle, and either the flash of her jewelry or the sense of her watching him had drawn his eye. Though the smile never wavered from his lips as he led the revelry, and his bare right foot still stamped perfect time, his blue eyes halted and burned through her like a white-hot flame.

Caught in the spell, April met his bold gaze with one of her own. It was as if his entire being challenged her to do something, both by his confident stance and the way his blue eyes beckoned her forth.

Taking a deep swallow, April came into the circle. Several of those watching, Marya among them, hissed angrily and stopped clapping. But the rest of the camp could feel the charged air, and the thread of excitement drawing the gypsy girl to the musician was felt and encouraged with a frenzied burst of clapping.

Damien could not look away from the beautiful nymph who had materialized again from the woods. She was like a brilliant jewel set against the dark velvet backdrop of the night. When she tossed her head and took a proud stance in the circle before him, her long hair

94

rippled like molten gold and almost caused him to falter.

For all her bare feet and unfashionably tanned skin, she was aristocratic, like a princess of wild but royal heritage. The uptilt of her chin and the flashing emerald-green eyes took him back to the day he had first encountered her, a little spitfire with a courage that had won his admiration.

April knew not what madness possessed her that moment, but she raised her arms and began to sway, her hips moving gently to the beat of the tambourines. Something in the night, the air, or the quivering music that flowed like silk, compelled her to dance, whirling slowly and then faster as the tempo increased.

Several of the other men took up their guitars to accompany Damien, and the women hummed in a low, sensual key that thrummed through the night. The leap of the flames seemed in perfect time to April's movements, and before long she found herself putting her heart and soul into the dance.

Green eyes locked to his, April danced for Damien. For now, it was enough that they shared a song. He played with increased fervor, the blood hot and surging in his every limb. His mind could do little more than wonder at the fate of seeing this young woman again. Was she the king's daughter? Her clothing was fine enough, but her fairness made it unlikely. A few of the others seemed to resent her presence, among them the lusty-eyed older woman who had boldly beckoned Damien several times before.

Yet there was nothing lewd about this girl's look. She simply held him in her direct green gaze until he was lost in her, and she in him. Faster and faster she spun, never once losing eye contact with him even as she whirled. Her green skirts flew, her jewelry jingled and gleamed. Then as the crescendo came, she curved into a perfect arch and threw back her head, her golden hair trailing along the ground.

His bow quivered to a stop. April dropped, exhausted, her breast rising and falling rapidly. Then, just as suddenly, she leapt to her feet, looking stunned and almost horrified at what she'd done before she bolted back into the darkness. All around him was a murmur of discontent, but Damien did not hear. His eyes were fixed on the spot where she had vanished, and his hand trembled on the neck of the violin as it dropped slowly to his side.

Five

In the morning, April awoke from restless dreams to find her mother hunched once more over the tarot cards in their wagon. The *phuri dai* did not seem to notice her foster daughter's high color, or the new uneasiness in the girl's voice.

"What do you see?" April asked softly.

The seer's golden agate eyes rose and fixed on her without a waver. "I want you to lay out the arcana, *chavali*. One last time if it must be, but it must be now!"

April's heartbeat quickened at the ominous words. "Will the decision be today? Have you heard something?"

Tzigane nodded. "Jingo came by while you were still sleeping. He has found someone he believes to be a fair judge. The *kris* will be called today within the hour."

The girl rose and sat on the edge of her bed to steady her shaking legs. "Will my fate be decided at the trial?" she whispered.

"Yes, it will be decided today, for better or worse. Now choose your cards!"

This time April did not hesitate. Taking the pack of colorful pictures in her trembling hands, she sorted and shuffled the deck until it fell into the "pattern of her soul," as Tzigane called it. Then, cautiously, she handed the reassembled cards back to the *phuri dai,* who looked pale as she began to lay out the arcana in the form of an inverted cross.

There were ten cards laid out, each representing different aspects of past, present and future. As always, the past was muddled with mystery and intrigue, but the present and future were revealed today with startling clarity.

The first card turned over was the King of Swords. "A dark man," Tzigane murmured thoughtfully. "A powerful man as well, but he has many dangerous secrets."

April did not speak, but she did wonder. Was it Nicky? Or Damien?

The reading proceeded, shortly revealing April's own card, but the last one caused Tzigane to let out a little gasp before she could stop it. Both she and the younger woman stared down into the face of Death, an evil grinning skull looming over April's near future. And though Tzigane tried to be optimistic by pointing out the King of Swords, the dark male soon to be in her daughter's life, neither woman could tear her eyes away from that awful gloating ghoul.

April's lips trembled as she said, "So I must expect the worst. I know that almost everyone in camp believes Nicky. Marya is angry enough not to care what is done to me, though she once claimed to be my friend."

"There are no friends when it comes to a man around here," Tzigane said. "Too many of the girls are looking for husbands." Then, as if hitting upon an insight, she mused, "Perhaps you should, too."

April laughed scornfully. "Who would have me? Already they call me *marhime,* dishonored. But they themselves act no better than the *gaje* they scorn. Were the Lowara always this way?"

Tzigane shook her head as she put the cards away, carefully wrapping them in the square of black silk that would protect them from evil influences. "No. When I first married Bal, the tribe was very small, and all were close. It did not pay to insult a friend, for you might need them the next day. I think it was when the tribes began to intermarry that we started having serious trouble. Some of the other Rom who came to us were not good of heart or soul."

April didn't need to ask whom her mother referred to; it was obvious enough by the darkening of her amber eyes.

"If the worst happens, I want you to keep the jewel and sell it," April said firmly, giving Tzigane no chance to protest. "It will do me no good if the worst happens. But whatever you do, don't let Nicky or his mother find out about it. They would kill you for less than that."

"Where are you going?" Tzigane looked alarmed as April picked up a shawl to warm her bare shoulders against the early morning breeze.

"I think it's almost time. I hear a crowd gathering outside. The *kristatora* will hear my side of the story too, not just Nicky's. They will hear the truth whether they like it or not."

Overcome by a strong sensation of something drastic about to happen, Tzigane reached out to her only child for a fierce hug.

"Let your heritage speak for you, *chavali*. You are not only Lowara, but also of noble blood of this land. No matter that we know not who your real mother was, it is enough that you are strong and able to endure your fate. Remember, you can survive."

April smiled sadly over her foster mother's shoulder. "At this point, there is little else left for me to do."

If ever he had regretted his impulsiveness before, the Earl of Devonshire had ample opportunity in the moments before he presided as the judge over a matter which had the entire camp up in arms.

For no sooner had Damien started for the large tent that had been specially erected for the trial, than gypsies began to flock around him, calling out pleas for mercy or vengeance as each believed to be due. He plastered a non-committal smile on his face, nodding politely to all who confronted him, trying to assure them that he would do his best to resolve the conflict. He dared not promise them anything. He already regretted having accepted Jingo's anxious request so readily.

As he ducked into the colorful tent, Damien was greeted by a solemn group of faces belonging to a select few older men of the tribe. They had apparently been invited to listen to the testimony.

Nodding respectfully to them, Damien took the space left for him and sat down beside Jingo. The king looked drawn and pale against the bright backdrop of the tent folds, and Lord Cross was sure it wasn't easy for Jingo to maintain such a calm expression as the trial began.

First to testify would be the aggrieved party, then the defense. Damien wasn't surprised to see the hard-eyed jade, who had tried for his attentions several times, enter the tent first, though he supposed she was the alleged "attacker." It wasn't difficult to imagine this hot-blooded *gitana* going after any man with a knife, and as he looked at her, he thought what an easy decision this would be after all.

Then to Damien's surprise, she went to sit away from the center of testimony, and a younger man entered moments after her. Like the woman, his dark eyes were flat and hard, and they passed swiftly over Damien with something close to contempt before he stiffly assumed his position before the *kris*.

"Vaivoides." The arrogant young man addressed Jingo curtly, with little genuine respect. "I am ready to tell my tale now."

"Yes, Nicabar." The king sounded weary. He nodded toward the woman, who had assumed a lounging position directly across from Damien and was displaying her bare legs to advantage. "And your mother?"

"Belita is also here to give testimony."

"I was not aware she was a witness to the incident."

Nicky's lips tightened in suppressed anger. "My mother is an important witness. She has proof that Tzigane and her daughter practice black magic."

Damien listened with interest. Now he could see the resemblance between mother and son, both darkly handsome, but in a hard way. The boy had taken obvious pains to make his facial wound more dramatic than it was, with a large fresh bandage taped over his entire cheek. Meanwhile, Damien irritably ignored the obvious efforts of the gypsy woman to draw his eye. First she pretended to fuss with her skirt, exposing bare legs up to her thighs, and then she displayed her ample cleavage as she reached down to readjust a toe ring.

Nicky appealed past Jingo's inscrutable expression to the other men present. "I have been with the Lowara now for several years. During all of this time, April has thrown herself at me. Sometimes I could not resist her. It was as if something else controlled me! My mother has seen this too, and she knows of the power of which I speak."

April. That was an odd name for a gypsy, Damien mused. Apparently the mystery woman was one intent on seducing men and then trying to stab them. Still, Damien wanted to hear more of the angry young man's story before he committed his opinion one way or the other.

"We will let the *kristatora* decide." Jingo suddenly gestured to their guest, and Nicky's dark eyes swung on Damien. "After all, Nicabar, when you asked for this *kris,* you agreed to any decision made by our visitor."

Damien was wise enough to add, "I will be fair. I will hear all who wish to speak."

With a grudging nod, seeing that was the only sensible decision, Jingo also agreed to hear Belita speak.

Nicky told his tale first, with initial calm and then increasing fervor as he detailed April's coy approach to him in the wood, just after he had told her he would marry Marya instead. Painting a picture of a wanton strumpet that would give a run for the money to any London bawd, Nicky exhorted his story to full effect, even gaining a few sympathetic nods and murmurs from the other five men present.

Damien did not react. In fact, he had lost attention for nearly five full minutes, recalling his own sweet encounter with another young woman earlier. He could not shrug aside memories of her glorious golden hair, her emerald-green eyes and the secretive half-smile when she had danced for him. He longed to be with her now, anywhere but in this stuffy closed tent with sweating bodies and the suggestive squirming of the lewd woman across the aisle.

Nicky's testimony finally ended, and looking smug, the youth surrendered the floor to his mother.

With a smile at her son that was anything but maternal, Belita rose with a shimmy and a jangle and haughtily took her place directly before Damien. Knowing full well he held Nicky's fate in his foreign hands, she gave the earl a direct burning look and struck a pose that might have been arousing on any other woman. It inspired only faint disgust in Damien.

"*Kristatora*. You have heard my son speak. He speaks from his heart, as his mother must do now." Belita wet her shiny red lips and continued in a husky voice. "This may be difficult for some of you to believe, but Belita must tell the truth. I have been with the Lowara for over two years. Never have I been brought before a *kris* myself." That much was true; she didn't bother to mention that she'd been banished from her birth band for attacking another woman in a fit of jealousy, and blinding her in one eye.

"I have seen the old witch and her spawn," Belita continued, her low voice mesmerizing every man but the earl. "At night they practice evil arts, chanting in their wagon and wishing ill upon any who cross them. I never did believe the story of the old woman finding the girl. April sprang to life from Tzigane's dark cards! Now she is a young witch herself, and that wild horse is her familiar!"

Belita continued like a building storm, until she had carelessly shredded every bit of April's character, who was not even present to defend herself. The language she used was vile, and Damien glanced at Jingo to see the king's disapproval covering his face like a thundercloud. Such viciousness was unworthy of Rom, a people who needed to band tightly together in a *gaje* world.

When she was finally through, her chest heaving proudly from the exertion, Belita shot one last seductive look of smoldering promise toward Damien and then followed her son out of the tent.

Jingo was inscrutable. "Next," he said, "we will hear from the other witnesses." He called out to have them brought in, and three giggly restless girls were thrust before Damien, blushing and stammering out their stories about how they had seen April throwing herself at Nicky, then slashing him with the knife.

"Do you have any questions for these witnesses?" was all Jingo asked when they were through, as he had with both Nicky and Belita. Damien asked them a few rote questions, still not certain of their credibility, but they seemed too stupid to concoct any fantastic stories that would persist unchanged for so long.

They had obviously witnessed something in the woods, but what? Had the girl really offered herself to Nicabar, or had the horse trader attacked her?

Damien mulled over the matter while the three girls left, the one called Marya taking a last angry moment to hurl a curse after April's name. Then the men were secluded for a time as they awaited the defendant.

Jingo said soberly, "I am sorry that you must see this side of the Lowara. But I am relieved that it will be over soon, and finally put to rest."

But would it be? Outside Damien could hear muttering in the camp, as the people grew restless and anxious for the decision. Then the voices rose and grew, as the defendant apparently passed toward the king's tent, and Damien heard Belita's coarse cry trailing after her.

Engrossed in his own thoughts, he could neither speak nor breathe when a slim silhouette of a young woman slipped into the tent, and the lamplight gleamed down the length of her rich golden hair.

Equally startled to see him, April stopped

106

and stared, shaking her head a little in disbelief. Surely the stranger so coldly assessing her now could not be the same man who had leapt naked from a stream, chased, and caught her in the wood.

April could not bear to feel Damien's blue eyes taking cool measure of her while she stood there waiting for Jingo to begin the questioning. She was furious, imagining what he might be thinking. She knew what Belita and Nicky must have said about her. At Jingo's order, she began to relate her defense. She had been so sure of herself earlier, calm and poised, ready to defend to the death. But Damien's presence unnerved her, and April faltered again and again, until a long silence broke in which he finally spoke briskly.

"I'm sorry, but I didn't catch your name."

He was needling her for having denied it to him earlier, she knew. "April," she conceded, a brief spark of defiance lighting her green eyes for a moment.

"That is not a *romani* name, is it, *Vaivoides?*"

Damien addressed the king with the respect due his station, and Jingo noted the younger man's curiosity as he replied, "No. April was named for the month in which she was found, a fancy of her foster mother, Tzigane. You may have seen the *phuri dai*. That is the woman who took April in as a babe, the one that Belita spoke of."

So, the girl was not true Rom after all. But the mystery in the woods intrigued Damien even more. Had April truly attacked Nicabar? The boy had the scar to show for it, exactly as would have resulted from a woman's strength used in anger. And as Damien already knew, the proud creature had a temper simmering underneath that silky golden skin, though whether it would drive her to kill, he wasn't sure.

As he questioned April in seeming impartiality, both of them were aware of the undercurrent of tension pulling them together even from several feet apart. The intensity of the night before, the playful escapade at the stream, all combined now to make them uneasily aware of each other in the close confines of the tent. The rapt silence of the others only made the world fall away the easier, and Damien found himself halting at times just to stare into her deep, still green eyes. Surely no lake had ever been so enticing, no sea ever beckoned so strongly to him. And yet there was nothing coy or obvious about April. She seemed wholly unaware of her power over men, and her few direct gazes at Damien were proud and defiant.

He held her very life now. What would Damien do, this stranger from another land, another world? Would her existence mean even less to him than it did to Belita? Would he let Nicky's cruel mother extract vengeance after all?

April knew that her tale had tumbled out too

quickly and too scattered to be believable. Nicky and his friends had had weeks to smooth their stories and accusations. With the deep despair of one who knows she is lost, April at last fell silent and simply stared at the ground.

"Have you nothing more to say?" Jingo prompted her anxiously. It was clear the king was worried she would leave it at that, a confused jumble of words, but April could only gesture helplessly back.

"I submit to the *kris,*" was all she could manage.

Everyone looked at Damien. His blue eyes never leaving the girl, he said slowly, "I must have time to think on this. At least a day." Jingo was reluctant to postpone the decision, but he understood their guest's hesitancy in making a rash ruling. He granted Damien the extra day, with the condition that he be excluded from the influence of any of the gypsies until then.

"You may go now, April," Jingo told the girl. She had not followed the others out of the tent, but still stood uncertainly before the gripping gaze of the blue-eyed man.

Then suddenly, she turned and rushed out, clearly fighting rising emotions. Jingo looked after her, and said in a low voice to Damien, "There's an old Rom saying you may have heard, *"si khohaimo may patshivalo sar o tshat-*

shimo . . . sometimes, there are lies more believable than truth."

And Damien knew that was the closest the king dared come to begging for the life of the beautiful gypsy girl.

Six

"April! What are you doing?"

In the darkness a male voice hissed softly behind her, and the young woman jumped and whirled around. Prince Adar snorted and side-stepped the halter she was trying to work over his nose.

"Petalo! You nearly scared me to death." April spoke in a fast, furious whisper, attempting to calm the stallion. She glanced at the young man she had practically grown up with. Though he was her age, Petalo was still far from grown-up. What he lacked in wisdom, however, he made up for in canniness, and April had always thought of him as a mischievous little brother.

"What does it look like I'm doing?" she whispered. "I'm running away just like you said I should last week!"

She thought nothing of it when Petalo's hand pressed down on her shoulder as a friend's would, and he recanted quietly, "I was wrong to

111

tell you that. It's too dangerous. The moon is full tonight and you won't make it far out of camp."

"Far enough to escape death," she muttered, as her anxious fingers finished securing the bridle on the horse. "Don't you see, I have nothing to lose?"

Petalo was silent for a tense moment, then his young voice broke as he said, "There is another way. I have talked to Jingo of it. I am ready to return to my band in the spring. I would be proud to take you back as my wife."

April knew what it cost her friend to make such an offer. Not taking him seriously, she said bitterly, "A wife accused of attempted murder! What a story that would make at the next Rom reunion! No, Petalo, there must be another way out, and I intend to find it tonight."

The young man reached out and restrained the black by the halter. "April, you know Nicabar will hunt you down if you try to leave."

"But I must try." Quick tears welled in her eyes. "Tzigane is in danger as long as I am here, and I will not see her suffer because of me. Already Belita's stories about black magic have made the others shy away from my mother. If I am gone, they will quickly forget everything. Let me go, Petalo. You will wake up the others!"

But the urgent whispers in the night had already roused Damien Cross. He had not been able to sleep anyway, but lay awake in the darkness musing upon the decision he must make about April. Lifting the canvas flap of the wagon, he glanced out and intently watched the scene unfolding before his eyes.

April was talking softly with a handsome youth with a shaggy black mane of hair. To his surprise, the earl felt a stab of jealousy when she reached up and gave the unfamiliar lad a chaste kiss on the cheek. A lover's assignation? He thought not, but the way the boy was speaking so low and urgently to April, he had to wonder.

Suddenly April reached out and gave the boy a firm push, urging him to go. It was obvious to Damien that she was trying to escape, but the question was, had she asked the other fellow to stay behind or to go get another horse?

He felt a twinge of regret at the thought of never seeing her again. And it seemed she might succeed, if she continued to keep her steed silent. She had taken care to wrap the stallion's hooves in canvas to muffle the noise, and kept feeding the horse a steady stream of tasty tidbits to quell his restless blood. She was certainly a resourceful young lady, he thought with admiration.

Only moments more and April would be on the black and away. Detesting himself even as he did it, Damien quickly knelt just outside the tent and reached out to retrieve a small, smooth pebble from the dirt.

Taking careful aim, he tossed it in the clump

of dry brush behind the wild-eyed stallion. As predicted, the horse shied and whinnied, raising an instant alarm and rousing the slumbering camp.

Obviously trapped, April made no move to hide. She was surrounded within moments and hustled off to a wagon at the other end of camp. The angry murmur among the gypsies told Damien he could not delay any further. First thing in the morning, he must settle the matter of April, even though it would cost them both their freedom.

"You have reached a decision?" Jingo sounded relieved. "Good. April's attempt to escape has upset everyone. Well, you may tell me first. Then I will tell the others, who will accept it more easily coming from me."

Damien nodded, feeling strangely uneasy for the first time among these generous people. He was betraying all of them, not just April and her apparent lover, but all of the Romany who believed him to be of their heart and mind. To a great extent he was, but his first loyalty still lay with the Queen of England and the Emperor of France, and he must never forget it.

Surprised to find his own voice emerge steady, Damien announced, "I find the girl guilty of attacking Nicabar."

Jingo winced, but eventually nodded, resigned. The evidence was such that nothing else could have been decided. But the king was a bit disappointed in Damien's decision to punish the young woman.

"The reasons for her actions are still unclear," Damien continued, "for April never denied slashing the boy, but said he assaulted her in the woods. I suspect there may have been some truth to that, but either way, she is still guilty. Now I will pronounce her sentence."

Jingo held his breath. He was fond of April, and the thought of her unnecessary death and what it would do the elderly Tzigane greatly saddened him.

Damien told the anxious king, "I know it is Rom tradition to ask an eye for an eye, but I must consider the circumstances. First, scarring April's face in return will do no good, but merely pacify Belita, who obviously has a grudge against the girl and her mother. I believe April can be punished in a more effective way, one that seems initially cruel but may, indeed, be kinder in the end."

"Yes?" Jingo urged.

Damien hesitated. "First there shall be a fine. That is customary, I believe, in most trials." The king nodded at that. "I understand Nicabar is a horse trader. Very well, then, April shall give him her finest possession in exchange for his damaged face. The black stallion."

Jingo sucked in his breath. "That alone will kill her. She raised the horse from a colt."

"Nevertheless, justice must prevail." Damien

disliked the sound of his own cold voice as he dictated this ruling to the king. "The horse has a good market value and will serve as a fair fine. Also, I saw the boy eying the animal earlier. I think he would accept the settlement."

"Perhaps you are right. But Nicky will delight in teasing April over the loss of Prince Adar."

Damien would not let himself be swayed by sentimentality now. He was too close to his own objective, one he had come upon with a flash of insight during the wee hours of the morning, and tossed and turned over all night. He needed a more secure cover with the gypsies, one that would not be questioned by the Russian authorities. And to that purpose, he needed April. It was too suspicious to have a man of his age unmarried among Romany, who reveled in family ties. It would draw dangerous attention to what otherwise would appear a natural situation, a man and wife traveling together to earn a living.

Drawing a deep breath, Damien plunged boldly on. "The girl must be married. It would settle her down, and would please those who wish to see the loss of her freedom."

"Yes, I suppose you are right. But it would crush her even more than losing the horse. Young men have offered for her before, but only because of her beauty. I knew they would kill her spirit, and curse my old bones, but I couldn't bear that. It would be wrong."

Damien agreed. "She needs an older man, someone worldly and experienced, who would be more tolerant than those young bucks. And most of all she needs to get away from the Lowara for awhile. No offense, *Vaivoides,* for I find your people kind and generous, but April will never have a normal life among you again."

Even the king was wise enough to see that much. "Yes, you are right. Marriage might hobble her enough, and perhaps stop the rumors. But who—" he stopped and looked shrewdly at Damien, finally understanding. "You?"

Damien shrugged. "I've a need for a wife." He did not reveal his true feelings for April. But it was the right thing to say, however unromantic; Jingo appeared to seriously consider it, and finally he nodded.

"It shall be done. By *solakh,* solemn oath, on this day, April will become your wife."

Damien could hardly believe it had been so easy. "What if she refuses?"

"There can be no refusal. I, her king, have demanded it because of her crime. And the horse will go to Nicabar to silence both he and his wasp of a mother. You may then take your new wife and go where you will."

"I doubt April will take kindly to this news."

"No, but it is better than the alternative. And I think she was prepared for even that today."

Damien was silent. Did April believe him to be so callous? He no more desired her death

117

than his own. Perhaps she would prefer to marry her lover instead. But it was too late now. No matter the cost to them both, the deed had been done.

"Marriage! He must be joking!" April choked out the words in response to Jingo's dry announcement.

"No. And that is not all. You must give Prince Adar to Nicabar."

"No!" She confronted the *Rom Baro* with wild eyes and a desperate plea. "Anything but that! I'll be Belita's slave, scrub pots and haul water till I die, but Nicky can't have my horse!"

Her broken cry carried across the camp, where Damien stood and watched. It clawed at his conscience to see the girl so ravaged by the decision, but she seemed more upset at the idea of losing her horse than at getting married, which boded some small hope for his plan.

But Jingo had forgotten to tell April who she would marry. Assuming she had her choice, the young woman mentally ran down the short list. It would not be so bad if she accepted Petalo's offer. Though she could only think of him in platonic terms, she was sure he would agree to it to keep her safe. And eventually they could part ways as friends. She opened her mouth to inform Jingo of her choice.

But the gypsy king spoke first. "You will be

wed today. You will find a mature man makes for a better husband."

Mature? As in old? Dear *Del*, had he promised her to one of the doddering widowers, like Samson the violin maker or Marya's drunken father Bruno?

Seeing her whiten, Jingo said, "But I thought you found the *romani rei* attractive. You danced for him the other night before the fire."

"Damien?" she whispered, staring up at the king with stricken green eyes.

"Yes. It is he who would have you. And I have agreed. My decision is final, child. It is far past time you were married anyhow. I hope you will not shame your mother with a refusal."

April's gaze flew from Jingo to Damien, who was watching her for her reaction. Was he worried that she would throw a tantrum? Scream and threaten to kill herself? Well, Rom women had more pride than that. Marriage she could endure, even if to a *gajo*. It was the loss of Prince Adar that cut her to the quick, and with a tight throat she turned to look upon the magnificent animal one last time before Nicabar led him away.

Tzigane did not even glance up at the shadow that fell across the inside of her wagon. "You must sit," she said graciously to Damien,

119

exactly as if she had expected him at that very moment.

Lord Cross found the interior of the smooth-walled oak wagon clean and neatly kept. Murmuring his thanks to the old woman, he sat across from her. There was a strong but pleasant scent of fresh herbs and dried flowers, and the glow of two hanging lamps cast a warm light onto the *phuri dai's* wizened features.

Though it was hard to estimate her true age, Tzigane's agate-colored eyes and fading cinnamon hair hinted that she had once been a beauty. She put aside the pack of worn, colorful cards she had been holding at his arrival and pinned him down with wise eyes.

"So. You wish to marry my daughter."

Tzigane did not seem surprised; on the contrary, she sounded satisfied. Since the decision had been made, and the wedding feast scheduled for that evening, Damien had sought out the seer to reassure her of April's fate. Of course, he could not confess his real reason for wanting the girl, but he did intend to be a decent husband to her in the short time they would be wed.

"How did you know? Did April tell you?"

Tzigane gave a mysterious shrug. "There are no secrets in a Romany camp."

"After April was told of my decision, she refused to speak to me. She has gone somewhere into the woods."

There was concern in his voice, and Tzigane

knew it. Her eyes keen on Damien, she said, "April has always been free. She was raised without a father, and it is hard for her to accept the ways of men. It has been said that I spoiled the girl. True, but she was all I had." Tzigane fingered her necklace as she spoke, and Damien saw a dreamy look stealing over the old woman's face.

"You were never married?"

"I was once. Ah, in my ancient youth." She smiled, but there was pain behind it. "You will no doubt hear of my foolishness someday. You see, I ran away to join the band when I was a girl just April's age. I loved the *Rom Baro*. Bal was young and handsome. He wooed me as no courtier ever could—" Aware of having said too much, Tzigane broke off, but not before Damien's curiosity was aroused.

No gypsy would have ever used the term "courtier" to describe a gallant gentleman. Only one versed in the courts, probably of gentility, would have made such a slip. Suddenly he wondered if the fortune teller was not hiding secrets even darker than his own.

He allowed her a graceful retreat. "What happened?"

"Bal and I were very much in love. I was his bride, his queen, for we came to rule at a young age. Alas, we were wed only five short years. The Lowara encountered a Turkish garrison near Constantinople—"

Damien could imagine the rest. The Turks

were brutal to the gypsies, whom they regarded as vermin among the holy of Islam. Tzigane echoed his thoughts.

"When they demanded our women be turned over to them for their pleasure, Bal refused. There were only ten Lowari men then—four were too old for fighting anymore—but they did their best." Tzigane closed her eyes in agony over the memory of the slaughter. Her voice caught as she rasped out, "They killed Bal before my eyes. And then, while he was newly dead, they threw me to the ground and—"

"Mother!" A sharp voice interrupted, and both of them looked up to see April had entered the wagon, and was staring at Damien with unconcealed suspicion. "Why is he here?"

"Does not your husband-to-be belong in our family now? We were just getting to know each other. Come, *chavali,* and join us before the ceremony."

"No. I want nothing to do with the *gajo* who took my horse away from me."

April stood defiantly before them, dressed in the lovely green skirt and white blouse she had worn the night she had danced. Her hair was loose in back but two slim braids dangled on either side of her face, secured with bits of green ribbon. She was not a blushing bride, she was a furious one, her green eyes shooting sparks at the man who had dared to give her beloved Prince Adar away.

"Where I come from it is bad luck to see the bride before the ceremony," Damien put in lightly, in an attempt to clear the air.

"No matter. That is the only sort of luck I have anyway." Anger darkened April's eyes to a moody forest-green. "Now that I have nothing to my name, not even honor, maybe you will release me from this foolish marriage!"

Damien did not flinch at her words, spat as they were out of hurt and upset. "You will find I am a decent enough man," he replied calmly. "And I shall see to it that you have another horse as fine as your first. You will not be denied much, provided you are a reasonable wife."

April flushed to the roots of her hair. "Reasonable! That is the word the Turks use when they try to barter for our women!" She saw her foster mother shake her head, and angrier at Damien for forcing her to upset Tzigane, April added in a voice trembling with fury, "I will wed you as I have been ordered, but I shall never be a wife to you!"

"Never is a long time," he responded, his blue eyes fixed upon her flushed face.

"April, *chavali*, do not start out on such bad terms. I believe this man is honest—"

"Honest as a snake! Can you tell me he did not plan to side with Nicky and Belita all along? Why else would he demand this of me?" April's voice and eyes were tortured, and the earl had to clench his teeth to keep from blurting out the truth, that he only needed her for a short while to assure his cover, and then she could go back to her lover as she obviously wished. His steady, calm gaze only seemed to upset her further.

"I want you to leave! This is still my home for another hour, and I do not want to see you any more than I have to!"

Not letting her get the satisfaction of seeing the insult had struck home, Damien rose and brusquely took his leave. Tzigane watched the man go with mixed emotions on her face. Then she began, "A bad sowing—"

"Will only reap a bad harvest, I know. But he is no different than any other *gajo!* He does not even know me and he wants to hurt me!"

"Perhaps he is worried about your fate," the fortune teller said softly. "Perhaps he seeks to save you from a worse one."

"I want nothing from him. How dare he give Prince Adar to that pig Nicabar! Why, Nicky can't even treat his own horses properly! And he'll be cruel to Adar, I know it. I will never forgive the *gajo* for that."

"Damien, you mean. He has a name, *chavali.*"

"So does the Devil in your cards. Oh, why wasn't I born a man? Then my destiny would be my own!"

"The ways of fate are mysterious. Daughter, you must guard against these dark thoughts that threaten to take you over." Then Tzigane continued in a gentler vein, "I sense this man is fair and kind. He will not beat or abuse you as even a Rom husband might. That is more than enough to be grateful for. And then, there is always the jewel."

April stiffened. "I think it is an unlucky thing. Maybe I should get rid of it."

"No, child. It is the only clue to your past, and someday you may wish to discover the truth for yourself. But for now it is safe in the pouch on my neck. Unless you would wear it this day?"

April shook her head violently. "No! I have been cursed enough of late. I could almost believe Belita has been practicing black magic herself!"

Tzigane did not laugh. "There are many strange and frightening things in this world, and even darker ones on other planes. Some can coax these evil powers to bring harm and ill unto others. You must guard yourself always." It sounded like a warning.

April weighed the words against Tzigane's expressionless face and decided to say nothing more of it. Instead she announced, "I want my mother with me on this supposedly happiest of days. Will you come to the ceremony?"

At last the *phuri dai* smiled, bright tears of emotion dotting her amber eyes.

"I would be honored, *chavali.*"

It was as if the darkness of the prior days had never been. Except for the obvious absence of Nicky and Belita, all the Lowara turned out for the impromptu wedding ceremony between April and the *romani rei*. Given any excuse, the Romany loved a celebration, and violins were tuned up and liquor brought out in anticipation of a rousing time.

But first, the *solakh,* an oath between marriage mates, was necessary. Everyone listened with bated breath as the couple exchanged the brief words at Jingo's instruction; Damien in a deep voice, April in a soft, defiant one.

Regardless of various feelings about the girl, all in the camp agreed that she was exceptionally beautiful this day. Her freshly washed golden hair shimmered down about her hips and the deep forest green of her skirt complemented her eyes. Some of the other gypsy girls had woven wreaths of wildflowers to adorn the bride, and unwilling to hurt their feelings, April wore a crown of daisies and carried a smaller bouquet of yellow sunflowers in her hands.

Damien gazed at his wife-to-be as she recited the vows. April was a natural beauty that needed no artifice to enhance her smooth complexion. Her slim, proud figure standing beside him made him wish for a moment that she really was his wife. He had never thought much of marriage before, but for some reason, imagining April at his side was almost euphoric. What would it be like waking up beside her each morning? To gaze into those sleepy green eyes? Soon, he realized with a tingle of anticipation, he would know.

Having never seen a gypsy wedding before, the earl was surprised to discover it was as long as any dreary church service. One by one, the Lowara each took a moment to wish fortune and fertility upon the couple, even those who had been cursing April just hours before. Everyone agreed this marriage would surely settle April down, and once she had a few young ones in her arms, she would be too busy to go thundering about on any horses.

Tzigane could not hide a small smile of satisfaction as she watched Damien take her daughter's hands in his. He was handsome, he was kind, and he seemed to understand the Romany way. What more could she wish for April except love? And that would come in time, she was sure. No matter what April said, Tzigane was sure the girl could not be entirely immune to the handsome *romani rei*.

Jingo pronounced the couple man and wife, and produced the *pliashka,* a bottle of dangerously aged brandy wrapped in silk and dangling gold coins for good fortune. Amid a round of hearty applause and cheers, everyone watched the newly married couple take the symbolic drink from a single cup.

"Well, wife?" Damien was unused to the sound of that word on his lips, but he found he could utter it easily enough. He set the marriage goblet aside. "Shall we retire?" The sun was dropping low in the sky, but there was no sign that the evening festivities would soon end.

April shivered as his warm voice caressed her. She looked at Damien in his black pants and the deep blue shirt that darkened the color of his eyes, and something in her belly uncoiled like a tightly-wound rope. His gaze brushed gently over her, while his hand moved down to guide her on the small of her back.

"No! I want to stay and watch them light the bonfire." Any excuse was good enough now. She desperately wanted to avoid any time alone with this man. April could not think of him as her husband. The shock had not worn off yet, and she was not ready to accept the consequences for her "crime."

Damien spoke softly against her hair. "There will be other fires, April. There will only be one wedding night."

He lulled her now in the same deep voice that he had used at the steam. It sent shivers up her spine, but she would not let him see that and misunderstand her very real desire to be alone that eve.

"Please. I'm not feeling well . . ." It was not a lie, but she saw with a sidelong glance at Damien that he neither believed nor appreciated it.

"We *need* to be alone. There has been no chance for us to talk, to get to know each other. I know this was all very sudden for you, April, and I'm sorry. But it is done now and we must make the best of it." Damien took her by the hand, intending to lead her somewhere where they might talk in private so he could reassure her of his intent.

But April, seeing only impatience and anxiety written on his face, assumed the worst. He was no better than Nicky, wanting to bed her at the first opportunity!

She was grateful when Petalo, having watched their tense exchange, hurried over to interrupt them on a pretense of good wishes.

When Damien took a measure of the younger man, April was startled to see her husband's eyes narrow. Then, with a curt nod to her, he said, "I am sure you two have a great deal to talk about. I'll be waiting in the wagon, April. Don't be long."

Damien left and Petalo gazed after him, puzzled. "What did he say to you? Are you fighting already?"

April laughed a little, appreciating her old friend's concern. She patted his arm in reassurance. "No, not yet. But I'm sorry you had to see me come to such an end. I had no choice."

"You should not have crossed Nicky."

"I think my fate was sealed even before that. But I suppose Tzigane is right, and I can only make the best of it. I must let go of everything I have known and loved."

A slow grin started to spread across Petalo's boyish face. "April, you are forgetting something very important. But there has not been a wedding in the Lowara camp since I have been here, so maybe it is different for your people."

"What is it?" She looked at him eagerly, ready to seize any excuse.

"You know that among Rom, it is traditional to have three nights of feasting before the marriage is—uh—"

"Consummated," she breathed, her green eyes sparkling. "That's right! I completely forgot about it. And who am I to break tradition?" April laughed in sheer relief as she tossed aside her bouquet and ran to remind the king.

Upon hearing her demure request, delivered as innocently as any Romany maid might, Jingo just shook his head and began to chuckle. April was right, of course—Rom tradition specified three days and nights of nuptial celebration before the couple was finally put to bed with much merriment and good-natured teasing.

It was considered a test of patience for the young husband, while letting a new bride receive instruction from her mother to lessen her fears concerning the marriage bed. Contrary to *gaje* beliefs, most Romany were celibate until marriage, and faithful thereafter. Jingo knew that April was innocent, and though she no doubt understood how children were produced, watching animals mate had surely given her no clue as to the wonderful and intimate pleasures shared between husband and wife.

Giving her a fatherly pat on the cheek, Jingo

nodded his consent. This time would give the couple opportunity to become better acquainted.

"Music!" The king cried out, and instantly three musicians jumped up eagerly with their instruments. "Now, a merry song in honor of the loveliest bride this side of *El'Bruz!*"

When Damien stormed back out of his wagon a short time later to find his wife, he could get no closer than three bodies deep from where April was whirling and clapping in time to the music.

For all his anger he could not help but stop and stare as she moved sensuously before the roaring bonfire. Framed by the night, she seemed an ancient goddess risen from the coals. Tongues of flame licked along each gold-crested curl tumbling down her back. At that moment April was a beautiful witch with no purpose but to mesmerize man. Damien stared at her until she blended with the crimson fire, whirling wildly in a crescendo to the beat of the tambourines.

As he was about to push in the ring and escort his errant bride gently but firmly out to his wagon, the king reached out and tapped him on the shoulder.

Beaming, Jingo shouted over the crowd, "She's a wonderful dancer, eh? April will bring you much money on the road! She is doing the Dance of the *Mule'*, honoring our ancestors!"

Before he could protest, Damien was swept aside as once again all attention focused on April. Drenched with the sweat of exertion, her eyes feverishly green, she seemed to glow with a secret inner power. She paused only to accept a sip of water from a cup held out by Petalo, while Damien cursed himself for not moving sooner to do the same. But soon she was dancing again, and he was caught up in her spell once more.

Jingo murmured in his ear about the Romany law regarding the three days. It was so absurd, and so obviously a ploy by April to avoid him, that Damien gave a grudging laugh for her intelligence.

"Patience I already have a great deal of," he told the king at last, who was surely expecting an outburst of some sort. "April will find that I'm prepared to wait as long as necessary. You can tell her that for me." He turned to leave.

"You're not staying to watch your wife dance?"

Damien shrugged and grinned. "I'll have plenty of time for that after three days. And then she can put on a private dance just for me."

Jingo winked back. He liked the witty *gajo*. It was too bad, really, that Damien hadn't been born a gypsy himself.

Seven

Three days passed more swiftly than she had anticipated, and April clung with dread to every passing moment with the knowledge that Damien still patiently awaited her in his—their—wagon.

She had learned from the others and from glimpses of him around the camp that he kept himself busy enough during their brief time apart, tending to his pigeons and haggling with the other men to obtain a fresher horse.

Meanwhile, the feasting continued in sporadic bursts, roast haunches of venison and beef cooking crisply over the spits, liberally doused with herbs and spices until they burned one's mouth. A great deal of liquor was also consumed to offset the tangy food, which meant that very little work was done around the camp for a few days, and even the king abandoned any notions of trying to get his people to move.

Tonight was the last night of feasting. Soon April would have no more excuses to avoid her

133

husband, and he would be demanding her presence in his bed every night. Feeling her skin go clammy, she shivered and rubbed at her bare arms. She remembered what her mother had told her.

"It will go easier than you think, April. Love between a man and wife is nothing to be frightened or ashamed of. It is a beautiful and natural thing, and full of pleasure. Don't worry, you will understand what I speak of after tonight."

But April knew she would be unable to concentrate for the rest of the day, knowing what awaited her when Damien came at last to claim his bride before the bonfire.

A three-quarter moon glowed lushly down upon the forest, turning the tree leaves silvery tan in the twilight. Damien looked up at the sky as he followed the well-beaten path from the stream on bare feet. He felt strangely content and full of exhilaration, wondering what the night would bring. He could have gone to fetch April hours ago, denying her the final night of song and dance, but he wanted no more bitterness than necessary between them.

Damien was surprised to find himself longing to please her in some small way. April did not deserve the deception he practiced, no matter her previous crime, and he was unwilling to hurt her any more than he already had. The matter of the horse was still a sore one between them, and she had not spoken to him at all during the three days. His one attempt to seek her out merely to get acquainted had been met with a cold shoulder.

He vowed she would soon come round. He had bathed earlier and donned fresh clothes. He was frustrated that every gypsy girl save April seemed to have cow eyes for him, while his new wife only tossed him scornful glances and wounded looks.

Lord Cross felt like a cad. Not even at his heights at court, breaking hearts left and right, had he ever treated a lady like this. He had given away April's most precious possession, then taken away her freedom, all in one fell swoop. No wonder she detested him. He had acted exactly like a *gajo*. He could see why the gypsies regarded outsiders with such contempt and scorn.

As he came closer to the camp, he could hear the revelry still going full-swing. Expecting to find April putting on another exuberant dance, Damien was surprised to see the fire circle was occupied this time with others. His beautiful young bride was nowhere to be seen.

Going to Tzigane's wagon, he knocked politely before asking admittance. The *phuri dai* was alone, but surprised at his inquiry about April's whereabouts. The girl had left over an hour ago saying she needed to bathe at the stream, Tzigane said. There was worry now in the old woman's eyes.

Confound the girl! Was she trying to run away again? Damien leapt down from the wagon and ran back down the trail toward the stream. He was sure April had lied, but passing through the camp on his way out he was relieved to see that Prince Adar was still there, securely tied to Nicabar's wagon. Damien was fairly certain that April would not leave without her horse.

As he backtracked in the growing darkness, he became increasingly worried about April. Though she no doubt knew these woods like the back of her hand, there were still wild animals and uncouth men who might waylay her. Soldiers had been known on occasion to blunder into a gypsy settlement, or seek them out on purpose, in order to molest the women.

Damien swore softly under his breath, wishing he had brought his pistol along. He crashed loudly through the brush, hoping to scare away any predators or other men who might be lurking in the gray shadows. The Georgian wilds were beautiful, but they were also dangerous. He felt a surge of adrenalin as he invaded the dark, brooding forest which had grown undisturbed for a thousand years.

Finally he could hear the splashing of cold water over rocks. Knowing that bathing was only permitted the farthest upstream, and the areas closer to camp reserved for washing clothes and dishes, he began to climb up an incline to the north.

Somewhere in the shadows, owls were already hooting, muffled slightly by the thick overgrowth. Here and there Damien heard other small night creatures scurrying, alarmed by his intrusion. He considered calling out for April, but he knew that she would not answer him. Cursing her for making him worry, and himself for being a fool, he continued his trek onward along the rough banks of the mountain stream.

After nearly a half-hour, during which the sun died in a final burst of orange-red fire, Damien became aware that the noisy rapids had fallen away behind him. Suddenly he broke free of the woods to find himself in a knee-deep grass meadow under a star-studded sky. He had stumbled across a lush little glen hidden in the bosom of *El'Bruz* itself.

The twisting and turning of the wild stream continued up the side of the mountain, and here in a vee protected from wind and rain lay a tiny paradise. From a snow-flecked ridge, a thin veil of water misted down to form a deep sapphire pool, eventually leading to a narrow outlet to the sea.

And it was here that the earl also found his young wife. He watched in spellbound silence at the figure of ivory and gold smoothly lapping across the pond. April paused once to scoop glittering water in her hands, and let it trickle down her face beneath the moonlit sky.

For several minutes more Damien watched her swim, as she flipped on her back and let the silver rays of night turn her proud breasts into glistening peaks of rose quartz. Her slim legs playfully churned in the water, propelling her along as she hummed softly to herself.

When April finally came to shore and walked from the water like Venus from her bath, Damien had to grit his teeth at the sight of her wet hair plastered like liquid gold to her nude form.

Not wanting to startle or embarrass her, Damien did not reveal himself until April had dried in the cool night air and slipped back into her clothes. Then, quietly, he walked into the glen and feigned surprise at finding her there.

"I thought you were a wood nymph at first," he greeted her softly.

"Have you been here long?" In the moonlight April's green eyes were very large and bright, a matched set of emeralds. He could see consternation in her face that he had found her at all.

"No, I just followed the stream up here. I was worried about you. Tzigane said you had left a long time ago, and it's dangerous in the woods at night. But I can see why you came here. I've never seen anything like this place."

Both of them fell silent, drinking in the beauty of the secret little paradise. For a moment it was as if they were the only humans in existence, a frightening and yet heady thought.

"We camped here once before several years ago, and I found it then," April said, very softly so as not to disturb the peaceful scene. "Nobody else knows about it."

"I'm sorry if I spoiled it for you," Damien replied. She suddenly noticed his clean hair and clothes. He was making an effort for her, she knew, but she still wasn't sure she wanted to accept it.

Damien studied April's lovely face by moonlight, wanting to reach out and trace her softly glowing cheeks and the full lower lip she worried between her white teeth.

"You have every right to resent me and the decision I made," he said, and she looked up at him in faint surprise. "But please try to understand, I had little choice. Many of your people thought you should be punished, some suggested banishment. It would have been foolish of me to let you off without any punishment at all, for Nicky would have revenged himself in the end."

She had realized that herself. "Yes, I know. I won't deny cutting Nicabar with my knife. But it was in self-defense, and I will not apologize for it." Her head rose proudly, and Damien smiled to recall the gypsy child he had rescued all those years ago.

"Then you see my problem. If I let you go free, someone might hurt you or your mother. This way, I satisfy everyone to some degree."

"Except me," April put in pointedly. "But then, my wishes don't count."

"Of course they do. I don't want to be unfair to you."

"Is that why you insisted on marriage? To be fair to me?"

Damien had to admit he had never been so completely cornered by a woman before. Even the court coquettes, so adept at their little mind games, could not equal April's straightforward challenge.

"I asked the king for your hand for several reasons. Yes, I needed a wife, and you needed a protector—"

"Perhaps you also need something else from me?" April interrupted, startling him with her insight. "Since you are not really Rom."

"Perhaps," he admitted. He changed the subject deftly to avoid going into detail about that. "But believe it or not, April, I do find you attractive. And I want you in the way a man wants a woman."

There. He had said it. Expecting to see fear or revulsion on her face, Lord Cross was surprised when she only looked at him frankly with her jewelled eyes and said, "Well, you have me now. By Romany law you can do with me as you please."

"And you won't fight me?"

Damien saw her swallow hard, but she shook her head. He suspected she was frightened, but no threat would make his little lioness tremble. Slowly, he raised a hand to touch her cheek. April stiffened, but did not bolt. Gently, very gently, Damien ran his fingers down the curve of her jaw to her throat, where a pulse fluttered rapidly under the smooth skin.

"What if I choose to take you now?" He could not resist the husky query, and saw an answering quiver run through her taut body.

Lips parted, April gazed up into Damien's aquamarine eyes. His touch sent strange thrills through her, burning almost, and for a moment she could do nothing but look at him in help-less wonder.

What kind of woman was she to respond to a *gajo's* touch? And worse yet, what wife wanted her husband to follow through on any threat? But April had a powerful urge to melt into his arms and surrender to the warmth and comfort he offered her now. Only her pride pre-vented her from caving in, and with a supreme effort she swallowed and replied, "You are my husband, and I will obey. But you will get no pleasure from me."

Damien chuckled, causing her green eyes to widen. "You vowed that much before, April. But surely you know a man can get pleasure from a woman even if she does not desire it? I think you are more innocent than you pretend."

Her moonlit cheeks flushed pink. "I know what happens between a man and wife!"

"The basics, perhaps. But what of the pleas-ure . . . the love?"

"Love!" she exclaimed scornfully. "You can-not expect me to believe that you, a *gajo,* care about such a useless emotion. Do your people not mock the Romany for their romantic songs? And your mother, did she teach you love is important in the *gaje* world?"

Damien hesitated, surprised. He had not thought about Marcelle for several months. It was as if being away from the glittering, brittle world of the European courts, he could easily put aside everything that went with that life.

"Yes," he said at last, deciding on a half-truth, "but it was before she died." That should satisfy any further curiosity over his past, he hoped. Actually, Marcelle did have a romantic streak. But then, she was French, and given to passion. His father, Edward, had scoffed at anything but marriages of convenience.

Sympathy flooded April's eyes. She asked quietly, "Did she die when you were young? Were you raised alone by your father?"

Damien silently cursed himself, realizing one lie bred another in quick succession. "Yes," he answered shortly. "But now he, too, is gone."

"I'm sorry." She suddenly touched his hand in comfort, a surprising but admittedly pleasant show of gentle emotion. Her fear and distrust had momentarily vanished, and he saw a side of her he suspected few others had seen.

"I have been alone for many years and am used to it now. I understand it has been much the same for you, since Tzigane is not your real mother."

April's hand quickly withdrew and her eyes

darkened unexpectedly. "I don't want to talk about that."

"Of course." Lord Cross cleared his throat, uncertain how to proceed. Damn the girl, why did she have to be so appealing? Gazing up at him with those bright green eyes, she was everything he had dreamed of, and more. Here was no petite French butterfly or refined English lady, but a strong, self-sufficient young woman fully capable of reducing a man to smoldering ashes.

Taking a deep breath, he tried to ignore the strong male instincts that urged him to make her his. "I expect nothing from you, April. You need not fear that I will take unfair advantage of you. That is the real reason why I was anxious to get you alone, to reassure you about the future. As to our—er—arrangement, it would be helpful if you would cook a little, perhaps, and wash once a week, or look after the horses. I'm not terribly talented in such areas." April would not admit to being disappointed in his suddenly practical air. She said stiffly, "That sounds fair enough. It will pay for my keep."

Damien started to protest. She had misunderstood his intent.

"No." April shook her head defiantly. "A gypsy wife earns her way in the world. I am no drudge to be lazing about. I will earn our living, and you may work or not as you please."

Damien knew she was serious, or he might

have laughed. He could hardly believe he had only found such a woman among gypsies, for in France or England, any lady would be thought quite mad to aspire to be anything beyond decoration in a drawing room.

He found he liked the idea of partners, uncommon though it might be. "We shall both contribute equally, I think. And I hope in time you will come to see that I'm a decent man."

"Why do you want to be a gypsy, Damien?"

He shrugged. "I'm sorry, but I just can't put it into words. When you saw me before in Constantinople, I was an unhappy man—rich and bored and lacking challenge in my life. Perhaps you'll think me mad, but I've always wanted to live as one with nature, with no limits but the sky. And," he admitted, "when I saw you again, I knew my decision was the right one."

How had he read her heart so easily? April drew in her breath, startled by Damien's revelation. He was turning his back on his other world for her, as well as for himself. Did he also feel the same powerful urge to link his body with hers?

April didn't know the answer to the question, but she could not quell the rapid beat of her heart or a soft moan when he suddenly leaned close and pressed his mouth down upon hers.

Thrilling, electric sensations pulsed through April at the almost innocent kiss. Damien did not try to thrust his tongue into her mouth or rudely grope her as Nicky had done. His lips were firm but gentle, subtly possessive and experienced. She knew in that moment what it was to be kissed by a man.

Nevertheless, when he finally lifted his head away, April said faintly, "You must understand, I won't sleep with you. You can't make me do those things."

Damien hid his amusement at her emphasis of "those things." What kind of horror was she imagining? But he said gently, "Don't worry about any of that right now. There will be plenty of days and nights ahead of us on the road where we can talk. Right now, we both must get some sleep. We need to think of getting an early start in the morning. I will walk you back to your mother's wagon. Are you ready to head back to camp?"

She nodded and got to her feet beside him. Almost shyly, April asked, "Will you hold my hand?"

"It would be my pleasure, wife." Damien's blue eyes sparkled like the pond lapping softly behind them, and with a sudden gallantry that made April laugh, he offered her a strong, warm hand and led her back to camp.

Eight

Goodbyes were said with tears and laughter, and many parting gifts were pressed upon Damien and April, even by those they had thought their enemies. Though Belita did not show up, Nicky lurked on the edge of the crowd, his dark eyes watching them closely as he passed up his own gift, a blanket for their new horse.

April did not want to part from her mother. She clung to Tzigane and cried, unashamed of her emotion as the others watched somberly. When Damien finally touched her shoulder gently indicating that it was time to go, she broke free from her mother and fled into the trees one last time.

"Let her go," Tzigane said, when Damien made a move to follow. "She just needs a few minutes alone. She has never been without me, and the change is hard for her."

"Why did she go to the forest?" Damien asked, his eyes fixed on the slim silhouette which vanished into a thick crop of shadows under the canopy of leaves.

Tzigane nodded toward the trees. "It was there that I found her. Somehow she senses it holds the secret to her life."

"And does it?"

A strange light appeared in the distant gaze of the gypsy woman. Without answering him, she murmured thoughtfully, "Perhaps the trees know the secret."

When April returned, most of the camp had already gone off to pack for their own move. As winter approached again, the gypsies sought a warmer climate, and the tribe's destiny was again Constantinople. To avoid the spillover of war, and a chance encounter with any soldiers, the king would lead his people in a roundabout course through Ankara, rather than directly along the coastline.

April climbed up onto the wagon seat beside her husband. Somehow she managed to keep from blushing at the randy wishes thrown up at them as they rattled out of camp, leaving deep tracks in the dark earth behind them.

She only looked back once, to be sure that Tzigane was still there watching them. She wanted to fling herself down and run back to her mother one last time, nudged by a sudden dread of losing the only relative she had ever had. Later, she would regret that she had not done so. But there was no time now, not when the rest of the world and an exciting new life beckoned just beyond the next rise.

By late afternoon, Damien and April had gotten as far as the outskirts of a small mountain town nestled near the rugged ring of the Caucasus. Damien had driven steadily, not taking April up on her offer to spell him off, and even their fresh horse was weary by the time he agreed they could take a break.

The trees surrounding them here were unfamiliar, twisted and half-dead and somehow frightening. April stayed close to the wagon without being told. She had been quiet during the journey, which concerned Damien deeply. He sensed that she was carrying a burden even greater than the one he had forced upon her, and it seemed to be bothering her more the farther they got from the Lowara.

"We'll camp here tonight," he suggested, watching her closely as he spoke. "The horse is tired and it would be foolish to try to travel in unfamiliar territory by night. I'll go look for fresh water."

April nodded, not really listening. Her gaze was fixed to the south, where the tribe had gone. "I will free the horse to graze."

He nodded and strode off with a tin pail in each hand, whistling a deliberately cheerful tune. He knew the girl was still afraid of him, if only a little, and he was determined to put her at ease and earn her trust. It was crucial for them to appear a loving couple when they arrived in Moscow, and somehow he needed to persuade April to adopt a sweeter attitude.

Sweetness was the last thing on April's mind, however, as she set the mare free and then restlessly combed the immediate area for firewood and a handful of edible nuts and berries. She was hungry and unwilling to wait for dinner. As she devoured the wild currants, she thought about the abrupt turn her life had taken.

She had lost Prince Adar, though she had gained a husband, and now she also had the awesome responsibility of safeguarding a priceless jewel that somehow held the key to her turbulent past. Tzigane had finally convinced her to take the gem. It was still in the green velvet pouch the gypsy woman had kept it in, but it was safely tucked away in the wagon where April did not have to look at it.

There was, however, no way to force it from her mind. Like Damien, the diamond teased at her with its secrets. It held the key to her past, but how did she begin to unravel a seventeen-year-old mystery?

April was startled from her thoughts when the mare, who was greedily grazing the grass, suddenly raised her head and whickered softly, urgently, in the direction of the forest.

April rose from the boulder she was sitting on, her eyes searching the thick grove of trees. She heard nothing. But only one thing would likely distract a hungry horse, and that was another horse.

"Adar?" she whispered, half in hope and half in fear, and she suddenly heard the distinctive rapid beat of horse hooves coming through the forest. April knew she was not mistaken when she saw a familiar flash of black and then the stallion, catching her scent, bolted wildly in her direction.

Upon the Barb's back a rider cursed and fought the reins unsuccessfully, breaking free of the cover with tree limbs whipping at his scarred, twisted face.

"Nicky!" April stepped back, not from fear of the plunging horse, but from uncertainty. Her first thought was that something had happened to her mother or someone else in the gypsy band, and Nicky had come to fetch her. Then the ugly leer of his lips told her otherwise. In his free hand, Belita's bastard gripped the steel-blue barrel of a gun.

"Where's your *gajo* man, eh?" His taunt carried across the clearing as Nicky dug his heels viciously into Prince Adar's sides and spun the frantic horse in tightly controlled circles.

It was obvious he had ridden at a breakneck pace, for the stallion's hide and muzzle were flecked with white foam and he rasped for air. The cruel bit Nicky had put on Adar caused April to clench her fists in pure rage, for the animal was obviously agonized every time Nicky yanked on the reins.

"They all said he couldn't be ridden, except by you," Nicabar jeered. April saw he wore wicked spurs, too, with which he had worn off strips of skin from the horse's ribs. "But as you see, I can tame anything. Even you!"

April knew Nicky had come after them with some twisted idea of revenge. He confirmed this with a soft, evil laugh that raised the hairs on the back of her neck.

"Think of it, April. You could be with me! Together we would be the perfect pair. You, with your dancing, could earn gold, while I would deal in horseflesh, fine as this beast here!"

"I want nothing to do with you!" April hissed, and when Nicky purposefully yanked the reins and the stallion squealed in pain, she cried, "Don't hurt him! Isn't it enough that I gave him up and left the tribe? You are rid of me now!"

His eyes glittered feverishly down at her. "No! It is not enough! And your weak-kneed *gajo* was wrong to think a Rom will sacrifice revenge for worldly goods! I will not be satisfied until you have paid your debt in full, witch, and I'm here to collect on it now! You can either come quietly, or I'll cut Adar's neck right now and you can watch him die!"

April gasped in outrage and disbelief. "Nicky! You cannot! Horses are protected by Rom law!"

"Damn the laws!" The young man snarled. "Are you coming with me or not?"

"She's not," a deep voice suddenly announced behind them.

Nicky answered Damien with a mocking laugh. "Well! If it isn't the high and mighty *rei!* I forgot to ask you before, *gajo,* if your brand of justice is learned or just bought! And don't get any ideas; this gun is loaded and there's a bullet in here with your name on it."

Nicky leveled the barrel at Damien and April cried out, "Nicky! No! I'll go with you—"

"The hell you will," Damien snapped. "Just so this animal can rape and kill you? Well, he'll have to come through me first . . . if he's man enough."

Nicky's eyes blazed at that. "Keep your mouth shut, *gajo!*"

"Oh, come off it, boy." The older man was suddenly the cool and austere Earl of Devonshire, giving advice to a hotheaded young swain. "If you fancy my wife, there's an easier way than that—and one with more honor, too. Though I suppose you wouldn't know much about honor, being a gypsy."

April nearly choked, sure that Nicky would blast the gun and she would see Damien crumple to the earth before her eyes. But she underestimated male ego, for Nicky actually took the insult and growled out, "Fine words coming from a filthy *gajo!*" He spat to emphasize his disgust. *"Rei* or not, you know nothing of my people!"

"I know that you are a disgrace to them," Damien retorted. He set down the brimming buckets and folded his arms as if to look down on Nicabar, even though the younger man was still atop the stallion. "If you truly want justice, you should go about this in a more civilized manner. A brutal killing may give you brief satisfaction, but why not think of the long-term benefits. A contest of honor would give you more to brag about to your friends, and might even earn you the respect of the king. And as for April—why rape, when you can persuade? You're a handsome lad—she's young, and girls are easily impressed."

April whipped her head around to stare outraged at her husband, but Damien kept his steady gaze fixed on the crazed gypsy with the gun.

Nicky actually seemed to be considering it. Damien nudged him by asking his wife aloud, "You'd go along with the winner fair and square, wouldn't you? Put the past behind and bury your grievances against this boy. He's more of an age for you anyway."

"You're mad—" April began, but Damien cut her off with a sharp hand movement underneath his folded arms.

Swallowing hard, unable to believe he asked it of her, she looked up at the gloating Nicabar and nodded.

The *gitano's* eyes sparkled dangerously, loving the power he held over them both. He couldn't wait to best the *gajo,* to cut his throat, then make love to April beside her husband's bloody corpse. His nerves raw with excitement at the thought, Nicky demanded, "What are you suggesting?"

Damien appeared to think a moment. "Well, if we intend to be gentlemen about it, a duel would be in order. However, seeing as how you're a gypsy and I'm certainly no gentleman, I think a knife fight would be more appropriate."

"No!" April cried.

Both men ignored her. With a slow, wicked smile, Nicky thought it over. "One hand tied behind your back," he added with obvious relish.

Lord Cross didn't flinch. "Fine. We'll each tie back our weaker hands—"

Nicky shook his head, still grinning a vile grin. "Not mine. Just yours."

"But the rules . . ."

"Devil take the rules, *gajo!* I've got the gun."

Damien nodded. The boy had a valid, if irrational point. And besides, haphazardly handling the gun as he was, Nicky was more dangerous right now than he would be with a knife.

Pleased with himself, Nicky steered the black stallion over to their wagon. Then, keeping his weapon aimed at April, he carefully dismounted and tied the horse. Stepping around to face the pair, he presented them with the muzzle of the gun.

"I'm ready." He smiled diabolically. "I've been ready to take care of both of you for a long time."

While he divested himself of his vest and rolled up his shirt sleeves, Damien listened to his young wife plead with him in a surprisingly worried voice.

"You mustn't do this! You don't know what Nicky will do. He is very skilled with a knife!" Her words carried across the clearing to the savagely grinning young man, who enjoyed hearing April exhort his skills to her husband.

Damien frowned. "Would you rather I surrender you to him? Or do you think I am so unskilled that I will put on a poor show and shame you?"

Color flooded April's face. "I—I don't want to see you hurt," she admitted haltingly.

"Well, at least this way we have a fighting chance." Damien spoke more quietly now so Nicky couldn't overhear. "As long as he has that gun, we are both in danger."

She shuddered, knowing Damien was right. It appeared Nicky had inherited his mother's bad blood, and would kill or maim without provocation. April already knew how he treated horses, and in Nicky's eyes, there was no difference between people and animals.

"Come on, hurry up!" Nicky shouted impatiently at Damien. "You're so hot to show me your *romani* tricks; what's holding you up?"

"I'm trying to comfort my wife," Damien replied dryly. "As you can see, she's about ready to swoon from all the excitement."

Damien suddenly grabbed April by the shoulders and drew her firmly against his chest. When her green eyes glittered dangerously, he flashed her a dimpled grin and inquired, "What, no good-luck kiss? I thought that was traditional among the Romany." As she opened her mouth to protest, his hard lips descended on hers with unerring skill. Jolted to the core, April clung to her husband's broad shoulders and absorbed the impact of his deep and unexpected kiss.

Aware of Nicky watching, and sensing the gypsy youth's smoldering fury, Damien prolonged the kiss with pleasure. In his arms April was rigid and unyielding for the first minute, but when he transferred his gentle kisses to her vulnerable neck, she gasped softly in surrender.

"While we're fighting," he murmured near her ear, "get Adar and ride away. Go back to your people. I won't risk you if I lose the fight."

She started to shake her head, but he thrust a strong hand into the thick gold mane of her hair and held her still.

"No arguments," Damien insisted. "Do as I say."

Then, just as abruptly, he released her, leaving April to stagger back against the wagon for support.

Her mouth tender and throbbing from the kiss, she stared after Damien as he walked out into the grassy clearing to meet Nicabar halfway. Her blood was pounding hot and fast after the unexpected thrill of his touch. Damien was handsome, but more than that, he was the part of her she had been forced to live without until now. Nicky had only revolted her with his crude gropings, but Damien's skilled assault had rendered her breathless and bemused.

Then suddenly, realizing that her husband of only a few days might die, April cried out after him, "Damien! Be careful!"

Lord Cross paused, drinking in the frantic tone of her voice. It was the first time April had uttered his name with something besides resentment. Feeling a surge of hope, he stepped forward to face Nicky.

Before the men could even discuss the few rules, April was at Damien's side again, her green eyes imploring.

"Here," she said to her husband, taking his right hand and thrusting the hilt of the ornate dagger Tzigane had given her into his palm. "Use this one!"

She saw Nicky's eyes narrow and his neck veins bulge as he recognized the weapon. But by Romany law, it was Damien's choice. The earl glanced down in surprise at the ivory-handled dagger, recognizing its workmanship as Spanish. It had the clean hone of Damascus steel. He was amazed that April had come into possession of such a fine piece, much less that she let him use it now—but she continued to surprise him. With a preoccupied nod, he accepted her offer.

After that, matters progressed swiftly and terribly. Nicky saw to the knotted rawhide that restrained Damien's left hand behind his back, tying it so tightly that the bonds cut into the earl's wrist. Then, using the other man's handicap to his own advantage, Nicky tried to grab April and give her a brutal kiss in front of her husband.

But she had been ready for something like that. With scarcely a flick of her skirts, April lashed out with a bare foot in a snap-kick that caught Nicky below the knee.

Cursing, Nicky hopped around and screamed obscenities for a full minute, waving the gun wildly about. To kill April now would be to deprive himself of the pleasure of raping her later, so he held himself in check and contented himself with calling her every vile name he could think of.

"It seems to me that your energy could be put to better use," Damien interrupted when a break in the cursing came.

"Yes! Killing you!" Nicky bawled back, his

dark eyes flaming with hatred. "Let's get on with it!"

Then, to ensure that April could not interfere, Nicky dismantled his gun and set it aside for the moment. Drawing out his own six-inch blade, sharpened to a razor-thin point that gleamed wickedly in the late afternoon sun, the horse trader dropped to the fighting crouch he had learned as a child.

April watched Damien assume a likewise pose. He was the taller of the two, but Nicky was strong and wiry and laced with muscle from working outdoors. Nicky's thighs were exceptionally strong, as he had ridden bareback from youth. The *gitano* emitted a low, mocking laugh as he circled his opponent. He intended to cut Damien to ribbons and enjoy every minute of it.

Damien gazed steadily at the boy. He didn't underestimate the younger man, but quickly sought for weaknesses in his opponent. Used to sizing up men for battle, Damien saw at once that the boy was unevenly gaited and possibly had one leg shorter than the other. This would have the effect of throwing Nicky off balance, if even a little, and could work to Damien's advantage, but the gypsy also had a longer knife and the benefit of two hands to his single one.

Knowing the real odds were in Nicky's favor, Damien had no choice but to make the best of it. Grimly patient, he waited for the boy to rush him first.

159

He didn't have long to wait. Nicky tried to distract him with a fancy flourish of his knife, then suddenly dodged and came at Damien's left, trying to capitalize on the other man's bound hand. Fully prepared, Damien pivoted smoothly and countered the attempt. Nicky hurled past, his knife slashing perilously close, but not touching.

Heart in her throat, April froze, completely forgetting Damien's order to flee. She could not choke down an outcry when Nicky tried to sneak up behind her husband to bury the gleaming dagger in his back.

Hearing his wife cry out, Damien hurled himself aside and rolled just in time to cause Nicky to stumble in mid-thrust. When the gypsy hit the grass with a hard thud, Damien saw his chance. He dove back for the boy, intending to end the deadly fight as soon as possible. But he had forgotten his own handicap. Wildly trying to free his tied hand, Damien hesitated a fraction too long. Nicky was soon back on his feet, his hoarse braying laugh carrying across the meadow.

"Nice try, *gajo!*" Nicky called out mockingly. "Maybe next time you won't be so foolish as to agree to a knife fight. But then again, there will be no next time for you!"

"We'll see about that," Damien muttered, sparing a moment to fling a furious glance at April, nodding his head sharply toward Adar.

To his dismay, she only stared stubbornly

back, refusing to take the hint. He understood then that she was here for the duration of the battle, for better or worse, just like a real wife would be. Infuriated by her obstinance, Damien was also a trifle amazed. It would have been so easy for her to leap up on her horse and ride away, leaving him to his fate alone. He had a fleeting suspicion that perhaps he meant more to her than he dared hope.

Both men tired as the hour dragged on. All the running, jumping, and dodging wore on their nerves and their muscles. Nicky was drenched with sweat, his dark eyes wild and desperate as he continuously circled his rival like a rabid wolf. Damien's blue gaze was still steady and calculating, but he could feel the telltale protest of every muscle, and knew his strength was beginning to give out.

I'm no longer a young lad, Lord Cross thought wryly, but concentrated on hiding that fact from his opponent. It mattered not that he had seen battles before this young whelp had been born; precious little good that did him now. Nicky was out to spill his blood, and it was patently obvious Damien couldn't talk his way out of this one.

Marshalling a final burst of adrenalin, the earl finally slammed into the younger man shoulder-first in a move that threw Nicky completely off-guard. Stumbling backward, the boy slipped in the slick grass and landed heavily on his back. He slashed wildly with his knife in defense, shredding the sleeve of Damien's shirt and leaving thin red slices on his enemy's exposed arm.

As he simultaneously ducked and attacked, Damien shoved a sharp knee into Nicky's chest, pinning the horse trader down. He leaned back just far enough to avoid getting a knife in the face, but Nicky quickly made mincemeat out of his right arm. Soon Damien's old war wound was reopened and gushing blood.

April cried out, not knowing to whom the blood belonged. All she could see was Damien's white shirt quickly turning to red. Both men's arms were a blur, weaving and clashing their gleaming knives together. Suddenly Nicky's weapon sailed away as Damien dashed it from his hand. Resorting to fists, the gypsy tried to punch his attacker. But it was here where Damien truly showed his skill. Trench warfare had been an everyday occurrence in Crimea, and he had learned how to dispatch an enemy quickly and effectively.

Bringing the square handle of the dagger firmly down, Damien knocked Nicky senseless in a single blow. The thrashing, cursing youth was suddenly rock-still beneath him. Panting harshly, Damien got up. He started to take a step, then wavered and nearly fell.

April was there to catch him. Grabbing Damien around the waist, heedless of the fresh blood staining her own blouse, she helped him to the wagon. There he collapsed, breathing heavily and looking slightly dazed.

"Your arm!" April exclaimed, seeing the terrible gash and pulled stitches. The puckered skin was angry and raw, laid back nearly to the bone. It had just begun to heal before Nicky had taken his knife to it. Fighting her own queasy stomach, April hurried to tear sheets from the bed in the wagon to tightly bind the cuts.

All the time she kept casting worried glances at Nicky's inert form, afraid the gypsy would wake up, and like a dark nightmare, come at them again. Seeing her concern, Damien finally managed a weak laugh. "I think we're safe for now. But just to be sure, why don't you untie my hand and use the rope to bind his instead?"

When Damien presented his back for her to free him, April's trembling fingers found the knot so tight she would have to cut it, and the binding had nearly sawed through his flesh.

She would make Nicky regret hurting her husband this way. Fetching the dagger from where Damien had dropped it, she freed him, and then took the cord over to where Nicabar lay.

It gave her savage satisfaction to roll the gypsy youth on his side and yank his wrists behind his back. Using every ounce of strength she possessed, April looped the rawhide twice and tied it in a double-knot. Then, for good measure, she gave Nicky a swift kick in the behind.

Watching his wife in action, Damien chuckled softly. He had never imagined such a woman existed. Every inch of April quivered with indignation as she exacted her vengeance. In the rosy glow of twilight she was like a wildcat poised over her prey, her tawny mane matched by flashing green eyes. When she came back to his side, briskly dusting off her hands for a job well-done, he congratulated her on her courage.

"But I should beat you for refusing to leave after I ordered you to," he teased her.

"Then you would be even more a fool!" April placed her hands on her hips and regarded him sternly. "Do you see now how easily you could have been killed?"

Damien only smiled, blue eyes intent on her and suddenly taking her breath away. "And do you realize how very green your eyes are, like the seafoam that rides the waves onto shore?"

Her lower lip trembled slightly. "What has that to do with anything?"

Damien gave her an penetrating look. "Right now, everything. At least, it probably explains why I suddenly want to make love to you."

Blushing, April whirled away. But not before she felt a sharp stab of anticipation that shot to her very core.

Nine

Having an uninvited guest didn't change Damien's intentions to spend the night in the clearing. When Nicky finally came to groaning consciousness, he found himself securely tied and bound to a sturdy tree trunk. In order to keep peace and quiet, the earl generously provided a gag as well.

To April's surprise, Damien gave her ample time to dress down and slip beneath the sheets of the bed, then blew out the candle and joined her. In the faint light she could just make out her husband's bare-chested figure as he got into the far side of the large bed. He moved stiffly, obviously suffering from the wound in his arm.

Softly she asked, "Are you all right?"

Damien made an affirmative noise. "Just a little sore." After a moment of silence, he inquired, "Do you regret coming with me?"

April didn't answer immediately. She knew she had not really had a choice, but so far, Damien hadn't been anything like she'd expected. "I think we can help each other," she replied, not willing to commit herself more than that.

Hearing the caution in her voice, Damien could fully understand the reason for it. April knew nothing about him, really, and what little he had told her was mostly lies. He had probably saved her life today, but then she had been an invaluable coach in the knife fight. April owed him nothing—not even loyalty. The thought for some reason disheartened him.

They would be spending weeks if not months in each other's company. Moscow was still a good distance away, and other than bandits and soldiers, they were not likely to encounter anyone else with whom to spend some time. Lord Cross realized as he listened to the girl breathing softly across the wagon from him that he suddenly did not want to be alone tonight. But he could not, and would not, hurt or betray her more than necessary.

At that same moment April was biting her lower lip in indecision. She was worried about Damien's injury, and also wondered if Nicky could escape. Sleep was too elusive, and she squirmed about trying to get comfortable for the next hour. When finally she heard Damien's soft snores, she rolled up on her elbow and looked across at him.

In the dim light her husband's features were dark and nearly indistinguishable, but she could just make out the closed lashes over his cheeks.

His broad chest rose and fell smoothly with each breath, and the sheet had somehow worked its way down to the narrow stripe of black hair at his waist.

Unabashedly taking this golden opportunity to study him closer, April slipped out of bed and crept over to Damien's side. His black hair was mussed and his mouth half-open like a little boy's. Wonderingly she extended a single finger to touch the silky waves that framed his clean-shaven face.

When April tentatively reached out to see if the whorls of black chest hair were just as soft, a hand suddenly shot out from beneath the covers and grabbed her wrist. She yelped softly as Damien's blue eyes suddenly opened on her.

"April? What are you doing?" he rasped, slowly recognizing the face above his. "I thought you were an intruder!"

She winced, and Damien realized he still had her wrist in a cruel grip. Letting her go, he sat up in the bed and demanded, "Is something wrong? Did you hear something outside?"

"No, I couldn't sleep. I just had to see if . . . if . . ." She trailed off, a hot flush flooding her face.

"What? You had to see if what—?" he prompted her. Suddenly Damien recalled the sensations of someone gently stroking his head and chest while he slept.

"If your hair was as soft as it looked." Choking on the words, April turned her face away so he could not see her shamed expression.

"But not just the hair on my head, hmm?" Damien laughed softly and didn't sound upset. "Well, it's your right, I admit. After all, we're man and wife now."

"I'm sorry," she whispered, ashamed.

Suddenly he understood that his laughter had wounded her. April wasn't half as worldly as she pretended to be. Taking back her hand in his own, he stroked it and said, "I'm flattered that you were curious enough to want to find out. You don't know much about men, do you?"

April shook her head. Her golden hair glistened under a veil of moonlight. Restraining his own desire to stroke her silken mane, Damien cleared his throat and tried to decide how a man of experience relayed the facts of life to an innocent like April.

"But you said you knew about—ah—men and women? Being together?" Lord Cross could have kicked himself at that moment for stuttering like an old maid, but *she* didn't seem inclined to laugh, thank God.

"Yes, Tzigane explained much of it to me as a young girl. But there's still a lot I don't understand."

"Like what?"

"Like why anybody wants to make love, when it seems so painful." It came out in a rush of soft breath. "When Nicky attacked me, I felt only like getting sick."

Damien listened gravely. "And how about when I kissed you, April? How did you feel then?"

"Different. Tingly, sort of, and a little strange. But it wasn't awful like it was with Nicky."

"Bien," Damien echoed dryly in French. But a tender smile hovered at the corners of his mouth as he gazed at the child-woman kneeling beside his bed. Any lesser man would not miss this opportunity to pull her into his arms, and even an English lord was not entirely immune to beautiful green eyes and a lovely upturned face. But he sensed April would be a woman won only by true love, and he could only offer her a lust of the moment.

"Get back to sleep," he said gruffly to disguise the longing he felt. "We need to get an early start in the morning."

Damien turned on his side away from her, while April wondered about his abrupt dismissal. Just when it had begun to get interesting, and when she hoped he would take her in his arms as she so desperately longed for him to do, he turned away from her! Damien had said earlier that he wanted to make love to her. What had changed?

"Come to bed, April," he repeated, patting the space across from him. "We both need our sleep."

How practical men were! With a bitter twist to her lips, April obediently sought the cold comfort of her own side of the bed.

"It will take me weeks to catch up with the tribe on foot!" Nicky snarled when Damien freed him the following morning. Rubbing his chafed wrists, he glared at the couple.

"You should have thought of that before you tried to kill me." Damien gestured toward the boy's knife placed on a boulder across the clearing. "But I am not entirely heartless. I realize you may have to defend yourself against wild animals like yourself, so I am leaving you one weapon."

"What about my gun? You can't steal it from me!"

"Can't I? You intended to steal my wife from me, and not for any honorable ends. No, I will not ride off with my back to a man with a gun. I am sure you will be able to survive without it."

"You bastard!" Nicky's jaw was taut with rage.

"My mother's morals have nothing to do with this, boy. I suggest you refrain from any more insults, considering I have a great deal to settle with you yet."

Nicky took a small step forward as if to test the earl's mettle, but he quickly regretted it. In a flash Damien placed the rifle barrel squarely on the gypsy's chest. And if he felt pain from his injury, his right arm never wavered.

Realizing he was lucky to escape with his life, Nicky nevertheless surged with black hatred as he watched the couple depart. Of course April had reclaimed Prince Adar, and now rode the prancing black proudly beside their wagon. She had exchanged her skirts for slim-fitting trousers and a blue peasant blouse. Her golden hair blew wildly about her shoulders in the brisk morning wind.

"I suggest you seek shelter," was Damien's final shout to Nicky before the wagon rolled away toward the north. "It looks like we're due for a storm."

The *gitano* did not reply. They left Nicky standing rigidly in the clearing, fists balled at his side, his face an ugly, twisted mask staring after them.

When the miles finally began to drop away, April slowly began to relax. She feared Nicky would try to follow them, or even come after her in one final, wild attack. But they made good time and there was no sign of him or anyone else.

Skirting any settlements they passed, Damien struck a path northwest toward Rostov, where he was sure April and he could hide themselves very quickly in the crowded streets. There, in a poorer quarter of the city, he could firm up his plans and perhaps begin to make the necessary contacts for his mission. He would also dispatch his first message to Raglan then, assuring the commander of his success thus far.

Glancing aside at the proud figure April cut upon the high-spirited stallion, Damien wondered again about the truth of her heritage. She was not Slavic, for her features were too fine and her skin too fair. Turkish was also out of the question. But for her riding attire, she could almost pass at the moment for an English lady out for a jaunty morning ride.

Damien smiled to himself. Actually, if he didn't know better, he could almost swear that April already knew she was the Countess of Devonshire. Her chin was high, her backbone so rigid as to imply great nobility. For a fanciful moment he imagined her bright beauty lighting up Mistgrove. There was no doubt she could turn heads at any European court. But that could never be. Soon, and the sooner the better, he must gently disentangle himself from the gypsy girl and carry on with his mission.

An ominous rumble preceded the icy downpour which chased April back into the wagon beside Damien. They continued their journey with Prince Adar securely tied to the rear of the wagon, but the stallion's wild whinnies warned of worse to come. Glancing up, the couple saw a flash of ball lightning roll across the heavens, and thunder shook the heavens and earth like an angry god.

Damien avoided the bloated rivers, which could not receive so much rain without washing out eventually, and headed west toward the Black Sea. Darkness had fallen again by the time they heard the faint roar of wind-capped waves. The earl headed instinctively for the shelter of cliffs he knew were clustered along the seashore.

"We'll camp here for the night. It should be drier."

Shivering, April quickly agreed. The rain was streaming steadily through the cooking vent in the back of the wagon, and puddling on the floor. Another flash of lightning showed most of their worldly goods were drenched, including the bed.

Damien lit a lantern in order to locate a weathered sea-cave below some cliffs. By then the rain had abated to a thin, cold trickle, but he and April were thoroughly soaked. Like a good Romany man, Damien saw to the horses first. After he hobbled them both under an overhanging shelter with sparse graze, he started a fire from pieces of dry driftwood he found in the cave. Then he went to lift his sodden wife out of the wagon.

"Hold tight," he advised April, carrying her swiftly through the rough weather to the brisk fire in the cave. Gently setting her down before the warm blaze, he peeled off the sopping blanket and wrapped her snugly in a dry one he had found in the wagon. She did not protest, even when his eyes lingered overlong on the gentle swell of her breasts and hips.

Frozen to the core, April sat in the sand and rocked herself to get dry. The wind had chilled her to her bones and she could not seem to get warm. Watching Damien as he moved about arranging their shelter, April realized she had come to desire the company of this mysterious, handsome man who was her husband. But Damien puzzled her greatly with his mood swings. One minute he seemed delighted to have her company, while the next he lapsed into a distant silence. And men called women the moody ones!

Feeling April's gaze on him, Damien glanced at her from the other side of the crackling fire and gave her a heart-stopping smile. His eyes reflected the electric blue of the lightning outside, and she swallowed hard. What had she seen in his look? A silent promise, perhaps smoldering desire? Hoping he was warming to her at last, after the past days in which they had spent so much time together, April waited for him to make the first move.

As if he had the power to read her thoughts, Damien suddenly spoke and startled her with his insight. "It's damned odd, but I feel like we've known each other forever, April. Does that sound strange? When I watched you dance, I felt as if you were calling to me somehow, and something in my soul understood, though my mind still doesn't."

She listened intently, waiting, and he finished flatly, "I don't believe in fate, and I don't believe Nicky's claim that you're a witch, either. So that just leaves chance."

There was a flicker of emotion in her cat-green eyes. "It seems unlikely that our paths should cross again after so many years, Damien. If I told you my mother's cards had even predicted our marriage, would you believe me?"

When Lord Cross considered the incredible odds against their relationship, he was forced to admit defeat.

"Perhaps I would, after all. I'm beginning to learn that there are stranger things in this world than I thought."

"I hope you don't include me in that," April laughed. "Do you find the bargain was not fair?"

"On the contrary," Damien replied, moving to kneel beside her and reaching out to entwine a golden strand of her hair around his fingers, "I find the bargain very fair indeed."

His husky voice shot warmth all the way through April's shivering frame to her toes, which curled at the look in his smoky blue eyes. Holding her breath, April dared hope that this time he would take her to wife. She longed to know of the love and wonders between a man and woman, something Tzigane had only hinted at, and which April suspected was even more interesting than her mother would admit.

Reading the anticipation in April's steady gaze, the earl was shaken. She was so open to him now, so incredibly vulnerable and trusting, with her lips slightly parted. This young woman wanted him, he realized. Wanted him in the way a wife would naturally turn to her husband for guidance in the matters of love.

Slowly Damien peeled off his wet shirt, laid it across a rock to dry by the fire, and saw April looking at the curling dark hair on his chest.

"You wondered once if it was soft," he said. "Would you like to find out now?"

Wordlessly April nodded, and he took her hand in his to place it on the smooth expanse of his broad chest. Her fingers were cold, but unerringly delved into the silky whorls of hair there as she smiled with shy pleasure.

"Like black silk," April murmured, and Damien felt a tremor run down his spine at her touch. She was too willing, her clear green gaze triumphant as she lightly tugged on his chest hairs.

"Careful, girl. That's very sensitive there," he rebuked her with a gentle grin.

"Oh? Have you many sensitive areas, Damien?"

She was teasing him, and once again he marveled that when this girl chose to be a coquette, she could do it quite well. Her intelligence was rivaled only by her beauty, and it made for a deadly combination.

Trying to take back control, Damien said briskly, "I imagine you're quite tired. Would you like me to roll out the other dry blanket for a bed?"

April just stared back at him, her expression as if he had slapped her. Alarmed, Damien reached out abruptly and grabbed her by the shoulders. The blanket slipped down and he felt her ice-cold skin under his own warm palms.

"*Jesu,* you're half-frozen! Why didn't you tell me? You must be in pain."

April did not answer, but drank in the sensation of Damien's arms holding her tightly to him. She knew it would not last. It seemed that he always set her aside eventually.

"Stay bundled up while I get more driftwood for the fire. We'll build it up so high you'll never be cold again."

"Please," she forced out before he could go, "don't leave me! I . . . I don't want you to go."

The vulnerability in her eyes convinced him at last. With a relenting sigh, Damien sat in the sand beside her and put his strong arm around April, holding the blanket up.

Tentatively, timidly, she leaned her head against his shoulder. Damien hated to admit it, but it was a pleasant sensation. Soon April's hand strayed out onto his thigh, resting atop the black trousers. He tensed but did not pull away, sensing she would be crushed if he did.

Lord Cross was in a quandary. The last thing in the world he, a renowned rake and womanizer, intended to do was to seduce his own wife! But certainly not because April wasn't lovely and tempting. It was almost funny, except he was in as much secret agony as she.

Damien was resolved not to hurt his little lioness, but April's whisper drove a stake so deeply into his heart that he knew the torment must show on his face.

"Why, Damien? Why don't you want me?"

A ragged groan escaped Damien as he clutched her even tighter. Suddenly he understood that in his "kindness," April had been hurt anyway. She only saw that she had a young, virile husband who did not desire her, and immediately assumed that the fault lay with herself.

"April, little girl, look at me." He sat back a bit and urged her to turn those tear-filled green eyes full on him, however much it tried him. "Remember back in the little glen? I told you then that I would never force myself on you. I meant that, and it still holds true. What you see as cruelty is only concern for your happiness. You have already lost your home with the gypsies. I would not have you lose your innocence as well."

His deep, tender voice wound through the channels of her heart until April thought she would burst for the emotion. This man cared enough about her feelings to subdue his own desires for her! In a flash she realized what she had suspected all along; she was beginning to love him, if even a little, and now she was ready to be a wife to him in every way.

"I am not afraid," she said boldly, her trusting eyes on his. "I know you are a gentle and good man. Please, Damien, I am so cold. Will you not warm me tonight?"

Once again April's hand moved upon his bare chest. Her golden hair tumbled over the dark blanket, gleaming like rich metal in the firelight. Damien had always longed to run his hands through that silken waterfall, and now she offered it to him.

Dear God, so this is what is meant by temptation, he thought, gathering the young woman fully into an embrace and stroking the satiny fall of her mane. April melted in his arms as if she had always belonged there, heedless of the blanket slipping to her waist.

Suddenly, with the sensation of taut young breasts rubbing against his own chest, Damien surrended to the flare of passion between them. He began by raining tiny kisses along the ridge of her brow, then down her sensitive neck until he dared to taste the smooth orbs that fit neatly into the palms of his hands.

At the first flick of his tongue upon a taut nipple, April gasped at the heat that burned through her body. She had never imagined such

179

pleasure, that a man might suckle upon a woman like a babe and render pure delight.

Damien lowered her gently to the sand, his teasing tongue moving upward again, to curl around the pink shell of her ear. It delved mischievously inside the ticklish canal until April begged him to cease the sweet torture. She wound her own hands into his ebony hair, loving the silky texture as she kneaded his head like a little cat.

Remembering Damien's recent injury, she was careful not to grieve him with an accidental bump. April contented herself with wrapping her arms lovingly around his neck, and then she copied his expert tutelage and began to press light kisses of her own accord against his neck.

Encouraging her with a faint moan, Damien delighted in the sweet willingness of this young woman. He knew April was not merely teasing him, but fully intended to go through with their lovemaking. He also knew he should be the one to stop it, to save her heartbreak in the end, but her softly glowing green eyes somehow told him that to deny her now would be a terrible mistake.

If he could bring her joy in the act of love, then perhaps she would no longer fear men. April would be free to take a lover of her choice then, once they had parted ways. But why did the thought of another man caressing this sweet Romany maid make him angry? Damien shook off his conscience to bury himself in her warm embrace, dragging the woolen blanket over them both where they lay in the sand.

Innocent and intoxicating, April's lips burned a fiery trail across his upper body. Obviously delighted to be able to touch and stroke him as she wished, she occupied herself for some minutes by rubbing her silken cheek against his darkly furred chest. Her pale hair spilled over them both, reflecting the fire's reddish glow. Damien stroked her head, fighting the rising desire to fully claim her as his own.

"Damien," April whispered, her soft voice stoking the burning coals in his loins. She mouthed his name so lovingly that for a moment the earl could actually see this beautiful young woman as his wife. Then, determined not to fall prey to her sweet wiles, he forced himself to look upon her as merely another desirable female. April need never know of his inner restraint.

Gazing deeply into April's eyes, he drew her up over his body, to mate their anxious lips. Lord Cross drank deeply of his gypsy bride, exploring the sweet cavern of her mouth with his tongue, holding her firmly against the shivers that shook throughout her frame.

Wave after wave of passion slammed into April as she succumbed to desire. Somewhere in the distant fog of reason, she was aware that the rain had slowed, and now she could hear the distant fall and crash of the surf upon the shore. How perfect, how right, that this should be their wedding night! Here, where man and woman had walked for centuries together along the shore, looking out to the sea in awe of its secret life force.

A tremor clutched her for a brief moment when Damien gently reversed their positions, putting her beneath him. He hushed her with soft endearments, quelling the fear in her eyes. April knew a little of what would follow, but she was still not fully prepared. Worrying her lower lip, she waited while her husband slipped out of his confining trousers. Romany girls were not shy by nature, and she gazed frankly upon the handsome male body revealed by firelight.

Del, but he was beautiful! As lithe as a panther, and lightly furred with the same jet hair on his legs as on his chest. Damien's eyes seemed to burn particularly bright blue this night, taking her breath away as she stared back at the man who would make her a woman.

The earl saw April blush a little as her gaze dropped to encounter his proud manhood, boldly upright in its own nest of curling black hair. But she did not draw away, even as he joined her again and murmured softly, "Are you sure, *ma chere?* It will hurt a little, though after that there will be much pleasure, I promise you."

At the unfamiliar endearment April smiled and snuggled closer to his delicious warmth.

"What does that mean, *"ma chere?"* Is it French?"

"It is," he grinned down at her, "and I confess I should have wondered if you had understood it, even as familiar with the language as you are. It means 'beloved.' "

April almost melted at the tender tone he used. It never occurred to her that endearments came as easily to men as their lust, and she finally answered him with a trusting smile.

"I am sure, my husband."

Casting away the last of his doubts, Damien took April as his wife in the deepest sense of the word. With a strong, gentle mastery that came naturally to a lover of women, he began by exploring her flawlessly smooth skin inch by inch, with his lips and tongue.

With a fist stuffed in her mouth to keep from gasping, April let the sensations bolt through her untutored body, causing her to arch and writhe for something she did not fully understand. One minute he was worrying her nipples, nipping and then soothing the inflamed peaks with a cool tongue, the next he gently stroked the insides of her silken thighs and made her moan with longing.

Any attempt she made to return such caresses only caused Damien to shake his head and still her pleas. "Tonight is for you, little girl," he whispered huskily as he licked her earlobe, "and I will not let you share it with anyone, not even me!"

Her head was spinning, her senses alive and aching with every touch of his hands. He brought her higher and higher, even insinuating his long fingers into sweet, secret places that caused her to protest faintly until he silenced her with firm kisses.

"Be still, April," he ordered. "Let me teach you! You need only relax and learn, that you might return the favor someday." Damien's eyes danced with flames, and for a moment he was a blue-eyed hawk, and April, his helpless prey. But still she would sacrifice herself to be caught. With an avid cry, she let him have full measure of her passion. Her head lolled from side to side, and her golden hair lashed his sweat-sheened skin. April felt burning wildfire in her belly, and begged her husband to soothe the unfamiliar ache.

Feeling the dew of her readiness, Damien edged his muscular frame atop April. She was no frail creature to be easily crushed, but still he held the brunt of his weight on his own arms as he settled his hips into hers.

The direct contact was almost too much. Sobbing with need, April clung to Damien and cried out for release.

"Easy, love, I want to take it slow. There may be pain at first . . ."

"I don't care! Please, please love me!" With an instinct deeper than she understood, April spread her legs wide and arched upward into him. Damien could no longer deny himself.

They fit too well together, and when she moved with primal sensuality, he brushed her warm entrance and eased slightly in.

Fighting himself for control, Damien's hands dug into the sand and he braced his back. But his young wife was undulating her sweet hips, urging him on, and with an anguished moan he thrust fiercely into her burning core.

April flinched slightly, but Damien cut off her gasp with a ravishing kiss. As he began to ride her, slowly and then with increasing speed, he released her bruised lips and let her cry out over the discovery.

Though there had been a moment of pain that had shot through her loins, April quickly forgot it in the breathtaking excitement of making love. Damien's hips settled against hers, and her long legs wrapped around his calves. Together they rode the waves of passion higher and higher until each felt the great crest crashing over them.

Damien was past reasoning, though he had intended to love his wife gently. Instead he had taken her like an animal, rutting desperately after months of celibacy. The fact that April encouraged his fierce efforts seemed only the more bewildering to his already hazy mind. Never had a woman clung to him so tightly, matching him thrust for thrust, the sheen of perspiration on her as bright as his own.

A burning, roiling sensation began to build in his loins, to Damien's dismay. He wanted to last the night through, to make April's first time wonderful, but like an untried boy he soon found himself crying out and spilling himself deeply into her womb.

April clutched his shoulders, which were taut for a full minute as he bore down upon her. The warmth of his love soon trickled down her thighs, but she would not release him from the leglock.

She nipped playfully at his shoulder, inquiring in a soft, mischievous voice, "Is that all, my teacher? Or would you kindly repeat the instruction so that I might learn it well?"

"Witch," Damien gasped against her ear, but her giggle eased his mind. He had feared she would be furious after such a clumsy assault, as any of his mistresses surely would have been. But he had forgotten April's innocence, and that she took anything he dished out as her proper due. Why did that make him feel even worse? She deserved better than this. Angry at himself, Damien withdrew and slid down to prop himself between her languid thighs.

"What are you doing?" Alarmed, April would have closed her legs and sat up, but suddenly his hands pinned her firmly to the sand, and before she could squirm or utter a protest, his mouth was loving her where his manhood already had.

First she tried to kick free, and then, when that didn't work, seized a handful of his silky black hair and yanked hard. But Damien would not be dislodged, and when she felt the first velvety stroke upon her secret woman's jewel, April cried out in startled pleasure.

He loved her, and he loved her well. In mere seconds she followed his example admirably, arching high with a piercing shriek. Then, as she drifted slowly back to earth, he moved up beside her again and branded her with lips that tasted faintly of sea-salt.

Holding her protectively to his side, Lord Cross studied April's serenely smiling face. Her green eyes aglow from lovemaking, she was a study in contentment. Curled up like a little cat against him, April nestled in his arms and laid her head upon his chest.

"I can hear your heart beating. It's so strong," she murmured sleepily.

Damien only patted her head in response. He was lost in thought, staring into the glowing coals of the fire that had since died down. It was getting cold now, but he did not want to break the spell by dislodging April and moving around. Now that he was restored to some sanity and reason, the earl could only curse himself for being a twice-tried fool. He had dishonored April tonight, but what's more, he had done so with the full knowledge of repercussions.

Knowing that she was not his wife in the eyes of either France or England, and that by virtue of her heritage, she could never be, he had nonetheless taken her innocence, and taken it well. Detesting himself as he did other men of his class who dallied with servants or easily impressed maids, Damien was at a loss as to what to do. By Romany law, he had had the right to take her, but now she was ruined for any other man. If King Jingo even suspected that Damien had wronged April thusly, he would not hesitate to kill him and leave his corpse for the crows.

As he well might, Lord Cross mused darkly. What fate for a girl like April, once he left her behind? Her beauty would always secure her a protector, but what of a husband, a happy life? She would never be more than a rich man's trull, or worse yet, die from childbearing before she was thirty.

Never before had he been so conscious of his own actions as now. The sophisticated courtesans he had amused himself with had never expected any more than they had gotten, nor had they gazed at him with such loving, open eyes. He knew that April's vulnerable heart lay full in his hand, and damn it all to hell, what would he do now?

She was already asleep, breathing softly against his chest, as lovely a wife as any man could ever hope for. So for the moment, Damien Cross dared dream too, and as he held his sweet gypsy tightly in his arms, he vowed that he would do whatever it took to keep from hurting her in the days to come.

Ten

It was late fall before Damien and April finally reached Moscow. Already the imperial city was lightly glazed with snow, like a spun-sugar confection with endless spires and steeples sparkling in the crisp air.

Damien glanced over at his young wife sitting beside him in the wagon, and could not restrain a grin at her obvious delight. With childlike wonder April pointed and exclaimed over everything, and the earl agreed to tour the sights.

They paid a few coins to leave the wagon and the horses at one of the cheaper stables, and April eagerly dashed into the core of milling humanity. Though they were dressed like gypsies, they blended in easily after they entered the poorer sections of Moscow. Here nobody looked twice at a gypsy girl stepping daintily over piles of manure and trash, except to remark upon her loveliness, or the scowl of the darkly handsome man at her elbow.

Damien dared not let April explore alone, and had to restrain her from running free as she had done since her youth. As a child she had been able to avoid notice by keeping to the alleyways, but here her blonde hair and uncommon beauty attracted the wrong sort of attention. Even escorted by a menacing, battle-scarred Romany man, April received stares that made Damien angry and uneasy.

Had they been in Turkey, where fair women brought a high price, he knew he should have never survived the day. As it was, he still cast frequent glances back over his shoulder, hurrying April along to her protests and cries of dismay.

"Oh, Damien, look at that cloth!" April stopped once to stare at an open stall where silks and velvets were displayed in a rainbow of colors. "Look, that's just the color of my wedding dress, remember? Tzigane used green to match my eyes."

Suddenly the owner of the stall came hurrying over, bleating in thickly-accented Russian, "Get away, gypsy! Do not touch my goods!" His verbal attack was accompanied with threatening gestures that caused Damien's eyes to darken. "You will drive away my honest customers!"

Though April withdrew her hand, her smoldering green gaze turned full upon the vendor without a trace of fear. Obviously, she was used to such prejudice from childhood. And, Damien thought with a chuckle, she already knew how to deal with it very well.

"A pox on you for cursing the daughter of a Romany king! May your days be fruitless and your loins equally so! May your goods rot before they sell! May your nights be dark and troubled—"

"No, no!" The man was suddenly pleading with her, holding out his gnarled hands in supplication. "Do not curse me, girl! I am a poor man and have many mouths to feed!"

"You should have thought of that before insulting the princess!" Damien put in, playing along for April's sake. "As it is, she must receive an apology at the very least."

April concentrated on looking aloof and offended while the vendor groveled piteously. Finally, in desperation, the man seized several bolts of material and, thrusting them at her, babbled, "I saw you admiring these trifles. Please accept them with my humble apology. I need you to bless my family, not curse us!"

Trying very hard not to smile, April hesitated as if weighing the gifts against the insult, and then nodded regally that she would accept the "trifles."

Later, as they walked on with the bolts tucked securely under Damien's arm, she could not help but grin, imagining how proud her people would have been of her performance.

"You are an excellent actress," Damien said.

"But not without your help! You are an actor

worthy of a prize yourself." April did not see Damien frown slightly at that, and she continued teasingly, "You have earned a reward of your own, I think."

His dark eyebrows rose with anticipation. "I wouldn't presume to argue, little girl!"

Together they hurried back to the stables. In the dark privacy of the wagon, bolts of cloth tumbled aside as they fumbled with each other's clothes.

Grabbing April by the shoulders, Damien drank deeply of her sweet essence. Perhaps she was a witch, for she kept luring him back to her bed time and time again. Even against his best intentions the earl could not resist her warmth, or the small hand that often strayed to touch him in the night. Since he had first initiated her, April had proven to be a quick and eager pupil, and there had been only one night thus far that they had not made love as man and wife.

Brushing his hands down her smooth, bare arms, he sighed with pleasure at the feel of her silken skin. April bathed every day, twice when she could, and was always perfumed and sweet for him. With a barely restrained moan, he lifted her up and laid her on the bed.

Her hands and lips were already busy arousing him. Now that she no longer feared lovemaking, April was impatient to become one with her husband again. They moaned softly in unison as they were finally joined. Rocking her gently in the bed, Damien perfected his timing so that when April finally saw the crest of passion, only then did he join her in the grand finale.

As they lay snuggled closely in the cold night, they murmured softly about their shared life and of plans to come. Damien, however, thought of other things that he dared not share with his lovely gypsy. He must release one of the pigeons to Lord Raglan the next morning, without April noticing or asking why.

His message would be brief, but smack of success. Finally he had the cover necessary to begin his covert activity, and Lord Raglan would be pleased. If all went well, Damien could probably complete his mission in as little as a month.

But as he nuzzled April's violet-scented hair, Damien once again felt the sharp twinge of guilt and regret. Were she anyone else, he should have been proud to take her back to England as his bride. April was lovely, bright, and a quick learner. She could likely sail through society with practiced ease. But he would never find out. Soon he must disappear, leaving his young wife bewildered and alone.

The whole plan reeked of deceit, which Damien did not like. It was one thing to dupe strangers into believing he was someone he was not, but April? How could he crush this young woman's dreams and ideals? Right now as her eyes closed and she snuggled up against him, he wavered in his duty to the Crown. He wanted nothing more than to bury himself in his new wife, to delight in her happiness and their life together, however brief.

Tomorrow was soon enough for breaking hearts. For now, Damien was content just to hold April and ease her gently into the wonderland of dreams.

With a glance at the forbidding gray sky over the city, Damien finished forking hay to the horses before he went back to the wagon to call his wife.

"April! Maybe we should put our performance on hold. It looks like it's going to snow."

He spoke up to the closed canvas flap, but when she whipped it back and smiled down at him, something in his chest tightened painfully. She was beautiful, her golden hair falling loosely around her, shimmering in the vestige of sunshine left. She had used the material the stall owner had given her to sew a new dress, and it fit her perfectly. The heart-shaped bodice was dark green velvet, the skirts, bright layers of blue and green taffeta.

"What, a few snowflakes stop our plans?" She laughed, a carefree sound. "And you supposedly a *romani rei!* Don't you know that Rom love bad weather? The wilder the better, for it only means our ancestors are taking note of our efforts!"

Her cheerfulness forcibly lifted the frown from Damien's brow, and he nodded in resignation. "I might need a tarp, though, or an overhang to keep my violin from getting water-damaged."

"That's no problem. The stallkeepers will no doubt give you a few feet once they hear the sweet music you make." April saw that her husband wasn't as optimistic as she, and wondered at the cause. Surely Damien wasn't shy about performing in public? He had done so well for the Lowara, throwing his heart and soul into the music as if he were full-blooded Romany.

Quickly she finished perfecting her attire, slipping on a few more gleaming bands of gold for her wrists. As Damien swung her down to the ground, she lovingly bussed his cheek. "Everything will be wonderful, don't worry, *mon cher!*" Her enthusiasm was contagious. Picking up his violin case, Damien accompanied her to the town square.

Already crowds were beginning to assemble. Besides the gypsy couple, other entertainers gathering promised a carnival of activity, complete with food stands and colorful vendors hawking a variety of goods. Always quick and clever to spot opportunity, April had overheard several merchants discussing today's event in the square, and she had immediately planned their appearance.

Though by no means the only gypsies present, she saw now that she and Damien were a breed apart. The other Romany had set up *ofisas,* fortune-telling booths, and *boojos,* where unsuspecting *gaje* lost untold amounts of cash in the money-switching games. Such things were not unknown to the Lowara, but as her tribe usually avoided large cities, April was not used to seeing deception practiced on such a grand scale.

At they passed through the crowd, she felt the eyes of the other Romany following her and Damien. The dark-eyed women stared boldly at her husband, and she felt a shudder of anger. She was startled to realize she was jealous, but now she finally understood why. She loved Damien with all her heart and soul.

April decided to ignore the others in the square and get on with her performance. She knew she was talented, and the new dress molded her figure to perfection. Men's eyes, Rom and *gaje* alike, had already found and marked her as a point of extreme interest.

Some feet away, a small childlike figure dressed as a harlequin in black and white watched the festivities. Behind the spangled mask, a pair of dark eyes intently followed the beautiful gypsy girl as she passed. The thick-set lips protruding thoughtfully beneath the nose-piece of the mask, however, were not that of a child. They twisted with satisfaction and slight cruelty as April ran lightly to the center of the square.

Damien brushed past the harlequin, hurrying

after his wife with the violin tucked under his arm. April jostled for position with a three-man ring of acrobats who were loathe to surrender the spotlight for even a moment. Finally, she ignored them and simply nodded to Damien. The violin rose to his shoulder and settled into place like an old friend. When the sweet peals of music wafted out over the noisy crowd, there was almost instantaneous silence.

Soon the acrobats shuffled aside a little sheepishly to make way for the roving musician. With a nod of thanks, Damien marked his territory in long strides as he walked about, wooing the crowd with his song.

April blended into the background for a moment, letting her lover take his due. She never tired of listening to Damien, or watching him coax the haunting strains from the worn old instrument.

A minute later she entered the charmed circle in a bright swirl of skirts. Pleased by the expectant murmur that ran through the crowd at her appearance, she nodded at Damien and he abruptly switched from sweet melancholia to torrid, rising crescendos that sent shivers up those who watched.

Suddenly April was no longer a beguiling wallflower, but a fierce and desperate dancer, demanding her audience's attention. In a blur of blue and green she cast a powerful spell over the crowd, her flying feet and hair too fast to capture in a blink, and the hypnotically clawing music gave a rush of adrenalin to all who listened.

The crowd pushed closer, drawn by some inexplicable magic, perhaps unconsciously noting the loving glances tossed between dancer and musician. For the handsome, dark-haired man played to the beautiful blonde, coaxing her body to respond with each slither on the violin, moving her like a marionette through the motions of his strings.

Of those who watched, the small harlequin was no less intrigued, and yet excited beyond the understanding of the others. His beady, dark eyes marked April from where he stood on the edge of the square, peering around a tall marble statue. He could feel the blood pounding and surging through his frame, giving him an intense, but welcomed headache. For here, after nearly four years, he had surely found a way to ingratiate himself into the services of Count Ivanov again.

The girl was perfection incarnate. Pavel had seen many beauties, but this one was special. He had nearly choked in shock when he had first seen her run laughing through the square.

Though he disliked women himself, the dwarf nevertheless saw his chance in her. This gypsy wench was the mirror-image of someone the count had lost long ago, his only love, and the woman who haunted him still.

Of course, the girl would likely demand a high price for her services. But so would Pavel, once Count Ivanov had caught a glimpse of this rarefied creature. The trick would be to lure the girl to Ivanov's residence outside of Moscow as soon as possible. Would she be willing? Pavel assumed so, but if not, there were ways to persuade gypsies, and he would see to it that she was taken to Count Ivanov, even if it was in chains.

A thin smile twisted the dwarf's lips as the crowd erupted into frantic cheers and encores for the breathless beauty now taking her bows. As if in echo, the overcast sky suddenly broke, and hard, fast flakes of snow began to fall. As the crowd scattered for shelter with a shout of dismay, the gypsy hurried to sweep up her shoes and her booty.

April's tambourine, set aside on the edge of the square, was overflowing with coins and cheap jewelry. A moment later, she grabbed Damien by the arm and they melted into the crowd.

As they ran laughing in the snow flurry, neither were aware of a small diamond-paned figure trailing them down the streets and alleys strewn with trash.

They thought themselves separate from the world, caught up in life and laughter and love. But soon, Pavel thought a little maliciously, soon he would prove to them both that nothing in life is free—especially love.

* * *

April was changing clothes inside the wagon when she heard voices coming from the nearby stable. Damien had left to feed the horses again.

She peeled off the new dress, quickly hung it up to dry, and donned warm, brown woollen skirts and a shawl over her blouse. She went to the wagon flap and looked out, just in time to see a pair of figures disappearing into the stables. One, she saw, was Damien. But behind him tagged a colorfully costumed child. She wondered if the lad was looking for work. Usually *gaje* children avoided gypsies, after being told horror stories by their parents. Curious as to the reason for the child's presence, she decided to join them in the stables.

Before April arrived, however, Damien had already exchanged introductions with the dwarf who had approached him as he was headed to the stalls. Pavel was trying to entice him into meeting his employer, a *boyar* aristocrat who lived on the outskirts of the city.

"There's money to be made, and plenty of it," the odd little man insisted. He removed his mask to reveal a misshapen, twisted face with an overbite and pointed yellow teeth that reminded the earl of his wolfhounds back at Mistgrove.

Pavel began to regale Damien with stories of riches and renown to be had if his music was favored by an aristocrat.

"I am Romany," Damien replied scornfully.

"No *boyar* would ever invite me out of the gutter!"

His disdain was believable enough, for Pavel hesitated. Then he cajoled, "But you are an exceptional musician, and your sister, a wonderful dancer."

"Sister!" Damien laughed. "Your mistake, little man. That is my wife, April. Is she not a prize?"

"Indeed," Pavel murmured, thinking that though their relationship might complicate things a bit, Count Ivanov need not know. Soon enough the girl would forget this gypsy oaf, once she had been showered with jewels and fine gifts. Women were easily bought, which accounted for much of Pavel's disgust for them. Even Damien, offered a good horse in trade, would probably not hesitate to turn over his pretty bride to Pavel.

Damien stopped to tend to a pair of steeds, one of which looked far too fine for a gypsy to own. The black snuffled and blew at his master's arm, while eyeing the little dwarf suspiciously. Pavel knew the animal had picked up the scent of his fear, for a man of his size was wise to avoid such unpredictable beasts.

Wondering at the cause for Prince Adar's nervousness, Damien gave the stallion his ration of oats and then tended to the mare. All the while Pavel continued to wheedle him, until in sudden exasperation Damien asked, "And what's in this for you?"

At the condescending tone, Pavel bristled. But he must maintain a friendly air until the gypsy agreed. With a nod of his overly-large head, the dwarf said, "A fair question, I'll grant! But you have surely heard of those who are given the arduous task of finding rare talent to amuse the courts? That is my mission, though I confess it is a difficult one. Once I was a court jester myself, and as you see I still have my costumes, but with my waning health I have decided to pursue a more dignified course."

"So now you ask others to play the fools, eh?"

Pavel could barely keep his full-sized temper in check. The gypsy was crude, unmannered, and certainly unworthy of the compliments being paid him. True, he was a talented violinist, but those were a dozen a ruble even in Moscow. It was the girl he needed to recapture Ivanov's favors, and first he needed to pacify her husband.

Seeing a different persuasion was called for, Pavel made a gesture toward the horses Damien was now grooming, noting slyly, "A fine brace of beasts, Damien. How interesting they should come into your possession."

"Why is that?" Damien instantly anticipated what the dwarf was driving at, and made his voice appropriately hostile. Now he understood the Romany resentment toward *gaje,* who assumed anything of worth or value in the gypsy realm must be stolen.

"It seems to me I heard rumor of a similar steed missing from one of the local nobles." Pavel indicated Prince Adar. "Surely black stallions are rare enough anywhere, but—" He shook his head, as if unwilling to say more. The untold threat was clear. Whether the horse was stolen or not was irrelevant, but Pavel was prepared to call attention to the obviously well-bred horse.

Damien wondered what the dwarf was really up to. The fact that he was trying so hard to get them to meet Ivanov made his curiosity grow. If it was true the dwarf only needed a commission, then he would have an excellent cover and an excuse with which to infiltrate the czarist realm. If not, then they were being lured into a trap of some sort. But what motive did Pavel have for wishing to waylay a pair of gypsies?

Pavel continued, "Of course, I will expect a small cut for my services in introducing you to the count. On your own, it is unlikely you would merit the attentions of nobility. But with my connections, you could find yourself a rich man in a very short time."

Ah, money. The eternal lure and curse of man. Perhaps the dwarf was being honest. He certainly stood to profit by such a deal. But something nagged at Damien, a sense of something not quite right.

Just then April appeared. She walked up to them quietly, her bare feet muffled in the scattered straw. Though plainly garbed now, she was no less lovely. Her face registered curiosity as she asked, "Who is your little friend, Damien?"

It was a good thing she had spoken in Romany, not Russian. For when Pavel turned around, April saw the mistake she had made, and colored in embarrassment. She had supposed the harlequin to be a child. Instead, a repulsive little man stared at her from beneath thick hairy brows, the ridge of his deformed skull protruding and giving him a strangely sinister look.

"April, this is Pavel." Damien introduced them in Russian as if she had never made the *faux pas.* "He has come to offer us work here in Moscow. Pavel, this is my wife."

"Charmed." The dwarf gave a short, comical bow. "May I say that you danced divinely in the square today."

April was unused to courtly compliments. She looked helplessly at her husband after murmuring a brief thank you.

"She is shy? But what a Romany rose!" Pavel gushed, privately thinking that the girl was probably only an excellent actress. Gypsies were known to be a bold and clever lot. If he did not despise women so, he could almost admire her. "I was just remarking to your husband that your stallion is exceptionally fine. Where did you come by him?"

Not seeing a trap in his query, April replied honestly. "Prince Adar was given to me by a gypsy king some years ago."

"Ah." Pavel's eyes gleamed wickedly. It was clear he did not believe her.

Damien interrupted, "Pavel is trying to get us an audience in Moscow. We might be asked to entertain at court."

"Might?" The dwarf looked offended. "No question of that, my Romany friend. Your talent is unsurpassed. While I admit I cannot recall the last time gypsies entertained at court, I am sure an exception can be made."

April's fine senses also picked up something wrong. Why was this stranger, this funny little man, trying so hard to win them over? She wondered if it was just his appearance which made her uneasy. But as a gypsy, she was used to seeing the ill-favored. They had never bothered her before. Now, however, something caused her skin to crawl, and trusting her instincts, she looked pleadingly at Damien. *I don't want to be around this man!* Her green eyes clearly told her husband. She moved closer to Damien so that his height gave her the illusion of safety.

Seeing the dilemma his wife did not, and knowing Pavel was not bluffing about turning them over to authorities, Damien had no choice. "I think it would be a good idea. We could get rich quickly and perhaps earn a ticket to other European courts."

"That's the spirit!" Pavel chuckled, also knowing why Damien had caved in so quickly. "I assure you, my friend, you will not regret your decision. Why, I'll even buy your pretty wife a whole new dancing wardrobe, of the finest silks and satins. You'll lack for nothing while you're under my care."

"Can't you just give us directions to Ivanov's?" Damien asked. He didn't like the idea of traveling with Pavel, whom he didn't trust.

"Nonsense. Without my introduction, Count Ivanov would never agree to see you. You'll also have to practice your act and refine it a bit. The court is easily bored these days. The distraction of war has upset the czar. When he is in residence, he always wishes to see something fresh and uplifting."

April couldn't believe Damien was agreeing so readily to this mad idea. She wanted to cry out, to plead with him to say no, but something in his blue eyes stilled her.

Something was terribly wrong. He was too easily guided by this odd, misshapen creature, who reminded her of an evilly grinning troll. Now was not the time to beg and wheedle her husband out of the deal. But the minute she had Damien to herself again, she would!

Instinct told April that to trust Pavel would bring disaster down around their ears. And she had never known those instincts to be wrong yet. Stifling her protests for now, she allowed the two men to discuss their plan, all the while wondering how she could convince Damien to refuse the dwarf's suspiciously generous offer.

Eleven

The ancestral home of Count Vasili Ivanov was built on the outskirts of Moscow, less than an hour's ride from the city proper. Soon after he left the gypsy couple at the stables, promising to return shortly, Pavel hopped in his sleigh and set off for Ivanov's residence. As he sliced through the bitter night, the dwarf quivered with anticipation, but he also recognized a thin trickle of fear in the pit of his belly. And he had good reason to be wary.

Once Ivanov's righthand man, Pavel Chevensky had been cast off five years ago after a servant plotting to secure his own favors with the count had betrayed the dwarf's dishonest handling of the estate accounts. Enraged, the volatile Ivanov had grabbed Pavel by his neck and flung him out into the streets, vowing to skewer him and serve him to his guests if ever Pavel should return to his home. Cowed, but not beaten, Pavel took up traveling, weaseling his way into the confidences of other nobles, until his own dwindling funds finally gave way to this latest madcap scheme.

Pavel would take great pleasure in giving April over to the count. Women found the dwarf repulsive and had always regarded him as a freak. His own mother, whomever she was, had taken one look at the son she had had and left him in a heap of trash some thirty years ago. If not for the soft-heartedness of an old peasant man, Pavel would have died. He had more in common with April than he would ever know, but he hated her simply because of her sex.

When Count Ivanov caught a glimpse of the gypsy wench, Pavel would be a very rich man. It would give him great satisfaction to see her taken in hand by Ivanov, knowing of the aristocrat's bizarre obsession with his love from long ago.

Pavel chuckled softly to himself, rubbing his mittened hands together. Perhaps he would dare to ask the count for a small favor himself. He would like to show April that he was as much a man as her husband, and when he was through with her, he would scar her as he did all the other women he used. Pavel made sure they never forgot they had been ridden by a little man with a huge ego.

The dwarf tingled with evil anticipation. He could hardly wait to exact his vengeance on womankind again. Each time he made one of them suffer, he could almost feel himself growing an inch taller.

When they left the paved roads and the comforting glow of the city street lamps, Pavel signaled his driver to light the lanterns he had brought. Perhaps he was foolish to set off so impulsively into a storm, but he could not wait to worm his way back into Ivanov's good graces. Of course, there was a small chance the count would refuse to see him, but knowing Vasili, he would be curious as to why Pavel had returned so desperately in the midst of a blizzard. Surely the dwarf would be assured a seat on the count's right again, and given all the rewards and boons such an honored position brought.

Soon Samarin House, as it was colloquially dubbed by the locals, rose before them in a blaze of lights and medieval peaked towers across the vast blanket of Moscow's north hills. Pavel banged on the window to urge the driver to go faster, his eyes gleaming with excitement as the sleigh raced across the snow banks. Pavel opened the window and cried, "Straight through the gates! Stop for nothing this night!"

Paid to obey, the driver ignored the pair of sentries who hollered in outrage at the sleigh that whipped past their posts. They made it to the front entrance before the guards could even get on their snowshoes, and Pavel executed a disembarkment worthy of the *boyar*, throwing back his shoulders and raising his knobby chin as if it were his own home he deigned to enter.

Even at this late hour it was not unusual to find the count awake. Seeing that that was the case when a disgruntled butler answered the door, Pavel moved swiftly past the minion to confront the man who was stalking down the hall directly at him.

"You!" Ivanov raised a threatening fist, his burgundy silk smoking-jacket flying open as he came. Pavel simply stood there, unruffled, briskly dusting the snow off his fur hat and mitts as he handed them to the lackey.

"I hope I have not disturbed you, my lord," Pavel said mildly as if Ivanov had just greeted him like a long-lost relative. "Though the hour is admittedly late, I have news which warrants your attention."

Still the silver-tongued court creature, Pavel's nonchalance caused even the count to hesitate. Ivanov looked barely older than when Pavel had seen him last; in fact, he noted that the slight ashen tinge to the count's sable hair was an attractive touch, and his figure was no less lean and admirable than the dwarf recalled.

"It must be news indeed for you to risk your life and limb in seeking me out again," Vasili said at last, weighing his old acquaintance with dark eyes. There was a veiled threat in his tone that squeezed Pavel's innards, though the smaller man did not react. Exactly as if he had

211

never been tossed out on his ear, Pavel said graciously, "It appears the storm may render me stranded for a time. Perhaps we could share a warm brandy by the fire?"

Pursing his lips, Count Ivanov considered. He was a shrewd man who knew Pavel would not have taken such a gamble unless the dwarf had something truly remarkable to tell. And, of course, Vasili understood there would be money involved, else he would not have come at all. The count knew his old friend well. Pavel had been his valet, secretary, and occasionally his lover in their younger days. It behooved him to hear what the little wretch had to say.

Nodding curtly, Count Ivanov spun on his heel and returned to the study where he had been relaxing before a roaring fire. Knowing Pavel would follow like a devoted puppy, Vasili did not even turn around, but gestured sharply to the worn velvet stool where the dwarf had perched for so many years like an eager pet. He had not seen fit to remove it since Pavel's dishonor. It might be said that even the count was prone to moments of sentimentality.

Quick emotion welled up in Pavel at the sight of his old fireplace roost. His initial bravado had taken a sharp turn now that he stepped back into time, into the very room of his undoing so long ago. Maintaining an outward calm, Pavel peeled off his coat for the hovering butler and let Vasili dismiss the servant with a short nod.

Left alone in the chamber, the two men studied each other warily as if uncertain of the next move. Finally Vasili broke the ice, saying briskly, "Well, what is it? What brings you crawling back this time?"

Pavel flushed, but held his temper in check. "I would recover your friendship, my lord. It has been an empty spot in my life for too long."

"Oh? And how do you propose to do that?" Vasili's scorn cut deep. He was not a man who easily forgave or forgot.

"Hear me out, if you would. I understand you have little reason to trust me, but in my exile, I have changed considerably."

"So you say. But my accounts have still not balanced since your treachery, and I am vexed beyond words at your abuse of my trust. Why should I listen to you now?"

"Because, my lord, I have a rare treasure in my grasp at present, one you will cherish and exult in beyond your wildest dreams."

"Treasure?" The count poured two snifters of brandy and grudgingly gave one to Pavel. He sampled his own, smacked his lips and said, "I have enough money to amuse myself with for years to come, even after your disloyal frolicking with my family funds. I have no wish for any other precious *objets d'art;* as you see I am fairly well represented now."

Ivanov's careless gesture indicated the gilt portraits and tapestries surrounding them, as well as a magnificent mahogany grand piano topped with jewel-studded candelabra.

"Yes, I know, my lord. However, it is an idle wish you expressed to me several times that prompted my search for this singularly rare treasure of sorts. Do you still recall the lady Ekaterina?"

Vasili stiffened. His nostrils flared slightly with the memory Pavel roused, that of the haughty and beautiful niece of the Grand Duke of Kiev. How obsessed he had been with her, almost to the point of agony. Her goldspun hair, her mocking emerald eyes, how they had driven him to distraction at court! Never had Vasili found any to match her; even after she had laughed aside his offer for her hand, he had burned with the desire of having her. Though the lady in question was no longer alive, he was haunted by the memory of the beautiful vixen she had been, and how much he had loved her, to her eternal scorn.

Ekaterina. His Katya. The golden lioness. There was no other way to describe such feline beauty. It demanded recognition, and he had sought to give it to her. Though Ivanov admired many women, he had never been able to recapture the elusive quality of the love-hate relationship they had shared. And to his eternal regret, he had never bedded the hellcat, though she had tempted him nearly to rape several times.

Only Pavel, damn his knowing sly eyes, knew of Vasili's burning obsession about the only woman he had ever loved. Now he had cruelly dredged up those memories for the count, and he would answer for it.

"Speak then, damn you!" Ivanov was grinding his jaw as he stared at the grinning dwarf. "What do you have to say about Katya?"

Pavel hesitated, driving the aristocrat to near frothing before he deigned to reply. "Not exactly *about* her, my lord. But like her. " Sensing the puzzled, angry stare pulsating from the count's dark eyes, Pavel took a deep gulp of the brandy and let it burn through his belly, bolstering his courage. "You see, I have found the lady's double. Tucked away in a disreputable inn with scarce else to recommend it—except this one creature of note. You will understand when you see her."

"Her? A woman? I do not need any more doxies, fool! And none could equal Ekaterina. You may throw all the mealy-mouthed blondes you like at me, but none will incite me as she!"

"I beg to differ," the dwarf said softly. "One look and you will regret your hesitation tonight."

The count stared hard at his unexpected visitor. Was it possible that Pavel was being honest? That he had found a woman to make him burn as Katya had? The past ten years had been hell for the count, alternately mourning and cursing the proud bitch. For that reason he had never married, along with the additional secret of preferring sexual acts even the city slatterns considered perverted, secrets he knew Katya had despised him for, when she had caught a glimpse of his darker side.

Beads of sweat dotted his brow as Ivanov demanded hoarsely, "Where? Where is this woman?"

"I intend to present her to you shortly," Pavel replied indirectly. "I will need your help in doing so, for she seems to distrust me. The mention of your noble name should be enough to assure she is lulled into coming here, and your reward will be her possession, if you so choose."

"And lest we forget, I assume you have a price as well, Pavel?"

The dwarf ignored the sarcasm, setting his empty snifter aside on a cherrywood table topped with smooth, pink marble.

"How well you know me, old friend. But I ask only a simple thing. To be restored to your side. Not even your accounts. I long to prove to you that I am faithful now, and intend to remain so."

Vasili considered the request with obvious suspicion. He knew Pavel better than that. The dwarf was not known for his goodwill. But then, he had always been amusing and an occasional comfort to the lonely count. If he did indeed know of a woman like the fiery Ekaterina, Vasili would consider the old debt paid in full.

Before he fully reasoned what he was getting

himself into, Count Ivanov found himself grasping hands firmly with Pavel in a desperate gamble to reclaim a love lost long ago.

Dawn slanted pinkly over the horizon, casting a soft glow on the glittering fields of deep, unblemished snow. An aching stillness ruled; after the blizzard, even busy Moscow seemed to slumber in peaceful respect for the full onslaught of winter.

As she looked out the back of the wagon, April marveled at what she saw. The night before she had not been able to appreciate the vastness nor the beauty of the city. Her breath emerged in crystalline little puffs that drifted away into the icy morning air. Above the rise of the imperial city, a vast, unbroken sky of wintery blue still shimmered faintly with the dying light of stars.

Behind her, Damien finished dressing and came to join his wife. "You'll catch your death of cold," he gently scolded, bringing a shawl to drape around her shoulders.

"Isn't it beautiful?" April said, awestuck by the imposing mounds of snow and the glittering white shroud it cast over the town. "If nobody moved, it should be perfect for years to come."

"But even perfection can be boring after awhile," Damien said, thinking for some reason of ladies at court, and their shallow personalities. "Are you ready to leave?"

217

April sighed. She did not want to let go of the memories of the night before, of just her and Damien secure from the storm in a world of their own making. Going outside would mean encountering Pavel again, and dealing with an unpleasant reality she would just as soon avoid.

"Come on," Damien urged, "Pavel is waiting for us."

"I'm hungry," April put in, hoping to delay the inevitable. "Can't we eat before we go to Ivanov's?"

"That's up to Pavel, I suppose. Perhaps he will buy us something to eat along the way."

With a cross acknowledgement, April bundled herself up and moved slowly out after Damien into the bitter cold. She tried hard to show optimism over their upcoming performance. Right now, though, she wanted nothing more than to be alone with her husband. Damien seemed more remote than usual, and she knew he was preoccupied by something.

April had tried to question him, but he had assured her he was fine. She did not believe that. Did he distrust Pavel as much as she did? Or was he still blinded by promises of riches and renown to be had?

When they found the dwarf waiting in the stables, the couple was surprised to find Pavel seemed in good spirits and in no hurry.

"Did you rest well?" he inquired pleasantly,

but April detected a sarcastic note that made her eyes narrow.

Damien returned the civility and accepted Pavel's offer to buy them a meal at a nearby inn. They all fell silent as they ate. There was hearty stew and biscuits for breakfast, with hot pressed cider to warm their insides. April found the food surprisingly good and ate hungrily. She kept darting suspicious glances down the table at Pavel, who seemed to be grinning to himself about something.

"I have some good news to share," Pavel said at last, wiping his greasy mouth with the edge of his shirt cuff. He addressed Damien, ignoring April as he usually did. "Ivanov has expressed interest in sponsoring you as new entertainment at court. Of course, he wishes to review your performance first. I have agreed to let him do so."

"When?" Damien asked around a mouthful of biscuit.

"Tonight. The ballroom there should be sufficient for your needs; if not, he has agreed to open the adjoining quarters for more space. He is an avid fan of music and dance, and always searching for the remarkable. I assured him that you qualify in every respect."

Not sure if it was a compliment or not, Damien said, "I don't know." He knew Pavel was expecting some hesitation, for they were supposedly sullen, shiftless gypsies, after all.

"Come now," Pavel continued patiently, but

with an edge of warning, "you seem to forget how far and how fast I have brought you! Where is your gratitude for my efforts? I promised you a great deal and I have delivered it all in a few short days. You should be humble at the very least."

This was too much! Unable to bear the dwarf's overbearing rudeness, April put in hotly, "Perhaps we do not fully trust you! After all, you threatened to report our horses as stolen to get us to stay here."

Judging by Damien's silence and Pavel's pinched look, she knew she had hit the nail on the head. What other dastardly things had Pavel threatened? Was that why Damien was so eager to comply with the dwarf on every matter?

"Your wife, it seems, is especially ungrateful," Pavel remarked in a brittle voice. He glared at April with obvious dislike.

"Romany women speak their minds," Damien said.

"Her sharp tongue may undo all of this, should his lordship be offended."

Lordship? Now Damien was intrigued. A peer of his own class? How strange that any lord, even a foreign one, should choose to sponsor a pair of rag-tag gypsies. Suspecting more to the story, he echoed with appropriate greed, "He is wealthy?"

"Indeed. The count is envied by nearly all the *boyar*. He came into a great inheritance in his youth, and as an only child, kept the estate intact." No thanks to me, Pavel thought, amused. "Alas, he is known somewhat for his eccentricities. He is forever searching for the unusual."

"So we are to be freaks to amuse him?" April inquired archly.

Pavel was forced to look at her now, but he did so with disdain, furious that the chit dared to speak so to her betters. "Hardly. He will no doubt appreciate you more than you know." That was followed by a smooth little laugh that did not reassure April in the least.

Damien also suspected Pavel had other plans for them, but this was an introduction to court circles after all, and he could hardly back down now. Thinking rapidly ahead, he said, "We will both need new outfits. Silks and velvets with gold braid."

Greed was something Pavel could understand. He granted the demand with a terse nod, so Damien pressed his luck even further. "Ribbons for April's hair, a silver belt for me. I want to look fine."

"As long as you perform just as well as you look," the dwarf said pointedly.

"I forgot to mention that my violin needs a new string. In the cold weather one has broken. There must be a shop close by that could attend to it for me."

Pavel looked annoyed but said, "You can take the instrument out for repair. I will stay here with your wife until the count summons us."

Lord Cross could not reveal his frustration openly. He needed to dispatch a message to the front, but he did not want to leave April alone with the strange dwarf.

"My wife comes with me," he said at last, in a low growl. "It will not take long."

Pavel frowned. "Remember, gypsy, in Moscow there are many fine horses missing. It would be better for you if no questions are asked." His open threat was accompanied with a dismissive nod, and Damien was forced to take April by the arm and lead her firmly away from the table. If he hadn't, she might have hurled her little dagger straight for Pavel, and Damien had a strong suspicion that she wouldn't have missed.

Twelve

The white bird squirmed in Damien's hand, its plaintive coos echoing in the wagon.

"Hold still, that's a good fellow, just a moment more," the earl muttered under his breath, finally securing the tiny metal cylinder to the pigeon. It puffed in indignation, flapping its strong wings in another attempt to dart free.

He had only moments more before April might return from the shop with the violin, and already his excuse that he had forgotten something in the wagon seemed too flimsy to be believed.

Cradling the bird under his arm, Damien walked to the rear of the wagon and drew back the canvas flap. With a flutter, the white bird burst from his hold, winging up to freedom.

"Fly swift and true," Damien murmured, watching it until it vanished into snow-laden clouds high above the city.

"*Ciel!*"

He heard April hurrying toward the wagon,

concern in her voice. "One of the birds just escaped!"

"I know." He adopted a wry tone as he leaned out to look at her. "I opened the cage to feed them, and it just flew out."

"Poor thing! It will freeze up there." She held his violin case in one hand, a paper-wrapped package in another. "I used the money Pavel gave us to buy you a new outfit. I hope it will fit."

"I have no doubts if you chose it," Damien said, jumping down to help her with her burdens.

"Did you remember what you'd forgotten?" she asked.

"Yes. I forgot to say I love you this morning. " Damien pecked a kiss on the end of her bright pink, icy nose, and April laughed delightedly. She completely forgot all about the pigeons then, just as the earl intended.

"She is here?" Ivanov faced the mirror as he spoke, fiddling with the stiff collar of his frilled shirt, but Pavel could detect the note of anxiety in the count's voice.

"Yes. Both she and the musician are dressing for the performance downstairs. I bought the girl a gown I knew would favor her. She should be ready within the hour."

Vasili lightly touched his graying, dark hair, patting it fastidiously into place though not a strand dared toy with his temper tonight. He trembled with anticipation, imagining and wondering if it could be possible, if a woman existed to compete with his Katya's perfection. His critical eye roamed over his appearance one last time, noting the excruciatingly correct lines of his black frock-coat and trousers, the finely embroidered waistcoat and highly polished shoes.

Though he knew by court standards he was still a handsome man, Ivanov resented the loss of his youth. At two score, he was eclipsed now by equally eligible, younger men. It gave his mouth a bitter twist, and his renowned acerbic wit had become harsh and cruel of late.

As he left his bedchamber, Pavel trotting alongside like a faithful dog, Ivanov shook his head and said again, "Gypsies! I just don't know, Pavel. Aren't they dangerous? Aren't the women renowned for witchcraft?"

"The only witchcraft this one has is with her eyes," Pavel gushed. "Such a shade of green as you've never seen—well, perhaps you have."

Idly Vasili recalled the collar of emeralds he had given Katya to match her flaming eyes. Considered priceless, the stones had been in his family for several centuries. She had worn them for a time, toying with his affections, then abruptly refused to wear them. Since then the necklace had been gathering dust in the gold chamber that he had once fashioned for her, in the same spot she had carelessly flung them in a fit of rage. Ivanov had forbidden any of his servants to touch anything in the room he had prepared for his intended bride twenty years ago.

Years ago, Vasili Ivanov had been teased by the *boyar* at court about his fascination with Ekaterina. Since her untimely death, he had shunned the court almost entirely, gaining the reputation of an eccentric and a recluse. He was tormented by the loss of Katya. She still existed in his tortured heart and mind, welcoming him in his dreams as she had never done in real life.

Even now, none dared mention Katya to the count. Her portrait hanging in the library was regarded with no little fear. Ivanov had once beaten a maid who had merely attempted to dust the frame.

Now he was desperate enough to let a compulsive liar persuade him that a gypsy, some blowsy backwoods wench, could possibly make him forget his Katya. Vasili doubted it, but he did suppose he would at least be entertained, if rumors about the gypsies' musical abilities proved true.

Pavel took a departure to check on the ballroom and the state of the performers. Vasili decided to avail himself of a smoke, and stepped outside on the stone path directly through the library doors.

It was bitterly cold outside, but the icy air refreshed him. He cupped his hands to light a cigarette, then blew a great white ring of smoke that spiraled up toward the dusky purple sky.

The count stood alone for a few moments, steeling himself for the night's events. As he finished his smoke, he overheard an explosive string of cries coming from a nearby room.

The voice was female, but he couldn't make out the words. Curious, Ivanov followed the gently curving path to the double glass doors that looked into that chamber. What he saw made him freeze and stare in heart-pounding disbelief. There, standing centered in a pile of snowy-white petticoats, was Ekaterina!

She was loudly berating someone, a maid perhaps, about something. The young woman wore only a thin, moonlight-colored silk chemise and her golden hair swirled to her waist, freshly shining from a bath. When she half-turned toward him, Vasili could see the angry green flash of her eyes.

Dear God. He sagged against a marble statue in the garden, the cigarette snuffed in the snow. In an instant he was transported back twenty years, to when he had similarly spied on his beloved at her toilette.

Suddenly he had to know what she was saying. Was her voice shrill, unpleasant? Or a low seductive drawl? He hurried back along the path, nearly slipping on his smooth soles. He entered the library breathless and with a complete loss of composure. From above the fireplace, Katya's portrait mocked him with knowing green eyes.

Witch! So she had come back to haunt and taunt him, eh? This time she would not succeed! One way or the other, whatever it took, Count Vasili Ivanov would make Katya his!

At that moment April had no idea she had nearly driven a man to the point of madness. She only knew she was consumed with rage herself, and her hands shook as she hurled the spangled red dress in a sorry heap across the room.

"I will not wear it! Tell Pavel to bring another! No Romany wears red. It is the color of death!"

The maid stared furiously back, outraged that a mere gypsy should scorn the hospitality of her master. She stalked out the door, slamming it emphatically on the stormy scene behind her. Zofia would never understand the count's desire to bring gypsies—trash!—into his home. Granted, the girl was beautiful, but such a temper! Almost as quick to blow up as Ivanov himself.

As she scurried down the hall, Count Ivanov stepped out of the shadows and halted the maid. "What is going on?" he demanded softly, gesturing at the room she had just left.

Zofia was glad to complain. "What a one!

Screeching at me about the dress Pavel brought for her."

"What was wrong with the dress?"

The thin, homely Zofia shrugged and threw up her gnarled hands. "Something about the color. It's death, she says. All that blather about nothing. And such a pretty gown it was, too!"

Ivanov was thinking fast. Distracted, he said, "Carry on, Zofia. Go tell Pavel she will be ready soon. I will see to it myself."

Bobbing a curtsey, the maid hurried off. Moments later Vasili hurried up the central staircase and opened another door on a host of memories, as he breached the dusty peace of the golden bridal suite for the first time in two decades.

Inside the row of closets, creased and pressed and carefully wrapped in protective tissue, was the entire untouched trousseau he had commissioned a Paris dressmaker to craft for Ekaterina. Blues, greens, and golds dominated the color scheme, those shades she wore so well. As if making a very important decision, the count went through the wardrobe carefully, setting aside any red hues.

There. Suitable for dancing, a flared knee-length skirt of green silk trimmed with gold fringes was attached to a golden-shot silk bodice over a lace chemisette. Though outdated in style, the material was as bright as if it had just been made. Taking it reverently from the closet, Vasili carried the outfit back downstairs and, after hesitating, knocked softly on the guest chamber door.

"Damien?" A sweet, clear voice inquired, and as she hurried to answer, "You won't believe what that rat Pavel has done now!"

As she flung open the door, April gasped in shock and embarrassment, trying to cover herself too late from the intense stare of a pleasant-looking older man. In his arms was a mound of glistening material, and before she could speak, he said gravely, "I would be very honored if you would wear this instead."

His Russian was fluent and very cultured. April felt like a clumsy country maid, but tried to overcome her shock by taking the dress he proffered and hugging it to her body.

For a moment, neither spoke. She wondered who this man was, why he was dressed so finely and most especially why he was staring at her so disconcertingly.

"You favor green, don't you?" He finally said into the tense silence.

She nodded, her eyes wide over the beautiful dress he had given her. "It's my favorite color."

Vasili smiled even as his heart pounded furiously in his chest. Her voice was musical, but more than that, the girl was a mirror-image of his Katya in her youth, even more stunning than his fiancée had been in the height of her beauty. There was some palpable quality to this girl that was similar, yet different. For certain she had the same formidable temper, but there was a softness in her eyes that had not been there in the frigid green pools Ekaterina had possessed.

"I have been terribly remiss," he said then, giving her a short bow. "I am Count Vasili Ivanov. I am delighted to welcome you to my ancestral home, Samarin."

April tilted her head curiously. She had never met a count before, of the nobility that she could recall. Yet this man put her instantly at ease, even half-dressed as she was. She was not afraid of him, and did not hesitate in returning a greeting in kind.

"My name is April. I am Romany." There was no shame in her voice, just simple pride.

"You are the entertainer for this evening?" Ivanov already knew as much but he wished to linger, drinking in her unsullied aura. Something about her innocence relieved a great ache in his breast.

"Yes, along with my husband, Damien, who makes the music for me."

At the mention of a husband Ivanov's spirits plummeted. Pavel had said nothing of that! Perhaps the dwarf did not know? Unlikely, knowing the shifty little fellow. Vasili offered an indifferent nod for April's sake.

"I will leave you now to prepare. Do you require Zofia again?"

"No, thank you." A small smile danced around the edges of her sweetly heart-shaped mouth. "I am not used to servants hovering about me like moths around a fire. You will have to excuse my country ways."

"Country, perhaps, but charming nonetheless," Vasili countered smoothly. "I shall see you later at the performance. Welcome to Samarin, my lady."

The way he emphasized the last two words struck April as strange somehow, but before she had time to muse on it, he had gone. Slowly pushing the door shut again, she shook her mind free of fancies and went to prepare for her dance.

"You must be Damien, the musician."

The suave voice that suddenly spoke behind him caused Lord Cross to tense and turn quickly around. He met the cool bland gaze of Vasili Ivanov, no doubt their mysterious host, finely dressed and fully mannered even for a gypsy's benefit.

Damien returned the aristocrat's intense appraisal with his own. It seemed the count flushed a bit at the even stare of a supposedly lesser man.

"Yes," Damien grudgingly acknowledged at last, returning his attentions to tuning his violin. "And who are you?"

"I am Count Ivanov, owner of Samarin House. I am your host, a grateful one indeed that you and your lady consented to entertain me on this dismal winter night."

Something in the count's smooth response bothered Lord Cross, though he couldn't put his finger on it just yet. The man seemed too cordial, especially after Damien's blatant disrespect. Why should one of Moscow's elite choose to sponsor a pair of gypsies, whether he was desperate or not? Surely such a fellow could have his share of doting females, and keep well-enough entertained during the long winter in the privacy of his own bedchamber.

Though the count was obviously ill at ease, he still pressed Damien for information. "I am told the dancer will be joining you soon. Your wife, I believe?"

Chill blue eyes turned on him at the observation, and Vasili tensed a bit. Did the gypsy fellow possibly sense his keen interest in April? He was certain he had kept his tone polite and noncommittal. Yet the scrutiny with which Damien examined him made the count feel as if he had just blurted his passions aloud.

"Yes. My wife." The words held obvious possession, thin as a knife and twice as sharp. To his chagrin, the count was the first to break gaze with Damien and call out, "Pavel! You have done very well."

Ivanov's gesture included Damien's new outfit, a rich ensemble that did not disguise the Romany's powerfully muscled, tall frame. The slacks were fine black linen, the white silk shirt topped with a dark blue velvet vest trimmed with gold braid and sequins.

There was thin disapproval in Ivanov's tone, the fact that he had also noted the cost to his coffers in buying this stranger new clothes. Pavel came hurrying over, content to ignore Vasili's censure with a falsetto gushing that made Damien raise one sardonic brow.

"I am delighted that you are pleased. Are they not a picture, him so dark and her so golden? Ah, but forgive me, of course you have yet to feast your eyes on the beautiful little dancer. Rest assured she is as light as this one dark, perfectly suited to him." Pavel enjoyed thrusting the little barb at the count, who was powerless before Damien to disagree.

Vasili kept an even smile pasted to his features. "I look forward to making her acquaintance as well."

"You shall not have long to wait. No, indeed, for here she is now." Pavel pointed at April standing hesitantly at the entrance to the grand ballroom, poised upon the checkered squares of onyx and ivory like a queen debating her move in the game.

As all three men turned to stare, her color heightened under their combined scrutiny. Quickly she read the expressions there; Pavel, disdainful as always, Damien, concerned and so grim, and the count's dark eyes veiled with some unreadable emotion.

She entered under an arch gilded with gold leaf and walked in a whisper of silk up to her husband. "Are you ready?" she asked him softly, taking hold of his sleeve for support and comfort.

"Whenever you are," he replied flatly.

Something was wrong. April sensed it stronger than ever, her finely tuned nature silently shrilling with alarm as she surveyed the ready room and its few occupants.

A cold chill caressed her skin, and she parted her lips to speak, to beg off the performance, but then Damien broke abruptly free and went to take his place across the room.

April was left alone with the count and Pavel, who both murmured meaningless compliments before departing to their own chairs placed squarely in front of her. As Count Ivanov sat back and studied her intently, she felt a rush of overwhelming trepidation, though whether from nerves or some imaginary danger she did not know.

Taking a deep, steadying breath, April swept the count a dramatic curtsey. Ivanov's narrow eyes noted that her grace was feline and a perfect unconscious mimicry of the Grand Duke's niece. Katya had been like a golden lioness, lithe and beautiful, and just as deadly. Known as the Circassian Cat among court circles, her exotic heritage had only made her the more desirable to men, and rumors that she was directly descended from the fierce 12th century Queen Tamar had never been questioned.

April was so similar that merely watching her made Vasili's blood rush and pound in his veins. One moment she was a simple gypsy girl, whirling and clashing her finger cymbals, the next she was that sultry court siren Katya weaving her timeless spell around him again. Vasili was so haunted by the resemblance that he soon had to force his gaze away and concentrate upon the musician instead.

Noting the count's sudden aversion, April assumed she had done something wrong. Her emotions plummeted, for it seemed that she could please nobody of late. Even Damien, whom she knew loved her, was cool and remote. Deciding to take a short-cut and end the humiliation, she gave one final spinning flourish and dropped to the floor in a puddle of green and gold silk.

Cut off in mid-draw, Damien looked at his wife in annoyed confusion. What was she trying to do? Her face was averted from him but he could clearly sense her intent not to continue. And if they did not please the count, he might toss them out. Not to mention the vengeance Pavel would extract, as the dwarf had already threatened more than once what should happen should they fail to amuse Count Ivanov.

Pavel's expression was thunderous, but he was intelligent enough to look to Vasili before he reacted. Seeing the predisposition to kindness in the count's eyes, Pavel merely glared at April until she finally raised her face to all the men and murmured one simple word.

"Please. I can't continue right now."

It was a plea and a statement, all in one. It was clear she either would not, or could not, go on. Damien didn't know whether to be angry or proud, but when Count Vasili rose and extended his hand to April, raising her slowly up with his dark eyes riveted to her green ones, he knew he definitely wasn't happy.

Jealousy clenched Damien, surprising him yet again. It was obvious that Ivanov was intrigued with April. And what man wouldn't be, the earl reasoned. She was living beauty, grace inborn, and as refreshingly innocent as court ladies were not.

Like a fawn, April quivered before Ivanov, unsure of her first instinct for flight. Her eyes obviously appealed to his greater male instinct to want to protect her. Though Damien knew April could fend for herself, he longed to break Ivanov's grip on his wife's hand with a brutal bodily thrust between them.

"Don't you feel well, my dear?" the count inquired in a solicitous, fatherly tone that didn't fool Damien for a minute.

"No, I don't," April responded breathlessly. "I'm a bit feverish and a little dizzy."

"Then I insist you immediately retire for the evening. You are my guests, and are welcome to reside in my home for the night." Count Ivanov turned slightly to include Damien in his invitation. "Of course I will provide you with separate chambers, so that your wife may rest undisturbed."

Damien's eyes narrowed at that suspiciously hospitable statement, but he could not speak before Ivanov had summoned one of the maidservants who was hovering near the foiled entrance.

"Zofia! You will show Madame April to the Gold Room for the night."

"But—" the woman began, obviously taken aback about something.

Vasili's eyes hardened. "If she needs anything, you will see to it."

Keeping her own gaze downcast, Zofia nodded and bobbed a mutinous curtsey. Satisfied, the count waited until April turned to follow the maid out.

Damien still stood clutching the neck of his violin as if he would strangle it. Amused, the count considered the imposition of the girl's unwelcome husband, but decided that the fellow had at least earned a hearty meal and a warm bed for one night. Tomorrow he could be paid or persuaded to relinquish his lovely young wife into the safekeeping of Samarin House.

Thirteen

The room that April was shown to had been hastily dusted and readied for occupation only moments before. Anticipating the count's commands, Zofia had seen to it that the Gold Room was at least presentable. Though April had no idea what caused the maidservant to regard her so darkly, she immediately picked up on the strange atmosphere within the room.

"Someone left their things here," she remarked, turning in surprise to confront Zofia.

But the maid slipped out, slamming the great carved oak door behind her. April was a little disconcerted, but not frightened. She assumed Zofia disliked her for her dancing, which was not so unusual. And she did not feel energetic enough right now to confront the woman.

With a weary sigh, April began to undress. She found the wardrobe conveniently full of beautiful gowns and chamber wear, and chose an ermine-trimmed satin wrapper to ward off the chill. She padded curiously around the

239

room, wondering who usually kept residence here.

On a Queen Anne vanity of deeply polished wood, she found an array of delicate crystal flagons and cosmetics, most still uncorked or in their original wrappers. There was a heavy ivory-handled hairbrush and matching carved comb, exquisitely designed and yet free of stray hairs, unused. She had no idea that only an hour earlier a priceless emerald necklace had been strewn across the same vanity, for it had been whisked away to safer quarters now.

April wondered if the count provided such homey touches for all his guests. Perhaps so. But as she circled the room, studying the huge velvet-canopied bed with its sable throw, she felt an icy shiver of fear that could not be fully explained.

Of course, she was still uncomfortable about imposing on the hospitality of a stranger, and about coming to Moscow in the first place. Even the elegance of this room and the beautiful gowns arrayed like so many jewels in the closets could not fully distract her from worrying about the future.

Surely sometime this chamber had belonged to a young lady like herself. The count's wife, perhaps, or his daughter? But he had mentioned nothing like that. Still, April's second-sense was finely tuned and she fancied she could catch the faintest whiff of a perfume still clinging to the room.

At last, too tired to ponder further, she sank into a deeply cushioned, gold satin chair that faced the only window. Unlike the room on the first floor, this chamber had no open door to the tiny balcony outside. Instead it appeared that it had been bricked off to create the smaller window instead. The view was currently limited to blowing gusts of snow and an occasional glimpse of an icy moon. April had not felt so lonely in a long time.

When a soft knock came at her door, she found herself anxious for company. Even if the unfriendly Zofia was only returning to check on her, she decided she would delay the maid with an excuse to talk.

"Come in!" she called, turning in the chair to welcome her visitor.

She was surprised when Count Ivanov himself appeared. In his hands was a beautiful silver tea tray and an array of tiny sandwiches.

"Oh," April began to get up, but he shook his head kindly at her as he paused to shut the door behind him.

"I thought you might welcome a bit of food and something warm to drink," he explained. "I doubt if you had time to sup before you came."

The sight of the sandwiches filled to overflowing with thinly sliced meat and cheeses did look appealing. Not thinking to consider her state of dishabille, April helped him to move over a small table between two chairs.

"You must join me," she extended, truly hoping he would stay for a minute. The storm outside and the dark night had brought a loneliness to her soul that could not be quelled even by the fire crackling merrily in the grate beside the bed.

Ivanov was trying all the while not to stare at the deep shadow that was revealed when the top of April's wrapper gaped a little. Though he knew her to possess a lovely body, this first glimpse of paradise nearly rendered him breathless. Had he been Damien, he knew he should have demanded his wife wear sackcloth to still the hungry gazes of other men.

April curled like a cat in the chair across from him, waiting for his cue to sink her white teeth into a sandwich. Then she rolled her eyes and exclaimed in delight, "It's delicious! You can't imagine what we've been eating all these weeks on the road!"

Ivanov was amused. Her honest enthusiasm thawed something in his heart. He hadn't felt this young in years.

"I hope you enjoy every bite," he said sincerely. "And rest assured, I had a platter twice this size taken to your husband. Cook will be furious if you don't eat every crumb. You see, I roused her even at this late hour to see to my guests' comforts."

"You are a wonderful host," April said.

"But surely you are thirsty after all the exertion of dancing. Would you take some tea?" He was poised to pour.

At her nod he commenced. "This is very fine Oolong, obtained at great length from the Orient. Or if you wish, I can ring for another kind." There was a tiny silver bell on the tray as well.

Hastily April swallowed and reached for her saucer. "No, this is perfect." She drank sparingly of the hot brew and studied him over the rim. The count was a very handsome and self-assured man. It seemed he had been around women before. Perhaps he often entertained married women in their bedchambers? Realizing the awkwardness of the situation, especially should Damien hear of it, she murmured, "I should be asleep by now."

"Indeed." Ivanov agreed readily. "Your dancing must be very tiring. My intention, however, was not to keep you up overlate. I merely wished to see to your comforts. I have a responsibility for my guests."

"Even when they are gypsies? Most people hate us."

A thoughtful smile played around the corners of his mouth. April studied him closely in that moment. Like her husband, Ivanov was clean-shaven, and also kept his hair a shade on the long side for fashion. His dark eyes seemed to burn into her as he murmured, "I appreciate such a candid question. But what reason have I to despise you? Especially one so fair as yourself. You must know that you are lovely."

Loveliness did not always equate with inner

beauty, April knew. But she accepted his compliment. "Thank you. I only hoped to bring a little light to you with my dancing. I am sorry I had to end it so early. But there was something . . ." Unexpectedly, she shivered.

Vasili automatically went to fetch the heavy fur spread off the bed. As he draped it about her shoulders, he noticed for the first time the silken cord looped around her neck and disappearing into the enticing vee between her breasts.

"You wear a special necklace?" he inquired lightly. "A gift from your husband, perhaps?"

She replied quickly, "No, it's just a lucky pebble, a talisman of sorts."

"May I see it?"

April tried to keep her tone equally light. "If you know anything of gypsies, then you know I cannot reveal it or I'll lose all my luck."

Ivanov laughed. "Good or bad luck?"

"Both! Life is not life without some of each. However, if you like, I can find another magic pebble for you."

He suspected by the mischievous sparkle in her green eyes that she was teasing him. "I think not. I have all I could wish for right now. A fine night and a very beautiful woman for company."

His words sounded a faint alarm in April, who, though young, was not easily led astray by pretty phrases. "But surely you must have an even lovelier wife hidden away somewhere," she said.

The words, even in jest, seemed to darken his eyes a bit. With a deep sigh he sat again across from her and said, "No, April, no wife . . . not even any illegitimate children that I could claim for my own. Mine is an isolated life at best. When I was younger I kept the courts gossiping, but of late, my thoughts have stayed at home. I daresay I shall remain a bachelor to the end of my days."

"I find it hard to believe there hasn't been someone special to you," she said softly. He saw then that he had struck a chord of sympathy in her gentle heart.

Thinking of Ekaterina, and her very likeness across from him right now, Ivanov said carefully, "There was once. I would have done anything for her. She knew that."

"And?"

"She took advantage of it. She never loved me, I know now. Still, it is hard for a man set in his ways to accept such a fact."

"How very sad," April said, and Vasili glanced sharply at her, but she was not mocking him. This girl had a heart, where her predecessor had none. How strange indeed that April should be the very image of a wicked tart like Katya, but her soul was as untarnished as the driven snow outside.

"What happened?" she pressed him gently.

"She left with another. Disappeared, left the

country, who knows? She was an ambitious girl and always wanted to whirl in other court circles. I'm certain she and her lover were well-received abroad."

April thought that was certainly rather wretched of the girl to desert the count like that. "Perhaps you are better off without someone like her," she suggested.

"No doubt you are right. However, it doesn't ease the pain much. So many years . . . and yet it seems like yesterday."

Seeing the sadness in his eyes, April hastened to change the subject. "What a lovely room this is," she said brightly. "It even looks as if it was specially prepared. But surely not just for me? There are clothes here . . ."

"For her," Ivanov explained abruptly. "This had been made ready for a bridal suite." He seemed morose at the memory, and April was horrified by her own carelessness.

"Of course I won't touch anything," she assured him quickly.

"But you misunderstand me, April." He smiled sadly at her, his dark eyes intent. "I want you to erase all memory of her for me. By wearing these clothes, these jewels." He gestured to a silken box on the vanity that she had not yet opened. "I wish to be your benefactor. Yours, and Damien's. I intend to be very generous with you both, and I am going to present you at court."

April flushed, not knowing what to say.

Surely it was too generous of the count, and she did not want to take advantage of his depressed state. It seemed he had not let go of his lost love yet. The poor man. She did want to cheer him a bit.

"I will perform at court if you wish, but I ask nothing for the privilege," she said firmly. "I know Damien will feel the same way, after I explain—"

"You must say nothing to him of this!" Suddenly, Ivanov's mood changed from melancholy to nearly outrage.

Seeing she was alarmed, he calmed a bit, but continued heatedly, "No, this must be between us alone. I do not want your husband to feel obliged or insulted by my hospitality. And the story of my fiancée—well, it too must be our little secret."

"But why? He is a sensitive man, he would understand—"

Vasili shook his head vigorously. "You are sweet, my dear, to be so concerned for me, but I would prefer my private life to remain exactly that—private. It was my own foolishness to confess my feelings over that girl."

"But," April put in practically, "how will I explain to him wearing these fine clothes and jewels? He will wonder at our relationship!" And she laughed a little uneasily at the thought.

Ivanov had also thought ahead. "It is my gift to you. My family coffers cannot support straight funds at present, so I have substituted these heirlooms instead in payment for your combined services. He will no doubt mutter a bit at first, but really the jewelry is quite valuable in itself."

What the count said made sense. Still, she wondered if Damien would accept the arrangement. He was doubtlessly as practical as the real Romany and would demand cash up-front.

Cautiously April said, "Let me ease it to him. It would come better from me, I think. He knows I didn't want to come to Samarin House, and a change of attitude would surprise and probably please him."

"You didn't wish to visit me?" Ivanov was surprised and a little hurt. "Why not?"

April pressed her lips together for a moment, debating whether to confess her antagonism toward Pavel or not. Finally she said, "I was a little suspicious of Pavel's motives. Oh, I know it sounds silly now, but—but he frightens me a little."

Ivanov did not laugh. He well knew the dwarf's hatred of women. "Do not worry, April," he said gravely. "Pavel is in my employment and subject to my orders. He will not dare to upset you in any way."

"Thank you," she whispered, obviously relieved.

"But now, my dear, I think I must leave you to your beauty rest. In the morning I will send Zofia with a tray. It will be very cold after the fire goes out and you will wish to stay under the furs. You are welcome to sleep as late as you wish. Your husband and I will discuss our plans in my study in the morning."

She nodded, suppressing a sudden yawn. "Thank you for the food. And for your kindness."

Ivanov merely smiled, pausing only to gather up the tray and look after her one last time. April was nearly asleep, surrounded by the rich sable throw over which her golden hair flowed like a mantle. He hoped she would fare better than Ekaterina in this house. And now that she was here, there was no room for the ghost of the other.

So decided, he quietly departed and went to remove the painting hanging in the library. In the morning, when Zofia went to dust, she was relieved to find she no longer had to endure the haunted eyes of Ekaterina gazing accusingly down on her head.

Damien was uneasy. He had not intended to stay overnight in the count's mansion, nor to be parted from his wife for even a minute. Though he was sure April was safe, something about Ivanov's manner bothered him. Not that the man was dangerous, for he was sure he would have seen that potential immediately, but for an aristocrat he certainly kept strange company.

Pavel, for instance, and now a pair of gypsies. Even his servants, the few that there were for running such a large estate, seemed to be a furtive lot. Tight-lipped Zofia, who had brought him his dinner on a tray, had not bothered to linger or to see further to his comforts.

It was possible the woman was only afraid of gypsies, but Damien did not think so. Pavel was far more intimidating for all his tiny stature than either he or April. No, there was something more, something very insidiously wrong beneath the smooth veneer of Samarin House.

So Damien decided that first night to check on April. He knew better than to alert the count to his intents, and he slipped out of his chamber to silently pursue his own course.

To his dismay, he found the chamber April had initially been given on their arrival was empty. It was closed and cold and obviously uninhabited this eve. Suppressing a sudden surge of foreboding, Damien tried to recall what Ivanov had said earlier. Something about a gold room. Where would that be?

A half-hour later, after cautiously testing a series of doors and peeking into chambers, he found himself upstairs and nearly frothing with worry. So far, he had not found so much as a golden hair to attest to April's presence. But he sensed she was near.

Luckily, the fourth door upstairs was that of the Gold Room. He cursed himself for not having spied it sooner, for it was draped round with a shimmering gold curtain roped back with thick silken tassels.

Not bothering to knock, he cracked the door and looked in. Only the fire highlighted the shadows, revealing a massive four-poster bed and a small sitting room. It was there that Damien tiptoed in and found his wife slumbering upright in a chair.

A relieved smile crossing his lips, he went forward and stopped to admire the view. She looked like a delicate figurine set against the velvet-flocked backdrop of the room. The entire chamber was done in glittering, almost garish, shades of gold. The bed was a hedonistic altar of saffron silk sheets and gold-fringed curtains, the oak headboard carved with cherubs and twined ribbons and hearts.

There was a plush bear rug before the smoldering fire, and a series of romantic Flemish tapestries concealing the cold stone walls. But for all its decadent beauty, Damien could not shake the feeling that it was very much a prison of sorts.

He moved to scoop April up in his arms, soothing her restless murmurs with his own gentle ones. Though wrapped in priceless sable, she felt cold. He carried her to the bed and deposited her gently there, grabbing another lynx throw and one of pale beige wolf to cover her with.

For some reason Damien decided to linger, and paused to brush back golden strands from her face. It was then, startled from her dreams by something else, April opened her green eyes wide with fright.

"Ssh, love, it's only me." Damien didn't know why he whispered, but he felt he was doing something forbidden by visiting his own wife in the night. "I've been worried about you."

April shook her mind free of cobwebs and sat up against the silk pillows. "I'm fine. I fell asleep by the fire, I guess." She shivered as she looked around the room lit with shadows now. "It's terribly cold in here."

"The fire died down. There's wood enough here to fix it. I'll do that before I leave."

"Leave?" Her eyes were suddenly frightened. "Why can't you stay here with me?"

"Ivanov—" Damien began, then corrected himself tersely. "Why not, indeed? My wife needs to be kept warm. And if he doesn't like it, he can go bay at the moon!"

April giggled as Damien impatiently tugged off his clothes and slid beneath the covers beside her. He reached for her, then recoiled at the fluff around her neck. "What is that thing?"

"A very elegant wrapper which you are trying to ruin," she huffed.

"Well, get it off. All this fur revolts me. What a waste of beautiful animals!"

Soberly April peeled off the wrapper and tossed it aside into the darkness. Naked, she snuggled next to the warm body of her hus-

252

band. "The count wants to see you in the morning," she said sleepily against his chest.

"I know. The sullen stick of a maid informed me of that earlier."

"Zofia? I don't think she likes gypsies."

"Who cares? We are Ivanov's guests, not hers. It is not up to a servant to like or dislike the master's choice of company."

April was silent a moment. "You sound like you speak from experience."

Damien caught his breath. He would have to be more careful. April was a very intelligent young woman. "Where I come from there is a great deal of nobility," he replied offhandedly, hoping that would satisfy.

"Where you come from—France. Oh, Damien, will you ever take me there? I want to see the place where you were born."

He smiled in the darkness at her sweetly wistful words. "Maybe someday. But now all I wish to do is get warm. Brr, woman, you have icicles for toes!"

"And you have one very large icicle yourself!" she tossed back tartly, and he grinned as he rolled onto her with his libido fully awakened.

Yet within moments, something in the strange gold room cut through Damien's passion like a finely-honed knife. The air was cooler than in any other room he had prowled through, and the atmosphere was oddly oppressive.

"Why did Ivanov put you in here?" he asked April abruptly, halting their lovemaking.

She was puzzled by his question. "I don't know. I imagine because it was larger than the one downstairs." She almost told Damien of the count's lost love, then remembered her promise not to embarrass their host.

"But it's not. And it's definitely not any warmer. I don't like this room." He suddenly sat up and gazed around at the long shadows streaming down gold-shot walls. "There's something wrong with it."

"Now who sounds like a superstitious gypsy?" April teased him, and touched his arm entreatingly. "Lie down and get some rest."

Slowly Damien complied. But it was a long time before he could close his eyes that night, and longer still before he slept.

Fourteen

The sound of his study door opening and closing prompted Count Ivanov to look up, although he fully expected the man who stood before him.

Damien wore his dress costume from the night before. He wasted no time on pleasantries, saying, "I hope you have good news for me. If not, April and I will be leaving this morning."

"I must admire a man who is direct," Vasili said, motioning his guest to the chair facing him. Reluctantly Damien sat, but he could not help noticing that Ivanov cut a dashing figure in a peacock-blue morning coat and striped gray trousers. The count was no young buck, but neither was he wasting away at his isolated estate.

"There is money to be made elsewhere," Damien said. "So far, I have seen no sign of it here."

Vasili feigned surprise. "But didn't Pavel tell you? My dear Damien, there seems to be a most grievous misunderstanding! I never agreed to pay you for the chance to appear at court. Why, it is as much my risk as yours. My patronage alone should be considered a sufficient honor by itself."

"I knew it was too good to be true," Damien growled, perfectly imitating an outraged Romany as he shot to his feet. "You must present us at court within a week, or I will take April and leave!"

"You dare to dictate to me?" The count's flaming eyes met those of flinty blue. "I do not usually make a habit of entertaining gypsies in my home, and do not intend to start now!"

"Then why did you agree to sponsor us?" Damien demanded, his heart sinking as he already suspected the reply.

Ivanov looked at him directly. "April."

"My wife, *gajo?* What has she to do with anything?"

"Everything, I'm afraid. For, you see, she is the only reason I agreed to this."

"What are you saying?" Damien's insides contracted sharply as he understood the count's implication. His fists unconsciously clenched in mute anger.

"I am saying that if you wish to be presented at court, you must agree to leave April here with me. The genteel life will suit her, and I find that she suits me. It could not be clearer, I think. I plan to handsomely compensate you for her loss, of course—"

Damien laughed incredulously. "As you would buy an old nag, Ivanov? Are you mad? I've seen no sign of her wanting this kind of life."

The count chuckled. "Be reasonable, young man. How can you expect any woman to prefer a life camped out under canvas to a fine estate like this? To a girl of gypsy extraction, who would never amount to anything without a kind benefactor, this chance is a dream come true."

"Or a nightmare."

Count Ivanov smiled thinly. "You cannot push me to the edge, Damien. Stronger men than you have tried." He drew a thin brown cigar from his jacket, lit it, and blew a stream of smoke at the ornate ceiling. Vasili gazed at the spot where Katya's portrait had hung and admired the elegant seascape which had replaced it.

"I do not expect a gypsy to understand," he continued in a patronizing tone, "but in court circles, a man is much admired for the company he keeps. And I believe that I am capable of passing April off as gentry here. Think of it this way, Damien; you will be relieved of the burden and responsibility of caring for her, and she will be secured a better life. Both of you will win. You have nothing to lose."

"Except my wife," Damien pointed out. Unfortunately, the count's proposal made perfect sense. It would ease his own worries about how to leave April behind once his mission was complete, and it would elevate her to a life beyond her wildest dreams.

"You may have a few days to think," Ivanov said, reaching for a velvet pouch which had been thoughtfully left on the table beside him. "Here, take this as a small token of my appreciation. I ask only that you leave for a time, in order for me to prepare April for the parting. I think it would be better coming from me."

So Ivanov could tell April that Damien had abandoned her? Lord Cross knew that was exactly what the Russian count intended, and yet he said nothing. He never despised himself more than when he snatched up the money pouch and left the study, hearing Ivanov's satisfied chuckle trailing him down the hall.

"Damien has left?" Exclaiming in disbelief, April rushed to the window of her room and stared after the sleigh whipping down the lane, churning up clouds of snow. "But where is he going? I don't understand!"

In the doorway of the Gold Room Pavel stood beside his employer and shrugged. "He asked to borrow a sleigh, and seeing how your horses were still here, I didn't see any harm in it."

Stricken, April looked back at Count Ivanov. Her green eyes begged him to take action of some sort.

The count said, "Send someone after him,

Pavel. Don't let him rush off without an explanation like that. I'm sure there's a perfectly logical reason for Damien's behavior, but he shouldn't have left his wife like this."

With regret, Ivanov saw that April loved her husband well and deeply. She was quite frantic over Damien's disappearance, and he saw that it would not be as easy as he'd hoped to tear them apart. But bit by bit, he was sure he could chip away at the trust and devotion until she would at last relinquish herself to his care.

"Don't worry, my dear. Damien will soon return."

April nodded, appreciating the count's understanding. But her voice trembled as she said, "This isn't like him at all. He has no family but me. He must come back!" She willed it to be so, her hands white on the windowpane where her fingernails sunk into the wooden frame.

"Of course he will," Vasili soothed her. "But come away from there, April. You don't want to catch a chill. The winters are very brutal here and you are not used to them, being from the sunny south as you are."

She turned, surprised. "Who told you?"

"Pavel, of course." He nodded toward the little dwarf, who promptly bowed and took his leave. Ivanov explained, "He told me he saw you dancing in the square, and he was charmed by your grace and beauty."

Pavel charmed? It sounded very unlikely, and

April frowned thoughtfully, but as if he knew he had used the wrong word, Vasili hurried to distract her once more.

"I think you need to get out into the fresh air. Though it is cold, it is still quite appropriate to go out and see the sights. Would you like to do that?"

She hesitated only a moment. Maybe if they went out, she would find Damien sooner. She accepted and let the count advise her on proper attire before they met downstairs again in the hall.

Taking his advice, April selected a heavy gown of plum velvet with full bishop sleeves, which when worn over horsehair petticoats, proved to be very warm. A black mink cape, complete with matching muff and circular hat, was procured at the door for her. She let the count help her into the outerwear as she was still too upset by Damien's departure to protest.

A sleigh was already waiting in the lane. Carefully guiding her on his arm, Count Ivanov, who was also bundled in dark fur, assisted April into the conveyance. She settled with a shiver and looked closer about the estate in the full morning light.

Set against the gentle swell of snow-flocked hills overlooking Moscow proper, Samarin House's medieval architecture of high stone towers reached for the ice-blue sky. On either end, slim turrets offered an unprecedented view of the land, and in the center April recognized the tiny single square window peculiar to the Gold Room.

"Do you like the manor?" Ivanov inquired as he wedged in closer beside her, and tossed a fox fur wrap over their legs. "It has been in my family since the reign of Ivan III, over four centuries."

"It is very grand," April said, avoiding a direct reply to his query, for although she found the estate impressive, she did not find it beautiful in the least. It seemed an appropriately frigid tribute to this northern city. For some reason, she also felt a cold tingle on her neck seeing the dark windows above them like so many staring eyes.

"Is most of your family gone?" she asked as the driver closed the door, stepped up in his seat, and made ready to go. They were only waiting on the groom now, who was checking to see that the harness on the set of matched grays was secure.

Ivanov kept his gaze straight ahead. "Yes. I am the sole survivor of many years and wars. I had one cousin, but he too was lost in this latest foolishness in the Crimea."

"I'm sorry." April offered her sympathy once again, and he felt his hard heart soften under her spell. Yes, she was the very image of Ekaterina, and just as beguiling. In a moment more she could have him eating from her hand.

Ivanov flicked open the window, whistled sharply to the driver, and they were off. The jingle of the harness and the sound of the runners hissing across the snow was a new experience for April, but she quickly warmed to its pleasures. The bitter wind from the open window stung her eyes and cheeks, but she felt immediate exhilaration in escaping the house. They moved swiftly, crossing only occasionally the recent tracks left by Damien's sleigh.

As she tried to follow the vanishing marks with her eyes, Ivanov cautioned her, "Don't stare so at the snow. You can go blind when the sun is so bright. There are many things you will need to learn about living in the north."

"We are not staying long," April said. However, she did as he asked and kept her gaze roving. Within a few miles they were sliding down a boulevard, alongside other briskly moving sleighs. She sat up and began to look around with interest.

All of Moscow was designed in a grid of concentric circles, Ivanov explained, and in the center of these rose the Great Kremlin Palace, just completed in 1849. There were also lesser palaces, the Granovitaya and the Terem, either of which she and Damien might be privileged to entertain in, he added.

April strained for a glimpse, but was cut off by other buildings along the Kutuzov Prospect, where they now slowed to a more sedate pace in the sudden glut of traffic. Even the inhospitable winter did not slow down business, she saw. There were street vendors and hawkers aplenty, and laundry strung out between buildings, frozen to a crisp. While Ivanov averted his eyes from the common peasants and beggars strung along their route, April stared curiously, searching for a familiar face or a sign that might betray one as Rom.

But foremost she looked for Damien. She soon recognized the area they had entered near the stables where they had stayed before, and tensed with expectation.

Just as April was about to ask the count to stop, he signaled the driver and they whirled abruptly right, cutting the corner before the stable. She sighed with disappointment and looked over her shoulder, but there was nothing to be seen but a few peasants and children playing iceball in the street.

Ivanov had been talking all the while of the history of Moscow, pointing out various landmarks as they passed, but April did not come around to listening until she could wrench her thoughts from Damien.

"We call it the city on five seas," Vasili said proudly, and ticked them off on his gloved fingers. "The White, the Black, the Baltic, the Caspian and the Sea of Azov are all accessible by means of canals leading to Moscow. You see why the French and English fools do not stand a chance in the war. We can easily ship supplies to our men overnight. In the end it will be their downfall."

"You sound certain of that," April remarked.

The topic of war mildly interested her, but men were always so obsessed by it. She was more intrigued with the sudden appearance of a mighty tower to the west, peeping above the mighty walls of the Kremlin area.

Ivanov followed her gaze and supplied, "Ah, the Tower of Ivan the Great. You have excellent taste. He is one of my direct ancestors."

"What of Ivan the Terrible?"

The count's smile dimmed somewhat. "Unfortunately for me, that one is also an ancestor. He was the grandson of Ivan the Great, and remembered now only for his atrocities, rather than his reforms. But both men were shrewd rulers and we owe much to them."

April was silent a moment, digesting the information. She knew little of history, only what Tzigane had told her in bits and pieces gleaned from bedtime stories, and she felt frustrated by her lack of conversational ability. Suddenly she asked, "Would you teach me about Moscow sometime?"

Vasili looked down at her with obvious tenderness and pleasure, and said, "I would be honored. It will be an enjoyable way to pass the winter hours."

"But we are not staying long," April reminded him again, a little more forcefully this time, wondering why as she spoke she had the distinct feeling that he was not really listening to her.

* * *

Damien was sitting at a crude wooden plank table, nursing a hot hard cider, when he picked up on the idle conversation between two peasant men at the nearest tavern window.

"There goes Ivanov and his latest whore," one of them remarked, and gave a clumsy salute with his slopping mug. The other patrons of the tavern guffawed loudly and stared after the passing couple. Damien rose abruptly but caught only a glimpse of the red sleigh and its occupants, one, a woman buried in black fur, her features indistinguishable.

His gut contracted with fury. It had better not be April, he thought, and took a full swig of the potent brew to calm his nerves. Surely she would not be so foolish as to agree already to appear with Ivanov in public and start wild rumors. Or would she?

As he paid for his drink and left the pub, Damien was bitterly conscious of the cold and his own feelings. He went immediately to one of the street stalls, using some of Ivanov's money to purchase a fur coat before striking out again. He still had a mission, one which was going to waste with every hour that passed.

After an hour of scouting and eavesdropping shamelessly on local conversation, he decided he had enough information to risk another message to Lord Raglan. By now the field marshal would be wondering what had happened to his inside man. Raglan must at least be warned of the impending attacks to the allied supply lines, for the Russians still held the only paved road, and they knew it was crucial to cut off their enemies before spring.

Blowing on his reddened hands as he walked along, Damien concentrated on the future. Everything was coming rapidly to a head. Soon he would be inside the Kremlin itself, given Ivanov's promises, and maybe he could make a difference for his two countries.

He must not think of anything except that now. But there was still something that made Damien tense when he remembered the words he had overheard in the tavern. "Ivanov and his latest whore . . ."

The last thing he needed now was a scandal about a gypsy dancer angling for the wealthy count. It would draw dangerous attention to April, and by association, to Damien as well. But if Moscow was anything like London, to be seen with a man in public was to be as good as sleeping with him.

He hoped April had not been the woman in the sleigh beside Ivanov. For if worse came to worse, and Damien was forced to choose between his mission and his wife, he already knew the choice he must make.

Count Ivanov came out of the stables shaking his head. "He is not here," he told the young woman waiting in the sleigh. "He has been by and gone, the man said. From my description they did admit seeing him walk past."

"But where?" April could not keep the despair from her voice. "Where would he go, and without word to me?"

The count shrugged, climbing back up beside her. "You must understand, he is a man, and Romany as well. He likely wanders where he will. He will return to Samarin House eventually."

His words were no longer comforting. It had been battle enough to persuade the count to stop at the stable and inquire after Damien. For some reason, he had been loathe to do so. But with April's piteous pleas, he finally succumbed. Now it appeared to be a waste of time, though she was too weary to cry. They had driven for over an hour, and she was nearly frozen through. Her feet were numb, and even buried in the mink muff, her hands were red and raw with cold.

Suspecting as much, Ivanov said, "We shall return to the house. A fire and a hot drink will soon revive you. It was careless of me to let you get chilled; as a dancer, your muscles will suffer for it." He called to the driver, and they raced out into the traffic as soon as a spot was clear.

April had only one desire; to be with Damien again. Her heart ached imagining where he might be. And if he did not appear soon, the count might decide not to present them to the court. He had tentatively set a date for three weeks hence, but without her music, April could not perform. She had no wish to appear without Damien anyway. It was the magic between them that brought the act alive, and nothing else.

Perhaps Damien was just another *gajo* after all. A cheat, a liar, a turner of pretty phrases. No! She would not accept that. Not as long as she had breath in her body. Her very soul cried out for him now, but her green eyes were filled with fading hope.

Ivanov drew the fox wrap more snugly about them both. "Our body heat will soon warm us again. That is another thing you will learn about Moscow. You must keep close quarter with friends."

He was trying to amuse her, April knew, but she could not force even a meager smile. All she wanted was Damien, and he had left her!

The journey back to the estate was long and cold. It had begun to snow again, tiny flakes that hinted at another lengthy storm. April opened her window with childlike wonder to taste them on her tongue like melting sugar, and felt them sting her eyes as they drove into the wind. She had never seen so much snow in her life, certainly never lived in it. For a moment it was delightful, but then she remembered that she had been abandoned to the care of a stranger. No matter how kind Count Ivanov was, he could not replace her husband.

"Ah, here we are." Soon the count was handing her down to the groom, who steadied her fur-wrapped figure. April was then passed back to the count like a side of beef, and she almost giggled. She could not have moved if her very life depended on it. Her feet prickled and burned with every step.

Shuffling her up to the door, Ivanov shouted for the maid. It was some minutes before Zofia appeared, not hiding her scowl of displeasure.

"Take the lady to her room, and see that she is brought a hot bath," Ivanov instructed.

"I cannot carry up the hot water by myself," the maid put in stubbornly.

"Then get the groom to do it after he has seen to the team." For some reason, the count did not pursue her insubordination, but turned to April and said gently, "Go with Zofia now. She'll get you warm again."

"I'm like a walking icicle," the young woman shivered, but forced herself to follow the servant upstairs. In the Gold Room, April went to toast her cold hands over the fire in the grate, not stopping to take off her wrap.

Zofia made a disapproving noise and hurried over, scolding, "You will scorch the fine fur so close to the flames!"

"Then you must take it off for me," April said coolly, disliking the tone the woman used with her.

Zofia pressed her lips together but said nothing. She waited rebelliously until the girl shrugged out of the fur on her own. Only then did she deign to accept the ensemble, smoothing it carefully over her arms as if searching for damage.

"You do not like me, do you, Zofia?" April inquired. "Is it because I am Romany?"

The maid's mouth trembled but she would not speak. Her eyes, however, spoke volumes. It was not a matter of dislike. It was a matter of hatred.

Startled by the realization, April did not understand. It was as if the woman actually loathed her, though Zofia did not know anything about her. Tentatively, she reminded the maid of that.

"I know that you look exactly like *her*, and I know what she was," Zofia spat at last, turning to leave.

"Her? Who?"

But April's voice only echoed off the stone walls back at her, as Zofia left and the door to the Gold Room slammed resoundingly in her face.

Fifteen

Damien knew by the time he reached Moscow that someone was following him. His movements had been casual, but several times he had caught a distant glimpse of a dark sleigh lingering just out of clear view a mile behind him.

And had anyone wished to pass him, they could have done so easily many times over. Thoughtfully, he chose to relinquish Ivanov's sleigh in the city limits and struck out on foot. He could move more easily without the conveyance which attracted undue attention.

Though the streets were busy and crowded, and people surged in every direction, Damien's senses were keen enough to soon detect the sensation of being watched. He had learned a long time ago to trust his instincts, and moved covertly around the side of a building to wait for his stalker to pass by.

Minutes passed but other than gaining strange looks from passersby, Damien did not see anyone who could possibly be tailing him. Puzzled that his instincts could be wrong, he cautiously stepped out into the street again and went on his way.

He started to cross an intersection in front of an elegant golden sleigh when sudden shots rang out. Hitting the pavement and rolling on his shoulder, Damien narrowly missed being grazed by one of the bullets being pumped out by a hidden assassin.

The stopped carriage was not so lucky. Inside, Damien heard a woman scream as the bullets chewed up the finely scrolled wood paneling inside the coach. Tracing the source of the gunshots with sharp eyes, Damien finally spotted a fur-bundled figure shooting from around the nearest corner.

With an oath, he leapt behind the sleigh for protection, shouting through the open window to the unknown woman, "Get down on the floor and stay there!"

He didn't know if she could hear him, or even if she was alive, for the screams had stopped. But then he heard the thump of a body inside the coach and trusted that was enough.

The street was empty now as other people had fled into shops or around corners. Only Damien was foolish enough to run after the gunman, but then he had a desperate need to know who it was.

Had he been found out after all? He had just

released his second pigeon to Lord Raglan, and although he had taken care to be discreet, there was always the possibility that he had been seen. Unknown enemies were the worst kind.

Damien moved toward the hidden gunman, carefully edging around corners, tasting the sour taste of fear in his mouth. He had no weapon, and right now the allies depended heavily on his reports.

Prepared for confrontation, Damien pressed flat against the cold stone of a building as he inched slowly toward his attacker. Finally he could hear the man's harsh breathing just around the next corner. His only hope was to grab and disarm him in one smooth move. Taking a deep breath of his own, Damien plunged into action.

A startled grunt was all the man managed to get out before Damien knocked the gun from his hands and then, in turn, dashed the fellow against a glass window that shattered explosively. The gunman was buried in bulky fur, even his face was covered so that only his eyes showed. He slid down in a sorry heap at the earl's feet, moaning painfully.

As Damien bent to uncover the unconscious man's face, a sudden outcry caught his attention. The sleigh that had been shot at was now open and a woman wearing rich red fox that matched her Titian hair was striding toward him now.

"Get him!" she ordered her footmen, and

they sheepishly rushed to grab the fellow passed out at Damien's feet. As the woman came closer, Damien felt memories clutch him like a vise.

He instantly recognized her lovely, brittle face, even though the years had not been kind to it. Princess Tatiana Menshikov had first initiated him into the ways of love when Damien had been only seventeen, on a tour of Moscow with his father. She was still regal, still arrogant, and obviously still quite vain. She eyed him boldly, but there was no trace of recognition in her eyes . . . yet.

"I must thank you," Tatiana said softly as the footmen began to haul the gunman off between them. Damien could hardly quell his frustration, wanting to tear from her probing gaze just as he needed to tear the face cover from his attacker.

"Don't worry about him," the princess said as she followed Damien's gaze, "I can assure you the filthy Cossack will never see the light of day again. This is twice this month that there has been an attempt on my life." She shrugged philosophically. "Such is the price one pays for being rich and beautiful, I suppose."

One thing had certainly not changed: Tatiana's supreme conceit. Damien found it hard to believe that he had ever found her attractive. He was trying to figure out how he could gracefully exit her attentions, but she was examining him closely and apparently liked what she saw. He could only hope she was jaded from enough lovers that she wouldn't recognize him after so many years. Still, he held his breath.

Then Tatiana said, "You don't look Russian. Are you visiting Moscow?"

He nodded, trying to disguise his voice when he replied. "I am Romany. A roving musician looking for work."

Damien could have cursed himself when Tatiana said thoughtfully, "You saved my life, you know. I owe you something . . ." she licked her lips in anticipation. He was a handsome, if crudely garbed fellow, and she was always one to spot potential a mile away. "What would you say to a hundred rubles?"

He raised a brow, considering. Yes, Princess Menshikov had the power to give him that and much more, and Damien would be mad to let this incredible chance slip through his fingers. He knew that, yet the cool touch of her fingers on his hand made him uncomfortable, and he had to think of April instead when he gave his reply.

"I say you can keep the money if you can give me an audience at the Kremlin," he stated boldly.

Tatiana's arched brows raised, and her red lips pursed on the verge of rebuke. He was terribly insolent, this one, not knowing what an honor she paid him by merely deigning to speak to him at all. But he had the most beautiful blue eyes, quite seductive under those long dark lashes, and she had always had a weakness for blue eyes.

"I'll see what I can do," she began hesitantly, but Damien started to turn away, suspecting that would force the decision. Suddenly she was grabbing his coat sleeve.

"All right! But there are conditions attached . . . I must have a private audition first, just you and me." Tatiana smiled like a hungry cat and pressed against his side as she led Damien to her waiting sleigh.

The earl had no time to demur, nor to curse when he saw the gunman break free from the lax footmen and sprint off running down the street. Now he would never know who wanted him dead. That, coupled with Tatiana clutching him in her claws, made Damien wonder if the odds against his success now were getting too high.

"So, it's true then."

A familiar voice spoke from behind April as she stood gazing at her reflection in the golden pier glass. She whirled and gasped, dropping the heavy white satin skirts looped with tiny golden bows. She had been holding them up in order to admire the matching embroidered silk stockings and white satin shoes.

"Damien!" Her cry was one of joy and relief, but something in his look stopped her. He stood at the entrance of the Gold Room, gazing at her with the coldest blue eyes she had ever seen. Then, faltering, she asked, "When did you get back? And what is true?"

He smiled a humorless smile. "I came back here only to get my violin. The truth I speak of is obvious. You are Ivanov's whore!"

Hot color rushed up April's cheeks, and she pushed back her mass of golden hair with an angry gesture. "Why would you say such a terrible thing to me?"

"Because it is true, even if you don't know it yourself yet. Why else did you show yourself on his elbow all about town yesterday?"

So he had seen them! And April's admittance caused Damien's mood to plummet even further. "There was nothing wrong with sightseeing," she said. "I was not on his elbow. We were in the sleigh the entire time. Nobody noticed us or even spoke to us."

"No doubt they were too busy gaping at Ivanov's latest doxy to find their tongues," Damien sneered, hating himself as the poisonous words poured out and April grew paler and paler. "Look at yourself! Draped in all this finery!" As he spoke his hand swept up a flowered brocaded silk dress draped across a chair, and he tossed it angrily at her. It fluttered to the floor like a broken butterfly, and her green eyes filled with tears.

"Is this what you want, April? Because you must know I can never give it to you. If you want to live a rich and idle life, then you have married the wrong man. Ivanov can offer it to you. I can't and I won't."

He was cruel, testing her love like that. But not knowing the reason, feeling only the pain and bewilderment, April came to him and sank in a puddle of white skirts at his feet.

"Please," she whispered brokenly, "don't be angry, Damien! I love you. I just wanted to try on the pretty clothes and play a little at being a lady. I—I used to pretend sometimes that I had lovely dresses and could parade around town."

"You used to pretend you were *boyar*," he put in harshly, knowing what it had cost her to admit such a thing.

"Yes," she murmured, ashamed. "But it's only a dream, Damien. I don't really want this. I want to be with you."

"Do you? Can you imagine life with me, year after year, traveling in a broken old wagon and eating hand to mouth?" There was a bitter twist to the earl's mouth now, for he despised this final lie most. "You are not being fair to yourself, April. You are clever and beautiful and far better suited to this life than you think. Here, there will always be a roof over your head and food in your mouth. You are still young . . ."

She raised a tear-streaked face to his, her eyes ravaged with pain. "Are you trying to tell me you don't want me anymore?"

God, no, he wanted her more than anything at this moment; wanted to sweep her into a fierce embrace and shelter her from everything but his love. And with a start, Lord Cross realized that he did love the gypsy waif, this innocent siren with the sea-green eyes who could make a man act rashly. He had wed her in a spurt of indecision, taken her to wife and never regretted it, except for those bitter moments when he was forced to remember the ugliness of war and what he must do to end it.

Now as he laid a trembling hand upon that bright gold hair, feeling its silken texture for perhaps the last time, the Earl of Devonshire felt a new grief and frustration rending his very soul. "Yes," he rasped at last, pausing to clear his tight throat. "I cannot want a woman who is destined for another path. Who aims for the world of *gaje,* which I gladly left years ago. You know of Romany ways as I do. We can be parted as friends still . . ."

April let out a sob, and clutched his hand. "No! Damien, please don't go! I love you . . . whatever I did, I'm sorry . . . please, take me away from here! Tonight. Now. We will go fast and far away. Don't think these things of me!"

But tenderly, for he could do no less, Damien pried her steadfast grip from his fingers, trying not to feel the hot tears scalding his flesh where they fell from her eyes like glittering diamonds. The Countess of Devonshire, if only she knew it . . . God, he ached so bitterly for her and what he must do.

"I'm sorry, April," he said at last, and in the awful stillness of the room even her beautiful features seemed to fade to misty gold shadows under the soft glare of the gas lamps. The Gold Room. He would remember it always with rage and regret. Somehow he sensed it had served its evil purpose in the end. For this was where he had surrendered April to another world, to a lush silken prison where she would be forever lost to him.

He could say or do no more. When he left, he did so as quickly as he had entered her life, and April never moved, because she was too dazed to yet believe that Damien would ever leave her. He was the only thing that mattered. For him, she had left her people. For him, she had come here. And for him, as she had just discovered, she would suffer greatly.

"You cannot lick your wounds forever," Count Ivanov said, staring at April intently as she paced before the crackling fire in his study. She was a vision in violet silk, the patina of the material reflecting the firelight when she turned. Her golden cascade of hair swirled down to her waist, over a tiny bolero jacket of deeper purple velvet with silver trim. As always, she stirred his memories with her haunting resemblance to his Katya.

"There is a grand ball being held at the Kremlin this eve, and I would be very honored if you would be my partner."

"I will not give Damien the satisfaction of driving me into another life!" April replied. "I will always be Romany. I do not belong in this world! On the surface you may see a *gaje* woman, but I am still of my people inside!"

"Of course," Vasili soothed her hastily. "I did not mean to offend you, my dear. I thought perhaps a little distraction might be welcome while you waited for news . . ."

Ivanov paused thoughtfully. His henchman, Dmitri, had returned cringing like a whipped dog after the first attempt to murder Damien had failed. But of course, Ivanov would send a more competent fellow next time. He had no doubt that Alexei, a professional assassin, would be equal to the task. When Damien was dead, and April had no possible avenue of escape, then . . . then the count could make his own move.

Taking a deep breath, Ivanov said evenly, "Who knows, Damien may yet come back. Why deny yourself pleasure when he is hardly doing so himself?"

At the implication of Ivanov's words, April stopped pacing and her figure tensed. The image of her husband in the arms of another woman made her burn with secret fury. Had he been so quick to turn to someone else?

"What do you mean?" she whispered, her voice shaking slightly.

Vasili feigned regret. "I'm sorry, it was indelicate of me to mention it like that . . . but one of my men, Dmitri, mentioned that he had seen Damien in the city with another woman . . ." Letting the brutal words sink in thoroughly, he then added hastily, "Of course, it could be perfectly harmless."

April knew the count did not really believe that, and neither did she. Had she ever really known Damien? He had been so vague about his past, and mentioned nothing of previous lovers, though there must have been some. He was too handsome and appealing to have escaped women's attentions that long.

April furiously rubbed her arms when she realized she was shaking. Not from cold, though she hoped the count would think so. She was overcome with raw, bitter hatred, a sensation so powerful and dizzying that she could almost taste the hard metallic edge of it in her mouth.

"Yes!" April suddenly said, startling Ivanov as well as herself. "Yes . . . I will go tonight." And if nothing else, she would have the satisfaction of proving that a gypsy could pass for a *gajo* as easily as the other way around!

Count Ivanov smiled with triumph. He could hardly believe it himself, but watching April descend the stairs with one hand running along the smooth mahogany banister, he could have sworn it was Ekaterina returned from the grave after all these years.

He made a mental note to congratulate the dressmaker he had hired in town. She had managed to transform a gypsy wench into a perfect courtesan. April's gown, a French import which proved that even in wartime Paris was still the center of *haute couture*, was guaranteed to turn heads at the Kremlin. They would all wonder who the stunning woman was, all but those who remembered Ekaterina, and those few would be shocked.

By design, Vasili had taken Katya's portrait to the dressmaker at Valenkov Square, and insisted that she use the painting as a model. Though April did not know it, she was wearing almost an exact replica of Ekaterina's most famous gown, the one which she had chosen for her portrait.

Of course, the style was updated, so it was not precise. The original gown had vanished with his fiancée, or Vasili would have insisted that April wear it. This near duplicate, however, was close enough to his satisfaction.

Instead of the high waistline of the earlier period, the gown had been modified to emphasize the tiny perfection of April's waist. The neckline was French, and very low off the shoulders, showing a tantalizing glimpse of her breasts. The full skirts were scalloped with velvet roses, a large one nestled at her bosom. But for those slight differences, the gown of midnight-blue velvet was as striking as it had been all those years ago.

At the count's specifications, April's hair was smoothly drawn up on her head, where a shower of golden ringlets cascaded to touch her bare shoulders. Days out of the sun had faded her skin to an acceptable pale golden cream, even more enticing than the powder-white flesh the other ladies possessed. Around April's throat, a glittering web of dark blue sapphires in gold filigree gleamed. It was like looking into the past again.

April smiled, searching for Ivanov's approval. He had been kind to her, and she wanted to please him.

"Lovely," he said huskily, forced to swallow his emotions and mask his intense desire. "Didn't I promise you that blue would be the perfect foil for your hair and eyes? I was fortunate I could find the material in time for tonight."

"But how did you get the dress made so swiftly?" April asked, reaching the end of the stairs and looking up at him curiously. "It must have taken twelve seamstresses all week to finish this for me!"

He shrugged modestly. "My connections occasionally assure me small favors in town. I merely convinced them to set aside some other less pressing projects for this one. I kept hint-ing it would please the czar, and that was enough for them."

April waited while Vasili produced a wrap of beautiful silver fox and eased it about her bare shoulders. Snuggling into the soft fur, she only half-listened to Ivanov's narrative as he reached for his own coat by the door. At every opportunity he gave her a history lesson. This time it was about the czar himself, but April was too distracted by the evening to come to concentrate upon his words. Instead, she found herself looking at Count Ivanov as a lady would assess her escort for the evening.

As always, the count was impeccably dressed, this time in a dark blue swallow-tailed evening coat and trousers. His smoke-tinged hair was neatly parted on the side, accenting the masculine cut of his features. When he leaned close to assist April to the sleigh, she could catch the faint whiff of ambergris he wore. It was a pleasant, musky smell that for some reason reminded her of the earthy smell of the woods, and a sharp ache seared her as she thought of her mountains so far away.

"You must not be melancholy tonight," Vasili said as they once again settled for the ride into town. It was already dark as midnight though quite early, and bitterly cold. He urged April to lean into him for warmth. "I intend for you to have a wonderful time. That will not be possible if you keep thinking of things that distress you."

She looked at him and tried to smile, but there was a sadness in her lovely green eyes that was impossible to ignore. The count knew the cause of it, but he did not wish to deal with the ghost of Damien any longer. Instead, he suggested gently, "You are very young yet and have your whole life ahead of you. I am offering you a chance to start anew! Do not throw it away, April. I sense you have the inner strength and resolve to be whatever you wish to be. Few souls can claim that right. You are destined for greatness, if you only reach for it."

Now she laughed, but with faint disdain. "I will always be Romany. That ends all chances for me before they can begin."

"It is a fact you can easily hide, with your hair and eyes. Your skin is so fair . . ." Vasili paused, almost touching her hand resting between them and then decided against it as he fought his own inner ache. "What I suggest, my dear, is that you let me do the talking tonight. Court circles move very swiftly, and I do not wish you to feel crushed in the madness. Just smile and nod and look as lovely as you do right now, and no one will be the wiser."

April had to admit that it sounded amusing. She had played at being a lady, and as Damien had so caustically suggested, why not try the real thing? It sounded like the very adventure to take her mind off a husband who did not want her anymore. Perhaps all men were not so immune to her. It certainly might prove interesting to find out . . .

Sixteen

The snow had stopped by the time Ivanov's sleigh moved through the massive gates and over the moat surrounding the inner circle of Moscow. Because there was no natural water barrier around the numerous palaces and cathedrals, the moat had been fashioned centuries ago with a slight diversion of the Moskva River.

Tonight the magical aura of the Kremlin was enhanced by darkness, and thousands of lights highlighted the gleaming onion-shaped domes and the eagles topping them. As the sleigh slowed, allowing for other traffic snaking toward the Great Palace, April peered through the coach window and stared breathlessly at the wonderland that awaited her.

Tapered gate towers flanked the entrance to the first building, the Cathedral of the Assumption. The white masonry was elegantly enhanced by curved arches that divided the stonework. A crown of five golden domes soared above them into the darkness.

Two other smaller, but no less beautiful, cathedrals were followed by the Granovitaya Palace, also of white sandstone, but faceted so expertly that it flashed and glittered like a precious jewel. Reminded of her own diamond, April touched her neck, but then she remembered that she had taken it off and hidden it in a secret space she had found in the vanity in the Gold Room.

Even Ivanov's fiancée had apparently not known about the little false bottom on one drawer, but April had decided her gem would be safer there then around her neck tonight in such a perilously low-cut evening gown.

Ivanov pointed out the Cathedral of the Archangel next, built in the early 15th century. It was the traditional last resting place of the czars. The building resembled no tomb April had ever seen, with six huge pillars of frosty stone, five gold domes, and scalloped friezes that stood as art alone.

Everything was white and gold on this magical night. She felt like a princess in the gold-trimmed sleigh drawn by four milk-white horses. The count had insisted that his driver wear a gold-braided uniform as well. The hateful little Pavel had been nowhere to be seen before they left, so perhaps it would be a perfect evening, after all.

The last cathedral, St. Basil's, was the most

magnificent of all just beside the Kremlin palace. April's gaze went immediately up to the garden of domes crowning the structure, each one different, in color as well as style. Floodlights rendered the onion-shaped domes into nine jewels this night. She drew her breath and Ivanov seemed both pleased and amused by her awe.

Finally the Palace itself, rose-colored brick with towers and turrets to spare, proved their destination. After all the unique cathedrals and their painstaking architecture, this building seemed almost plain. But the count cautioned her to withhold judgment until she had seen the interior.

Instructions were given to the driver as they waited in line behind other brilliantly decorated sleighs. So many of the vehicles, April noted, were red. So, too, were many of the ladies' gowns revealed as they dashed laughing inside on their escort's arms. Even though red would always mean the color of death to her, April was able to appreciate the stark contrast of the shade against the sparkling snow this night.

Soon it was their turn to disembark. Vasili carefully lifted her down, folding her hand over his arm and assisting her up the icy stairs. It seemed forever before they reached the entrance, and the doors were wide open to admit the glittering throng.

She chose not to relinquish her wrap to the doorman but asked to keep it until she could get warm again. Then her breath was struck from her. Never, in all her wildest flights of fancy, had April ever imagined such lush opulence.

An ornate portal, gilded blue and gold, opened into the main chamber lit by massive chandeliers. Soaring columns imbedded with precious jewels and spiraling icons struck toward the round ceiling high above them. Everything was painted with excruciating detail of motifs, flowers and fans and tiny human figures. Even the floor was jasper and agate, polished to a high shine.

Dazzled, April clutched Ivanov's arm and let him lead her into the swirling gaiety. There were at least three hundred people present, though it was not pressing the limits of the room yet. Heads began to turn, whispers to thread among the masses, as the renowned Count Ivanov made his appearance with April at his side.

Within minutes, her resemblance to the former court beauty Ekaterina was noted and exclaimed upon. There was clearly a shock to be had for those who recalled the green-eyed Circassian Cat. Rumors whirled wildly as to this young woman's identity.

Surprised by the intense stares, but not shaken, April kept her head high. She was such a vision that even those who did not know of Ekaterina or the count's notoriety gazed with fascination upon the proud, obviously titled young lady.

Everyone but Princess Tatiana Menshikov, who was interrupted in her husky oratory with a handsome young nobleman by someone who rightfully predicted her outrage.

"Katya!" The hiss escaped her lips as her dark eyes widened with shock. Then, realizing there was no way her old rival could have returned from the dead, Tatiana stared hard at Ivanov and his unpleasant surprise. "What is Vasili up to? I certainly must find out."

She brushed past her own fawning admirers to stalk directly up to the count, who had paused to speak with another aristocrat.

April was the first to see the fox-haired woman storming toward them. The lady was small, but commanded great presence, especially in a blood-red silk dress. Her neckline was shockingly low, nearly baring the entire rounded upthrust of her bosom. And there, nestled in the valley of her breasts and surrounded by a soft ruff of red fox, was a ruby as large as an egg.

Wondering what twisted the pretty features of the lady into such a scowl, April glanced up to Ivanov. But it was not he whom the other woman had fixed her furious stare upon.

In a moment, silver fox and sapphires clashed with rubies and red fox in a dazzling display. Tatiana halted and took in her rival's French gown and fresh young beauty with an insolent up-and-down perusal and then turned on Ivanov with a soft snarl.

"How dare you presume to bring your whore here!"

April gasped, hardly daring to believe she had heard such speech from a lady. Who was she? And why didn't Ivanov confront her for the insult? Instead, he emitted a low laugh that seemed to enrage the woman more.

"My dear Tatiana, I must correct the mistake. This is a distant relative of mine who has come to visit. I can assure you her bloodline is as flawless as her face."

"Relative! A likely story." Still, the princess paused as she took in April's regal bearing. The little vixen was matching her stare for stare, and clearly had no sense of manners. Draped in deep blue, with the Ivanov family sapphires dripping off her slender neck, she did indeed resemble royalty.

Tatiana was further incensed seeing her guests were so intrigued by Vasili's lady. The vixen could have been Kayta in the flesh, and the princess recognized the gown that Ivanov had chosen with care, just as she had never forgotten the insults that Katya had dealt her so long ago. The Circassian beauty had always made Tatiana feel like a clumsy peasant. And now she was confronted with her virtual double!

"If you wanted a stir, you have made one," Tatiana granted Ivanov in a nasty tone. She continued to ignore April, who was beginning to bristle. "I suppose I cannot throw you out, seeing as you are one of the *boyar*, Vasili, but see that you keep the chit in hand tonight, hmm? And if you behave yourselves, you can stay for the special entertainment I've commissioned tonight." The princess licked her lips, thinking of the musician. "I guarantee you will be as enthralled as I."

April tried very hard not to say something rude to the woman, and the only thing that stopped her was that Tatiana was of royal descent. She was glad she was not Russian and subject to this angry woman's rule. Tatiana surely made life very miserable for anyone she disliked.

April was relieved when Vasili suggested they move on. He had no intention of abandoning her to the curious stares of the crowd, who were all wondering what his mistress had done to infuriate the princess. A few of them rightfully suspected that it was not April herself, but her beauty and her uncanny resemblance to Tatiana's old rival that had caused such an upset.

Nevertheless, Tatiana's scene only attracted more, not less, notoriety for the latest arrival. The men were eying April with open speculation. The women, understandably less pleased to be overshadowed, were anxiously trying to win back their escorts' attentions.

After he coaxed April to surrender her fur wrap, Count Ivanov swiftly led her away from the main floor where the crowds milled restlessly, to a more secluded passageway beneath a series of marble pillars.

Leaf-embossed arms and ornate shell designs covered the beautifully carved stone that yawned to the ceiling several stories overhead. Tiers of icons, lit by the chandeliers, reflected dazzling jewel-like colors overhead. April craned her neck to take in all the wonder of it, but Vasili urged her along to a decorative stairway of mosaicked lapis lazuli stone leading up in a graceful spiral.

April's velvet skirts flowed after her as they ascended, and she was prompted to ask, "Where are we going now?" It seemed they were the only ones headed in such a vertical direction.

"You will see," he said mysteriously, and smiled at her curiosity. He was privy to a great deal of knowledge about the Kremlin, and intended to presume upon it fully in order to win the lady's admiration.

Soon they were standing in a long, seemingly endless hall, whose filigreed walls of reds and blues were heavily overlaid with golden friezes and depictions of various saints. It was the most beautiful place April had ever seen, and she was overwhelmed by the opulence of it. Life as a Romany under the open sky had never prepared her for such magnificence. She felt she could drink it in forever, parched for knowledge as she was, and for once she had no trouble concentrating upon Ivanov's words.

"Now you see why the first *boyar* and bishops that stood here swore that they had a glimpse of heaven," Vasili said softly. To speak loudly would have shattered the moment, as he seemed to understand.

"It is so beautiful! It must have taken years," she whispered, hearing her voice echoing endlessly down the foiled corridors.

"The palace is new compared to the rest of the buildings in the Kremlin. The others took centuries to design and perfect. But all serve to remind man of his insignificance, I think."

"I can hardly believe men designed this," April said, daring to reach out and touch a depiction of a praying saint on the nearest wall. "It seems the work of angels."

"You know of angels? I assumed Romany were godless," Ivanov remarked with surprise.

"We know of many different religions. My mother, Tzigane, had been Christian once. She often told me stories from the Bible."

Vasili was pleased. "It will be important for you to attend church while you are in Moscow. Others will be watching for that. I am relieved that you are not totally ignorant in that area."

April's eyes flashed as she looked at him. "Have I proven myself ignorant in so much already?"

He was taken aback but secretly thrilled by her show of spirit. This was working out better than ever he had dared to hope. Katya was not gone, she was here right now staring at him with those fiery green eyes he knew he could not resist. Ah, to crush her in his arms again, to bite her flawless neck, to make her his . . .

"Have I?" April repeated sharply, wondering why he was gazing at her so oddly. Sometimes she felt as if he was seeing someone else, or not paying attention at all.

"Of course not," Vasili soothed her, taking her hands in his own and patting them in a fatherly fashion. "I just want you to be happy, my dear. And if others ostracize you, you will find acceptance very difficult. You agreed to let me guide you into Moscow society. I am only advising you on the proper course to take."

"And what should I know about tonight? Will someone try to trick me into revealing who I really am?"

"Perhaps," he admitted. "We must be careful at any rate. The Princess Menshikov unfortunately took a dislike to you. She will look for any opportunity to effect your downfall."

April was beginning to enjoy the challenge of it. She would dearly love to frustrate the vicious Tatiana. If she was found out, little harm would be done anyway. But if everyone truly believed she was one of the elite . . . who knew what chaos she could wreak? It sounded like justice to her. For too many years *gaje* had maligned and injured her people. It was time they received what they so often gave.

With a brilliant smile, she said, "Don't worry. The princess will not succeed. Tonight, at least, I am here to stay. Will you please take me back downstairs?"

As they turned to leave, April's glance took in a portrait hanging nearby. She paused, struck by the man in the picture. He was a tall, dashing aristocrat wearing a red-sashed uniform. His hair was blonde and his eyes, kind and merry. When she sucked in her breath, Ivanov glanced over and immediately tensed, recognizing the portrait.

"Who is that?" April whispered, inexplicably drawn to the painting with a pull too powerful to ignore.

Ivanov forced a shrug. "I believe that is Prince Andrei Petrovna. He died a long time ago. Now come along, April. Your admirers are waiting . . . and so am I."

Reluctantly tearing her eyes from the man's in the picture, the young woman let the count escort her back to the festivities.

The red velvet seats were plush and comfortable. April sat beside Ivanov and arranged her skirts, looking curiously about the hall. Most of the crowd had emerged in this large auditorium of sorts, above an onyx and marble parquet floor. On the second tier, they were just above the center stage.

All around them chairs creaked and groaned with *boyar* nobility. Ladies tittered behind their hands, whispering and exchanging final juicy bits of gossip before the performance. The men craned their necks for another glimpse of the new beauty at Ivanov's side. April felt the weight of their stares but did not return any of them. She knew Ivanov sensed them too, and a half-smile played about his lips.

"This entertainment will be over soon," he assured her softly. "Afterward there will be dancing."

"It will be a very long evening then," she murmured back, seized by the knowledge of something about to happen when the lights overhead gradually dimmed. Then a spotlight appeared on the stage below them. April watched impassively.

Suddenly she clutched Ivanov's sleeve like a vise. "No," she whispered fiercely.

But he grabbed her hand and restrained her where she sat. Her aching heart was forced to recognize Damien striding across the stage, handsome and proud as a panther. She could hear the soft *aahs* of the ladies around her as they drank in his savage good looks. Yes, that was what *gaje* hussies liked, a real man! April fought the bitter stabs of jealousy and longing as Damien struck a pose and began to play.

She was scarcely conscious of the music this time. It was haunting and lovely but it flowed over and around her without penetrating her to the core. April refused to let it do so. What they had was over, gone. He had left her without a backward glance. She tried to summon unconcern.

Instead, tears threatened. Ivanov looked at her sternly. She could not help it. She began to tremble, the tears spilling silently over her cheeks. It took every ounce of strength she possessed to stay there and listen to Damien perform.

But the music floating over the crowd had drawn their attention away from the new beauty. Few had heard such pure strains in their lifetime. He had a rare talent, in that he played with passion, not mechanically. It touched their hardened hearts and brought tears to eyes besides April's.

In the prime seat over center stage, Tatiana preened like a red bird. Czar Nicholas himself shot her a glance of appreciation and an approving nod. Though Moscow boasted of being the cultural center of Russia, it had been sorely deprived of quality performances during the war.

Still, everyone could sense a slight something missing. The music Damien played was for dancing. In the mind's eye, the vague shadow of a beautiful girl whirled to the lively refrain. It seemed only right somehow.

And Damien himself was conscious of the empty spot beside him, where no laughing green eyes challenged him to play faster and faster. His grip tightened vise-like upon the bow. Where was she now? In Ivanov's bed, gracing the saffron sheets of that vile Gold Room?

Glancing up, he almost faltered. Surely he was imagining things. The harsh glare of the spotlight was nearly impossible to look past, and for the most part he kept his eyes fixed on his violin, but for a moment he thought he had seen a familiar fair face reflected in the crowd above him.

No, April would not be here. She would have refused to come. As she should have. To be near Damien now was to court danger, as he was very close to his goal. Just yesterday he had sent another missive to Lord Raglan regarding the latest movements of the Russian army. He had only two birds left now, and he must make them count. He also knew what a veritable fountain of information Tatiana would be, for she was General Alexsandr Menshikov's niece. It would be foolhardy of him to pass up the opportunity.

Of course, it was not without dire risk. Tatiana might recognize him eventually. If she did, it would mean terrible consequences for both him and his countries. But he knew he must take the chance. If necessary, Damien would find a way to silence her. The thought repulsed him, but so did the lusty stares the princess had been giving him all week. He would have no difficulty getting her alone tonight, he suspected. And as he also recalled, she drank a great deal. He remembered the fiery redhead of twenty who had talked his ear off after a liberal dose of vodka.

Finally he finished, having played nonstop for nearly an hour. The applause was stupendous. Damien bowed and waved, but was anxious to escape the spotlight. The moment he had left, the buzz of conversation filled the hall.

Who was the musician? Where had he learned *A Night in Madrid?* Had he studied under Mikhail Glinka, perhaps? Speculation flew as the *boyar* stood for an encore, but Damien did not reappear.

"Take me out of here!" April begged Ivanov under the cover of clapping and cheering.

"Nonsense," he said as he leaned close to her, "it will only confirm the rumors that you are my mistress then."

"What? You cannot mean they believe the princess?"

Vasili laughed at her. "Are you really as innocent as you seem? They have been thinking that ever since you first appeared by my side in the sleigh! That is what I meant by opportunity, April. Either you are my mistress or you are a relative, but at any rate you are fit to be among the *boyar.*"

"You tricked me," she said, finally yanking her hand free of his possessive grip. "but your little game is over. I want to leave!"

"Will you cause another scene so easily? I assure you they are all still quite fascinated by your little duel with Tatiana earlier. You have opportunity to have them at your mercy now, if only you listen to me."

"As you have me at yours? I am not a weapon to be used against those you hate!"

With surprising swiftness Vasili recaptured her hand, and crushing it painfully under his arm, he murmured, "Are you not? We shall see." And he rose then, dragging her with him down the aisle, making it look as if she clung to his arm of her own free will.

There was no opportunity to protest. Hundreds of eyes watched them leaving. April was helpless and furious at the same time. How could she have been so foolish as to trust Ivanov? It was clear he was only using her as a tool to strike back at the *boyar* who had laughed at him so long ago.

Instead of leading her to the exit, as she had hoped, the count took her to the ballroom for dancing. Other musicians were already set up, playing a lively ensemble. Flocks of people were arriving by means of various entrances after Damien's performance.

"Now we will see what you are made of," Ivanov told April in a low voice. "I know you can dance, but can you waltz?"

"I can do anything I wish," she shot back angrily. April carefully observed the couples whirling gracefully in triple-time to the lilting music. "It does not look so difficult."

"We shall put you to the test shortly. But for now, I think I must revive your color with

some punch. I trust you will not wander off."
His voice was genial, but his eyes were hard.

April nodded curtly and he left her standing alone for a few minutes. The Strauss music, though lovely, was beginning to make her temples ache. She sought for a place away from the curious eyes of the aristocrats around her. Some of the men had begun sidling closer to her the moment the count had gone.

Slipping into an adjoining small chamber that hinted a brief respite, April paused to catch her breath away from the crush and the stares. She closed her own eyes and tried not to think of the man she still longed for and loved.

"You are creating quite a stir, little girl."

Damien! She opened her eyes and stiffened to see him appear on a circular staircase above her, walking down and studying her with cool blue eyes. "I did not recognize you at first in all those jewels . . ."

"What are you doing here? I thought you had left."

He reached the bottom of the stairs and regarded her indifferently. "But I was invited to attend the ball by the princess herself. How could I refuse?"

How indeed? April glanced just outside the antechamber then and saw the volatile Tatiana presently distracted with another gentleman across the ballroom. Otherwise she knew the woman would not have hesitated to create another scene.

"You are lovely tonight," Damien said softly. And it was true. His wife—if she still was—did not look out of place in the slightest. What a beautiful countess she would have made at his side! Her bearing was as regal as a queen's. For a moment, Damien wondered if he could pass her off in England as a Russian princess. Then he saw the fury in April's eyes and he knew she would never agree to it now.

"Please leave," she said, her hands clutching the blue velvet folds of her skirts. "You are only making things worse. I am doing what you told me to do—"

"Whoring for Ivanov? It certainly seems you are dressing the part." Damien took in her low-cut gown with faint disgust. "Perhaps he is selling you to the highest bidder even now." He gestured into the ballroom again at a paunchy, whiskered *boyar* who was talking with Ivanov at the refreshment table.

"That's not fair! Count Ivanov has been kind to me since you left, and there is nothing between us—"

"Yet. But he is not doing this merely out of the kindness of his heart, *ma chere*. Surely you realize that?"

"Kindness is not something you understand," April shot back. "You left me, remember? Where else was I to go?"

She had a right to be angry, Damien knew. But seeing April coiffed and perfumed like some damned porcelain doll for men to drool over made him furious. He had made a mistake in leaving her. She was an innocent surrounded by wolves.

"I thought you were better off without me," he admitted after a brief silence. "I was wrong, April."

April refused to be swayed by Damien's words. He had wounded her too deeply, too abruptly. The shock of his desertion would scar her for a long time, and the time that had passed had only made her more bitter and resolved that she would never love so trustingly again.

"The count is returning," she observed coldly. "I think you should go now."

Damien's eyes burned into hers. "I will be back, April. You cannot avoid me forever. And you know you won't forget me . . ."

He stalked away just as Ivanov came in search of her. She stepped out of the antechamber with the breathless excuse that she had felt faint. Damien disappeared back up the stairs and Vasili was none the wiser.

"You are too pale," the count agreed critically. "Here, drink this."

April took the punch he proffered and quaffed it in one unladylike gulp. It burned all the way down and brought tears to her eyes, but her color returned as two bright spots on her cheeks.

"Dance with me!" she said, aware that Damien emerged on a inner balcony and was watching her from above. "I wish to try this fancy whirling in circles."

"It will make you giddy," Ivanov warned, but April was not to be swayed. He saw she was even prepared to return an encouraging glance to any of the men who lingered hopefully nearby, and with a sigh he swung her out onto the floor.

It had been years since the count had danced, but he had not forgotten. Ivanov guided her smoothly into the next refrain, and April followed his lead flawlessly, watching the other dancers. She was gifted with a natural ability that made her appear light as gossamer, born to glide across fine floors with her belled skirts swirling.

The punch, which was not much more than colored vodka, went to her head as Ivanov had predicted. She smiled and enjoyed the breeze blowing across her face as they spun gracefully around the huge floor among the other brilliantly-costumed dancers.

Suddenly, another *boyar* cut in unexpectedly. The man was unfamiliar to April and Ivanov purpled, but was forced to relinquish her to avoid a scene. Soon the interloper was replaced with another and yet another enchanted nobleman.

All of them tried to coax personal information out of April. Who was she? Who was her family? She laughed and chatted easily, avoiding any direct questions. They were all too charmed by her dazzling beauty to note how she adroitly failed to reply. April left many a man standing bemused after she whirled off with another courtier, realizing he knew nothing more about the mysterious beauty than her first name.

Soon it was like spring inside, and even the hothouse flowers lining the bowls about the room seemed to brighten under April's spell. She was indeed a breath of fresh air to a court long since grown stale, and her various admirers sighed and stared after her. At least half a dozen men were convinced they were in love, even two older gents who distinctly recalled her predecessor Katya and the heartbreak that one had wreaked as well.

Only two persons were totally immune to April's magic that eve. One was Damien, glowering helplessly as his wife was swept laughing from arm to arm; and the other was Princess Tatiana, thoroughly enraged and inconsolable that she should be so upstaged at her own fête.

"Mikel!" she snapped to her escort, who hurriedly tore his own gaze from April and rushed to do her bidding. "I find I am weary of this night. It seems that Ivanov's slut has all the men slathering after her. But I have my own entertainment that will prove far more amusing." And she flicked a pointed fingernail in the direction of Damien standing rigidly on the balcony, watching the dancers. "That one. See that he follows."

Without waiting for the young man's reply, she raised her Titian head and sailed from the room. Mikel gulped and hurried to do the princess's bidding. It was not up to him to approve or disapprove of her lovers, as she often scolded him. As many young men, he was enthralled by Tatiana and her potent personality. Her willingness to take on all comers was common knowledge, but morals in czarist Russia were very different from other European courts.

"Sir?" Mikel approached Damien, stammering in polite Russian, receiving an ice-blue stare in return. "The—the princess Menshikov requests an—uh—audience with you." The boy colored, not knowing what else to say. To his surprise, Damien let out an abrupt laugh and slapped Mikel on the shoulder as he passed. "That much I understand, boy. Now go find a less dangerous woman to play with. You would do well to learn from my mistake."

Damien found Tatiana out in the reception hall, where she stood impatiently waiting and tossing her brazen hair like a high-strung filly.

Whirling by the gilded portal a moment later, April's eyes widened to see Damien take the princess's arm and murmur something low against the lady's ear. Laughing huskily, Tatiana shot a seductive look up at her handsome partner. Damien was helping her into a luxurious red fox coat that nearly reached the floor.

April's own grip tightened on her dancing partner so noticeably that he made an exclamation of delight, supposing she urged him closer. Then they were on the other side of the room, and April looked about in vain when they passed again. Damien and Tatiana had left, obviously together. She was so distraught she could hardly choke down her tears when her escort gushed passionate compliments to her under his breath as they parted.

In a daze, April sought the only refuge she knew. Count Ivanov smiled archly as he took her on his arm, having seen what she had. It suited his cause well that the insatiable Tatiana had taken a liking to Damien. Though he was annoyed that Dmitri had failed to dispose of the gypsy as he had ordered, the fact that Damien had caught the princess's eye would surely keep him out from underfoot until Alexei could be sent to finish the job.

Count Ivanov had April all to himself now, body and soul. And when he saw her tortured green eyes, he knew too that he had his beloved Katya back.

Nuzzling closely into her chosen lover inside the gilded sleigh, Tatiana murmured, "You played divinely! I know I shall never forget the sound of your music. It even brought tears to my eyes. I know my uncle felt the same, for I watched him during the performance."

"Uncle?" Damien repeated stupidly, probing

for more information, which she provided with a willing little laugh.

"Do you not know who I am? Of course I am more than just a princess, I am Alexsandr Menshikov's niece!" Tatiana waited for his reaction, and when met with a puzzled stare, she supplied patronizingly, "The commander of the Russian armies at the front. You must have seen him. The large, glowering man sitting by me at your performance."

Damien had indeed, and he had also managed to brush close enough to Menshikov during the dancing later to overhear a few interesting comments about the latest troop movements.

He shrugged in apparent ignorance. "I am Romany. War does not concern me."

"How fortunate for you. It seems that I am always being tugged about in political discussions nowdays." She sighed petulantly, then blinked her large dark eyes up at him. "I would much rather be tugged about in matters of love, wouldn't you?"

Instead of being enticed by her obvious ploys, Damien was repulsed. He could not help but contrast April's fresh, unsullied air with that of Tatiana, who had known so many men that it had become a sad addiction with her. He recalled her as an insatiable lover, demanding and tireless, and with no shred of modesty.

Tatiana had not changed, he soon saw, when on the seat beside him she suddenly unlaced

311

her gown and let her full breasts spill out in full view of any passerby.

Enjoying his obvious shock, Tatiana murmured throatily, "Touch me! Take me if you want. Here and now. Why wait?"

Once he would have jumped at the chance to couple almost anywhere with a willing woman, but Damien carefully masked his revulsion with a fierce look that shot thrills through the obviously jaded princess.

"Cover yourself! You will not do anything tonight without my orders." He saw in a flash that his gamble paid off. Tatiana was startled but scrambled to do his bidding. She apparently craved a strong man, subject as she was to endless court fops with weak wrists and wills that could not match her own.

Her dark eyes gleamed with excitement as she whispered, "When will you take me?"

"When and where I decide," Damien responded curtly, suspecting correctly that his little game only thrilled her further. Suddenly submissive, Tatiana remained silent for most of the ride, only asking once, "Why did you choose to be a gypsy? You could pass for nobility, given the right clothes and manners."

"Does it matter?" he asked, trying to quell her curiosity with a smoldering glance.

Tatiana took the ruby-encrusted combs from her hair and shook the flaming red locks out over her shoulders. "No," she said huskily, "but just for a moment you reminded me of someone. I can't think who."

Damien's blood turned to ice as the princess snuggled against him, boldly running a hand up his thigh. "Don't worry," she assured him softly, tauntingly, "I'll remember eventually. I never forget a face."

Seventeen

Old men, young men, thin and tall or short and lumpish, it seemed that April had danced with them all. She was not sorry to leave the ball, but welcomed the chance to rest her aching feet in the coach as they left. Beside her Ivanov sat stiffly lost in his own thoughts, and she was secretly glad that he was not in the mood to subject her to another history lesson.

Some of the night's magic had worn thin for her since Damien's appearance. She could not tear him from her thoughts, though she refused to dwell on the last memory she had of him, leaving the festivities early with Tatiana Menshikov on his arm.

Surely he was not charmed by that snake of a woman! Perhaps the princess had lured him with promises of more concerts or *boyar* sponsorship. Certainly, Damien had played exceptionally well. It almost seemed as if he had put more emotion into his music this night than even April remembered hearing before. But she could not let herself get carried away into supposing he still wanted her, no matter what he had said there at the ball.

She must have made a weary sound, for Ivanov suddenly said, "I know you are tired, but I hope you'll join me for a final toast when we return to Samarin."

April glanced at his inscrutable face half-hidden by shadows. "Are we celebrating something?"

"In a way, yes." But he would offer her no more than that. "You certainly were a success tonight. So many men were entranced by you." He sounded a little sad for some reason.

Seeking to cheer him, April agreed to stay up a little later on this special night. She did not admit her bone-weariness but thought of her host instead. Count Ivanov had been very generous in giving her beautiful clothes and a new start in life if she chose to take it. He had unerringly offered the simple explanation time and again to the overly curious *boyar* at the ball that April was his distant cousin, recently orphaned but of the same fine lineage as he. He did not lie about her origins in that he acknowledged she came from a small Georgian province in the south. Given her fairness and her exquisite bearing, nobody had questioned it. April had quickly discouraged a few persistent suitors on her own.

Soon they were back at Samarin House, but April wished to change her attire before reappearing downstairs. Ivanov seemed disappointed, but agreed, retreating directly to the study himself. They had arrived earlier than planned, and most of the house was silent and dark. The hall itself had not even been lit when they came in.

Following the faint light from a few gas lamps, April gathered up her velvet skirts and went up the series of stairs, her slippers making no sound on the smoothly polished mahogany.

When she came to the Gold Room, she was surprised to find the door slightly ajar. She was sure she had closed it firmly before she had departed. Then, seeing a rustle of movement through the crack, she hesitated and peered in. Perhaps Zofia was only turning down the covers or stoking the fire. But what she saw made her heart begin to pound furiously. Someone—mostly hidden in darkness, so she wasn't sure who—was frantically riffling through the contents of the vanity table. As if they purposefully looked for April's jewel!

Though she was frightened, April was more outraged. She knew the count would expect her to confront a thief, and he would surely stand behind her in doing so. She only hoped the intruder did not have a weapon. When she heard the scrabbling of anxious fingers beneath the vanity, right where the secret drawer held her diamond, she knew she must act swiftly.

Pushing open the door, April cried, "What are you doing in my room?"

As she had half-suspected from the beginning, it was Zofia who whirled around and stared back at her with crazed eyes. Without answering, the maid turned back to the vanity one last time and gave a triumphant tug on the drawer she had just found.

"No!" Desperately April threw herself at the woman and the impact knocked them both to the Aubusson rug on the floor. But it was too late. The drawer had been pulled out, and the diamond fell with a muffled thud on the rug, and rolled some distance away.

Tangled in her voluminous skirts, April was unable to get a good grasp on the wild-eyed Zofia who lunged after the gem and its betraying sparkle. The maid finally crawled to grab up the jewel just as April came to her feet again and darted for the open door to try and cut off Zofia's escape.

Cupping the gemstone in her violently trembling hands, Zofia stared at it a long moment and then raised her gaze to April's. Suddenly she hissed, "I will not let you destroy him!"

"Who?" April cried, seeing wild emotion in the woman's eyes. Clearly Zofia was demented and reliving some terrible nightmare in her head.

But Zofia only clenched the jewel so tightly that her fist whitened, and shook it in April's direction. "You thought you could come back and haunt him as *she* did! But I will not let you hurt him! No, I shall kill you myself first, and you can molder in your graves together then!"

Horrified by the maid's ranting, but at the same time curious to know what Zofia knew about the jewel, April played along for a daring moment. Softly she said, "I don't want to hurt anybody, Zofia, as I am sure you don't either. But you seem to be determined to have the diamond. Do you need the money so badly?"

Zofia stared at her a second and then laughed with a twisted fierceness that took the young woman aback. "You thought you could hide it from me, eh? As if I couldn't figure out your games, hiding the jewel and pretending to be a gypsy! I recognized you at once. Your mother swore she would have revenge one day when I took the babe from her dying arms, but I never believed it! And I will not let you destroy Vasili as she vowed to do even from the grave!" Zofia drilled a stare full of hatred deep into April's shock-widened eyes, and slowly the girl began to gather the facts.

"Baby?" she breathed, her own thoughts like lightning as she remembered the circumstances of her own birth almost eighteen years ago. "That diamond was found around my neck as a baby, Zofia. Why?"

"Because I put it there!" The maid nearly shrieked at her. "In my youth I was soft and foolish, and could not bring myself to kill a helpless babe! So I left you in the snow for

318

God to take you instead. And when I returned, you and the diamond were both gone!"

Almost staggering with the impact of the knowledge, April whispered desperately, "Who was my mother, Zofia? Why was she dying? You must tell me!" She clutched at the bed poster for support, knowing the terrible truth was rising to drown her in a matter of moments.

Zofia shook her head impatiently. "It is not important now. What matters is that I have the diamond back, and that you can be revealed for what you really are!" She gave a diabolical little laugh. "Do you know what will happen when the count finds out who you are?"

"Yes! He will have you branded and hung as a thief! And he is right downstairs, Zofia. Don't be foolish! Give it back to me now and I will plead leniency for you."

The maid only shook her head wildly and suddenly lunged past April, knocking the girl roughly aside.

In her tight stays and full gown April could not catch the woman. She kicked off her satin slippers and sprinted after Zofia in a valiant attempt, but the maid disappeared down the maze of shadowy halls.

Breathing hard, April headed for the stairs. She must alert the count! Ivanov would be concerned having such a madwoman in his house. As she flew back down the staircase with the blue velvet gown bunched in her hands, April could hear a soft cackle of crazy laughter somewhere up above her. The hair rose on her neck but she hurried on, arriving dazed and breathless at the door to Ivanov's study.

"My dear!" The count was sitting by the fire and rose, concerned, when April bolted into the room with her hair half-tumbled down to her shoulders and her green eyes wild.

"Zofia!" April managed to gasp out, pointing back the way she had come.

"What has happened? You are distraught. Come and sit by the fire." Ivanov spoke strangely and yet April was too distressed to notice the odd glaze that had suddenly filmed over his dark eyes at the sight of her in the blue ball gown.

"I found Zofia in my room! She was going through the vanity, and when I confronted her she began to say all sorts of mad things—"

But Count Ivanov only turned, reached down to an ornate table beside the chair he had been sitting in and picked up a pair of matching fluted glasses which reflected rainbow colors as he extended one to her. "Shall we have that toast now?" he proposed pleasantly.

Was everyone mad? April shook her head. "How can you call for a drink at a time like this?" Then she wondered if Ivanov had perhaps been drinking on his own while she was upstairs, and was overcome with the effects now. But his speech was very precise as he raised a quizzical brow at her.

"How? Because I have waited forever for this. You see, it is time to announce our engagement. I wish to seal our love tonight with a toast, and something you will cherish even more." He smiled indulgently at her, as if to a child, and then exchanged the goblets for a long flat velvet box. "Come now, Katya. I know you will be delighted—"

April pressed her hands to her head, trying to stop the waves of dizziness that threatened to weaken her now. What kind of game was he playing? When he snapped open the box she could only stare at the beautiful collar of emeralds glittering against the black velvet.

"They match your eyes, beloved," Vasili said in a voice thick with emotion as he took the necklace out. "Let me put them on you. I want to see them gracing your lovely neck tonight. It would make me the happiest of men."

April shook her head wildly, choked with fear and unable to scream as he advanced, murmuring softly.

"I forgot to tell you what a princess in truth you seemed tonight," he smiled. "I am sure your uncle would be most proud, had he lived to see your coming-out. You stole the spotlight and the hearts of many men this eve, Katya. It is no wonder that you are hailed as the Circassian Cat. You are very clever, my dear."

Suddenly Count Ivanov was before her, just a handspan away, and his hot breath came hard and fast upon her cheek. April froze in a mixture of indecision and fear, and he took the advantage to trail his icy fingers upon her neck. In a moment the sapphire necklace she was wearing slid off into his hand and he set it aside. Vasili substituted the heavier emerald choker and secured the clasp.

Suddenly his smile abruptly faded. His brow creased with darkness, and he said in a low voice very close to her, "However, I did not approve of Prince Andrei dancing close attendance upon you tonight. It seemed you encouraged him, Katya. Have you forgotten so quickly that you are my betrothed?"

"I'm not—" April began in a desperate attempt to pull Ivanov back to reality, but he misinterpreted her words and cut her off with a savage growl.

"You are mine! Mine and no other's! You may flirt with princes all you please, Katya, but in the end you will be my wife! Must I impress this upon you again? I have respected you and bowed to your wishes to hold off my attentions until our wedding night, but when I see you playing the coquette with other men, I burn to have you myself!"

April had no chance to scream, only whimper, when Ivanov suddenly yanked her fiercely into his arms and crushed his hard lips into hers. Struggling wildly, she tried to throw him off but could not. He gave her a painful, punishing kiss, roughly kneading her breast all the while, as she quivered with revulsion and rising hate.

Only one brute before had dared to treat her so—and Nicky had gotten his just due. Though she was too close to the count to kick effectively, April whipped her elbow between them and punched him sharply in the solar plexus. With a muffled grunt, Ivanov broke off the attack.

April whirled to run, her long skirts hampering her again. She dashed gasping from the study into the dark empty hall, her blood surging in her ears. Behind her he called, "Katya! Come back. You cannot hide. And if you persist in fighting me I shall lock you in the Gold Room again!"

Her head throbbing with urgency, April glanced right and left for escape. She knew it would be foolish to head out barefoot in the darkness and the merciless snow. She would not get far. Then, remembering a series of rooms she had wandered through before on a tour, one of which led indirectly to the stables, she turned left and ran for all she was worth.

Behind her footsteps rang out in the dark hall as Ivanov looked for her. "Katya! I am getting angry!"

Quelling a sob, April continued to flee. The last she heard was the count cursing and searching for a lamp as she finally found a doorknob and yanked open the entrance to what appeared to be the conservatory.

To her surprise, a series of candelabra had been lit and rested upon the black harpsichord in the corner. The candles were low but the light served to guide her directly across to another door that linked to yet another passageway.

Suddenly a scale of notes tinkled out as someone ran a hand over the harpsichord keys. April jumped in fright and whirled around, startled, to face the grinning visage of Pavel.

She had not seen the dwarf sitting there. Once again Pavel had chosen to don the bizarre spangled costume of the black and white harlequin. Though he still repulsed her, for once April was glad to see him.

"Pavel!" she cried softly. "You must help me!"

"But of course." He jumped down from the bench and gave her a ludicrous bow. "I am always happy to help a lovely lady in distress."

"Please listen. Count Ivanov is coming after me! He seems to think I am someone else . . . he has been saying the strangest things tonight, and Zofia too!"

"Really?" The dwarf seemed genuinely concerned. "Then certainly we must see you to safety." He hurried to precede her through the door she had found. "Follow me!"

Almost sobbing with relief, April followed Pavel through a dark passageway and down a series of narrow, spiral stairs. She did not consciously decide to trust Pavel, but merely wished to escape the madness she had left behind. Her thoughts were whirling wildly as she remembered the things Zofia had said. If she could have stopped and gotten sick, she would have done so. Her nerves were on razor-edge and she could not think straight.

"Here we are!" Pavel announced. "It is very dark but we shall find our way. I will light a candle. There is one in the corner, as I recall."

"Hurry!" April whispered, disliking the feel of damp, cold stone under her feet where she stood. "What is this place?" she called after his retreating figure.

There was no answer. A sudden flare from a wick lit what appeared to be a gruesome stone cellar of sorts.

"Just a moment," Pavel called back reassuringly before she could panic further, "I will bring the candle to you and you can hold it over my head as I lead the way out." He came back toward her and with trembling gratitude April took the taper-holder in her hands.

As she concentrated on keeping the wick alight, Pavel slipped past her and back through the door they had entered. Abruptly it banged shut behind. She cried out and whirled to grab the knob, but there wasn't one. Then she heard an oily chuckle as the dwarf slid the bolt home on the other side.

"Sweet dreams, *princess*," Pavel crooned to her. "You'd best hope Vasili calms down before

I tell him where you are! There will be no reasoning with him then."

April felt her fear give way to a surge of rage. "You little rat!" she cried.

"You'll know more about rats before the night is through down here," Pavel sniggered back. "If I keep Ivanov from killing you, you will owe me! I intend to make you pay dearly for the favor."

"Never!" April hissed, sensing his implication and feeling the chills streak up her spine. But there was only the sound of retreating footsteps, light and mischievous as a troll's, and then terrible silence.

With despair April noted the candle was hardly more than a stub. It would not last more than a half-hour. And what then? In this house of madness, who knew what would happen next?

When Damien arrived with Tatiana at her estate on Poltava Circle, the mansion was fully ablaze with the entire staff waiting up for her safe arrival from the ball.

Along the way, the princess had been desperately trying to persuade Damien to spend the night. He finally agreed, letting Tatiana think it was the lure of her overripe body that drew him into her private bedchambers after she haughtily dismissed the servants for the night.

While Damien toyed with her bright hair

upon the huge bed strewn with fur pelts, Tatiana complained about the war and Damien listened sympathetically. He found several bottles of vodka, and kept filling her glass as they talked. Tatiana drank it down like water and became quickly philosophical. They talked for an hour without making love.

At first, the princess was annoyed, but when she realized Damien was showing the first genuine interest in her that any lover ever had, she was touched and content to let him just stroke her head.

Finally, when she was drunk enough to talk about anything, Damien risked the most dangerous questions of all. He found Tatiana knew a great deal of Menshikov's plans, since her uncle came and went frequently to her house. She raged about Czar Nicholas's threat to replace her uncle with someone he considered more suitable, Prince Michael Gorchakov.

"Can you imagine? Gorchakov!" she snorted with disdain, lolling about on the bed beside Damien, red hair askew. "That weak-kneed Cossack and his horse-faced wife have never done anything of note, certainly not at court! And they both look down their noses at anyone who cannot trace their lineage back a thousand years. What matter when you go back to a plow horse and a rutting Mongol anyway?" Tatiana shrieked with laughter at her own wit and Damien was forced to bring her back to the subject.

"I am sure your uncle's and your bloodline is much finer," he said.

Tatiana stopped laughing, and her dark eyes glowed with some secret resentment. "Some say—" she began, and hiccupped indelicately, "—some say that I am not fit to be a princess! Can you imagine? Cruel, jealous peasants that they are . . . like Ivanov and his ilk."

"Count Ivanov?" Damien prompted, interested to hear what she had to say about the mysterious nobleman.

Tatiana made a face. "Mad old fool! He lost his wits long ago over Katya." At Damien's puzzled look, she seized eagerly on the tale, asking, "Didn't you notice the little whore he paraded around tonight? The blonde in the blue gown?"

"She was striking," he admitted cautiously.

Tatiana sniffed. "Straight from the grave, that one! I'll admit she even gave me a start at first. It was like looking at a ghost!"

Damien felt a prickle of foreboding at her words. "What do you mean?"

"She looks just like a girl named Ekaterina—Katya—who held sway over Ivanov's heart twenty years ago. The fool was obsessed with Katya. But so was half the city." Tatiana was obviously miffed by the memory. "Anyway, Vasili decided to marry her. He pursued her relentlessly. I think even Katya was frightened of him after awhile."

"What happened?" Damien urged, thinking of April still living under a madman's roof.

Tatiana shrugged with *boyar* indifference. "Katya left. It was right after she told Vasili that she was going to marry some prince—I can't remember his name—and they wed and were off to his estates somewhere south. I heard years later that they had been killed in their travels by brigands. I can't help but wonder if Ivanov had a hand in it . . . he was so obsessed with her."

Tatiana yawned hugely, almost falling asleep, and Damien started to rise from the bed. His heart pounded with a nameless dread. He had but one thought: to get out of there and find April, to wrest her from that madman's grasp. For he knew with a horrible certainty that he had uncovered the reason for his own uneasiness at Samarin House—Vasili Ivanov was possessed by demons from the past.

When Damien rose and made a move to go, Tatiana reached out with claw-like fingernails to clutch his sleeve. "Make love to me!" Her gaze momentarily cleared as he plucked her hand from his arm, and suddenly the princess focused on his dark blue eyes.

Tatiana had never quite believed that his name was Gregorio, for she had seen him fail to respond to it several times. It had not mattered to her what he called himself, as long as he was a good lover. But as she stared up at him, the alcoholic haze suddenly lifted, and the knowledge of what she had just told him rang throughout her head.

"Damien," she whispered. "Damien Cross!"

"You're drunk," the earl said, taking a step back away from the bed. "You need to sleep it off, woman!"

Tatiana did not fall for it again. "I never forget a face," she repeated, rolling over onto her elbows, her dark eyes narrowing on the handsome Englishman. "What are you up to, Damien? Why are you trying to get me to betray my country?"

Damien did not answer her for a moment. Looking down at the once-vital woman with the glorious red hair, he saw only the shell of the beauty she had been. Drink had taken her looks as well as her soul, and for that he was sorry. But he would not allow her to interfere with his mission.

"If you do not answer me, I will scream for my guards," Tatiana threatened softly. "They are just down the hall, and they will not bother to ask questions. Or perhaps I should just turn you over to my uncle, hmm? He knows how to make spies speak!"

"What do you want to know?" Damien asked her, with a resigned air.

"First, what you are doing in Moscow? Are you with your father on this trip also?"

"Edward is dead," Damien informed her flatly.

"Then you are Lord Cross now." She licked

her red lips greedily. "Oh, Damien, I can be very good to you, if you don't anger me. We can help each other—"

"You're right, princess." He looked thoughtful as he raked a hand through his thick black hair, and then returned to her side. "I've never forgotten our time together, and I will make it even better tonight . . . if you let me."

Tatiana smiled with triumph, catching him by the lapels to pull him down over her body. "I still don't know why you're here," she whispered fiercely, "but I don't care! Love me, Damien! Tomorrow is soon enough for matters of war, but tonight, the only thing that matters is love!"

Eighteen

Before her candle went out, April made a brief and useless search of the cellar room in which Pavel had locked her. As she suspected, there was only one door, and that was the one he had slammed behind her. But she was not the only living creature trapped in the awful, musty prison.

Soon after Pavel had gone, she heard the tell-tale scurrying and thumping of rats nearby. In her search to escape she saw old crates of broken wine bottles and various junk that had been tossed down here by the house staff over the years. It was there that the rats had made their home, and they came and went by way of a broken air vent across the room.

Fortunately April was not afraid of rats, as Pavel had assumed all women were. When an indignant thump came close to her bare feet, she raised the candle high and looked down at a rodent eyeing her in apparent interest.

It was not a sewer rat but a wood rat, with

a fluffy tail and large round ears that gave it a comical appearance. It regarded her for a moment with its large, curious eyes, then darted off to join its companions once again in searching for interesting bits of glass and shiny objects to carry back to its nest.

As a gypsy, April had long grown used to a variety of animals and she was almost glad of the company in comparison with that of the people upstairs. Were all three of them trying to drive her insane? It could not have worked better if they had planned it!

Just after the candle sputtered out in a hot pool of wax, April heard footsteps ringing down the stairs again. Tensing, she backed away from the door and waited to see who it would be. If it was Pavel, she planned to knock him over and rush out. He was small enough that she was sure she could do it. But as she steeled herself to take him off guard, the door opened and she saw Count Ivanov holding a gas lamp high, swinging its light rays into the room.

Seeing April regarding him angrily, he said in a grim voice, "I wish Pavel hadn't had to do this, Katya. But he told me you were trying to run away again. I won't accept that. You know everything is settled, even the matter of your dowry."

"Settled with whom, count?" April inquired, for some reason more furious than afraid of him. "You seem to assume that I want to marry you!"

"I realize you are young and easily impressed by titles," Ivanov said through gritted teeth, "and that Andrei Petrovna may seem quite a catch to you right now. But while the young prince may be your age, he is scarcely your equal. It was agreed by the Grand Duke himself when you were only twelve that I would be considered a candidate for your hand someday. As he put it to me, he said you would be in need of a firm hand when the time came."

As the count rambled on, April came to her own swift deductions. In her hour alone she had finally gathered enough of her thoughts to begin piecing the fantastic tale together. What Zofia had said, along with Ivanov's delusions, seemed to paint a portrait of a woman, her real mother perhaps, who had once had the misfortune to be considered Count Ivanov's fiancée.

Taking a gamble, she said haughtily, "What makes you think I will settle for a mere count?"

It was the wrong thing to say, though perfectly correct in character for what an infuriated Ekaterina had hurled at Vasili twenty years ago. His eyes darkened, and he took a step into the cellar room nearly shaking with rage. "I am claiming you for mine, Katya! No man dares gainsay what I have already put my mark upon!"

"Oh? And what if Andrei has put his mark on me first?" In her own desperation to find the answers to her identity, April flirted with a man's sanity and her own life.

Suddenly Vasili raised a hand and slapped her lightly, his nostrils flaring. As April cradled her cheek, he hissed, "So! It is as I feared! You have already given yourself to the prince. But if you think that will save you from my claim, you are wrong, Katya!" He paused as if hearing a voice respond from long ago, though April had spoken no words. He retorted harshly, "Will you beg me to release you from our betrothal? What do you mean, there is none? I decided I would have you the first moment I laid eyes on you twelve years ago! You knew of this and still you encouraged Petrovna!"

"Please," April sobbed, "please stop!" Like a play, she could see the characters dancing in her head. The count angrily berating a young woman who resembled herself. And Ekaterina—Katya—trembling with terror then as her daughter did now, pleading for Ivanov to cease the madness.

"We shall see," he threatened, reaching out to grab April by the arm and yank her behind him, dragging her stumbling up the stone stairs out of the cellar, holding the light ahead as he went. "We shall see how deep your so-called love for Andrei goes, my dear, once you have spent a few weeks in the bridal suite I made just for you!"

"No!" April cried, fighting him uselessly, her

335

strength inconsequential against his maddened determination.

Soon he had her up to the main floor, and then up to the bedchamber in turn, where he hurled her not gently across the Gold Room and she fell against the bed post, grabbing it to keep her feet just in time.

Pushing back her tangled mass of goldspun hair, April cried at him, "You are insane! You cannot treat people like this!"

Vasili glowered at her from the doorway. "I can and I will. I am the master of this house. When you agreed to be its mistress, you agreed to obey me in everything. You will stay here and rot before I let Andrei Petrovna have you!"

So saying, he pulled the door shut and turned the key, and for the first time April saw that it had been designed only to be locked from the outside. With a cry of despair, she ran to pull on the knob and beat on the door. Yet the wood, too, had been cut thicker than that of the other chambers, muffling her voice almost completely from the other side.

She understood suddenly the horrible purpose of the Gold Room. A luxurious prison—a gilded cage—it held her now as it had once held her mother, Katya. And like the duke's niece, she was smart enough to realize that until Ivanov chose to be lenient, there was no escape. Curbing an impulse to cry, which would be of no use, April searched through the vanity

336

and the closets for something, anything, that could serve as a weapon if need be.

She decided on the heavy ivory hairbrush, and hid it in the folds of her skirt as she paced, waiting. Hours or days, she did not know how long before the count would return for his final vengeance. But she suspected that he could not keep away from his "beloved Katya" for very long. And when he returned, she would be ready. Her very life, like that of her mother's, depended on it.

Damien glanced down with distaste at the dark red stain spreading across the ermine furs of Tatiana's bed. He suspected when she awoke she would be more furious seeing he had spilled wine on her bedspread, than discovering the bump on her head where he had knocked her unconscious.

Unfortunately, the princess had a hard head, and the bottle had cracked before she had finally sagged limp in his arms. Damien lowered her gently to the bed, with a murmured apology for treating a lady so outrageously. But he didn't dare risk exposure so late in the game. Who knew where Tatiana's true loyalties lay? And with April in serious danger, he didn't intend to dawdle the night away here.

Slipping from the mansion was easier than he'd imagined. Thinking their mistress was immersed in love battles for the night, the staff had gone to bed. Even the guards were slumped snoring in the hall, full of mead and good food. Damien took the back stairs, and then presumed further to take the servant's sleigh parked outside.

Though Samarin House was only a mile out of Moscow, it seemed liked leagues by the time Damien broke fresh snow and the lights of the city receded dimly behind him. The awning over the driver's seat provided little protection from the biting, bracing winds, but thankfully the snow had stopped and everything lay in icy stillness. He had only to contend with the threat of exposure and frostbite, which, he soon found, were not far removed.

When his hands became so numb that he could no longer feel anything, he realized the foolishness of his plight. At least his coat was warm enough, and he knew he wouldn't die. But once he reached April he should be incapacitated in helping her. Unfortunately, it was the best he could do now, and time was of the essence.

Damien was not far afield when he heard the hiss of runners close behind his own sleigh and the telltale jingle of fine harness. Whipping his frozen face around, he peered back to recognize one of the count's sleighs, headed in the same direction as his.

Perhaps he would be fortunate enough to find April aboard it! Purposefully slowing his team, who were no match for the four fine blood bays that drew the count's sleigh, Damien watched alertly as the other driver veered sharply to pass him.

When the second conveyance was half past, the light of two lamps swinging from the seat highlighted the count's manservant Dmitri at the reins, his large beaked nose protruding characteristically between his muffler and fur wedge hat. But while Damien noted that the carriage itself was empty, he also remembered that the coach he had seen outside the Kremlin had been drawn by white horses instead. Apparently Dmitri was out on his own tonight. In a sudden daring move, Damien drew his own team close on the runners of the passing sleigh.

Dmitri glanced back and appeared to curse, wondering if the other driver was drunk. But he did not recognize Damien in the darkness, and made no move to slow or stop.

Enjoying his own chance for revenge, Damien purposefully edged the front runner of his own sleigh up against that of the other. When the metal met, sparks flew and he could hear Dmitri curse as both sleighs squirreled in the snow.

Undaunted, the earl extended his team, knowing he must act swiftly before the faster coach could pull away. His team was weary but surprisingly big-hearted. Steam rushing from their distended nostrils, the grays pursued the set of bays that were slowly extending the distance. His own aim needed to be precise,

Damien knew, to force Dmitri to stop without inviting disaster. He had no wish to kill or injure any of the horses.

Suddenly, Dmitri branched off on his own in a wide sweep to the right that forced Damien to quickly gather in his own reins to avoid a collision. In doing so, the other driver miscalculated and the ornate sleigh rocked dangerously, nearly rolling over. The lead bays knocked together, upsetting the entire team and tangling the leads. The well-trained horses immediately slowed and soon came to a rasping stop in the darkness.

Shouting obscenities in Damien's direction, Dmitri leapt down and ran back to check the damage. Opportunity knocked boldly on Damien's door in that moment of providence. With a wry, regretful grin, he stopped his own sleigh within a few feet of the other man's.

Dmitri was more worried about the damage done to the newly-painted red runners than he was about himself. He had scarcely time to straighten and face Damien Cross when the earl swung out, catching the other squarely in the jaw.

As the driver dropped like dead weight, Damien caught him. He immediately recognized the coat Dmitri wore as the one the gunman in town had been wearing. The fellow also had scars from the glass slivers that had slipped down his collar and cut his neck when Damien had thrown him into the store window.

"Sorry, old man," Damien said in a return of brisk British humor, "but I think I owe you that one. And I need to borrow your sleigh. Hell of a way to ask, I know, but I haven't got time for polite pleasantries tonight!"

Lugging Dmitri's heavy inert form to the older sleigh, he then removed the man's gloves and hat and quickly put them on. They were still warm from the driver's bodyheat and felt delicious against the brittle night chill. Damien hefted Dmitri's body inside the enclosure of the other coach and shut the door. It would keep the cold from killing the man before the other team returned to town and he revived.

Lastly, but with great appreciation, Damien patted the grays who had shown great courage in their pursuit. Then he brought the team around facing Moscow again. Trusting they would swiftly find their way back to Tatiana's stables where warmth and hay awaited, he slapped the rump of the nearest steed and sent the sleigh flying back toward the lights of the city.

The blowing bays still stood patiently in their traces. Damien swiftly untangled the reins and harness, checked the sleigh and found the paint chipped on the runners. Otherwise, the coach was undamaged.

Leaping up in the seat, he slapped the reins with a crack and felt the rush of exhilaration as the powerful animals instantly responded. Within moments, he was racing toward Samarin

House again, confident that he could fly directly to the count's front door now and none would dare try to stop him this night.

To Damien's surprise, there were not even any guards on duty when he drove through the open gates. Going directly to the stables, as Dmitri logically would have done, he slowed the team and brought the sleigh to a smooth halt on the snow. There was a light on inside the stables, but it was otherwise deserted.

Cautiously getting down and going to inspect, Damien found the staff had long since departed for warmer quarters indoors and left a light on only for Dmitri's sake.

A soft whicker greeted Damien as he walked down the row of stalls. Prince Adar thrust out his great black head and eyed Damien with interest. Putting a hand on the stallion's silky nose, he murmured, "Where's your mistress, hmm? Has she been out to see you tonight?" Damien guessed not, noting the absence of any spilled oats on the floor beneath the horse. April was always diligent about giving her horse a treat after her own supper. It made him doubly uneasy to note that Adar stood in piles of his own droppings, which April never would have permitted.

"Something's wrong, isn't it, boy?" Damien comforted the horse, who began to impatiently bang a hoof on the door of his stall. "I think you know it too. Tell you what, you and I are going to get April out of here tonight. I know she won't leave without you, so let's get you ready."

Quickly and furtively, knowing he might be disturbed at any time, Damien gathered together Adar's riding gear and readied the horse. Anxious to escape his confinement, the stud did not fight the bit but let Damien settle it in his mouth and throw several blankets over his back. Damien eased the horse out of the stall and finished saddling him, having no qualms whatsoever about borrowing Ivanov's finely-tooled silver tack.

Then he led Adar down the aisle and outside to the sleigh, where he secured the black behind the coach. As he finished, Damien glanced around to ascertain that nobody had seen the sudden activity at the stables. Fortunately, the uncommonly bitter night had dissuaded any servants from wandering out for trysts or anything else.

Samarin House itself was almost entirely dark, except for a single light downstairs and one upstairs where the Gold Room was located. Wondering if April had turned to the count's arms for comfort, Damien felt a biting stab of resentment that had grown increasingly more frequent of late.

Perhaps seeing her at the Kremlin ball, as poised and lovely as a princess, had finally convinced him that he must take the risk of keeping her at his side. It would be easy enough to smooth over the real facts of her heritage, and since she already spoke many languages with ease it would be enough to convince most inquisitive folk. And knowing his mother, Marcelle would be delighted enough with the marriage itself and April's beauty that she would accept Damien's choice without a qualm.

The thought of returning to either France or England without April had become more and more impossible. Damien would be the first to admit that she had enchanted him, and that he was deeply in love with the girl. Several weeks ago April would have been more than ready to follow him to the ends of the earth. But now . . . ? He would just have to find out.

Damien knew he could not merely stride up to the front door and demand his wife. Soon enough Dmitri would awaken and alert those in town that the count was in danger. With a measuring glance at the height of the Gold Room, Damien considered trying to scale the manor, but there was no balcony to receive him and it was a gamble that April was even there.

With a frustrated noise, he began to circle Samarin House, keeping in the shadows so as to avoid detection. As luck would have it, he was directly before one of the rear exits when the door suddenly flew open and someone stumbled out, gasping white clouds of breath as she looked frantically about.

Damien recognized the maid Zofia. The woman had not seen him but furtively struck out across the snow. She turned toward the stables, but the snow was ankle-deep and in her heavy skirts she could not move very swiftly.

Sensing trouble, Damien moved to follow her. He caught up with Zofia and grabbed her arm from behind, and the maid loosed a feral snarl as she whipped around.

Recognizing Damien, her glittering dark eyes went wide. Then, before she could scream and alert any others, he clapped one hand over her mouth and with his other twisted her arm high up behind her back.

"A little late to be out and about on such a cold night, *nyet?*" he hissed in her ear. "Somehow I get the feeling you aren't out for a casual stroll!"

She struggled soundlessly for a moment, and he continued in a low voice, "As you may guess, I'm looking for my wife. And by the looks of you, there's some trouble inside that house. Am I right?"

When she stubbornly refused to reply, Damien shook her a little and hissed, "Don't toy with me, woman! I've already had enough of your insolence while staying here, and if you were on my staff, I'd have dismissed you long ago! Now I'm going to take my hand away, and you're going to tell me everything. But I warn you, I'll have no second thoughts about striking a woman, especially where April's life is concerned. So make it quick and make it good!"

Damien unmuffled her mouth then and saw that Zofia had tried to bite him. Fortunately, the thickness of the hide in his gloves meant that he had not even felt it, but there were teeth marks in the leather and he was not amused.

"Well?" he demanded. "What are you doing sneaking out here like this? Where is April?"

Zofia gave him a triumphant look. Though he still held her arm cruelly twisted back, and she must have been in pain, she refused to speak.

"Very well," Damien ground out, "then I'll just have to take you in with me and together we'll pay our respects to the count!"

"*Nyet!*" Zofia suddenly reacted, her voice a hoarse and desperate cry, "Don't take me back in there!"

"Why not?" Damien demanded.

"Because he will kill me!"

"What have you done to deserve that? It must be pretty good. Or did your disrespect finally annoy him as much as it does me?"

Zofia would not answer, and he gave her a hard shake. "That does it, "he said coldly. "I've no time for these games tonight. You can dance around in circles all you please, but in the end you'll answer me!"

Damien dragged her back to Samarin House, to the door through which she had crept. It was no easy task. Zofia fought him, silently but de-

346

terminedly, and she was thin but strong, of peasant stock. Luckily she did not seem to want attention drawn to them either, and in the end Damien won, forcing her through the door which was still unlocked.

"Now," he ordered her quietly when they were inside, "take me to April!"

Unwillingly Zofia nodded and began to move ahead of Damien in the darkness, up a series of wooden, back stairs that appeared to be for servants' use only. Before they went very far, he clamped his hand around her wrist and warned, "If you try to trick me, I'll not go lightly on you. Remember that."

Soon they were on an upper landing, about the same height as he judged the fourth floor to be. Relaxing his grip long enough to let Zofia crack a door into a dark hall, Damien then reasserted his control over the woman and escorted her directly to the Gold Room.

Once there, he tried the knob and found it locked. It would not be locked without a reason. Damien motioned for Zofia to open the door and she grudgingly reached for the ring of house keys tied to her waist.

A moment more and the door clicked open. Pushing the maid ahead of him as a shield of sorts, Damien entered the bedchamber. It was only a fraction of a second before a white object came whizzing toward them, smacking Zofia soundly in the forehead and causing the maid to buckle to her knees. Throwing himself inside against the wall, Damien looked to the source.

"Damien!"

With a soft cry of disbelief, April gathered up her skirts and ran toward him, halting only when she remembered that she was still angry with him. But her green eyes were alight with hope and he longed to crush her in his arms in that moment.

She was more beautiful than ever, though Damien frowned to see the state of her gown and her hair. He closed the door and stepped over the faintly groaning Zofia on the floor, noting the deadly accuracy with which the ivory hairbrush had been hurled.

"What's happening?" Damien asked, and a second later against all her intents, April was in his arms, shaking like a terrified child.

"The count—Zofia—Pavel—they're all mad!" April gasped into his fur coat. "Ivanov locked me in here after he ranted and raved at me like I was someone else. He kept calling me Katya—"

As the story tumbled out, wild and almost unbelievable except for Tatiana's confirming tales, Damien glanced around the Gold Room. He saw by the black marks on the beautiful velvet gown that April had put her time to good use and had not only lit a fire in the grate herself, to keep warm and provide light, but had also begun assembling a variety of furniture and boxes with which she had probably intended to block the entrance to the room.

He was thankful that he had gotten there in time, not only to rescue her but to prevent Ivanov from frightening her any further. Smoothing back her hair, he murmured, "You're safe now. I won't let him or any of the others hurt you."

Then, with a glance to assure Zofia was still stunned, he asked his wife, "I found her outside. Do you know why she was trying to escape the house?"

April pulled back and nodded vigorously. "She stole my jewel from me! I—I never told you, but when Tzigane found me as a baby, there was a little pouch around my neck that held a valuable gem. A diamond. But there was no clue as to where it came from . . ." Trailing off, afraid that Damien would resent her for not being honest before, April blurted, "I didn't want you to think I had stolen it myself! But I was going to tell you someday . . ."

"Never mind," Damien said, still feeling guilty enough about his own deception. "I understand why Zofia would want to have such a jewel. She probably intended to sell it and live comfortably for the rest of her life."

"But that's not all!" April cried. "She told me she had stolen it from my mother, when she also took me. She said that my real mother—whom I think is named Katya—was dying! Zofia confessed she didn't want to kill a newborn baby too. But isn't that horrible? Why would she have any reason to kill my mother in the first place?"

"Maybe she didn't." Damien was grim. "Have you ever considered that perhaps someone else arranged for it, and Zofia was only an accomplice?"

April shuddered. "There's only one person who could have wanted my mother dead. Ivanov! The way he carried on tonight, raging about her and another man, I expected him to kill *me,* too!"

Damien looked down into his wife's beautiful green eyes, suddenly understanding why she had always seemed of such noble bearing to him and others. "April," he said softly, hesitantly, "I think you may be the daughter of *boyar* parents. Tatiana told me the story of Ekaterina—Katya—leaving Ivanov to marry a prince in the south. She also said they had both been killed by brigands on a journey somewhere later. Nobody was accused of the crime, but Tatiana believes that Ivanov had a hand in it."

At the mention of the arrogant Princess Menshikov, April's eyes darkened. Instead of seizing eagerly on what he had just told her, she demanded, "Why did you leave with Tatiana tonight?"

Damien made an exasperated noise. "April! Don't you understand? You are probably a princess yourself by birth. It makes sense now.

Zofia apparently coveted Ekaterina's prized jewel, which by the sound of it was probably a family heirloom. She saw her chance to get rich and took it, after the prince and his wife were murdered. As for you—" and he ran his hand down the satiny fall of her golden hair with great tenderness, "—it seems she was soft-hearted enough to spare an innocent babe, thank God!"

Suddenly Zofia began to stir behind them, and the couple turned to watch her come round.

"Perhaps the story would come better from someone who knows the whole truth," Damien suggested, as Zofia opened her eyes and gingerly touched the great bruise darkening on her forehead. "Why don't you tell us now, Zofia, about the jewel and who was murdered almost eighteen years ago in the wilds of Georgia?"

Having heard snatches of their conversation, the maid knew it was fruitless to feign ignorance. With dark eyes smoldering, she hissed, "Yes! I took the jewel from her neck as she died. The beautiful Ekaterina, and her handsome prince!" Her lip curled with loathing at the memory. "They were so happy, two fools in love! But for that she destroyed Vasili. I knew the moment I laid eyes on that woman that she would only hurt him!"

"But Zofia," April put in curiously, "why would you care whether the count was hurt or not?"

"Because," she snapped, "family looks out for itself!"

The young woman gasped. Damien was not so surprised. He had noted before the slight resemblance between the maid and her master, and it explained why Ivanov had always failed to chastise her properly in her servant role.

"You are brother and sister?" April guessed.

Zofia grunted a yes. "My half on the wrong side of the blanket. We had different mothers. So he is a count, and I am nothing!"

Feeling sorry for the woman now, April prompted gently, "But you don't seem to resent him. After all, you stay and work here of free will, don't you?"

With a sigh, pressing her hand to her aching temple, Zofia said, "He was always kind to me growing up. I am five years younger and he would not let anyone be cruel to me. I think he knew all along who I was, too, and how we were related. It has never been spoken between us, but I am sure Vasili knows. Over time I came to see what a good man he is. That is why, when he fell in love with Katya, I tried to warn him. She did not understand the kind of man he is, or what he needs."

Damien glanced at his wife. She was entranced, kneeling by the maid's side. Her nods and pats on the woman's shoulder kept Zofia going.

"So," the maid continued in a shuddering breath, "when in spite of all his begging and pleading, Katya left him for Prince Andrei, I went to Vasili and told him he was better off. But he would not be consoled. He raged and wept for days, weeks, thinking of her wed to the prince. And after nearly a year passed I thought he must be over it, but then I overheard him and Pavel discussing their—plan."

Damien supplied grimly, "To waylay the couple somewhere and murder them?"

Zofia nodded. "I was horrified . . . at first. Then I remembered how ungrateful Katya had been when she was here, how vain and selfish. She never thought of Vasili. She only wanted to escape him. It was for her own good that he kept her in the Gold Room, until the prince found out and came with his soldiers to rescue her." She clenched her fists in righteous indignation for her half-brother. "The count was the better man! He would have given her everything. As it was, all she got from young Andrei was a ticket to her grave!"

Zofia went on to explain how she had posed as a servant in the Petrovna's retinue in order to help the count exact his bloody vengeance. "It was just before the trip south that their first child, Natasha, was born," she said, with a meaningful glance at April. "I rode behind the others in the caravan, and when I knew the attack was coming in the next pass, I left on an excuse to relieve myself in the woods. Then I waited while the travelers were attacked and killed. After the robbers left, I hurried to the overturned coach. I heard nothing but the squalling of a babe." She did not seem to notice how white April had become. "I tugged open the door and climbed inside. Anything of value was gone. It was necessary to make it seem the work of thieves." Zofia swallowed hard and went on. "The prince was dead and Katya seemed to be. They were both covered in blood. But she still clutched the screaming baby. I looked for the diamond, but I knew Katya did not keep it with her other jewelry, which was already gone anyway. Then I saw the baby was clutching something sparkling in its little hand. Before she died, Katya had put it around her daughter's neck."

"I heard someone coming back to the scene. So I took the baby and ran. I was afraid that whoever was coming might find me by following the child's cries, so I left the baby in the snow and intended to come back and get the jewel when God had done his work. But when I went back later, the baby and the diamond were both gone!"

"Where is the diamond now, Zofia?" April asked.

"In a safe place. And I intend to keep it!"

April exchanged a frustrated glance with Damien, and then the lovely young woman rose and brushed off her skirts.

"Zofia, if you cannot give me back my jewel, then at least help us get out of here alive. You know Count Ivanov better than anyone. And you know he is capable of murder. I don't know when he will be coming back upstairs to check on me. We need to be gone by then!"

"It could be days or weeks," Zofia told them. "He left Katya up here for an entire month once, just sending up meals and gowns to keep her amused. She put them away and refused to wear them. She was as ungrateful as ever. If Vasili had only listened to me there would not have been such trouble!"

"You would not have left Samarin House in such a hurry if you did not have the jewel on your person," Damien said.

Zofia stopped sniffling and stiffened, confirming his words. April knew her husband was prepared to take a direct approach and perhaps search the woman, but she stilled him with a quick hand on his arm.

"Wait," April said, and crossed the room to the vanity where she had thrown the emerald choker earlier after clawing it off her neck. Picking up the heavy necklace, she returned to show it to Zofia. The servant recognized the piece instantly.

"That is the Ivanov family heirloom. By tradition it goes to the bride of the eldest son."

"But you, Zofia, are an Ivanov too," April said. "You have as much right to this necklace as anyone else now. The count has not married and I will not wear it again willingly. What would you say to exchanging our prizes? After all, the diamond is all I have left of my heritage, and these emeralds are all you have of yours."

Damien admired his wife's quick thinking. As Zofia stared fascinated at the firelight winking off of the costly stones, he added, "Emeralds are more valuable than diamonds anyway. And the necklace could be easily broken up and sold a stone at a time as you need the money. Hadn't you ever considered how difficult it would be to find a buyer for a diamond so large? Most jewelers would shy away from something obviously gotten by ill-means."

It was soon apparent that Zofia had not thought that far ahead. Without further ado, she reached down and promptly pulled off one of her ankle-high winter boots. The gem had been rolled in layers of soft hide to cushion her sole.

But she did not surrender it immediately. She demanded that April give her the necklace first, and once that was safely clasped around her own neck and hidden beneath her overcoat, only then did she grudgingly unwrap and hand over the jewel.

Taking it with new reverence, April gazed for a moment down into the icy fires of the diamond. In the firelight it threw off a rainbow of colors, the perfectly cut facets scattering tiny pinpoints of light across the ceiling.

"Put it somewhere safe," Damien advised her. He could see the conflict playing across April's features, and he knew she had not fully accepted her heritage yet. With a shivery little breath, she extended it to him instead.

"Please," she said. "I—I want you to keep it safe."

Her complete trust after all that had occurred moved him deeply. Nodding, Damien accepted the stone and tucked it carefully in an inside pocket of his coat. "We'd best be leaving now," he announced. "I don't care to find out what will happen should Ivanov find me up here."

Zofia unconsciously touched her own neck where the weight of the emeralds lay. "I can't go with you. My place is here. If you don't betray me to Vasili, I will tell him nothing. It is best that you, like Katya, disappear forever from his life. He would have been furious had he known I had taken the jewel. Anything of Katya's was precious to him. After you go, I will tell him that you stole the emerald necklace too. He will be angry . . . but not at me."

April agreed. She said gently, "I know your life must have been a hard one, Zofia. I'm sorry you had so much unhappiness. You deserve the necklace, though I don't know if I can ever forgive you for playing a part in my parent's deaths. But I won't betray you. You spared my own life once and only because of that small mercy am I alive now."

For the first time, they saw genuine tears sparkling in the woman's eyes. Suddenly, Zofia looked very old and tired.

"Go," she said gruffly, to mask her emotions.

"The sooner you are gone from here, the better." She made no move to get up from the floor. "I will tell Vasili you attacked me and escaped." She pointed to the large bruise on her forehead. "I don't think he will doubt *this*. Now go!"

Nineteen

April took only enough time to don horsehair petticoats under the blue velvet gown, and a heavy wool coat and snow boots. Together she and Damien edged to the door of the Gold Room and peered out into the dark hall. The coast was clear.

Motioning April out first, Damien followed closely on her heels, directing her back to the servant's stairs that he and Zofia had used earlier. But before they could slip out unseen, a macabre chuckle echoed across the wide hall.

"Pavel!" April exclaimed, an involuntary cry of horror remembering how he had locked her in the cellar earlier.

Damien turned and saw a shadow headed for the stairs. Instinct told him the dwarf was running to warn his master.

"I have to stop him. You keep going!" he told April.

She shook her head. "Not without you!" There was no time to waste on arguing. Grabbing her by the wrist, Damien sprinted for the stairs. They had three landings in which to catch Pavel before the little villain reached Ivanov.

To Damien's relief, April could keep up, having removed the cumbersome hoops from beneath her dress sometime earlier. Just ahead he could make out the dwarf jumping stairs two at a time in his haste to escape them. Already Pavel regretted giving himself away, but it had been just too delicious to see the stark fear in the girl's eyes when she realized he was there. The surge of power it had given him was incredible. Pavel felt as if he could do anything. Now he outsprinted a full-grown man who was in excellent shape!

Only one floor to go! Pavel heard the desperate gasps of the couple behind him and it gave him a spurt of over-confidence, so that he leapt in a brash effort to take three stairs rather than two.

But he had forgotten one critical thing. The harlequin costume—of which Pavel was so proud—was sewn in a single piece. Thus his feet were also encased in the material. And without shoes on the highly polished stairs, he was bound to meet with disaster.

One moment after he hurled a vicious laugh up at the pair who followed at a more careful pace, he tumbled head over heels down the last flight, striking his knobby head with a sickening crack upon the last stair. His scream echoed through Samarin House, and Damien and April halted uncertainly on the lower landing. Below them, Pavel lay sprawled like a clown doll broken in a child's temper tantrum.

There was no time to run back upstairs. The awful death screech brought Count Ivanov running from his study, where he looked from the unmoving dwarf to the couple who clutched each other now.

"So," Vasili said with chill dignity, glaring furiously at them. "It is not enough that you steal my bride-to-be, Petrovna, but you also murder my servants in cold blood! Do you think your title will protect you even now? I vow that it shall not!"

"Hear me out, Ivanov!" Damien shot back as he thrust April bodily behind him for protection. "We've both had enough of your sordid games in this house. Enough is enough! I know you arranged for the murder of Prince Andrei and his wife Ekaterina seventeen years ago. It will not save you to plead insanity. Let us by peacefully and we shall be quickly gone from here. But I will not let you molest my wife any further!"

"Wife!" Ivanov shrieked, as if he had picked out only that much from all that Damien had said. "Is it true, Katya? Did you wed the prince?"

April pressed her face against the collar of Damien's coat. Only her large green eyes showed over his shoulder, huge with consternation and fear. She knew how pointless it was to try to reason with the count, so she merely nodded and confirmed the man's irrational outrage.

"Betrayal!" Ivanov's features twisted with rage, and he screamed the word at them like a curse. "But you will not take my fiancée without a fair fight, Andrei! I shall take you down where you stand if you do not give me one last chance for honor!"

When Vasili reached into his smoking jacket to remove what appeared to be a cigar case, Damien tensed. The earl had seen such paraphernalia before. Inside the cleverly designed case, he knew, was a small but very effective pistol.

"Get down!" he ordered April, and when she obediently sank down on the stairs, Damien began to step slowly toward Ivanov, suddenly speaking very congenially to the count.

"You are right, of course. Honor dictates a fair course of action at this point. But what do you propose?"

Ivanov hesitated in opening the case and gave Damien a cold smile. It seemed he had been hoping for just such a chance. "I have been called old-fashioned by some, and by you in particular, Petrovna. But I have the blood of a dozen czars flowing in my veins, and they cry out for vengeance now. While I could shoot you down—and I see by your eyes that you know what I hold in my hand here—I am prone to be nostalgic, and also, you might say, gallant. The nobility has settled scores for centuries by a very effective means."

"You speak of the duel, naturally." Damien refused to let Ivanov intimidate him. "I understand it is outlawed in every modern country now."

"Country?" Ivanov laughed. "You speak as if someone rules Samarin House besides me, which is certainly not the case! Here I make the law, and I decide what is permitted. And you know as well as I that duels continue to happen behind many closed doors among the *boyar*."

The same was true in England and France, though laws had been in effect for years to try to halt such practices. Conceding the fact, Damien noted, "However, the weather would seem to negate the attempt this evening. And I doubt you wish your—humiliation—to become public knowledge."

Ivanov's brows furrowed darkly at that. He gritted out, "I am not speaking of duelling with pistols, which would not be appropriate in any case. No, I challenge you this night to a far more amusing sport—fencing."

Damien arched an eyebrow back at the count. "Indoors?"

"Why not? I have several antechambers which will serve. But you understand, this is not merely for satisfaction. It is for honor, and shall be to the death."

"No!" April's cry rang out behind them. She would not allow such madness to take place, for what could Damien possibly know of sword-fighting? She had seen the outcome on occasion when the gypsies had strayed across a body run through and left to rot where it fell. The crazy ideas men had about honor made her furious!

But both of them ignored her protests. Ivanov put his case away and shrugged out of his silk jacket, setting it carefully aside on the banister. "You will follow me," he said almost cordially to the man who still appeared in his tortured mind to be Prince Andrei. "The ballroom, though unused these many years, has the best floor and the space necessary."

Ivanov began to roll up his shirtsleeves, and after stepping over the small body of the dwarf at the bottom of the stairs, Damien removed his coat and did likewise.

Suddenly April flew down the stairs beside him. "How can you be such a fool? It was bad enough with Nicky, and your arm is still sore from that! You know nothing of a duel!"

"On the contrary, little girl," Damien returned with a regretful smile, "I know more than I should like about fencing."

"What do you mean? Why are you looking at me so strangely?"

Damien waited for another moment until the count was out of range. Ivanov walked away and was not listening to them in any case, wholly concentrating instead upon murdering his old enemy and the satisfaction it would bring him.

Finally Damien said, "Now is not the time or place, April, but if worse comes to worse, you will need to know that I, too, am not entirely who I seem to be."

She gazed up at him, puzzled. "I already know you aren't Romany. You said you had turned your back on the *gaje* world. Is that what you're trying to tell me?"

"Yes and no," he continued in a low voice. "Listen to me and don't interrupt. If I am killed, you shall need to find refuge. Whatever it takes, you must make your way to the north of France. Go to Chateau de Villette—"

"Where?" April cried, stalling him with a frantic hand before he could turn to follow Vasili who had thrown open the great double-doors to the ballroom.

"Just ask anywhere. It is well-known. You must go to my mother, Marcelle Cross, the Countess of—"

"Mother? You told me your mother was dead!"

"I lied." Damien spoke curtly, adding, "Time is so short, *ma chere!* Don't keep cutting me off. I hate for it to come out like this, but my full name is Damien Cross. It also so happens that I am the Earl of Devonshire. It is a long story how I came to be here. But listen, my love. Get to France. Marcelle will take you in. Tell her you are my wife—"

The stunned look on April's face pained Damien, but he was forced to go on. "—and if the worst happens, tell her I died in battle. Not a word of the truth, do you hear? She must never question your right to Mistgrove." For a moment his blue eyes visibly softened at the memory of his English home. "You need not lie, April, in telling her that you are of royal Russian descent. She will take care of you, I promise."

"But . . . why?" April drew away and her voice, though a whisper, carried volumes of reproach. "Why did you marry me then, Damien? You could have had any woman you wanted!"

"I discovered that I wanted you," he said gently, looking more handsome than ever she remembered as he gazed tenderly down into her upturned face. "I will explain it all to you . . . soon. You must trust me once more, little girl. Trust me now as you never have before. I have told lies, but it was never a lie that I love you."

Her lips began to tremble and he could not read beyond the anguish in her beautiful green eyes. Would April desert him now? Because even if she did, he would still fight to the death for her, and without regret. Suddenly, not knowing if these last moments they shared were their last, Damien took her by the shoulders and kissed her fiercely and desperately.

"Remember," he said as they parted, and she shook with devastated sobs, "Chateau de Villette! You are the Countess of Devonshire now and have rights to all my holdings. You will be provided for . . ."

"Petrovna!" Count Ivanov interrupted with a tense and angry shout. "You have accepted the challenge and now must pay the price!"

The count stood in the center of the ballroom holding two sabers and extending one to Damien. "I assure you they are perfectly matched. They once belonged to Czar Ivan himself!"

"Which Ivan?" Damien asked as he strode over to accept the weapon, and tested it with a few slashing movements through the air. It was well-balanced and deadly sharp, and he was not surprised when Ivanov laughed and said, "Ivan the Terrible, of course! He had a lust for fine weapons as he did for the deaths of his enemies. And I hope that you lust for Death as well, Petrovna, for you are about to taste from His cup!"

There was no warning when the count suddenly spun around on the smooth floor and lunged for Damien. April cried out, but Ivanov's running attack was effectively countered when the earl parried with a quick block that caused both blades to ring with a metallic clash.

Then, with artistic savagery that surprised both April and his opponent, Damien began a riposte that set Ivanov back in a desperate scramble for defense.

In the French Legion Damien had excelled at swordplay, and had even taught several classes at the *salle d'armes* in Rocroi. He felt a fierce satisfaction in being able to display his skills now, and he tested Ivanov's abilities as he had once done that of his students.

As Damien had suspected, the count was not unschooled, either. But Ivanov's style was more Italian, straightforward and full of bravado. He lacked the feline finesse of the younger man.

April soon saw that the two men merely toyed with each other. They each pressed wild attacks only to subside to a more controlled pace as the minutes wore on. Damien had initially been the defender, but a quick turnabout occurred with his successful parry and now a series of clever feints occurred that clearly enraged Ivanov and made him more reckless than ever. When he found himself driven further back and almost pressed to the left wall, Vasili abruptly resorted to a stop-thrust that finally caught Damien off-guard.

Now it was the count's turn to grin wickedly as he brutally drove the other man back with wide slashes of his saber. Sweat poured off both men, and Damien's old injury was beginning to ache. Still, he could sense Ivanov weakening, and he let the older men vent his last bursts of adrenalin on a final savage flurry.

Pride drove the count to attempt anything. In the fantasy of his mind, he was scoring brilliantly over a desperate young prince, while

Katya watched and cheered him on. Torn by the bloodlust and the vengeance in his soul, Ivanov began to lose control. His lunges became wild, undisciplined, and his saber hissed through the air like a furious serpent.

April watched in mute horror as Damien was driven back toward the great windows that revealed a snow-covered landscape bathed by the glow of an icy moon. The few lamps which Ivanov had lit for the duel cast an orange glow onto his murderous expression. He no longer reasoned, but fought only to kill. As he continued whipping his saber wildly from side to side, it suddenly snagged high in one of the red velvet curtains roped off beside the window.

With an enraged cry, Ivanov yanked it free again, but Damien seized the opportunity to assume a more favorable stance and moved farther from the count's reach. A final series of flurries between the two men occurred as both marshalled the last of their strength. Damien took a thin cut across one shoulder, laying open his shirt to reveal a bright line of bloody beads. Ivanov dropped to one knee when the earl scored a hit and flayed the skin open there.

Before the count could gain his feet, Damien sent his opponent's saber skittering across the room with a clatter of steel. Only then did he glance over to see April had left, once she was assured of his victory. Too exhausted to pursue her, he looked down at the man at his feet.

Ivanov collapsed groaning onto his side. The

wind had been knocked out of him, and the duel had taken its toll. Damien saw the count for what he really was, a broken old man still living in the past and facing an empty future. As empty as his own. With a frustrated sound, he tossed his own weapon aside.

Outside in the bitter night, April paused to gaze back for a second at the lights still burning in Samarin House. Something deep in her soul cried to remain, to try and accept Damien's explanation of deceit, but her Romany pride surfaced when she remembered how he had used her. Never again would she trust a *gajo*, nor would she attempt to enter a world in which she did not belong.

Prince Adar whickered a soft welcome and April turned to him for comfort. Burying her face in the horse's silky mane, she whispered, "Home, Adar. Take me home. There is no other place for me now . . . you and Tzigane are the only real family I have ever had."

Somehow in her dazed state she managed to mount the stallion and steer him south. After that, everything seemed a blur. But no matter how fast she rode, or how far, April could not leave her memories behind.

April lost all concept of time during her long journey. Somehow, by keeping off the main roads and resorting to her wits in order to find food and shelter, she avoided being accosted by anyone. Later she would look back and realize how lucky she had been. But she was thankful enough when she found her people again, camped outside Constantinople in their usual winter haven.

As April rode toward the gypsy camp, her eyes instinctively sought for Tzigane's brightly-colored wagon. A slow feeling of panic began to surface when she could not locate it. The spot which Tzigane had always favored, underneath some sheltering trees, was alarmingly bare.

Adar began to whicker, scenting the mares hobbled nearby. April slid down from his back, pausing to tie the stallion to a stout young tree. She continued toward the camp, occasionally tripping over the soiled and torn hem of the blue velvet gown. She could not see anything beyond the ominously empty space beneath the distant clump of trees.

Then a familiar voice startled her from her daze.

"April! What are you doing here?"

She looked up into the wide eyes of her old friend, Petalo. His boyish face mirrored concern and surprise, and something else she did not want to see.

"Tzigane," she whispered. Her green eyes began to glaze with bright tears.

Petalo was silent a moment. He cast a quick, furtive look over his shoulder. "On the journey here," he rasped, "she got very sick. There was nothing anyone could do."

When April let out a soft cry and started to move toward the camp, he reached out and restrained her. "No, April, you must not be seen. Nicabar is still furious over the loss of you and the horse. And with Jingo gone to the city today, there would be nobody to protect you from him."

She shook off his grasp. Her voice surfaced at last, proud and determined. "I belong here!"

"You belong with your husband," Petalo corrected her gently. "Where is he?"

"Dead." She lied quickly and easily, avoiding her friend's knowing dark eyes. "So I came back to my people."

"Don't be foolish. You can never take Tzigane's place, and you will only stir up bad feelings in the camp." Petalo informed her of the facts sorrowfully, and though she did not want to hear it, April knew he was right.

"Tzigane's wagon and all her possessions were burned and buried with her," Petalo continued. "But at her last wish, the money she had was set aside for you. It is strange, is it not, that she gave it to me for safekeeping?" He paused for a moment, watching April's shoulders shake with silent sobs. "I have it hidden safely away. Stay here and I will get it for you."

April could not have moved if she wanted to. She sank down in the lush grass, quietly

372

keening for the loss of the only mother she had ever known. A moment later she pummelled her fists on the ground in helpless rage, feeling the bitterness of betrayal yet again. Tzigane had left her! Why now? How could she? Now April was truly, terribly alone, with nowhere to turn.

When April raised her tear-streaked face a short time later, Petalo was gazing down at her with pity. In his hand he extended a leather pouch clinking softly with gold coins.

"Tzigane said your destiny lay over the water," he told her softly. "I think she wanted you to use this money to get there."

The coincidence seemed too incredible to believe, yet as April took the surprisingly heavy bag, she accepted once and for all that fate did indeed deal out some unexpected cards. She nodded with new resolve. "Thank you, my friend. I think I understand what I must do now."

Petalo helped her up, regret in his dark eyes. "I wish things had been different, April."

"So do I," she murmured sadly. "So do I."

Twenty

"Ciel!" Marcelle Cross gave the train of the black taffeta gown an angry shake and critically studied her reflection in the pier glass once again. "I do not believe the new court style flatters me, Henriette! What do you think?"

The younger woman had barely opened her mouth to speak when there came a sharp rap at the bedchamber door.

Guy Fontblaine's droll voice came through the wood. "Madame, there is a person asking to see you downstairs."

"Send them away!" Marcelle did not hesitate and quickly returned her attention to her gown. "Do you think my pearls would improve it, Henriette?"

After a brief silence the knock came again, louder this time. "Madame, this—this person is really quite insistent. She will speak only to you and refuses to leave until she has satisfaction."

"Mon Dieu! Of all times, why now? We

must be at Fountainebleau within three hours! No doubt some peasant is peddling her wares." She gave her sleek black chignon a final pat as she turned to Henriette. "I suppose I must deal with it before we go. Would you prefer to wait here?"

"Au contraire," Henriette Dupre purred, rising from the velvet divan. She was a strikingly lovely, raven-haired woman with flashing dark eyes. Her voice was low and throaty. "Perhaps she has something of interest to sell me."

"Very well." Marcelle led the way to the polished mahogany staircase, gliding gracefully down with her black skirts flowing a full length behind. She dismissed the perplexed steward and moved to confront the young woman at Chateau de Villette's entrance.

Marcelle gazed in surprise at the wraith-like vision standing there, wrapped in a cloak of good quality. The young woman would have been beautiful, except she looked deathly ill, her green eyes huge against the pale oval of her face.

"Madame Cross?"

The question was barely more than a whisper. Puzzled, Marcelle nodded. *"Oui.* What do you want?"

Her affirmative answer caused the young woman's shoulders to sag in relief. *"Merci Dieu!* I have found you!" she murmured, more to herself than the countess.

Henriette Dupre moved forward from the

shadows. "What can the bold creature want? Send her away! She looks half-dead and may have the pox!"

But Marcelle was more inclined to be curious. "Speak up, child. Who are you?"

Tears began to streak the wax-white cheeks of the young woman in the doorway. *"Bonjour,"* she whispered, taking a single, trembling step forward. "I am April Cross."

And she promptly fainted at Marcelle's feet.

The voices in the parlor were hushed, only one of which rose occasionally on an anxious note.

"Of course she's lying!" Henriette hissed, leaning toward the countess with her dark eyes narrowed. "The chit cannot possibly be Damien's wife! Where is her wedding ring, and a copy of the banns?"

"She said her trunks were lost on the journey," Marcelle repeated patiently. "And I know from personal experience it is commonplace enough."

Reminded of the deathly-pale young woman lying upstairs, the countess felt another pang of pity. When April had recovered sufficiently to be questioned, she had relayed enough knowledge of Damien to ease Marcelle's mind. There was no doubt the girl had known Damien quite well, but Henriette kept casting suspicions on the notion of any marriage.

"And the ring, Madame?" Henriette persisted. "Was she also set upon by brigands, as well?"

"There was no time for a formal ceremony, with the war and all," Marcelle answered curtly, disliking the challenge in the other woman's voice. She had invited Henriette to spend the weekend at the chateau out of respect for her son, but now she was beginning to regret it. Though she came from a fine family, Henriette's manners had always been coarse.

"The family doctor examined April, and said she was merely stressed from the long journey," Marcelle continued. "I had Guy check her story out, and it is true that she did arrive upon the *Eastern Star* from Constantinople. There is little reason she would lie about the rest, Henriette."

Damien's former mistress rose to agitatedly pace the elegant parlor. *"C'est impossible!* You know as well as I that your son refuses to marry. And I doubt he would choose such a creature if ever he did!"

"April is quite lovely, as well you know, Henriette. And as for Damien vowing never to wed, men are prone to change their minds. Love strikes quickly, and where it will."

"You are such a romantic, Madame," the younger woman said disparagingly. "I cannot believe you would take a total stranger into your home and accept whatever she chooses to tell you! Mark my words, you will regret it. She is playing you for a fool."

The countess suddenly glanced at the crystal

timepiece upon the fireplace mantel. "Why, my dear, I see that your weekend is over. You should think about returning to town before it grows dark. I shall send Guy for your things." She picked up a silver bell from the table and rang it sharply. Henriette could not possibly miss the hint this time.

"I would advise you to check out the girl's story more thoroughly, Madame," Henriette said just before she left. "She claims she is descended from Russian royalty. That would be easy enough to disprove!"

"I have no doubts," Marcelle replied coolly. "I shall leave the fretting to you, my dear. *Au revior.*"

Henriette departed angrily, following the steward out to the waiting coach. Before she embarked, she glanced up at the window to April's room, the same bedchamber Damien used when he was in residence at the chateau. Her eyes narrowing, Henriette murmured, "We shall see, Mademoiselle April, just how blue your blood really is!"

Feeling slightly assuaged, she climbed into the coach and waved to the driver. But her black eyes remained fixed on the upper window until the chateau faded out of sight into the winter dusk.

"C'est magnifique!"

Marcelle clapped her hands in delight like a

little girl, watching April slowly revolve before her in the crinoline gown of golden gauze. The wide skirts were sewn with tiny seed pearls, the bodice low and shaped to fit her wasp-waist. Small embroidered puffed sleeves matched the gold-trimmed train of the gown.

"This one!" Damien's mother told the seamstress, who smilingly nodded and rushed to help April out of the lavish creation. Several hours later, after April had been fitted for dozens more gowns and dressed in a lilac-print day dress, she rejoined Marcelle in the drawing room downstairs.

"Madame, I cannot thank you enough. You have been too kind," April said as she took the hands held out to her.

"Nonsense. I have not had such fun in years! I always dreamed of the day I would be able to dress Damien's bride. It is my good fortune that your trousseau was lost at sea!"

April was silent a moment, feeling guilty over deceiving this wonderful woman. Marcelle Cross had been nothing but supportive and generous since her arrival, and though much of what April had told Damien's mother was the truth, how would the countess react if she knew her daughter-in-law had been raised by gypsies?

Lies had multiplied so quickly when Marcelle had questioned April about her upbringing. The tale that she had been orphaned young and raised by a foster mother seemed to satisfy Lady Cross. But what would April tell the others who had been invited to a chateau ball in her honor tonight? She had tried without success to dissuade Marcelle from the idea, but the countess was proud of her son's wife and wanted no unsavory rumors over April's sudden appearance.

"Wait here, *ma petite,* I have something to give you," Marcelle said, smiling mysteriously as she moved to the sideboard where her fine china was displayed. From behind one of the plates she produced a tiny foil-wrapped box, and presented it to April with a fond kiss on the cheek.

The younger woman untied the silk ribbons and opened the box. A simple gold wedding band glimmered up at April through her suddenly moist eyes.

"It was my mother's," Marcelle explained. "She was a staunch old matron in her later years, but when she was young she was quite a romantic. And her marriage with Andre de Villette was a love match. I know she would be happy to see you wear this tonight."

The thoughtfulness of the gesture warmed April to the core. She embraced Marcelle, constantly amazed at the tiny Frenchwoman's insight. Much of Damien's sensitivity could be attributed to Lady Cross, April decided, and it was easy to love them both. But she reminded herself of Damien's deceit, and that she had come here only out of desperation. She wanted nothing from him or his family, and soon she must surrender her dreams of belonging here and leave to find a new life of her own.

April openly wiped away the tears from her cheeks as the two women went upstairs together to dress for the fête. Marcelle thought it was only because April was so moved by the gift that she cried. She had no idea that her son's wife had also learned from the family doctor on his last visit that in less than seven months she, too, would be a mother.

Henriette Dupre watched spitefully as the young woman calling herself April Cross charmed the countess's friends and guests that evening. Wearing the gown of golden gauze, April moved like a fairy princess through the crowd, her crown of pale hair sparkling with diamond dust. She had the men bowing and the women simpering, and Henriette was even more convinced that the girl was nothing but a talented imposter.

Henriette's father, Henri Dupre, soon moved up beside her and noted where his daughter's malignant gaze lay.

"Ah, the young Lady Cross. Destined to be rich as well as beautiful. As long as Marcelle continues to believe her tale."

"What did you find out?" Henriette hissed under her breath, in no mood to be reminded of April's loveliness.

Her portly sire only smiled for a long moment, as a couple paused within listening range and then moved on. Like his daughter, Henri Dupre had long aspired to be the relative of an earl. This latest turn of events was quite unsettling as it directly affected his own future. Drawing a scented handkerchief from his pocket, he mopped his sweaty brow and murmured, "You were right, *ma doux*. The girl is merely an excellent actress. There was indeed a young prince by the name of Petrovna, but he and his bride were killed many years ago. They were childless."

Henriette's red lips curved upward in a tight smile of satisfaction. It had been worth waiting a month for the information to arrive from her father's Russian connections! Her dark eyes glittering with malice, she murmured, "Now for the right moment to expose her!"

Henriette had, of course, every intention of letting the entire crowd absorb the impact of what she had learned. Tingling with anticipation, she moved forward to intercept Marcelle.

"Madame, I have an announcement to make to your guests."

The countess was not pleased, especially since Henriette had not been invited to her fête. "Not now, my dear. It is time for the dancing to begin." Marcelle motioned for the doors to the ballroom to be opened, and the guests began to stream away through the doors.

Seeing her audience slipping away, Henriette looked desperately about for her father. Instead, she spotted April moving discreetly into the ladies' toilette room. Seizing her chance, she moved quickly. She found April alone in the room, doubled over with an arm across her waist.

"*S'il vous plait,* mademoiselle, would you help me to loosen my laces?" April begged her, and took deep gulps of air when Henriette grudgingly complied. The color flooded back into April's face, rendering her even more beautiful. Henriette felt a rush of jealousy as she stared at the younger woman.

"You don't know who I am, do you?" she purred. "I am Henriette Dupre."

April straightened slowly and met the burning black gaze of the lovely Frenchwoman in the jade-green silk gown. She realized she had seen the woman before, but she could not remember where. Then Henriette's husky laugh stirred up unpleasant memories for her.

"That's right, I was the one who told Lady Cross to throw you out when you came crying at her door!" Henriette hissed. "And had she any wits about her, she should have! For I know what you are, and once she learns it too, you will be tossed out on your laurels!"

"I don't know what you mean," April whispered.

"Indeed? Shall we go together and explain to her how the Petrovna family died? *Oui,* girl, don't look so shocked. It is not important how

I learned the truth. It is enough that I can and will expose you for the liar you are!"

"Why?" April asked, feeling the hostility emanating from the other woman in waves. "Why do you care?"

Henriette laughed incredulously. "Can you be as innocent as you pretend? Not if you knew Damien, and I don't doubt that you did. For, you see, Lord Cross has a great appetite for beautiful women. In any court!"

April felt as if she would be violently ill. She understood at last who—and what—Henriette Dupre was. And she was horrified to realize even Damien's mother apparently accepted Henriette's presence with ease.

"I congratulate you on your cleverness," Henriette went on, "but I won't see Damien robbed blind by a scheming chit. If you leave at once, I might not betray your secret. But I have little sympathy for a lightskirt who would try to pass off her bastard as an earl's son!"

April gasped. How did Henriette know she was with child? As if reading her mind, the courtesan smiled archly at her.

"A tiny waist thickens quickly when one is *enceinte*," Henriette said. "When I loosened your ties I could not miss the fact. And Guy mentioned you no longer ride the magnificent black stallion you brought with you. I hope you will not be so foolish as to try and make anyone believe it is Damien's child you carry!"

April did not answer. She sought desperately

for a way out. Henriette's appearance was shocking enough in itself, but the woman threatened to destroy her and any future her innocent child might have.

"You need not worry," she told the woman at last in a low voice, "I will be leaving soon."

"Bien!" Henriette echoed with satisfaction. "Take your bastard and go. You are not wanted here!"

April turned and rushed out of the room, trying to lose herself in the crowd. Her head was ringing with all she had learned, and she could think of nothing but Damien lying in that other woman's arms. She had always planned to leave eventually, but now it seemed she had no choice. It must be soon, before Marcelle guessed what Henriette Dupre already had. April felt her heart sink when the countess spotted her across the room and hurried over.

"Ciel! I have been looking everywhere for you," Marcelle scolded her lovingly. "The orchestra is here. The Emperor has just arrived and wishes the honor of the first dance with you."

There was no polite way for April to refuse. She forced a bright smile and executed a deep curtsey when presented to Louis Napoleon III and the Empress Eugenie. She masked her surprise upon finding the emperor to be half-ahead shorter than herself. He was not a handsome man, either, with a high forehead and thinning hair, a bushy moustache and unkempt beard. His dancing ability was his only impressive talent. April found he could waltz as if born to it, and she enjoyed the brief time they shared on the floor.

A short time later she escaped the fête with the plea of a headache, and Marcelle dotingly agreed that she might retire early. April escaped to her room, where she quickly packed and then wondered where she might flee. Suddenly she recalled several conversations she had shared with Guy Fontblaine upon her arrival. The steward had gone out riding with her, before she had learned she was with child and ceased any risky activities.

Guy had mentioned a remote estate in Devon, which had been shut down upon the earl's departure. The way he had described it, isolated and on the edge of the sea, had instantly appealed to April's need to escape. There would be no servants to question her arrival, no neighbors to invite themselves over. And it was also quite unlikely she would ever be found there, by Henriette or anyone else.

April paused in thought to run a hand over the velvet bedspread she sat on. It had been difficult to sleep in the bed she knew Damien occupied when he was here, harder still to force him from her thoughts whenever she saw his likeness in Lady Cross. But though time had dulled the pain of his betrayal, she knew she could never forgive him for it, and now the fact of Henriette Dupre only made her more resolved never to trust a man again.

April rose and walked to the window. The view of gently rolling green hills was dazzling in daylight, and softened now by the veil of moonlight cast over the land. She placed a hand across her lower stomach and felt the light flutter there, like butterflies in a jar. Soon it would be too awkward and dangerous for her to travel. She must leave now, before Henriette betrayed her or Marcelle refused to let her go because of the child.

April tried to imagine what Lady Cross's reaction would be when she found the empty bedchamber in the morning. Would Marcelle be hurt, angry, relieved? April realized she would never know. She laid her cheek against the windowpane and felt her hot tears frosting to the glass.

Twenty-one

Damien hesitated slightly before he stepped down from the open landau. Something was very wrong at de Villette. The windows were shuttered and the chateau dark, as if it had been closed up for the season. Which was extremely unlikely just before winter.

He frowned as he walked up the path, noting the unkempt gardens and empty stables. It was not like his mother to let anything go unattended, even in her absence. Damien had been gone almost two years, but it was not such a span of time that he expected any glaring changes. He felt a prickle of foreboding, wondering if something terrible had happened. The door knocker echoed through the empty chateau several times, and he found the door securely locked.

Immediately returning to the waiting coach, Damien gave brisk directions to the Dupre residence. Henriette would know what had happened to Lady Cross. The earl sat back against the cushions, trying not to let his imagination get the best of him. It was possible Marcelle had simply gone abroad for awhile. He found himself tapping his fingers impatiently on the armrest. He simply was not in the mood for any guessing games after returning from the war.

It had been trial enough to learn of the slaughter of the Light Brigade after his return to the field quarters from Moscow. If it hadn't been for his old unit, a French division of the Chasseurs d'Afrique, the loss in the North Valley would have been even greater.

The war was over now, and a temporary truce signed, but the wounds would remain forever, especially the loss of Lord Raglan, who had passed away in the spring. Damien smiled a little sadly, recalling his old friend's last words to him. James had thanked him for the covert information he had obtained, and assured the younger man that it had made a great difference in their tactics against the czar. Damien doubted it, but he had accepted the praise silently, no longer caring about winning a war when the cost was so dear.

Now he gazed broodingly out at the French countryside, wondering if the first skiff of snow had settled on Mistgrove yet. He had planned to visit England first, but realized his mother must be frantic for word of him since the war ended. So Damien had stopped in Normandy first.

Finding the countess gone was both alarming and annoying. Damien knew first-hand how flighty Marcelle could be, but now was not the time he felt like chasing her all across the countryside. He let out a sigh of relief to see that the Dupre mansion in Rouen had several carriages parked out front.

Damien disembarked, paid the driver to wait, and hurried to the front door. He was forced to exchange pleasantries for several minutes with the old boor, Henri Dupre, while his daughter was called down.

Recognizing the handsome earl standing in the hall, Henriette squealed softly and flung herself into Damien's arms. "Is it really you?"

While Monsieur Dupre moved discreetly away, she stepped back for a closer look, failing to notice that Damien's arms had not returned the embrace. She was too busy drinking in his dashing appearance in a black swallow-tailed coat over a white waistcoat. He was as handsome as ever, but there were tiny lines near his eyes she had not seen before, and a smoky cast to his night-dark hair. Damien looked dispirited. Even his blue eyes were weary as he greeted her formally.

"Henriette, you're looking well."

She made a pretty *moue* with her red lips. "Oh, Damien, aren't you even going to kiss me? It has been years since we were together!"

"And if you will recall, the last time we were together was mutually agreed to be the last," Damien replied. "I only came here tonight to find out if you know where Marcelle has gone. If so, please tell me."

With an unhappy sigh, Henriette relented. "She has gone to Paris for the winter. She said she did not want to be all alone at the chateau this year."

"Why not?" Damien frowned. This was indeed a drastic change in Marcelle's behavior. The last time she had refused to be alone at de Villette was right after Edward had died. Was she mistakenly grieving for her son?

"I don't know." Henriette sounded petulant. "Maybe it had something to do with the chit who played such a cruel trick on her last year."

"Chit?" Damien gazed at the dark beauty curiously.

"A girl came to the chateau while I was there, claiming to be your wife. I knew at once she was lying, and I tried to convince the countess as well. She was eager to believe the chit's clever story about you wedding her, though. She took the girl under her wing for a time, until she learned her lesson the hard way."

Damien's hands moved to urgently grip her upper shoulders. "What girl, Henriette? What did she look like?"

"You're hurting me!" she whined, and when his grip slackened, she rubbed her shoulder and muttered, "She called herself *Avril.*"

Henriette used the French word, but Damien

knew at once whom she meant. His blue eyes softened, and he murmured hopefully, "April! My wife was here?"

At the longing in his voice the other woman felt a stab of bitter jealousy. So, he had really wed the chit after all!

Henriette quickly changed her tactics, babbling, "I finally realized she was really your wife, Damien, but by then it was too late. She fled, without so much as a *merci* for all Lady Cross had done for her! And your poor *maman* was so devastated she moved into an *appartement* in Paris. She could not bear the thought of such betrayal."

Damien suspected there was more to the tale than that, but he merely nodded. Why had April come to France? He thought she had gone back to the gypsies after learning of his own betrayal. He had tried to find her in the band camped outside Constantinople, and though Jingo had insisted he knew nothing of April's whereabouts, Damien could tell the gypsy king was lying. The earl assumed they were helping April to hide from him. Now he had to wonder, and he gazed thoughtfully down at Henriette Dupre, not missing the gleam of cold satisfaction in her eyes.

"Where did April go? Do you know?"

"*Non.* Marcelle tried to find her for several weeks, and then gave up. It is just as well, Damien. The girl only came here to take advantage of your good name!"

He brushed her aside as he turned to leave. "I will find her, Henriette," he vowed softly. "If it takes a hundred years, I will find her again!"

The countess moved to extinguish the oil lamp on the desk where Damien had finally fallen into an exhausted sleep while writing more letters. She glanced down at the half-finished parchment pinned under his elbow.

> . . . *and if you should hear word of a young woman fitting such description, or of any lady calling herself April or Lady Cross, please contact me immediately at the following address* . . .

Marcelle smiled sadly, patting her son gently on the head. His soft snores echoed in the den. She knew how many months he had spent writing letters, following up on any leads about April. She herself had felt the same desperation when she had found the girl had taken her stallion and gone. But April had executed her flight with incredible skill, because generous bribes and greased palms had failed to produce any word of her whereabouts.

Marcelle had been hurt at first, but then she listened to her heart instead and understood that April had felt it necessary to leave. She suspected that reason had something to do with Henriette Dupre, because the other woman had not seemed surprised that Damien's wife had suddenly vanished.

And now, too late, Marcelle learned April was truly the love of Damien's life. She felt a mother's sympathy and a sense of helplessness that she could not magically restore her son's wife to his side.

Damien had convinced the countess to move back into the chateau in case April should return there. But Marcelle's womanly intuitions sensed April was long gone, possibly never to return here. She had not shared the feeling with Damien, not wishing to dash his small hopes. But it was spring again, and over a year had passed since April had been at Chateau de Villette.

With a soft sigh, Marcelle moved to look at the portrait of the previous earl hanging above the fireplace. Edward Cross seemed to be gazing sternly down upon his son, and she raised a finger to waggle it up at him.

"This is one time when you shall not have your way, *Edouard!*" she scolded the frowning visage. "I always said Damien should marry for love, and so he has! I only wish you were here to find the girl now for your son."

"Maman?" Damien's head rose with a jolt, and he gazed blearily at the woman across the room. "Is somebody here?"

"Non. Why don't you go up to bed. You fell asleep with the lamp on, which is dangerous."

Damien rose, his shoulders seeming to sag

with a hidden weight. He blundered past Marcelle unseeing, as if he could not bear the pain of reality. She felt something prompt her then, and she called out softly after him, "Why don't you take a little trip? Visit Mistgrove. It has always been your favorite place."

"I haven't the heart for it anymore, *Maman*," Damien muttered as he headed up the stairs.

Marcelle glanced up at the portrait again. Was it her imagination, or did Edward actually seem to be smirking down at her?

"Bah!" she said forcefully as she departed the den after her son. "You'll see, old man! Love always triumphs in the end!"

Damien reined in the prancing, dark bay just above the last rise over the sea. Already he could taste the salty tang in the air, and his skin tingled with anticipation. Home! Marcelle had been right after all. Mistgrove was just the thing to restore his spirits.

He prompted the restless steed beneath him and they galloped down the last stretch of road, sending dark clods churning up behind. Damien felt his coattails flying in the brisk spring breeze and grinned. The English weather was as ungodly as ever, already starting to drizzle as he approached the mansion, but he felt a contentment he hadn't experienced in months.

Damien drew the bay stallion down to a ringing trot across the cobblestones of the drive.

The mansion was dark, but he noted with consternation that the staff had failed to shutter the windows properly when they had left.

The earl dismounted and started to hitch his mount to the iron post. Then a shrill bugle came from newby and his own stallion responded to the blood-curdling squeal with one of his own.

"Bloody hell!" Damien cursed, trying to control the fractious bay. His horse laid back its ears and skittered on the cobbles, wildly trying to free itself in order to answer the challenge that echoed across the misty yard.

Finally, he managed to herd the animal into a nearby stall, bolting it securely. The bay immediately thrust out its head and bugled again, nostrils flaring as it caught the scent of a rival stallion.

Now Damien was able to turn and see the black horse galloping out in the pasture, neck arched proudly, mane and tail flying. He watched Prince Adar pause and paw the wet ground, steam rushing from his distended nostrils, a knowing glint in his wild, dark eyes.

The earl felt a rush of euphoria. "I know just how you feel, boy," he said, and turned toward the house. A light upstairs had just flicked on. April was here! Somehow it made perfect sense, and the months of painful separation and sleepless nights were instantly forgotten.

Damien moved toward the mansion, conscious of being watched from a window above. He mounted the steps with mixed emotions, a sense of foreboding and excitement combining to set him on razor-edge. He hesitated slightly before he entered the mansion. What had prompted April to run away from the chateau and come here?

He was surprised when he stepped into the hall. The downstairs furniture was still covered with protective sheets, and obviously unused. He glanced up the staircase, toward the single light burning up there. She had taken only a small corner for herself, like an animal in hiding.

Slowly Damien began to ascend the staircase. He was only halfway up when the slight figure came barrelling down toward him.

April froze on the landing, her green eyes huge in the dim light. She was dressed in a forest-green velvet riding habit, her blonde hair tumbled loose about her shoulders. Her posture was defensive, as if by virtue of living here in isolation she had again retreated to the wild.

"April." Damien spoke her name softly, like a caress, and saw her shiver with emotion. "Why did you run away from Chateau de Villette, little girl?"

For a moment April could not find words. She could not believe Damien was here, after so long, after she had given up daring to hope or even to dream. She had hidden herself here, totally absorbing her mind and body and secret longings in creating a safe haven. She had not intended to stay at Mistgrove longer than a few months, but she had become a part of it. And Damien threatened to take that away from her now.

Her eyes flashed at him like a cornered cat's. "I thought I could forget you, and the lies you told," she whispered. "But when I went to France, I found I couldn't. Everywhere I turned, there were reminders. Sleeping in your bed, seeing your mother each day, talking to your mistress—"

Damien started to protest, but she shook her head fiercely at him.

"Listen to me! I came here only because I had no choice. I tried to go back to the Lowara, but Tzigane had died and I was no longer welcome. I will never be able to forget that she died alone."

Damien's face reflected sorrow to match her own, and for a second April was thrown off-guard. She did not want to accept the fact that he could care about anyone except himself, and yet his eyes met hers with understanding reflected in the dark blue depths.

April swallowed hard and forced anger into her voice as she finished. "Because my people no longer held their arms open to me, I had nowhere to go, but I remembered what you told me about France. And I thought, why should I suffer anymore? I will make a new life for myself in a new land."

She raised her chin proudly, as if daring him to dispute her decision. To her surprise, Damien only nodded. Her voice dropped to a whisper again. "For over a year I have succeeded in forgetting. I live here alone, bothered by nobody. And now you shatter my world around me like glass."

"No," Damien corrected her gently. "I will take nothing more from you, little girl. I've damned myself a thousand times for hurting you like I did. For using you to try to end a war that would have finished on its own, sooner or later. Desperate men do desperate things, and I had to do something . . . find an end to the madness." His eyes darkened in memory of the horrors he had witnessed, and he shook his head to force the images away. "To that end, I used you. I never intended for it to happen."

"You must have planned it!" April put in desperately.

"No. I never intended to fall in love with you."

She stared at him, feeling the deep words melt into her soul. How she wanted to believe! But she was afraid, so afraid . . .

Damien continued in a husky voice, "I've told you before that I love you. Nothing has changed since then."

April fought her rising emotions, trying not

to let Damien lull her into believing him again. She had opened her heart and soul to him once, and the resulting pain had been almost more than she could bear. Did she dare trust again?

She whispered, "And now, Damien? What happens now?"

"I hoped you would ask that," he said, coming a step up on the stairs and looking intensely at her. "I want you to stay here as my wife. We both have a right to be here, April. This is my home . . . yours too now if you choose. Is it possible for us to begin again?"

"I don't know," she answered him honestly.

Damien nodded with resignation. "Will you at least listen to my reasons for what I did?"

April moistened her lips a little nervously. It would be unfair of her to refuse him that much. She agreed, asking only, "How did you find me at all?"

"Sheer chance. Marcelle suggested I come here for a respite. I don't think she knew you were here, either."

At the mention of his mother her eyes softened slightly. "Is the countess well?"

"Yes, but as anxious as I for word about you. She grew very fond of you in the short time you were at the chateau."

"Others were not so kind as she!"

Damien nodded grimly. "I'm sorry Henriette Dupre hurt you. I knew her a long time ago, and believe it or not, it was over long before you came here. There is nothing between us now, nor will there ever be again." He paused, sensing her anger receding, and then forged on. "We have a lot to discuss, little one, if only you are willing."

He started to move up the stairs and April quickly raised a hand in protest. "Not the bedroom!"

Damien assumed she felt uncomfortable about being in any intimate quarters with him again. He nodded shortly, and waited for her to join him downstairs. They were halfway out the door when a thin, high wail wafted from upstairs.

April froze in indecision, looking quickly to Damien to see if he noticed.

He mused, "Cats?"

She nodded jerkily. But one step more and the cry was unmistakably hungry—and human.

"What the devil!" Damien exclaimed, heading back up the stairs before April could stop him. He burst into the west wing bedchamber, where he saw a crackling fire in the grate and a bassinet beside the canopied bed.

"It's a baby!" he said almost accusingly, swinging to face April with shock on his handsome face. "Where in the world—"

"The servant girl who helps me out just gave birth," April said quickly, moving to intercept him. "Ssh, you'll just upset the baby more."

"It's already fit to be tied," he complained, as the wails grew progressively louder and more insistent. Damien stepped around April and peered down into the bassinet. He chuckled down at the beet-red, miniature human face screwing up for another lusty howl. The baby was no newborn, judging by size, but at least several months old. It already had a full head of curly black curls.

"I declare, that's got to be the ugliest infant I've ever seen!" the earl exclaimed, and the baby's howls rose in volume as if understanding his remark.

"She is not!" April reached into the bassinet and snatched up the child. The little girl quieted to hiccoughs as April cradled her on one shoulder and paced back and forth. "She's really quite pretty when she isn't all red in the face. There, there, love, it's all right." She patted the baby's back and glared at Damien as if daring him to make fun of the infant again.

He threw up his hands in exasperation. "Where's the mother? Can't she look after her own child properly? We need to talk."

"She's gone to town for some things," April muttered evasively. "We'll just have to make do." But as if on cue, the baby began to wail again, louder than ever.

"Oh, for heaven's sake—" Damien began in exasperation, but when he glanced at April again he saw a dark shadow spreading across her velvet bodice. He walked over and incredulously touched the milk-soaked material, and looking closer at her face, saw the tears glistening on her cheeks.

"I take it back," Damien said in a low voice. "She's the most beautiful baby I've ever seen."

Tenderly, he led April to the bed and unbuttoned her bodice so she could feed their child. Embarrassed, she would have looked away, but he turned her chin and placed a warm kiss upon her lips as the baby happily settled in place and began to nurse.

"Why didn't you tell me?" he rasped thickly.

"I didn't know," she murmured, eyes downcast. "I found out after I arrived in France. And . . . Henriette convinced me nobody would believe it was your child. She also threatened to expose me to your mother if I stayed. In my eyes, I had little choice but to leave."

The baby made a snuffling noise and Damien wonderingly extended a finger to stroke the downy hair on her head. "She looks like Marcelle, doesn't she? What did you name her?"

April smiled, tears making her eyes bright green as she gazed at him. "Mistelle. In honor of your mother and this wonderful place."

"You like it here?" Damien was amazed. Every other woman he had brought to Mistgrove had ceaselessly complained about the cold, the damp, the isolation.

"It is the only real home I've known," she said softly, "and this is the one place I knew Misty and I would be safe."

"You were all alone?" Damien mentally berated himself for not thinking of Mistgrove sooner, but she placed a hand consolingly upon his clenched fist.

"No. There's a young girl named Maggie who moved out from town to stay with me. She is sworn to secrecy, and she thinks my plight is terribly romantic." April smiled a little wistfully as she spoke.

"Well, so it is." Damien dropped a quick kiss on the sleeping baby's head, and waited while April placed Misty back in her little bed and buttoned her bodice up again. Then he took his wife by the hand and drew her over to the window. "Let's give your Maggie a happy ending if she's out there watching us."

April shivered as Damien drew her into his arms. She wanted so desperately to forgive him, and to gladly step into the new role awaiting her. But she was still afraid.

"Damien," she whispered, "Henriette knows. Others will find out I'm not who I say I am. And they might hold that against Mistelle, too . . ."

"Then we'll never leave England again. Nobody knows you here. I won't let you go again, April. I can't." Damien spoke fiercely as his mouth moved to claim hers. He pulled her slender body against his own, his hands moving to trace her curves in the velvet riding habit.

April's soft moan echoed Damien's. Her head whirled wildly, feeling the familiar warmth and longing stealing over her languid body. Now she understood what Tzigane had tried to tell her about the love between soul-mates, the ceaseless circle of fate which would bring them together time and time again, no matter the obstacles.

When they parted a moment later, Damien saw the love shining in April's eyes. He understood how deeply hurt she had been by his betrayal of her trust, just as he saw now with a rush of pure joy that she had forgiven him. There was only complete devotion and a genuine desire to build a life together reflected in her beautiful green eyes now.

"I love you, Lady Cross," he said softly, before his lips moved against hers again. A second later an explosive cry came from the bassinet, and April laughingly broke off their passionate kiss. "Your daughter is still hungry, Lord Cross!"

"Nonsense. She's merely jealous!" Nevertheless Damien moved quickly back to the cradle, and grinned down at the wide-eyed baby who fell abruptly silent and looked hopefully up at him. "I have something I think you'll like, Misty."

From his coat pocket Damien withdrew a long golden chain with a familiar gem dangling from the center.

April gasped and moved up beside him. "My diamond!"

"Our daughter's now, if I don't miss my guess," Damien chuckled, watching the baby's chubby hands waving wildly to catch the sparkling prisms of light. "I think she's safely entertained for the next hour or two." He looped it securely to the hood of the bassinet, letting it dangle enticingly just out of Misty's reach.

"Now," Damien murmured, turning to take April in his arms, "I think I should see about entertaining her mother, don't you?"

"Oh, most definitely, my lord."

April sealed the suggestion by raining kisses down Damien's neck, and next she knew, she was high in the air, being swiftly carried to the bed.

The dowager countess disembarked from the shiny coach bearing the Cross coat of arms and promptly let out a small screech. Flying toward her on a great black horse came a young girl, black ringlets bouncing, a sparkle of mischief in her green eyes.

"Grandmere!"

The girl gathered up her steed, bringing it to a sliding stop within inches of the countess on the lush summer lawn. Her young voice was filled with the joy of life and love for the feisty little Frenchwoman glaring up at her.

"Mistelle! Where are your manners? Get off that wild beast at once. What are your parents thinking, to let you ride a stallion?"

In deliberate defiance, the young girl leaned down to stroke the glistening neck of her horse. "Azize is not a wild beast, *Grandmere*. He is my pet, my baby. Isn't that so, Azize?"

The young horse sired by Prince Adar snorted softly as if in agreement, and Marcelle threw up her hands in a dramatic display as she glanced toward the mansion. "Where are your parents?"

Misty's mischievous grin quickly turned to a pout. "It's Jamie's third birthday today, *Grandmere*. Such fuss simply because he is a boy!"

"He is the fifth earl of Devonshire," her grandmother reminded her, and then she smiled in sympathy up at the pretty little girl still astride her horse. "Can you keep a secret, Mistelle?"

The eight-year-old bounced in the saddle with delight. "Oh, you know I can, *Grand-mere!*"

"Bien. I am here to ask your father if you may return to France with me. It is high time you learned how to be a young lady."

Misty let out a soft squeal, slid down from her horse and flung herself into the older woman's arms. *"Oui,* I want to go!"

"Then we shall ask your father." Fondly Marcelle patted the black curls so like her own, and hand-in-hand they went into Mistgrove.

They found Lady Cross and several servants decorating the great ballroom for the children's party to be held later that afternoon. April looked lovely in a soft rose-colored gown, her golden hair twisted into a gleaming chignon at the nape of her neck. She wore a single strand of pearls around her throat, and had matured into an elegant beauty. Exactly as an earl's wife should look, Marcelle thought approvingly, opening her arms to return April's loving embrace.

"Maman!" The endearment warmed the dowager countess's heart. "When did you arrive?"

"Five minutes ago, to be exact," Marcelle laughed. "Just in time to watch *ma petite-fille* thundering across the moors!"

April looked down and noticed her daughter's wind-kissed cheeks and the missing hair ribbons. There was also a conspicuous mud stain on her frilly white party frock, but Mistelle endured her mother's inspection with an innocent expression.

"Is Damien here?" the countess asked.

"*Oui,* he's upstairs battling with Jamie." It seemed only natural to speak in French when Marcelle was here. A small smile teased at April's lips. "For some reason, your grandson no longer wishes to wear short pants. Or any pants, for that matter."

Misty giggled and both women turned just in time to see a blonde haired, chubby toddler come tearing down the stairs with his sire in exasperated pursuit. James Edward Cross had not a single stitch of clothing on, but the fifth earl of Devonshire seemed happily oblivious to the fact as he came barrelling into the ballroom to fling himself into April's skirts.

"Up!" he demanded, and his chuckling mother complied as Damien came to a puffing halt before the small group.

"That little devil," the earl accused with a wagging finger at his son, who peered back at his father with huge blue eyes from the safety of his mother's arms, "is entirely Romany! He acts as if clothes are a penance!"

"Well, aren't they?" The countess laughed, enjoying the joke since she had learned long ago the truth of April's upbringing. "I daresay he would start a new trend in France. With the way the latest court fashions look, I might prefer such *au naturel* attire myself!"

Misty was ready to burst. She tugged on Damien's coatsleeve. "Papa," she announced excitedly, *"Grandmere* wants me to go to France with her!"

"What!" Her startled parents spoke in unison, and the dowager countess gave her granddaughter a playful wink.

"Pouf! So much for secrets, eh? But it is true. I think it is time Mistelle was introduced to another part of her heritage. After all, Damien was going back and forth across the channel when he was still in nappies."

"Maman, I don't know—" April began uneasily.

"Henriette Dupre has gone abroad," Marcelle announced with satisfaction. "In fact, the entire Dupre family has immigrated to Mexico at the request of the Emperor himself. They will not return." Her black eyes glinted with mischief.

"What have you done, *Maman?"* Damien demanded.

Marcelle shrugged. *"Moi?* Nothing much. Simply mentioned to Louis that the Archduke Maximilian and his wife might like some company on the journey. Can I help it if the Dupres were the obvious choice?"

Damien knelt to his daughter's height. "Do you want to go, poppet?"

"Ever so much! I want to see the chateau and the vineyards and learn how to dance—"

He laughingly held up a hand to cease her chatter. "If it's all right with your mother, you have my permission."

April felt the weight of three pairs of eyes on her and relented with a sigh. "Very well. But you shan't be able to take Azize along, you know."

A moment of indecision flitted across Misty's face. Then, turning to the dowager countess, she asked slyly, "Might you find me another horse in France, *Grandmere?*"

Marcelle grinned. "I think we might, *ma doux.* We shall stay the weekend, and then be off on a new adventure." She looked gratefully at her son and his wife. Her grandchildren were her whole life now, and they understood.

Several days later, after the earl and countess waved goodbye to Mistelle and her grandmother from the front steps of the mansion, April turned and buried her face in Damien's lapels.

"I don't think I can bear it!" she gasped tearfully.

Damien chuckled as he stroked her golden hair. "Little ones grow up, my love. But we still have Jamie."

"Not for long." April sniffled and raised her head. Her green eyes were imploring as she gazed up at her handsome husband. "I want another baby, Damien."

A slow smile curved the earl's sensuous

mouth. "You know I can't deny you anything, Lady Cross," he said huskily before he captured her lips beneath his.

Out in the pasture, Prince Adar paused to stare a moment at the couple embracing in the mist. Then, with a shake of his mighty black head, he raced off to find his mares.

AUTHOR'S NOTE

While GYPSY JEWEL is, of course, fiction, it may interest my readers to know that much of the background for the novel is based on real events and people. Lord Raglan, for example, did indeed exist, and died shortly after the end of the Crimean War (some historians think due to grief).

For those who are interested in learning more about the Romany people and their heritage, I highly recommend THE GYPSIES by Jan Yoors. While small bands of gypsies still roam the modern world, nearly half-a-million died in Hitler's concentration camps during World War II. I dedicate this book to the Rom and all others who have paid such a great price for freedom.

I would enjoy hearing from readers. Please feel free to drop me a note at P.O. Box 304, Gooding, Idaho, 83330.

PASSION BLAZES IN A ZEBRA HEARTFIRE!

COLORADO MOONFIRE (3730, $4.25/$5.50)
by Charlotte Hubbard
Lila O'Riley left Ireland, determined to make her own way in America. Finding work and saving pennies presented no problem for the independent lass; locating love was another story. Then one hot night, Lila meets Marshal Barry Thompson. Sparks fly between the fiery beauty and the lawman. Lila learns that America is the promised land, indeed!

MIDNIGHT LOVESTORM (3705, $4.25/$5.50)
by Linda Windsor
Dr. Catalina McCulloch was eager to begin her practice in Los Reyes, California. On her trip from East Texas, the train is robbed by the notorious, masked bandit known as Archangel. Before making his escape, the thief grabs Cat, kisses her fervently, and steals her heart. Even at the risk of losing her standing in the community, Cat must find her mysterious lover once again. No matter what the future might bring . . .

MOUNTAIN ECSTASY (3729, $4.25/$5.50)
by Linda Sandifer
As a divorced woman, Hattie Longmore knew that she faced prejudice. Hoping to escape wagging tongues, she traveled to her brother's Idaho ranch, only to learn of his murder from long, lean Jim Rider. Hattie seeks comfort in Rider's powerful arms, but she soon discovers that this strong cowboy has one weakness . . . marriage. Trying to lasso this wandering man's heart is a challenge that Hattie enthusiastically undertakes.

RENEGADE BRIDE (3813, $4.25/$5.50)
by Barbara Ankrum
In her heart, Mariah Parsons always believed that she would marry the man who had given her her first kiss at age sixteen. Four years later, she is actually on her way West to begin her life with him . . . and she meets Creed Deveraux. Creed is a rough-and-tumble bounty hunter with a masculine swagger and a powerful magnetism. Mariah finds herself drawn to this bold wilderness man, and their passion is as unbridled as the Montana landscape.

ROYAL ECSTASY (3861, $4.25/$5.50)
by Robin Gideon
The name Princess Jade Crosse has become hated throughout the kingdom. After her husband's death, her "advisors" have punished and taxed the commoners with relentless glee. Sir Lyon Beauchane has sworn to stop this evil tyrant and her cruel ways. Scaling the castle wall, he meets this "wicked" woman face to face . . . and is overpowered by love. Beauchane learns the truth behind Jade's imprisonment. Together they struggle to free Jade from her jailors and from her inhibitions.

Available wherever paperbacks are sold, or order direct from the Publisher. Send cover price plus 50¢ per copy for mailing and handling to Zebra Books, Dept. 4306, 475 Park Avenue South, New York, N.Y. 10016. Residents of New York and Tennessee must include sales tax. DO NOT SEND CASH. For a free Zebra/ Pinnacle catalog please write to the above address.

EVERY DAY WILL FEEL LIKE FEBRUARY 14TH!

*Zebra Historical Romances
by Terri Valentine*

LOUISIANA CARESS   (4126-8, $4.50/$5.50)

MASTER OF HER HEART   (3056-8, $4.25/$5.50)

OUTLAW'S KISS   (3367-2, $4.50/$5.50)

SEA DREAMS   (2200-X, $3.75/$4.95)

SWEET PARADISE   (3659-0, $4.50/$5.50)

TRAITOR'S KISS   (2569-6, $3.75/$4.95)

Available wherever paperbacks are sold, or order direct from the Publisher. Send cover price plus 50¢ per copy for mailing and handling to Zebra Books, Dept. 4306, 475 Park Avenue South, New York, N.Y. 10016. Residents of New York and Tennessee must include sales tax. DO NOT SEND CASH. For a free Zebra/ Pinnacle catalog please write to the above address.